£1-50

Fault Location
Radio and Televis

(City & Guilds and

VOLUME 1

K. J. BOHLMAN

T.Eng.(C.E.I.), F.S.E.R.T., A.M.Inst.E.

Senior Lecturer in Radio and Television
Lincoln College of Technology

LONDON

NORMAN PRICE (PUBLISHERS) LTD

NORMAN PRICE (PUBLISHERS) LTD
17 TOTTENHAM COURT ROAD, LONDON W1P 9DP

Third edition 1977

ISBN 0 85380 059 6

Printed in Great Britain by
Biddles Ltd., Guildford, Surrey.

AUTHOR'S PREFACE

THIS is the first of three volumes originally written for the student service engineer following a course of study for the City and Guilds of London and the Radio Trades Examination Board certificate in radio and television servicing.

Questions have been added to embrace the syllabus of the MECHANICS' COURSE IN RADIO, TELEVISION AND ELECTRONICS (222). The multiple-choice type of question has been retained as this technique is favoured by the examining bodies for the course.

Volume 1 will be found suitable for use by first-year and second-year students and will exercise their theoretical and practical knowledge of simple circuits and components. Those questions suitable for first-year students are denoted by an asterisk immediately following the question number. Second-year students should be able to answer most of the questions in the book.

CONTENTS

SECTION (I) COMPONENTS AND ACTIVE DEVICES

Those questions suitable for first-year students are denoted by an asterisk (*) immediately following the question number.

(1)* Give the values of the resistors shown in the table below which are colour coded by the BODY–TIP–SPOT method.

RESISTOR	BODY	TIP	SPOT
R_1	RED	VIOLET	ORANGE
R_2	BLUE	GREY	RED
R_3	ORANGE	ORANGE	ORANGE
R_4	BROWN	GREEN	BROWN
R_5	BROWN	BLACK	GREEN
R_6	YELLOW	VIOLET	YELLOW
R_7	GREY	RED	BROWN
R_8	ORANGE	WHITE	GREEN
R_9	BROWN	BLACK	BLUE
R_{10}	BROWN	BLACK	BROWN
R_{11}	WHITE	BROWN	BLACK
R_{12}	BLUE	BLACK	BLACK

(2)* Give the values of the resistors shown in the table below which are colour coded by the RING method.

RESISTOR	1st RING	2nd RING	3rd RING	4th RING
R_1	BROWN	BLACK	ORANGE	—
R_2	BLUE	BROWN	BROWN	GOLD
R_3	RED	GREEN	YELLOW	SILVER
R_4	GREEN	BLUE	BLACK	SILVER
R_5	RED	RED	RED	—
R_6	GREY	RED	YELLOW	—
R_7	BROWN	GREEN	GREEN	SILVER
R_8	BROWN	BLACK	ORANGE	GOLD
			(5th	RING PINK)
R_9	ORANGE	WHITE	BLACK	SILVER
R_{10}	YELLOW	VIOLET	ORANGE	GOLD
R_{11}	YELLOW	VIOLET	GOLD	GOLD
R_{12}	GREEN	BLACK	SILVER	GOLD

(3)* **Give the values of the three resistors shown.**

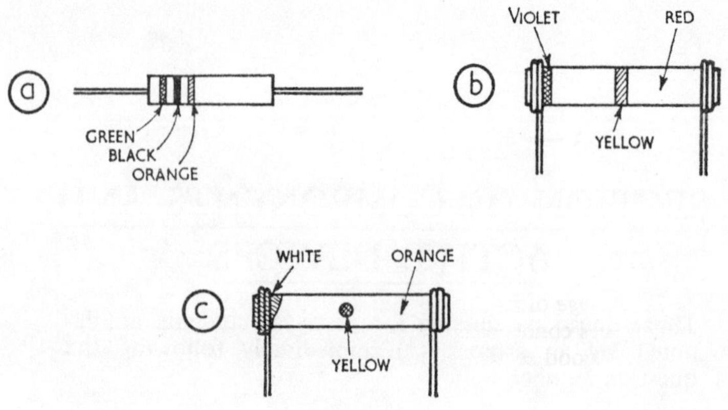

(4)*

A — R1 10kΩ ±5% — R2 22kΩ ±10% — B

When an ohmmeter is connected across R_1 it reads 11·5kΩ and when connected between terminals A and B it reads 35·5kΩ. Are resistors R_1 and R_2 within tolerance?

(5)*

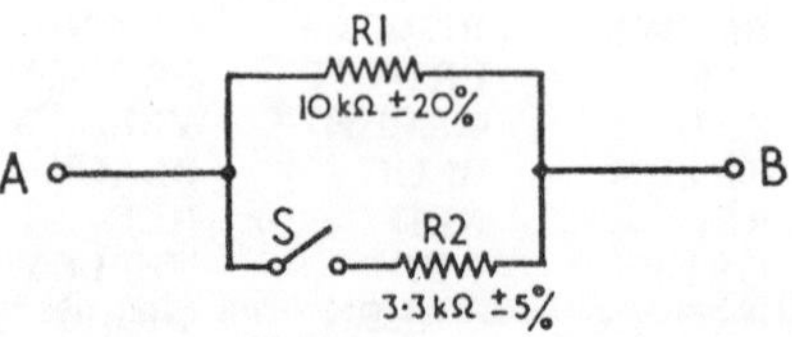

With the switch S open, an ohmmeter connected between A and B reads 9kΩ.
With the switch S closed, an ohmmeter connected between A and B reads 2·25kΩ.
Are resistors R_1 and R_2 within tolerance?

(6)*

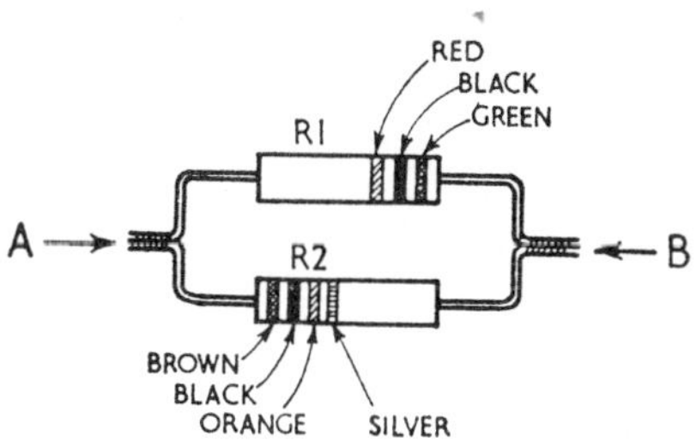

Give the *range* of resistance values that might be indicated when an ohmmeter is connected between *A* and *B*. Before the measurement is made a good service engineer always ensures that ....?

(7)*

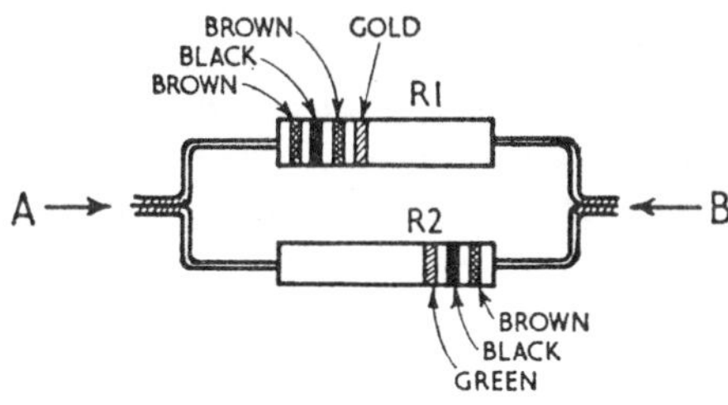

What would be a typical resistance reading if an ohmmeter is connected between *A* and *B*?

(8)*

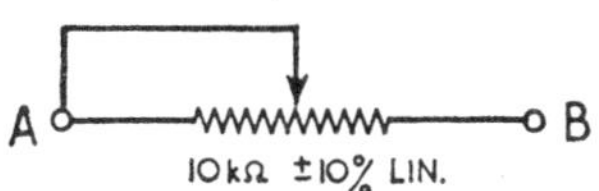

(a) What will an ohmmeter read when connected between *A* and *B* if:

(*i*) Slider is set to extreme right
(*ii*) Slider is set to extreme left
(*iii*) Slider is set to the centre of track.

(b) What name is given to this component symbol?
(c) In what other way is it often shown in circuit diagrams?

(9)*

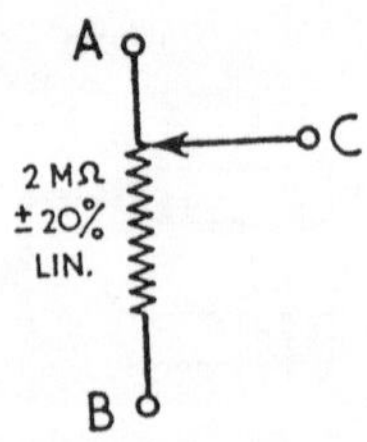

(a) When the slider of the potentiometer is in the position shown, what resistance readings will be obtained if an ohmmeter is connected between:

(*i*) *A* and *C*
(*ii*) *C* and *B*
(*iii*) *A* and *B*.

(b) What resistance readings would you expect between *A* and *B* when the slider is in the following positions:

(*i*) In the position shown (top of track)
(*ii*) In the centre of the track
(*iii*) At the bottom of the track.

(c) If 1 volt d.c. is applied across terminals *A* and *B*, what position will the slider be in to obtain across *C* and *B*

(*i*) Maximum p.d.
(*ii*) Minimum p.d.

(d) The current flowing in the track under the conditions in (c) will be:

(*i*) 0·5mA
(*ii*) 5mA
(*iii*) 0·5A
(*iv*) 0·5μA
(*v*) 5μA.

(e) Will the position of the slider affect the current reading?

(10)* On what range of an Avometer (Model 8) would you measure:

(*i*) 10Ω ± 5% resistor
(*ii*) 5MΩ ± 20% resistor
(*iii*) 20kΩ ± 10% resistor
(*iv*) 100kΩ ± 20% resistor
(*v*) 100Ω ± 5% resistor.

(11)* When checking the resistance of a *new* 5MΩ resistor, an engineer was surprised to find that it read 100kΩ. To confirm the result he repeated the measurement and this time it read 5MΩ. He rechecked it several times and on each occasion it read 5MΩ.

Give a possible reason for the 100kΩ reading he obtained.

(12)* Before carrying out some measurements on a radio receiver, an engineer commenced to "zero" the ohms ranges of his Avometer. He adjusted the R × 100 zero adjust knob for zero reading but found that he could not make the pointer fall right to zero. However, he was successful in "zeroing" the *R* and *R* ÷ 100 ranges.

What do you suspect was wrong with his Avometer?

(13)* What type of resistor would you expect to find used for the following:

(a) H.T. smoothing resistor
(b) Cathode bias resistor of an a.f. output valve
(c) Mains dropper resistor
(d) Grid leak of a.f. power amplifying valve
(e) Anode surge resistor of h.t. rectifying valve
(f) Volume control of a radio receiver (valve)
(g) Volume control of a radio receiver (transistor)
(h) Screen grid feed resistor of an a.f. preamplifier valve?

Give an approximate wattage rating for each type.

(14)* A replacement was required for a 5kΩ linear variable resistor. The only value, of suitable physical size, that was available was a 10kΩ linear variable resistor. A stock of assorted carbon composition resistors was also at hand.

Say how you would carry out a temporary repair using the 10kΩ variable resistor.

(15) The anode load resistor *R* of the triode valve shown was suspected of going high in value when the valve was conducting.
Give a method of determining the "hot" resistance of *R*.

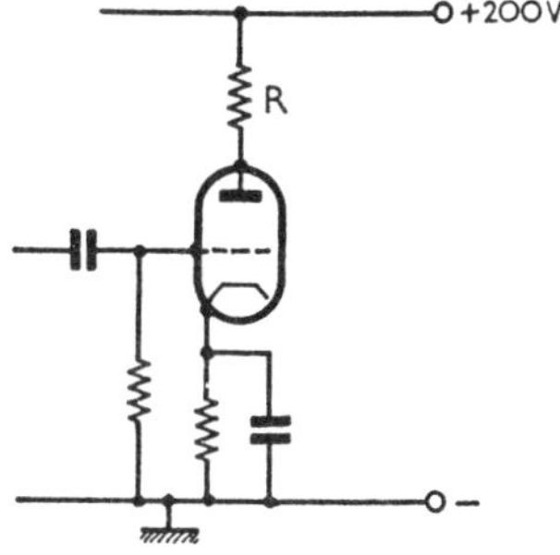

(16)* Why may wire-wound resistors be unsuitable for use at high frequencies?

(17)

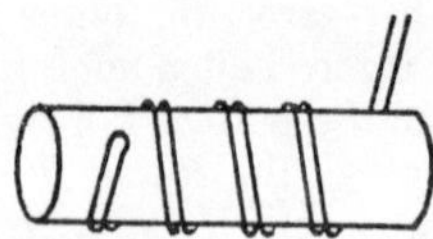

The wire-wound resistor shown employs a special type of winding. What name is given to this form of winding and for what purpose is it used here?

(18) Draw the component symbol for a thermistor.

(a) What kind of temperature coefficient of resistance does a thermistor have?
(b) Why are thermistors used in series heater chains?
(c) State the approximate "hot" and "cold" values of resistance that you would expect a thermistor, of the type used in series heater chains, to have.

(19)* If one section of a mains dropper went open circuit, how would you carry out a temporary repair?

(20)* A replacement was required for a 500Ω 5W resistor; the only ones available were the four shown.
Show how you would arrange any number of these to provide a replacement.

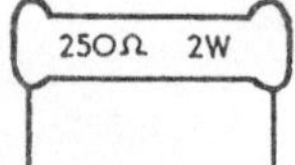

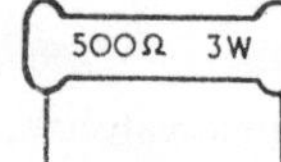

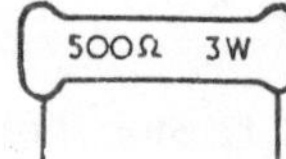

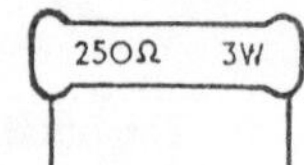

(21)*

(a) What dielectric would be used in the capacitor shown above
(b) What significance has the band shown on the right
(c) What does "500V d.c." convey to you
(d) How would you measure its capacitance.

(22)* Which *two* of the following types of capacitor would you say possessed the most inductance?

(a) Silver Mica; (b) Electrolytic; (c) High-K Ceramic; (d) Paper; and (e) Ceramic.

(23) (a) What "losses" occur in capacitors?

(b) What is meant by the "loss angle"?

(24) Give a typical application for the following types of capacitor, either in a radio receiver or a.f. amplifier.

(a) 0·05μF Paper 500V d.c.
(b) 25μF 25V d.c. Electrolytic.
(c) 100pF 250V d.c. Ceramic.
(d) 16μF 500V d.c. Electrolytic.
(e) 0·01μF 500V d.c. Hi-K Ceramic.
(f) 500pF + 500pF variable air-spaced.
(g) 50pF compression type trimmer.

(25)*

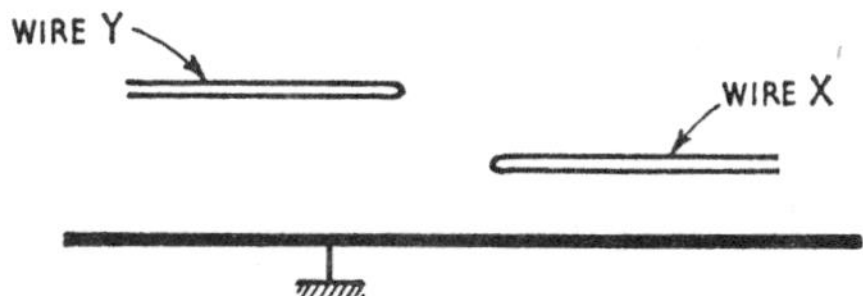

Which wire will have the larger capacitance to chassis?

(26)* How would you reduce the capacitance *between* the coils *A* and *B*?

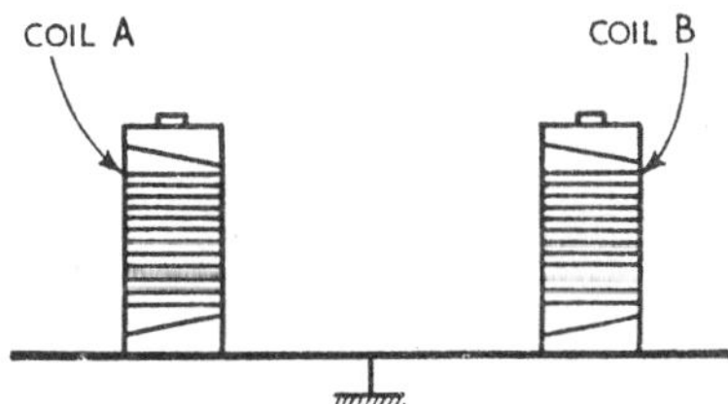

(27) Which of the following arrangements will give minimum capacitance between primary and secondary?

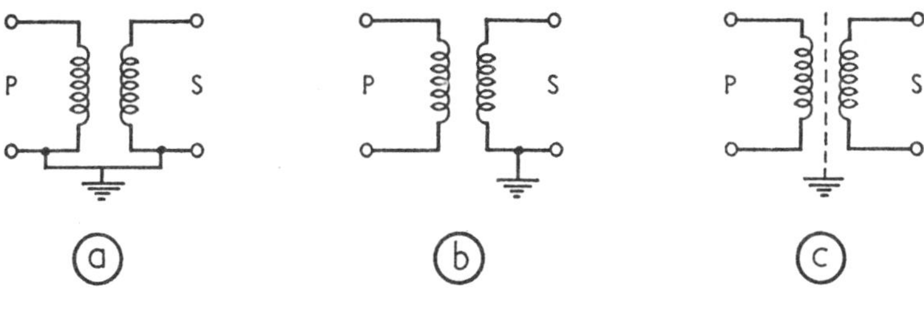

(28)*

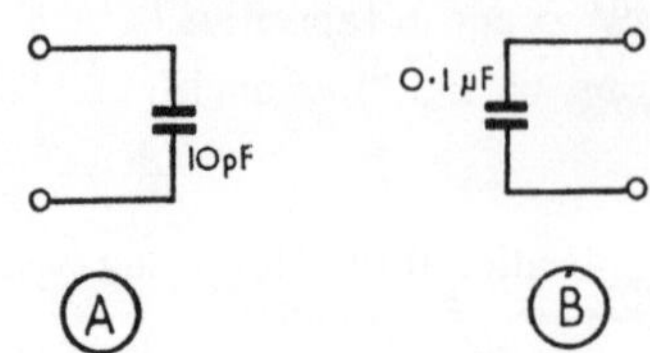

The two capacitors shown are serviceable. When an ohmmeter is connected between the terminals of (A) it will read:

(a) Zero ohms
(b) Infinity
(c) Kick up and quickly fall to infinity
(d) Depends upon meter lead polarity.

When the ohmmeter is connected to terminals of (B) it will read:

(a) Zero ohms
(b) Infinity
(c) Kick up and quickly fall to infinity
(d) Depends upon meter lead polarity.

(29)* When three different 0·1-μF capacitors were tested on the highest resistance range of an Avometer, the following readings were obtained:

CAPACITOR NO. 1: Kicked up and quickly fell to infinity.
CAPACITOR NO. 2: Instantaneously read 10kΩ.
CAPACITOR NO. 3: Instantaneously read infinity.

Explain the significance of each reading.

(30)* How would you test the insulation resistance of a 100-pF 500-V ceramic capacitor?

(31)

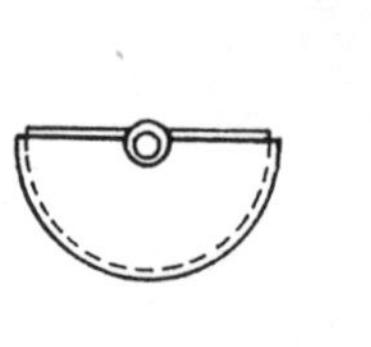

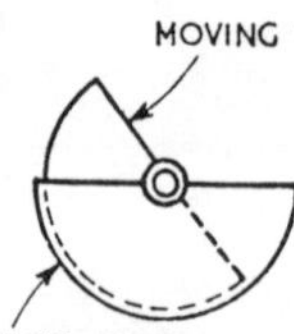

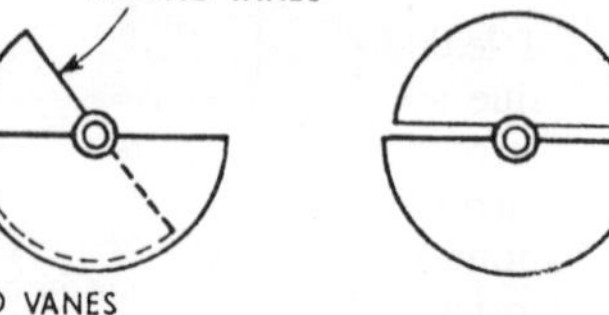

The figures represent three positions of the moving vanes of an air-spaced variable capacitor.

(a) Which position will result in maximum capacitance between the moving and fixed vanes?
(b) If a coil is connected across the capacitor, which position will give to the tuned circuit, formed by the coil and capacitor, its highest resonant frequency?

(c) Which plates are normally connected to chassis potential?

(d) What would be the approximate $\frac{\text{max. capacity}}{\text{min. capacity}}$ ratio for a 0·0005μF tuning capacitor when it is connected in circuit?

(32)* What would you say were typical tolerances for the following capacitors?

(a) 0·01μF 500V d.c. Paper Tubular.
(b) 16 – 16μF 450V d.c. Electrolytic.
(c) 0·01μF 500V d.c. Hi-K Ceramic.
(d) 10pF 500V d.c. Standard Ceramic.
(e) 10pF 500V d.c. Silver Mica.

(33)* Would you consider a capacitor rated at 275V d.c. safe for operation on 200V a.c.?

(34)* Why is it important to mount capacitors away from sources of heat?

(35)* Which of the following will pass the greatest "leakage" current when connected to, say, 500V d.c.?

(a) 0·05μF 500V d.c. Paper.
(b) 0·01μF 500V d.c. Ceramic.
(c) 0·0001μF 500V d.c. Silver Mica.
(d) 8μF 1000V d.c. Electrolytic.
(e) 0·05μF 1000V d.c. Paper.

(36)* (a) What forms the dielectric of an electrolytic capacitor?

(b) Why is it important to make sure that the polarity of the voltage applied to an electrolytic is correct?

(c) What is meant by "etched foil"?

(d) What is meant by "re-forming" an electrolytic capacitor?

(e) How would you measure the leakage current of an electrolytic capacitor?

(37)* Results of leakage-current tests on three different electrolytics (of similar value and working voltage) are given below:

C_1: Current initially 20mA and then falling to about 10μA.

C_2: Current 100mA and remaining reasonably constant for about 10 minutes.

C_3: No leakage current.

Say what you can about the condition of each capacitor.

(38)* The 16μF reservoir capacitor of a radio receiver developed a short circuit despite frequent replacement. The reason for this was eventually discovered to be excessive surge voltage (550V) from the mains transformer during the switch-on period, the safe surge voltage rating for the capacitor being 525V.

It was decided to replace the 16μF by an arrangement using 32μF capacitors, to prevent the fault from recurring.

Make a diagram showing how you would arrange the capacitors.

(39) Which of the following connections would you consider as being "safe"?

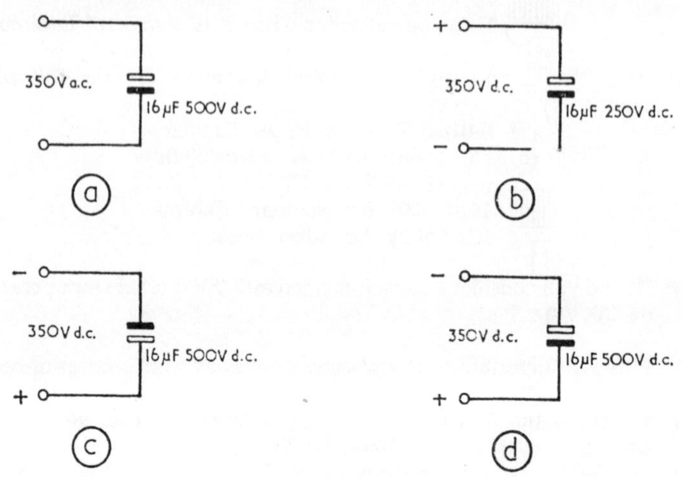

(40)* Identify the following component symbols:

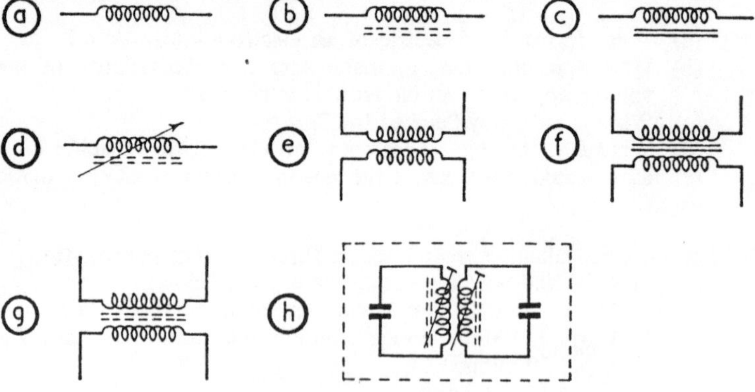

(41) The figures on the opposite page show several positions of the iron-dust core when tuning a coil which has a capacitor across it. Which positions of the core will give:

(a) Maximum inductance
(b) Minimum inductance
(c) Highest resonant frequency to L and C
(d) Lowest resonant frequency to L and C.

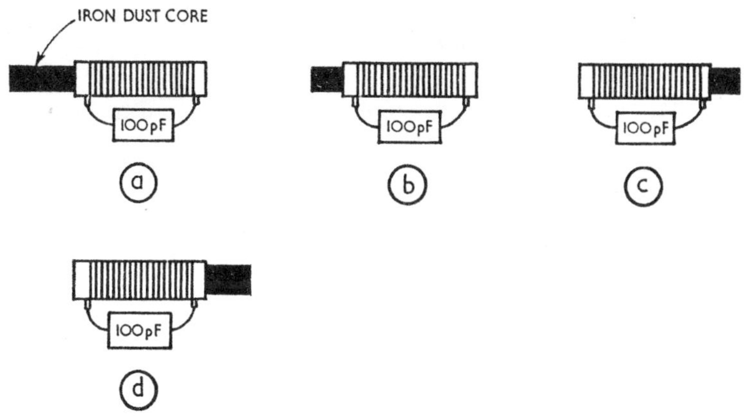

(42) If the iron-dust core of question (41) is replaced by a brass core, which position will give:

(a) Maximum inductance?
(b) Lowest resonant frequency to L and C?

(43) Say which of the following will increase the inductance of a coil:

(a) Increasing the number of turns.
(b) Increasing the diameter of the former.
(c) Decreasing the number of turns.
(d) Decreasing the diameter of the former.

(44) What do you understand by the following terms as applied to coils?

(a) Self-capacitance.
(b) Q-factor.
(c) Skin effect.
(d) Litz wire.

(45) A tuned circuit in a certain receiver is required to be sharply tuned The coil used should preferably have a Q of:

(a) 10
(b) 100
(c) 200
(d) 1
(e) 5.

The capacitor should possess:

(f) A low Q
(g) A high power factor
(h) A large loss angle
(i) A low power factor.

(46) (a) How would you determine the inductance of a coil?
(b) How would you test it for continuity?

(47) The inductance range of *radio frequency coils* is approximately:

(a) 1mH to 10H
(b) 1H to 100H
(c) 100H to 1000H
(d) 1μH to 100mH
(e) 0·01μH to 1μH.

(48)

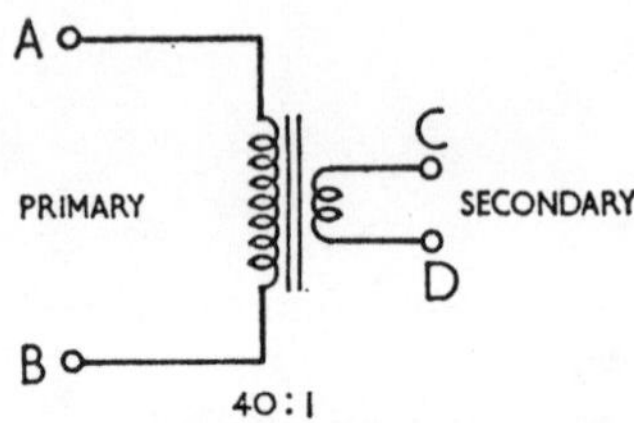

(a) Resistance measurements across the primary and secondary windings of a serviceable audio output transformer would be typically:

(*i*) *AB* 50Ω—*CD* 1kΩ
(*ii*) *AB* 2Ω—*CD* 1kΩ
(*iii*) *AB* 500Ω—*CD* 500Ω
(*iv*) *AB* 500Ω—*CD* 2Ω
(*v*) Depends upon meter polarity.

(b) The ratio 40:1 indicates that:

(*i*) There are 40 turns on the primary and one turn on the secondary
(*ii*) The voltage across the primary is 1/40th of that across the secondary
(*iii*) The voltage across the primary is 40 times greater than that across the secondary
(*iv*) For every 40 turns on the primary there is one turn on the secondary
(*v*) The current in the primary is 40 times greater than the current in the secondary.

(c) The resistance between primary and secondary should be:

(*i*) Zero ohms
(*ii*) Infinity
(*iii*) Depends upon core size
(*iv*) Depends upon meter polarity.

(d) The purpose of the iron core is to:

(*i*) Increase the losses
(*ii*) Prevent eddy currents.

(*iii*) Obtain the required primary inductance using the minimum number of turns
(*iv*) Prevent magnetic hysteresis
(*v*) Reduce capacitance between primary and secondary.

(49)

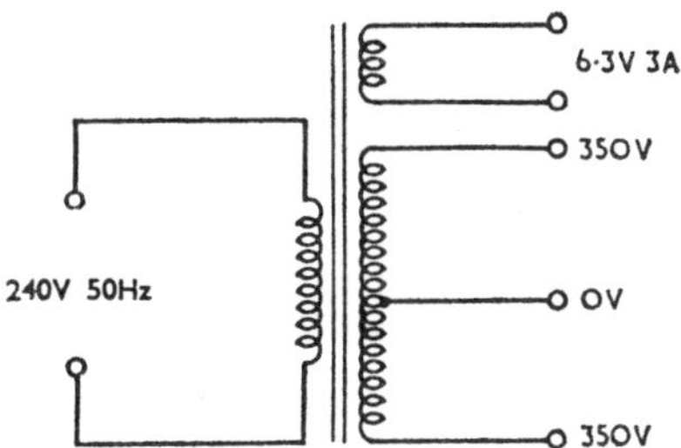

(a) What would be typical resistance readings between:
(*i*) Primary terminals?
(*ii*) H.T. secondary terminals of a mains transformer?

(b) What would you expect the insulation resistance to be:
(*i*) Between primary and secondary windings?
(*ii*) Between primary and core?
(*iii*) Between secondary and core?

(c) What instrument would you use to determine the insulation resistance?

(d) The h.t. secondary winding may be quoted as "350-0-350, 100mA". What does this mean?

(e) What type of rectifier would be used with the transformer above?

(f) How would you distinguish between the h.t. secondary winding and the heater winding without the use of instruments?

(g) Give reasons for the core of a transformer getting rather hot.

(h) What would be the *peak* voltage across:
(*i*) Full h.t. winding
(*ii*) Heater winding?

(50)* Below is a list of the code letters and numbers of valves, etc., using. the European valve-coding system. Say all you can about each type.

(a) EF80	(f) EM81	(k) OC44	(p) MW43-80
(b) UCL83	(g) UAF42	(l) OA81	(q) AW43-80
(c) EY86	(h) EB91	(m) OC78	(r) PCL82
(d) PCC84	(i) UCH81	(n) GZ32	(s) DK96
(e) EZ41	(j) EL34	(o) HF93	(t) DL96

(51)* Draw the valve circuit symbol using the information given by the valve base pin connections for each of the following shown overleaf.

(51)

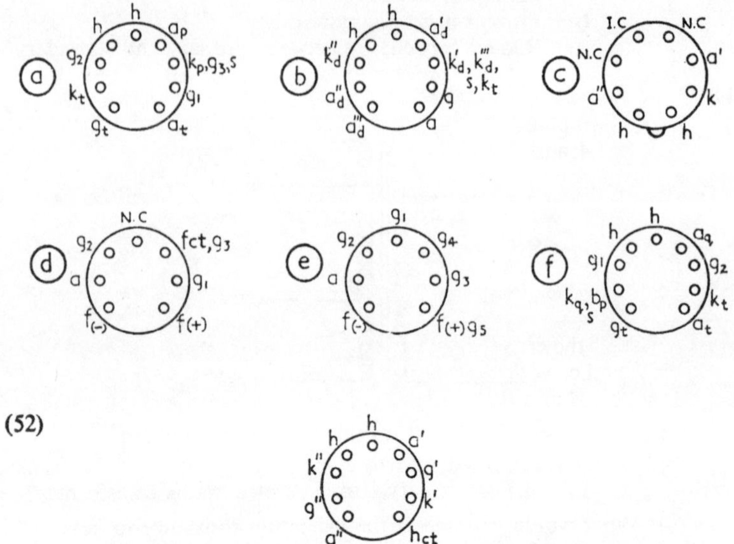

(52)

The figure shows the valve base pin connections for an ECC81 valve.

(a) Comment on the heater arrangements for this valve.
(b) Which electrode of the valve will be connected to pin 3?
(c) State the resistance readings you would expect on an ohmmeter connected between the following pins of a serviceable ECC81:

(*i*) Pins 4 and 5.
(*ii*) Pins 1 and 2.
(*iii*) Pins 5 and 9.
(*iv*) Pins 2 and 7.
(*v*) Pins 3 and 8.

(53)* Identify the component shown in the diagram.

(a) Give a typical use for the device.
(b) What does the + sign indicate?
(c) What precautions should be taken when mounting this component in circuit?

(54)

If the component shown is serviceable, the measured resistance between *A* and *B* would be:

(a) Infinity
(b) Dependent upon meter polarity
(c) Zero ohms
(d) $\simeq$ 100kΩ.

(55) Which of the circuits will result in forward conduction of the diode when a d.c. voltage, with polarity as indicated, is applied to the terminals *A* and *B*?

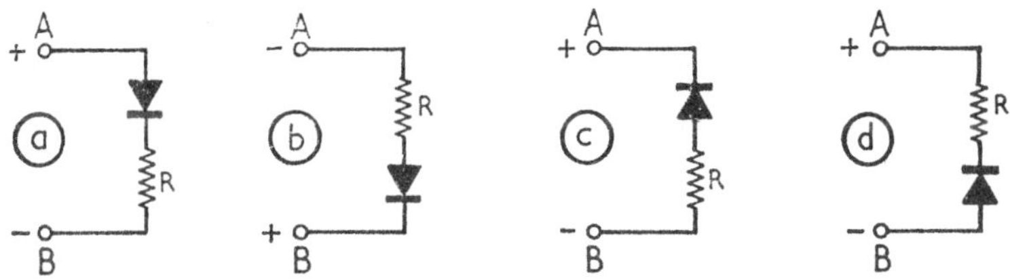

(56) Identify the component shown in the diagram.

(a) What name is given to each of the three electrodes of this device?
(b) What does the spot indicate?
(c) Why must a heat-shunt be used when soldering it into circuit?
(d) Which electrode would be n-type?
(e) A possible code for the device would be:
(*i*) OA70 (*ii*) EB91 (*iii*) OC71 (*iv*) EF80.

(f) What resistance readings would you normally expect between the following, assuming that the meter-lead polarity was the same as the polarity of voltages normally applied to the device?

(*i*) Two outer wire leads.

(*ii*) Centre and right-hand wire leads.

(*iii*) Centre and left-hand wire leads.

(g) Why is a light-proof container an essential feature of this device?

(h) How would you determine the leakage current $I'co$? This would be in the order of:

(*i*) Tens of mAs? (*ii*) Hundreds of mAs? (*iii*) Tens of amperes? (*iv*) Tens of μAs? (*v*) Thousands of μAs?

(i) What is thermal runaway? How is it prevented by the circuit designer?

(j) Draw the circuit symbol of an n-p-n transistor.

(57)* The frequency of the signal shown in the diagram is:

(a) 1kHz (b) 500Hz (c) 10kHz (d) 50Hz.

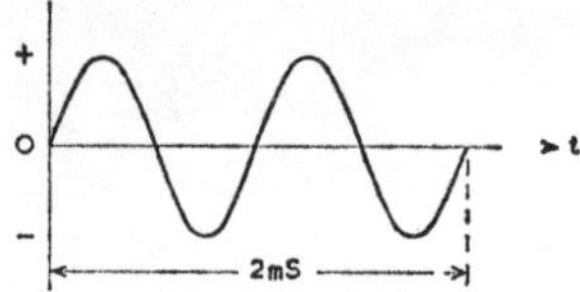

(58)* Identify the wave shapes given below.

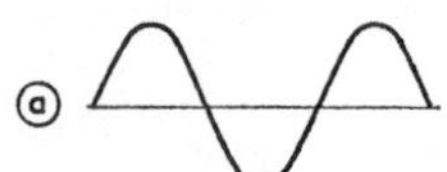

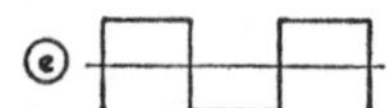

(59)* The velocity of radio waves is:

(a) Dependent upon their frequency.

(b) 3,000 metres/second.

(c) 3,000,000 metres/second.

(d) 300,000,000 metres/second.

(60)* A signal has a frequency of 1MHz. Its wavelength is:

(a) 300m (b) 30m (c) 10^6m (d) 300cm.

(61)* Which of the following waveforms have a d.c. value?

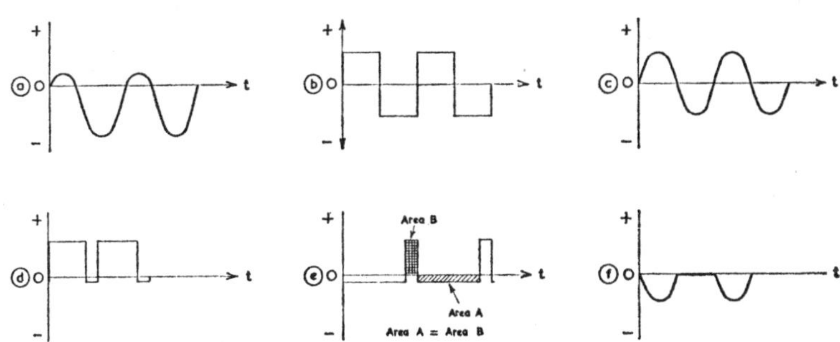

(62)* The voltage between any phase and neutral of the normal 3-phase supply is:

(a) 240V (b) 415V (c) $\sqrt{415V}$ (d) 707V.

(63)* A d.c. amplifier will amplify:

(a) d.c. only
(b) only frequencies within the range 20Hz—20kHz
(c) a.c. and d.c.
(d) a.c. only.

(64)* An a.c. amplifier will amplify:

(a) a.c. only
(b) frequencies in the range 0Hz—5·5MHz
(c) a.c. and d.c.
(d) d.c. only.

(65)* (a) What type of gate does this symbol represent?

(b) If the output of the gate is binary 1, the binary inputs to *A*, *B* and *C* will be:

(*i*) 000; (*ii*) 111; (*iii*) 110; (*iv*) 101.

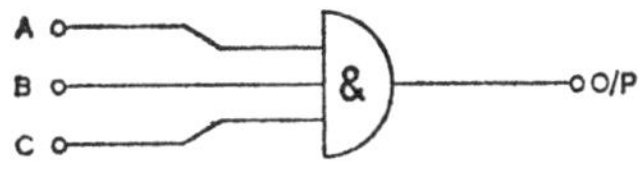

(66)* (a) What type of gate does this symbol represent?

(b) If the output of the gate is binary 0, the binary inputs to A and B will be :

(*i*) 11; (*ii*) 10; (*iii*) 01; (*iv*) 00.

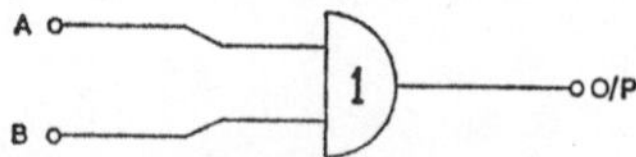

(67)* (a) What type of gate does this symbol represent?

(b) If the output is binary 1, the binary inputs to A and B will be :

(*i*) 11; (*ii*) 00; (*iii*) 10; (*iv*) 01.

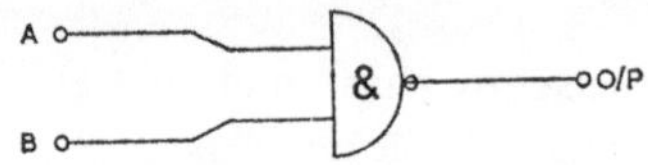

(68)* What type of gate does this symbol represent?

(b) If the output is binary 1, the binary inputs to A, B and C will be:

(*i*) 111; (*ii*) 001; (*iii*) 101; (*iv*) 000.

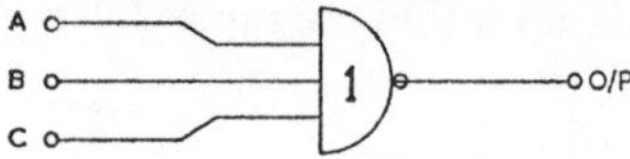

(69)* If the output of the figure is binary 1, which of the following binary inputs to A, B, C and D will result in this condition?

(*i*) 0010; (*ii*) 1100; (*iii*) 1010; (*iv*) 0110; (*v*) 1000.

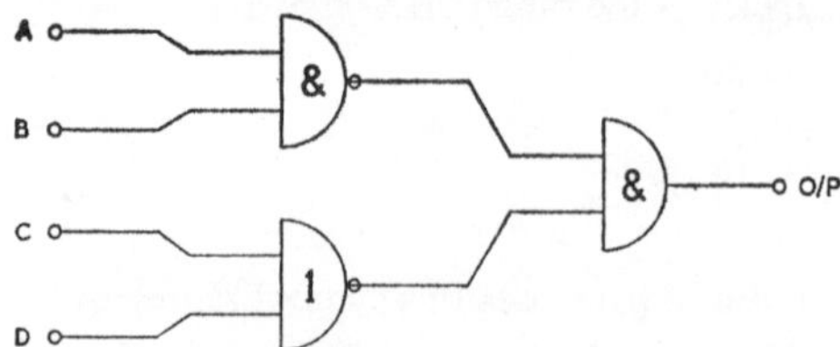

(70)* Supply the missing word to the following statements:

(a) In a photo.....................cell electrons are emitted when light falls on the photo cathode.

(b) When light falls on a photo.....................cell its resistance varies.

(c) A photo.....................cell generates a small voltage when light falls on it.

(71)* Identify the component symbols below which are to British Standards (BS3939).

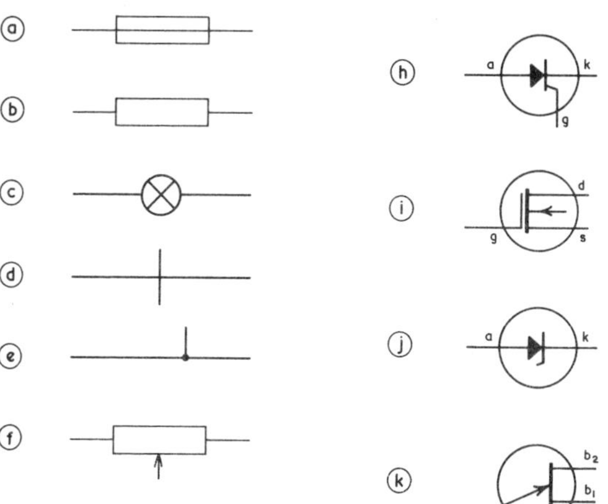

(72) The usual base-emitter voltage drop at low forward currents for a germanium transistor is:

(*i*) 500mV to 800mV
(*ii*) 1mV to 5mV
(*iii*) 5mV to 10mV
(*iv*) 100mV to 200mV.

(73) The usual base-emitter voltage drop at low forward currents for a silicon transistor is:

(*i*) 0·1V to 0·2V
(*ii*) 600mV to 700mV
(*iii*) 0·01V to 0·02V
(*iv*) 40μV to 60μV.

(74) In order to obtain a 6V stabilized supply from the O/P terminals of the circuit below, the input to terminals *A* and *B* must be:

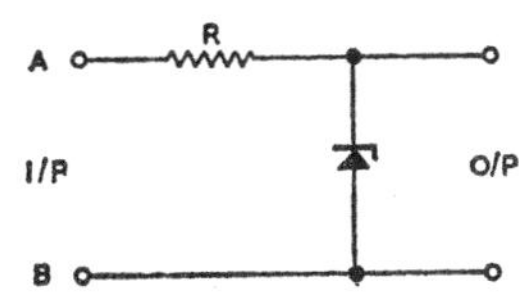

(*i*) Less than 6V with terminal *B* negative to terminal *A*
(*ii*) Greater than 6V with terminal *A* positive to terminal *B*
(*iii*) Less than 6V with terminal *A* negative to terminal *B*
(*iv*) Greater than 6V with terminal *B* positive to terminal *A*.

(75) With reference to the diagram below which of the following statements are true?

(*i*) The slope resistance of the device at A is less than the slope resistance at B

(*ii*) The slope resistance of the device at A is greater than the slope resistance at B

(*iii*) The slope resistance of the device at C is less than the slope resistance at B

(*iv*) The slope resistance at A is the same as the slope resistance at B

(*v*) The slope resistance at A is the same as the slope resistance at C

(*vi*) Voltage and current are linearly related.

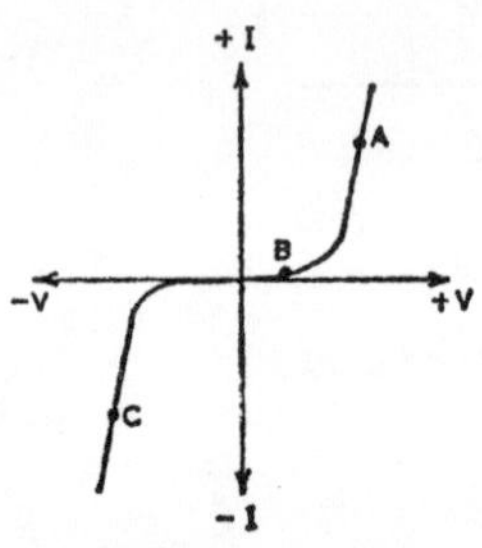

V.D.R. CHARACTERISTIC

(76) Give the probable names for each of the blocks shown in the diagrams below.

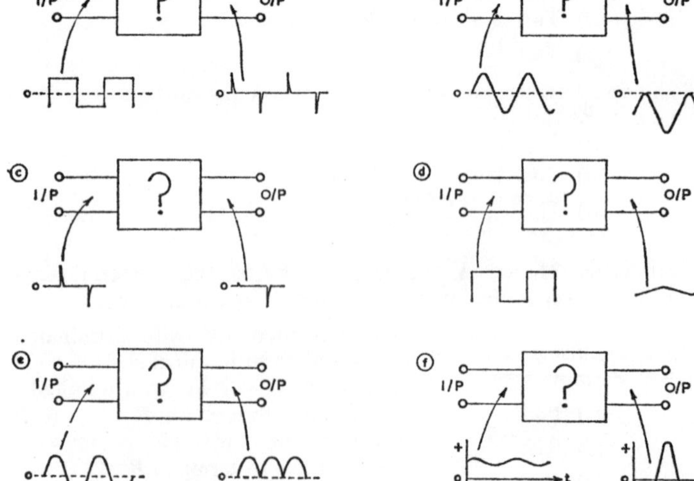

(77)* The three primary colours used in colour television are:

(*i*) Red, yellow and blue
(*ii*) Red, blue and green
(*iii*) Red, cyan and yellow
(*iv*) Cyan, yellow and magenta.

(78)* What will be the resultant colour when the following are additively mixed in suitable proportions:

(*i*) Red and green
(*ii*) Blue and red
(*iii*) Blue and green
(*iv*) Red and cyan
(*v*) Red, blue and green.

(79) (a) A vari-cap diode is normally:

(*i*) Reverse biased
(*ii*) Forward biased.

(b) If the bias applied to the diode is increased will the capacitance:

(*i*) Decrease
(*ii*) Increase
(*iii*) Remain the same?

(80) A thyristor is a semiconductor device having:

(*i*) Three P-type and one N-type layers
(*ii*) Four P-type layers
(*iii*) Two P-type and three N-type layers
(*iv*) Two N-type and two P-type layers.

(81) Appreciable current flows in a thyristor when:

(*i*) The anode and gate are both positive to the cathode
(*ii*) The anode and gate are both negative to the cathode
(*iii*) The gate is negative and the anode positive to the cathode
(*iv*) The anode is negative and the gate positive to the cathode.

(82) A gating pulse is applied to a thyristor causing it to "fire". When the pulse is removed the current in the thyristor will:

(*i*) Fall to zero
(*ii*) Rise
(*iii*) Remain the same
(*iv*) Rise a little then fall to zero.

(83)* (a) Give the probable names of the unlabelled blocks of the diagram below.

(b) What change would be necessary to block 5 to receive f.m. signals?

(c) Would changes be necessary in blocks 4 and 6 to receive f.m. signals?

(d) What will be the frequency of block 7 when receiving a signal of 1·11MHz if the i.f. is 470kHz?

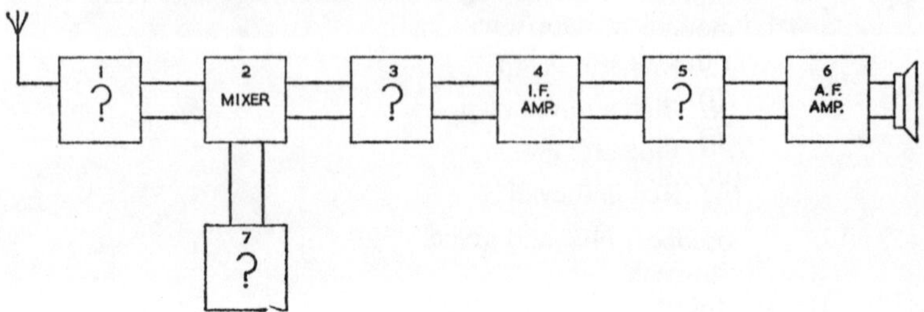

SUPERHET RECEIVER FOR A.M. SIGNALS

(84) (a) State the effect that the potentials applied to the deflector plates will have on the electron beams for each of the diagrams.

(b) What type of deflection is suggested by the diagrams?

(c) What type of deflection is used in cathode ray tubes employed in:

(*i*) Television; (*ii*) Oscilloscopes.

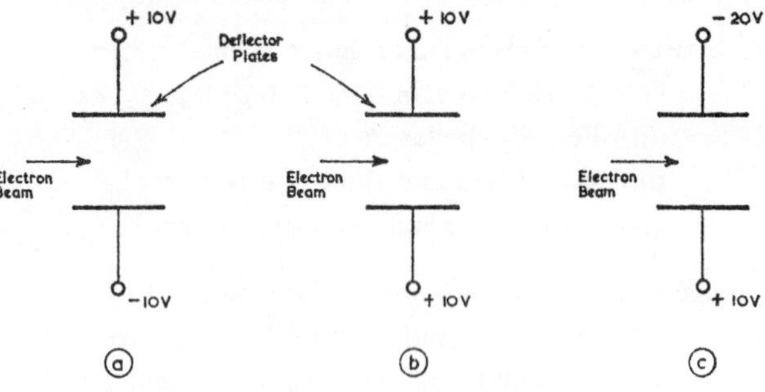

(85)* A high potential is used on the final anode of a c.r.t. to:

(*i*) Eliminate secondary emission
(*ii*) Accelerate the electrons to a high velocity
(*iii*) Decrease the beam current
(*iv*) Increase the sensitivity of the tube.

(86)* The final anode potential of a television tube would be of the order of:

(*i*) 500—600V
(*ii*) 1—5kV
(*iii*) 15—20kV
(*iv*) 50—100kV.

(87) To produce a linear scan across the face of a c.r.t. using magnetic deflection requires:

(*i*) A deflecting current of sine wave shape
(*ii*) A deflecting current of sawtooth shape
(*iii*) A deflecting current of square wave shape
(*iv*) A steady deflecting current.

(88) The Y amplifier of a c.r.o. usually incorporates a switch marked AC/DC mounted on the front panel. When switched to DC, what effects on the trace will the following Y inputs have:

(*i*) +20V d.c.
(*ii*) −20V d.c.
(*iii*) 30V a.c.

(89) An oscilloscope Y amplifier has a sensitivity of 100mV/cm. What is the peak-to-peak value of the signal applied if the beam is deflected a total of 5cm when the Y amplifier gain is increased by a factor of ten (×10)?

(90) Maximum power will be dissipated in the load resistor when:

(*i*) *R* has a value of 7·5kΩ
(*ii*) There are 5 volts across *R*
(*iii*) There are 7·5 volts across *R*
(*iv*) *R* equals twice the internal resistance of the generator.

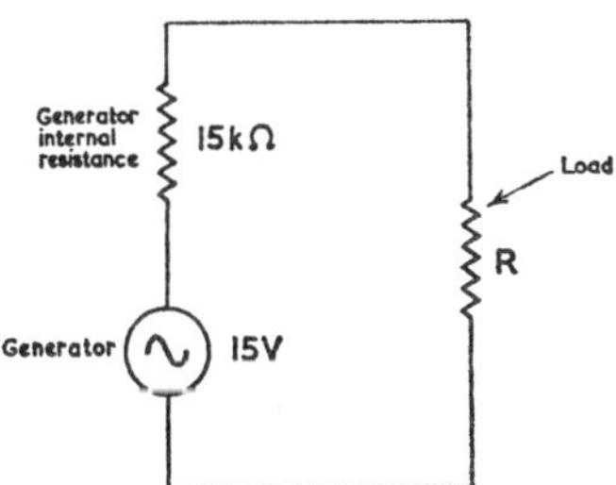

(91) In a klystron having two resonators, electrons from the gun are:

(*i*) Intensity-modulated by the second resonator
(*ii*) All slowed down by the first resonator
(*iii*) All collected by the second resonator
(*iv*) Velocity-modulated by the first resonator.

(92) In a two-resonator klystron the electrons arrive at the second resonator:

(*i*) In bunches
(*ii*) At a steady rate
(*iii*) To receive energy from the resonator
(*iv*) Give up their energy and then accelerate.

(93) A typical operating frequency for a klystron valve would be:

(*i*) 200MHz (*ii*) 5000kHz (*iii*) 100Hz (*iv*) 1500MHz.

(94) In a magnetron valve, the electrons emitted from the cathode follow a curved path because:

(*i*) They are bent by the radial electric field between anode and cathode
(*ii*) The anode is a cylindrical block
(*iii*) They are influenced by radial electric and magnetic fields
(*iv*) They are acted upon by a radial electric field and an axial magnetic field.

(95) The resonant circuit elements of a magnetron oscillator are formed by:

(*i*) Very short lengths of wire
(*ii*) Cavities in the anode block
(*iii*) Inductors and capacitors
(*iv*) Transmission lines.

(96)* What is a transducer?

(97)* Which of the following measuring instruments are analogue devices?

(*i*) Mercury column thermometer
(*ii*) Wrist-watch
(*iii*) Digital voltmeter
(*iv*) Pointer type ammeter
(*v*) Tyre pressure gauge.

(98)* Which of the following are digital type signals?

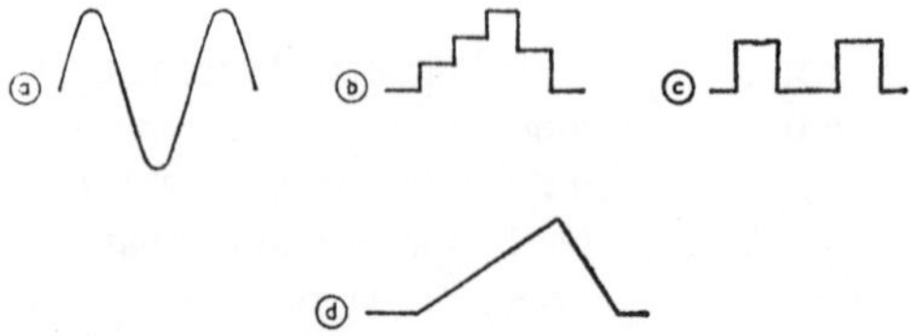

(99)* Suppose that in the interest of safety it is important that a large machine does not start until all of its five safety guards have been fitted. If each guard is fitted with a switch which closes when the guard is correctly placed, what type of gate could be used to give a starting signal to the machine?

(100)* Say whether the following statements are true or false:

(*i*) The eye is equally sensitive to lights of different colours

(*ii*) In general, photoelectric cells do not respond to electromagnetic radiations of different wavelengths by the same amount

(*iii*) Sound waves travel at the same speed as radio waves

(*iv*) Pulse radar is normally used to locate an object and measure the object's speed.

(101)* When a capacitor is discharged *via* a resistor, the voltage across the capacitor will take the form of one of the following. Which will it be?

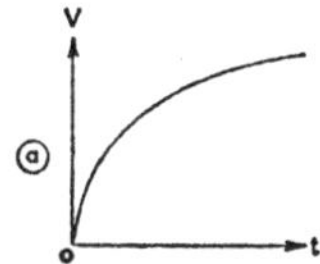

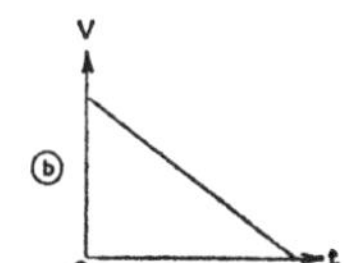

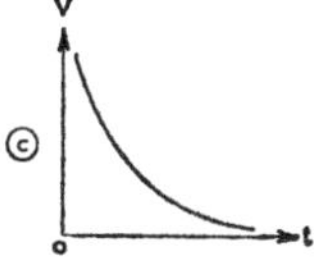

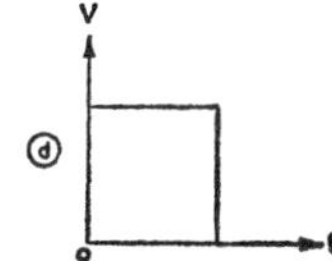

(102)* A fuse is normally fitted into an electrical circuit primarily to:

(a) Prevent fire

(b) Protect the components from damage

(c) Increase the stability of the circuit

(d) Counteract mains fluctuations.

(103)* A fuse is marked 2A on its end cap. It will:

(a) Blow with 550mA passing through it

(b) Blow with 2A passing through it

(c) Pass a steady 2A without blowing

(d) Blow with 1A flowing.

(104)* A fuse normally blows at its centre because:

(a) The resistance is higher at the centre

(b) Heat is conveyed from the fuse more quickly at the ends than from the centre

(c) The resistance is lower at the centre

(d) There is a greater current flowing in the centre.

(105)* A 1kW electric fire is operated from a 13A socket. The plug fuse should be rated at:

(a) 13A; (b) 1A; (c) 1000A; (d) 5A.

(106)* The electric plug used with a television receiver operating on a 240V mains supply should be fitted with a fuse rated at:

(a) 2—3A; (b) 3—5A; (c) 5—7A; (d) 7—10A.

(107)* A square wave may be considered as comprising :

(a) A large number of parabolas of diminishing amplitude
(b) A fundamental sine wave and a large number of even harmonics
(c) A fundamental sine wave and a large number of even and odd harmonics
(d) A large number of odd harmonics and a fundamental sine wave.

(108)* The binary number 11011 represents:

(a) 11·011; (b) 1101·1; (c) 4; (d) 27.

(109)* In binary form the number 31 would be written as:
(a) 310; (b) 11111; (c) 1111; (d) 10110.

(110)* The side frequencies present in a frequency-modulated carrier wave are:

(a) Always two; $f_c + f_m$ and $f_c - f_m$
(b) A number depending on the modulation index
(c) A number depending on the frequency of the modulating signal only
(d) Dependent on the frequency deviation only.

(111)* Which of the following instruments would you use to test the insulation between the element and body of an electric kettle?
(a) Capacitor bridge; (b) Ohmmeter; (c) Lamp and battery tester; (d) Megger.

(112)* The diagram below represents a moulded silicon bridge rectifier. Draw a circuit diagram of the rectifier bridge and number its four connections according to the information given on the diagram. Indicate the supply and output terminals.

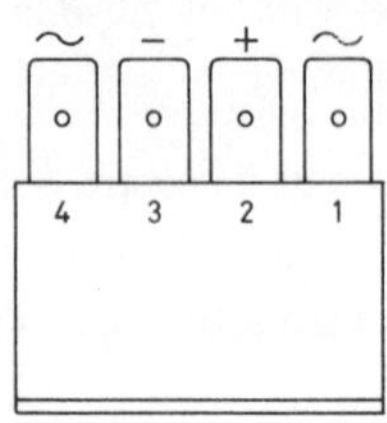

(113) A transistor connected in common base will probably have an h_{fb} of:

(a) 50
(b) 200
(c) 1000
(d) 0·97

(114) The a.c. output resistance of a common emitter amplifier is 20k Ω. Its output conductivity will be:

(a) 50×10^{-6}S
(b) 200×10^{6}S
(c) 20×10^{-3}S
(d) 5×10^{6}S

(115) The h_{fe} of a transistor connected in common emitter will probably be:

(a) 1·1
(b) 0·98
(c) 2×10^{6}
(d) 60

(116) A transistor connected in common collector will probably have an h_{fc} of:

(a) 50
(b) 0·5
(c) 0·98
(d) 10^{-3}

(117) Separate resistance measurements made on three transistors produced the following results. The second set of readings in each case were obtained with the meter leads reversed.

	COLLECTOR-BASE RESISTANCE	BASE-EMITTER RESISTANCE	COLLECTOR-EMITTER RESISTANCE
Transistor	400Ω	200Ω	200Ω
No. 1	400Ω	200Ω	150Ω
Transistor	1·2kΩ	Infinity	Infinity
No. 2	Infinity	Infinity	Infinity
Transistor	1·2kΩ	1·2kΩ	230kΩ
No. 3	Infinity	200kΩ	Infinity

Comment on the condition of each transistor. If faulty, state the nature of the fault.

(118) Why are heat sinks sometimes painted black?

(119) Determine the effective capacitance between terminals A and B.

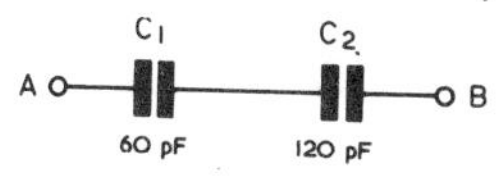

(120) What is the effective capacitance of the capacitor combination?

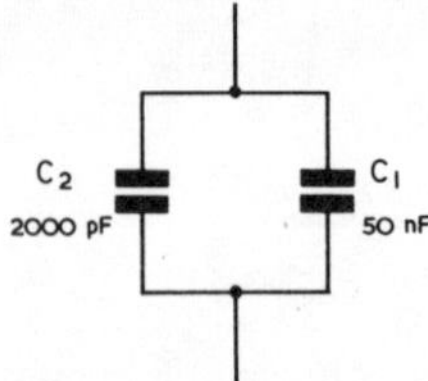

(121) Neglecting the effect of leakage resistance, the voltage across C_1 will be:
(a) 300V
(b) 200V
(c) 100V
(d) 1000V

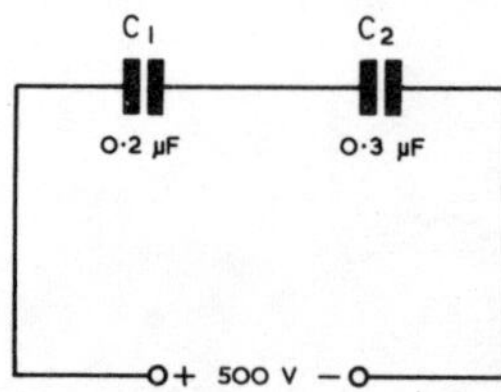

(122) Neglecting the effect of leakage resistance what is the maximum d.c. voltage to be applied between terminals A and B?

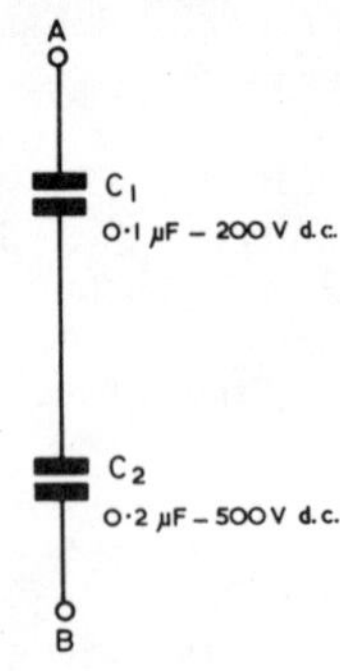

(123)* Using diagrams show what is meant by the following terms as applied to switches:
(a) Single-pole single-throw
(b) Single-pole double-throw
(c) Double-pole double-throw
(d) Double-pole single-throw

(124)* What is the value and tolerance of the following resistors which bear markings conforming to the BS 1852 resistance code:

(a) 4R7K
(b) 68KK
(c) 2M2M
(d) R68J
(e) 1ROG
(f) 27RF

(125)* When fitting the component shown in the diagram into circuit, what particular precautions should be taken?

ANSWERS TO SECTION (I)

(1) $R_1 = 27\text{k}\Omega$, $R_2 = 6{\cdot}8\text{k}\Omega$, $R_3 = 33\text{k}\Omega$, $R_4 = 150\Omega$, $R_5 = 1\text{M}\Omega$, $R_6 = 470\text{k}\Omega$, $R_7 = 820\Omega$, $R_8 = 3{\cdot}9\text{M}\Omega$, $R_9 = 10\text{M}\Omega$, $R_{10} = 100\Omega$, $R_{11} = 91\Omega$ and $R_{12} = 60\Omega$.
All resistors $\pm 20\%$ tolerance.

(2) $R_1 = 10\text{k}\Omega \pm 20\%$, $R_2 = 610\Omega \pm 5\%$, $R_3 = 250\text{k}\Omega \pm 10\%$, $R_4 = 56\Omega \pm 10\%$, $R_5 = 2{\cdot}2\text{k}\Omega \pm 20\%$, $R_6 = 820\text{k}\Omega \pm 20\%$, $R_7 = 1{\cdot}5\text{M}\Omega \pm 10\%$, $R_8 = 10\text{k}\Omega \pm 5\%$ HIGH STABILITY (GRADE 1 RESISTOR), $R_9 = 39\Omega \pm 10\%$, $R_{10} = 47\text{k}\Omega \pm 5\%$, $R_{11} = 4{\cdot}7\Omega \pm 5\%$, and $R_{12} = 0{\cdot}5\Omega \pm 5\%$.

(3) (a) $50\text{k}\Omega \pm 20\%$.
(b) $270\text{k}\Omega \pm 20\%$.
(c) $390\text{k}\Omega \pm 20\%$.

(4) R_2 is within tolerance, since actual value of $R_2 = (35{\cdot}5 - 11{\cdot}5)\text{k}\Omega = 24\text{k}\Omega$.
R_1 is outside tolerance.

(5) R_1 is within tolerance.

Knowing that R_1 is actually 9kΩ, we may calculate the true value of R_2 from

$$\frac{1}{R_T} = \frac{1}{R_1} + \frac{1}{R_2} \quad \text{where } R_T = 2{\cdot}25\text{k}\Omega \text{ and } R_1 = 9\text{k}\Omega$$

$$\text{Hence} \quad \frac{1}{2{\cdot}25} = \frac{1}{9} + \frac{1}{R_2}$$

$$4 = 1 + \frac{9}{R_2} \quad \text{(multiplying out by 9)}$$

$$\textit{i.e.} \quad \frac{9}{R_2} = 3 \text{ or } R_2 = \frac{9}{3} = \underline{3\text{k}\Omega}$$

Hence R_2 is outside ±5% tolerance.

(6) From the colour code:

R_1 = 5kΩ ±20%. Hence resistance may lie anywhere between 4kΩ—6kΩ.

R_2 = 10kΩ ±10%. Hence resistance may lie anywhere between 9kΩ—11kΩ.

Therefore lowest resistance obtainable for the two resistors in parallel

$$= \frac{4 \times 9}{4 + 9} \text{k}\Omega = \frac{36}{13} \text{k}\Omega \simeq 2{\cdot}8\text{k}\Omega$$

and highest resistance

$$= \frac{11 \times 6}{11 + 6} \text{k}\Omega = \frac{66}{17} \text{k}\Omega \simeq 3{\cdot}9\text{ k}\Omega$$

Hence possible range of resistance values is approximately

from <u>2·8kΩ—3·9kΩ</u>

A good engineer will ensure that the ZERO has been set on the resistance ranges.

(7) From the colour code:

$$R_1 = 100\Omega \pm 5\%$$
$$R_2 = 1\text{M}\Omega \pm 20\%$$

Since R_2 is a very large resistance value compared with R_1, the reading obtained will, for practical purposes, be that of R_1.
Hence a typical reading would be

100Ω ±5%

<u>*i.e.* 95Ω—105Ω</u>

(8) (a) (*i*) Zero ohms.
(*ii*) 10kΩ ±1kΩ.
(*iii*) Approximately half the reading obtained in (*ii*).

(b) Variable resistor.

(c)

(9) (a) (*i*) Zero ohms.
(*ii*) 2MΩ ± 0·4MΩ.
(*iii*) 2MΩ ± 0·4MΩ.

(b) (*i*), (*ii*), (*iii*) In all positions 2MΩ ± 0·4MΩ, since there is no resistance path from *C* to either *A* or *B* externally to the potentiometer.

(c) (*i*) As shown in diagram (top of track).
(*ii*) Bottom of track.

(d) ≏ 0·5μA. (Answer is only approximate as resistance may lie anywhere within ±20% or 2MΩ).

(e) The position of the slider will not affect the current reading.

(10) (*i*) Ω ÷ 100 range; (*ii*) Ω × 100 range; (*iii*) Ω range; (*iv*) Ω × 100 range; (*v*) Ω ÷ 100 range.

(11) The most likely cause for the 100kΩ reading is that during the first reading his *fingers* were probably touching the prods of the meter—hence the resistance of his body was in parallel with the 5MΩ resistor.

(If you haven't observed this before—try it! You will be surprised how low the resistance of the body is, especially if the fingers are moist).

(12) The most likely cause would be that the internal meter battery was low. (NOTE: A separate battery is used for the Ω × 100 range, e.m.f. = 15V. On the Ω and Ω ÷ 100, e.m.f. = 1·5V).

(13)			
(a)	Carbon or wire-wound	1—5 watts	fixed
(b)	Carbon	½ or 1 watt	fixed
(c)	Wire-wound	30—50 watts	fixed
(d)	Carbon	¼ or ½ watt	fixed
(e)	Wire-wound	3—5 watts	fixed
(f)	Carbon track (log)	¼ watt (0·5—2MΩ)	variable
(g)	Carbon track (log)	¼ watt (5kΩ)	variable
(h)	Low noise resistor (*e.g.* "Cracked" Carbon or Oxide-coated type).	½ watt	fixed

(14) A temporary repair could be achieved by "bridging" the 10kΩ variable resistor with a 10kΩ fixed resistor. The wattage rating for each type should be double the wattage rating of the 5kΩ variable resistor.

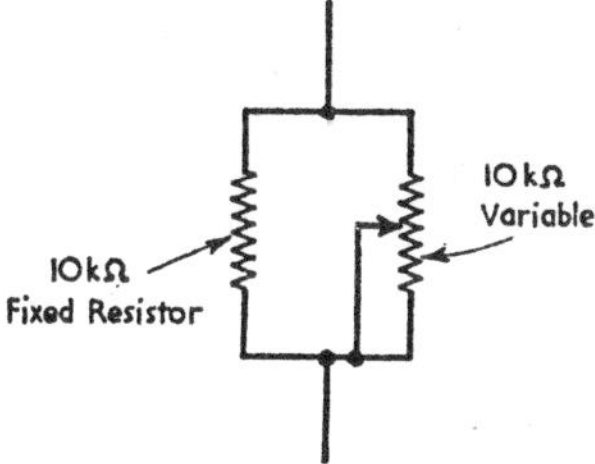

(15) The "hot" resistance may be determined by measuring the volts-drop across R and the current passing through R. The resistance may then be calculated from

$$R = \frac{V}{I} \quad \text{(where } I \text{ is in amperes).}$$

(16) Wire-wound resistors take the form of a coil and as such will possess inductance. The value of the inductance may be small, but it can be of significance if the frequency of the current flowing through it is high enough; the effective resistance of the resistor would increase due to the reactance of the inductance. Also, between the turns of the winding and between layers, there is capacitance. If the frequency is high enough the capacitance will shunt the resistor and its effective resistance would be lower than its stipulated value. Manufacturers utilize special winding techniques to reduce the self-inductance and capacitance of wire-wound resistors. [One such method is to use a bifilar winding: see answer to (17)]. Ordinary carbon resistors possess negligible inductance and capacitance, and on this account they are more suitable for use at high frequencies.

(17) The winding here is a BIFILAR winding and is used to reduce the self-inductance of the resistor. The resistance wire is first doubled and then wound on the former. Thus, adjacent turns carry current in opposite directions, and since the turns are close together, their external magnetic field is very small, consequently the self-inductance is also small.

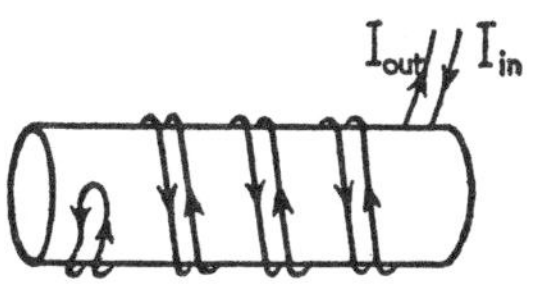

(18)

THERMISTOR CIRCUIT SYMBOLS

(a) A thermistor is a thermal sensitive resistor. It may have either a positive temperature coefficient (p.t.c.) of resistance, *i.e.* its resistance increases as the temperature increases; or it may be given a negative temperature coefficient (n.t.c.) of resistance, *i.e.* its resistance decreases with an increase of temperature.

(b) An n.t.c. thermistor in a series heater chain offers protection to the valve heaters against the large surge current that would flow through the chain at switch-on. It performs this function by virtue of its high resistance when cold which limits the current flowing in the chain and allows the valves to warm up gradually. The current, in passing through the thermistor, raises its temperature, causing its resistance to fall, thereby allowing the current to rise slowly to its operating value.

The valve heaters in thermistor-protected circuits will naturally take a longer time to warm up, but the heaters will have a longer life.

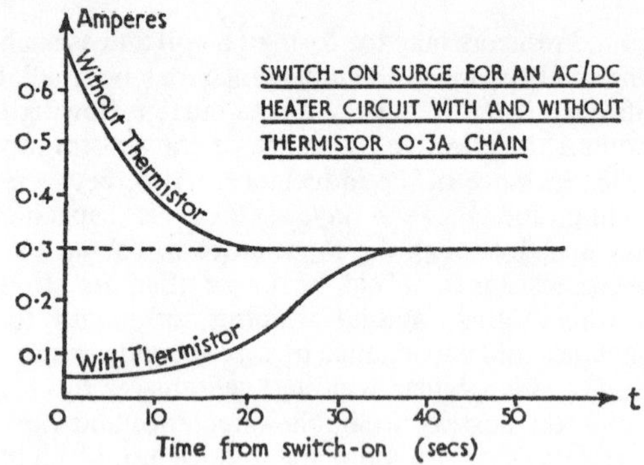

(c) Typical values:

COLD RESISTANCE	=	600Ω—3000Ω
HOT RESISTANCE	=	10Ω—40Ω

(19) Supposing that the 300Ω-section of the mains dropper rated at 30W shown at (A) was open-circuited. A temporary repair could be achieved by replacing the 300Ω-section by a separate 300Ω 30W resistor and connecting it in the manner shown at (B).

The resistor should not be bridged directly across the 300Ω section as the break in this section may "remake", in which case the resistance would be reduced to 150Ω and subsequent damage would occur to other components.

Generally, it is expedient to replace the mains dropper by a complete new unit at the earliest convenient time, as the resistance wire in the

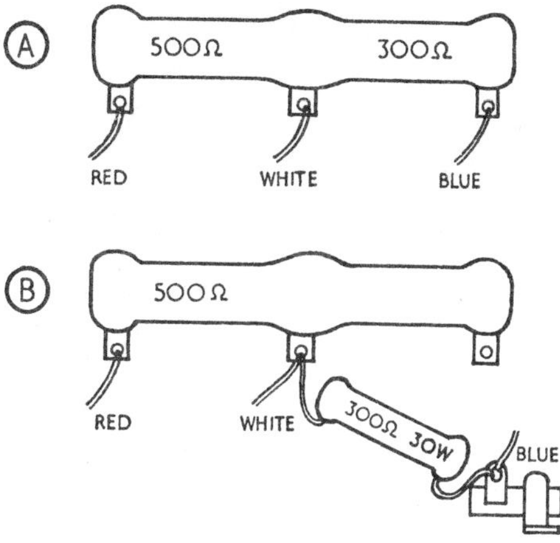

other section will most likely be "tired" (especially if it has been in use for several years) and subsequently go open-circuit.

(20)

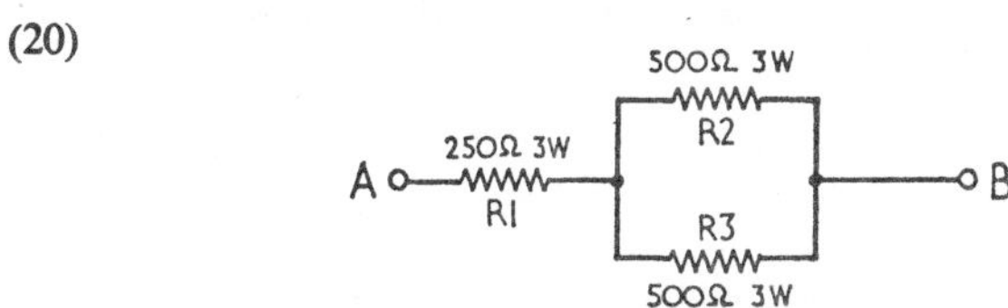

The resistors should be arranged as shown in diagram. R_2 and R_3 in parallel will give 250Ω, and this in series with R_1 will produce 500Ω between *A* and *B*. The wattage rating of the resistors will not be exceeded, since any voltage existing across *A* and *B* will be shared in equal proportions by R_1 and the parallel branch formed by R_2 and R_3.

(21) (a) Paper dielectric.

(b) This indicates that the lead-wire nearest the band is connected to the *outer foil* of the capacitor, and should be connected to the "earthy" side of the circuit. In this way the outer foil acts as a screen for the capacitor.

(c) 500V d.c. is the working voltage for the capacitor, *i.e.* the *maximum safe continuous* voltage that should be applied to it.

(d) This is best carried out on a capacitance bridge. It usually takes the form of a Wheatstone bridge with the "ratio arms" formed by a large potentiometer (see diagram overleaf). The potentiometer carries a pointer which moves over a scale calibrated in microfarads. The capacitor to be measured is connected to the test terminals, after selecting the appropriate range. The potentiometer is then rotated until "null" indication occurs (the null indicator usually being a magic eye) and the capacitance is read directly off the potentiometer scale.

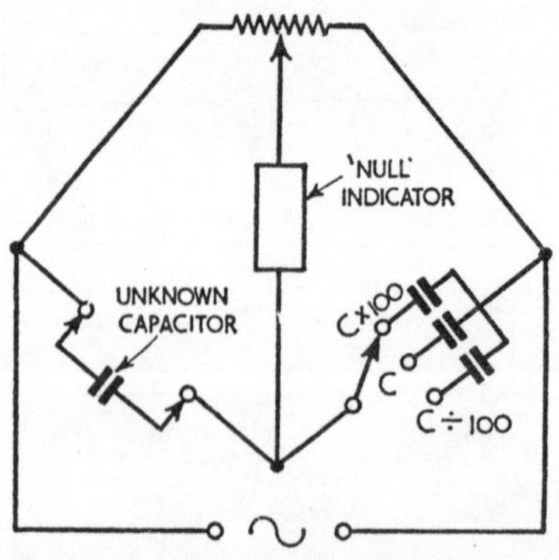

CAPACITOR BRIDGE

(22) Electrolytic and Paper—although manufacturers do their best to keep the inductance to a minimum, because it restricts the decoupling action of the capacitor at very high frequencies where the inductance may have appreciable reactance.

(23) (a) The losses which occur may be due to the following:

- (*i*) The radio frequency resistance of the lead-wires and plates.
- (*ii*) Imperfections, moisture or impurities in the dielectric, lowering the insulation resistance of the capacitor.
- (*iii*) Leakage across the surface of the dielectric.
- (*iv*) Dielectric hysteresis loss due to alternating dielectric currents.

(b) All of the losses of a capacitor as given in answer (a) may be lumped together and represented either by a small resistor R_s in series with a loss-free capacitor C_s; or by a large resistor R_p in parallel with a loss-free capacitor C_p.

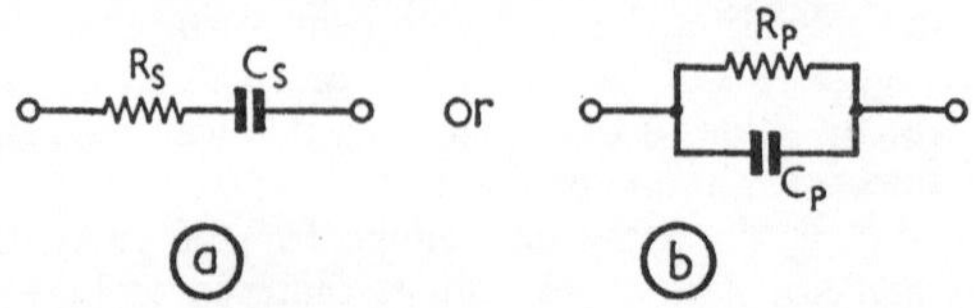

Considering circuit (a):
If a voltage V is applied to the terminals, a current i will flow. A volts-drop will occur across R_s and C_s; these quantities may all be represented by vectors in the usual way.
From the vector diagram we see that the loss angle is a small angle the size of which is governed by the losses in R_s, increasing as R_s increases. Therefore, a high-Q type capacitor will have a very small loss angle since R_s will also be very small.

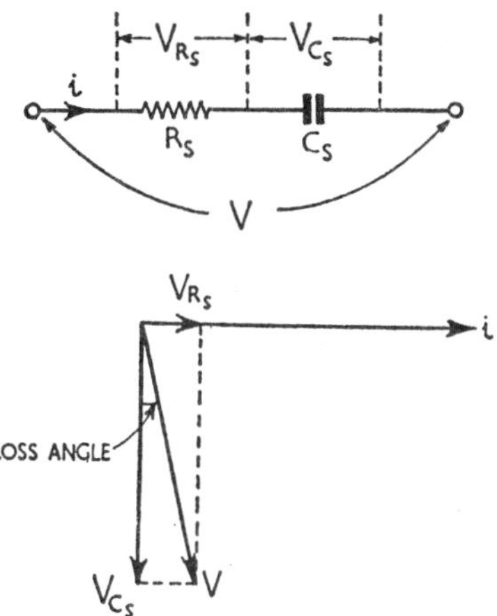

(24) (a) Audio frequency coupling capacitor.
(b) Cathode resistor by-pass capacitor in an a.f. amplifier.
(c) R.F. or i.f. filter capacitor in the demodulator stage of a receiver.
(d) Either h.t. reservoir or smoothing capacitor.
(e) R.F. decoupling of the heater chain.
(f) Signal and oscillator circuits main tuning capacitor.
(g) Oscillator or aerial circuit trimming capacitor.

(25) Wire *X* will have the larger capacitance. If *X* forms one plate and the chassis the other plate, the capacitance will increase as the distance between the two plates decreases.

(26) The capacitance between the two coils may be reduced by moving them farther apart, or by interposing between them a metal screen connected to chassis.

(27) Arrangement (c). This has an electrostatic screen placed between the two windings and is usually employed in mains transformers for the very reason of preventing capacitive coupling between the primary and secondaries.

A capacitance between each winding and the screen will exist (*Cx*), but there will be very little between the windings.

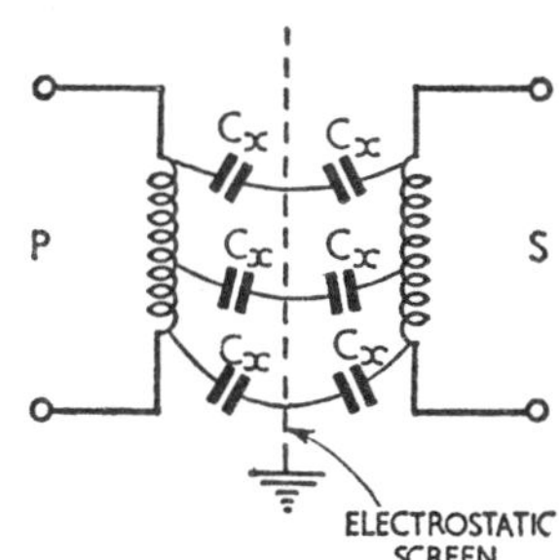

(28) CAPACITOR (A): (b) Infinity. Initial kick will not be apparent owing to the very small current taken by the 10-pF capacitor from the meter battery.

CAPACITOR (B): (c) Kick up and quickly fall to infinity as capacitor charges up to the e.m.f. of the meter battery.
One can usually perceive the initial kick in values above about $0{\cdot}002\mu F$.

(29) CAPACITOR NO. 1. This is a normal indication on an ohmmeter for a capacitor of this value; the fact that it kicked up indicates that it was charging, *i.e.* it has capacitance.

CAPACITOR NO. 2. This indicates a leaky capacitor which should be discarded.

CAPACITOR NO. 3. This indicates an-open circuit capacitor which should be discarded.

(30) This may be carried out either by using a 500V Megger (a good capacitor will normally read infinity); or by testing it on the insulation range of a capacitance bridge which will test capacitors under voltage stress.

(31) (a) Position (a).
(b) Position (c).
(c) The moving plates.
(d) The maximum capacitance (in pF) of a $0{\cdot}0005\mu F$ tuning capacitor is about 530pF, and the minimum capacitance about 30pF. When it is connected in circuit, the stray capacitance formed by the wiring and the valve may increase the maximum and minimum capacitance by about 30pF.

$$\therefore \frac{\text{max. C}}{\text{min. C}} \simeq \frac{560}{60} \simeq \underline{9:1}$$

(32) (a) $\pm 20\%$;
(b) $+50\%$ to -25% (low voltage types sometimes have a greater tolerance, *e.g.* $+100\%$ to -25%);
(c) $+50\%$ to -25%; (d) $\pm 10\%$; (e) $\pm 10\%$.

(33) No. Generally speaking, the maximum safe a.c. voltage working is about $\frac{1}{3}$ of the d.c. working voltage.
For example, a capacitor rated at 500V **d.c.** should not be used on a.c. above $\frac{500}{3} \simeq \underline{165 \text{ volts.}}$

(34) Because the capacitance varies with temperature, as do the losses. Manufacturers usually specify a working temperature range for their capacitors.

(35) (d) the electrolytic. The others should pass negligible leakage current.

(36) (a) The dielectric in electrolytics is aluminium oxide. The oxide forms on the positive electrode as a very thin film. The thinness of the film accounts for the large capacitances which can be obtained with this type of capacitor.

(b) If the polarity markings on the capacitor are not observed, reversal of the connecting leads will cause the leakage current to increase. The capacitor will then overheat and may possibly explode. Always make sure that "positive volts" are connected to the + terminal on the capacitor.

(c) This refers to the chemical etching of the positive electrode (the anode) of an electrolytic capacitor. An increase in surface area results, which enables larger capacitances to be obtained.

(d) After a period of idleness (*e.g.* several months in stock), the leakage current of an electrolytic is noticeably greater. A re-forming period is required to reduce the leakage current to an acceptable level. This is best achieved by connecting the capacitor to a source of d.c. voltage, the value of which is gradually increased in steps up to the working voltage of the capacitor. The process is known as "re-forming". Some capacitance bridges have facilities for re-forming electrolytics.
As a rule, the leakage current after periods of idleness is greater for wet than for dry types.

(e) The leakage current may be measured by using the arrangement shown. A series resistor is used to limit the maximum current to 250mA in case the capacitor is short circuited.

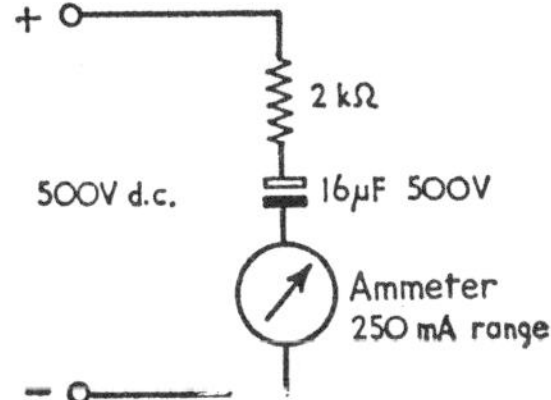

(37) C_1: Capacitor in good condition.
C_2: Very large leakage current: discard capacitor.
C_3: Capacitor open circuited, as all electrolytics pass *some* leakage current: discard capacitor.

(38) The 32μF capacitors should have a surge rating of 525V each. The resistors are included to equalize the voltages across the two capacitors. This arrangement will withstand surge voltages up to ≏ 1050V.

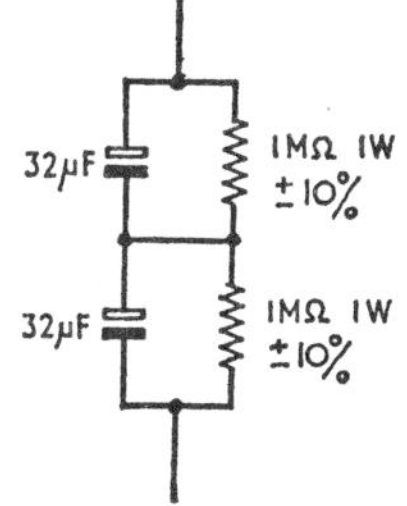

(39) Connection (c) is the only one that is "safe".

(40) (a) INDUCTOR (air-cored). (b) INDUCTOR (dust-cored or ferrite-cored).
(c) INDUCTOR (iron-cored). (d) INDUCTOR (variable dust-cored or ferrite-cored).
(e) TRANSFORMER (air-cored). (f) TRANSFORMER (iron-cored).
(g) TRANSFORMER (dust-cored or ferrite-cored). (h) TRANSFORMER (i.f. type with variable iron-dust cores or ferrite-cores and screening can).

(41) (a) Positions (b) and (c) will both result in maximum inductance.
(b) Position (a) will result in minimum inductance.
(c) Position (a) will result in highest resonant frequency. (Minimum inductance).
(d) Positions (b) and (c) will result in the same lowest resonant frequency. (Maximum inductance).

(42) (a) Position (a) will result in maximum inductance.
(b) Position (a) will result in lowest resonant frequency.

(43) (a) and (b) will both increase the inductance.

(44) (a) Between adjacent turns, and between each turn and all others, there exists capacitance; a few of these separate capacitances are shown in the diagram. When these individual capacitances are lumped together, they form what is known as the **self-capacitance of the coil.** Manufacturers try to keep the self-capacitance to a minimum as it may restrict the tuning range of a coil. Also, it forms with the inductance a resonant circuit which may, for example, produce undesirable peaks in the output of an amplifier.

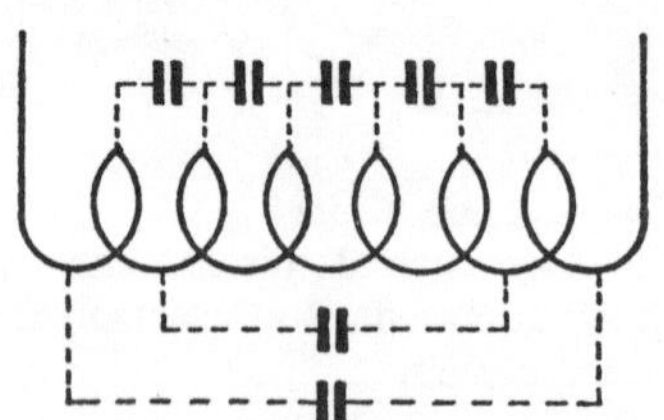

(b) The Q-factor of a coil is basically a ratio of the energy stored in the coil compared to the energy lost in the coil, per cycle. The energy stored in the coil exists in the form of a magnetic field around the coil when a current flows through it; the energy lost in the coil appears as heat and is due to the resistance of the coil. This ratio is usually expressed as

$$\frac{2\pi fL}{R}$$

i.e. it is a ratio of the reactance of the coil to its resistance.

(Note that R includes all the losses, not just its d.c. resistance). Q is therefore a measure of the "goodness" of the coil, and a high-Q coil will possess a large reactance and a small resistance. Its energy loss will therefore be small.

(c) "Skin effect" is a phenomenon which occurs when a conductor carries high frequency alternating currents. The current is not distributed evenly over the cross-section but tends to concentrate near to the surface of the conductor; the current that flows in the centre tends to decrease as the frequency of the alternating current increases. This means that the effective resistance of the conductor is increased when it carries high-frequency alternating currents, and accounts for R [see Answer (b)] being greater than the d.c. resistance of the coil. The effect may be reduced in two ways: (*i*) using tubular conductors; and (*ii*) using Litz wire.

(d) Litz wire is a multi-stranded wire, each strand being insulated from the others, and specially wound so that the outer strands lead into the centre of the conductor. It is used to reduce skin effect. Care must be taken when soldering this type of wire in circuit to ensure that *all* the strands are soldered properly, otherwise the benefits to be gained by using the wire will be lost.

(45) The coil should preferably have a Q of 200 (c)—since the higher the Q the sharper the tuning.
The capacitor should possess a low power factor (i).

(46) (a) Measurement of the inductance of a coil is most conveniently carried out by using an inductance bridge employing the principle of the Wheatstone bridge. It is usual to balance out the positive reactance of the unknown coil with the negative reactance of a calibrated standard capacitor placed in the opposite arm of the bridge. The resistor R is adjusted during the balancing to compensate for the resistance losses of the coil.

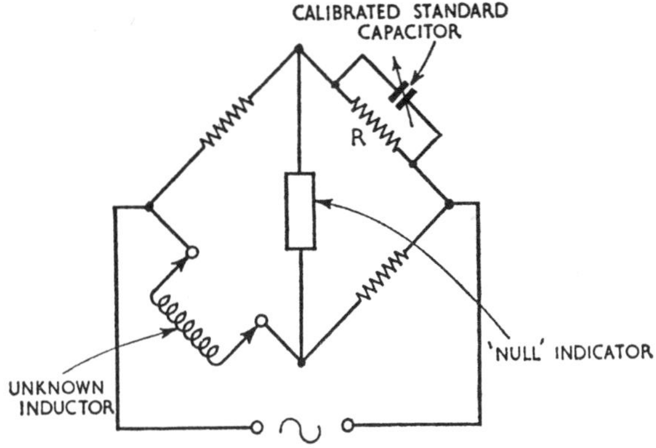

(b) The continuity of a coil may be tested by connecting the leads of an ohmmeter to the ends of the coil and noting the resistance reading obtained. The value of the resistance will depend upon the purpose of the coil, *e.g.*

TUNING COILS: from a fraction of an ohm up to 50Ω.
R.F. CHOKES: from about 200Ω up to 1,000Ω.
L.F. CHOKES: from about 100Ω up to 1,000Ω.

The continuity of a coil should not be checked with a Megger as the breaks which may occur are very fine, and the high voltage from a Megger may "arc" across a break and register continuity on the scale of the instrument.

(47) (d) 1μH to 100mH.

(48) (a) (*iv*) *AB* 500Ω—*CD* 2Ω.
(b) Both (*iii*) and (*iv*) are correct: the others are incorrect.
(c) (*ii*) Infinity: the others are incorrect.
(d) (*iii*) To obtain the required inductance using the minimum number of turns to keep the size of the transformer reasonable.

(49) (a) (*i*) 20Ω—100Ω.
(*ii*) 100Ω—500Ω.
(b) (*i*) Infinity.
(*ii*) Infinity.
(*iii*) Infinity.
(c) The Megger.
(d) This means that the h.t. winding is electrically centre-tapped, and across each half of the winding there is a voltage of 350V r.m.s., *i.e* across the full winding there will be 700V r.m.s. This will be the voltage present when the winding is carrying its full rated current of 100mA. If the current drawn from the secondary is less than this, the voltage will be slightly higher. If the current is greater, the output voltage will fall, the transformer will overheat, and damage will result. For this reason the secondary is normally fused in the centre-tap connection to protect the transformer against accidental overloads.
(e) A full-wave rectifier.
(f) The heater winding will be wound with a heavy gauge wire, as it will be carrying heavy currents; whereas the h.t. winding will be wound with a lighter gauge wire, since it is carrying much smaller currents.
(g) Excessive heat may be caused by:
(*i*) Shorted turns on primary or secondary.
(*ii*) Short present on heater wiring, or valve with s/c heater.
(*iii*) Short, or partial short, on h.t. line to chassis.
(*iv*) Low insulation between primary and secondaries, or between core and either primary or secondaries.
(*v*) Transformer inadequate for load current requirements.
(Not a fault found in a well-designed power supply).

(h) (*i*) Peak voltage across full h.t. winding $= 700 \times 1{\cdot}414 \simeq \underline{990V.}$

(*ii*) Peak voltage across heater winding $= 6{\cdot}3 \times 1{\cdot}414 \simeq \underline{9V.}$

(50) (a) EF80. R.F. pentode, requiring 6·3 volts on its heater, using a B9A valve base.

(b) UCL83. Triode and output pentode, heater series connected, 100mA, using a B9A valve base.

(c) EY86. Half-wave e.h.t. rectifier, requiring 6·3 volts on its heater, using a B9A base.

(d) PCC84. Double triode, heater series connected, 300mA, using a B9A base.

(e) EZ41. Full-wave rectifier, requiring 6·3 volts on its heater, using a B8A base.

(f) EM81. Tuning Indicator, requiring 6·3 volts on its heater, using a B9A base.

(g) UAF42. Single diode and r.f. pentode, heater series connected, 100mA, using a B8A base.

(h) EB91. Double diode, requiring 6·3 volts on its heater, using a B7G base.

(i) UCH81. Triode heptode, heater series connected, 100mA, using a B9A base.

(j) EL34. Output pentode, requiring 6·3 volts on its heater, using an Octal base.

(k) OC44. P-N-P junction r.f. transistor.

(l) OA81. Germanium diode.

(m) OC78. P-N-P junction transistor.

(n) GZ32. Full-wave rectifier, requiring 5 volts on its heater, using an Octal base.

(o) HF93. R.F. pentode, heater series connected, 150mA, using a B7G base.

(p) MW43-80. T.V. tube, 17″ screen, 6·3V heater, B12A base.

(q) AW43-80. T.V. tube, 17″ screen, 6·3V heater, B12A base.

(r) PCL82. Triode and output pentode, heater series connected, 300mA, using a B9A base.

(s) DK96. Heptode, requiring 1·4 volts on its filament, using a B7G base.

(t) DL96. Output pentode, requiring 1·4 volts on its filament, using a B7G base.

(51)

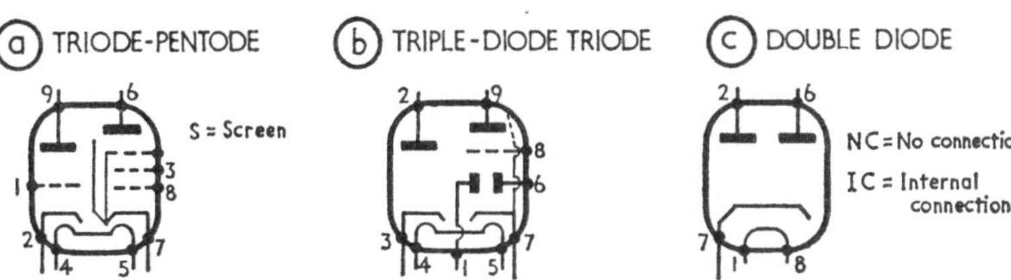

—continued

(51) *cont.*

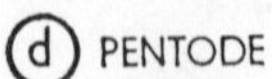

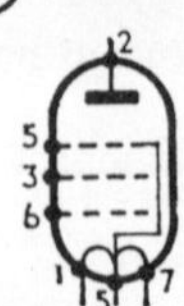

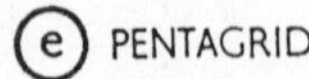

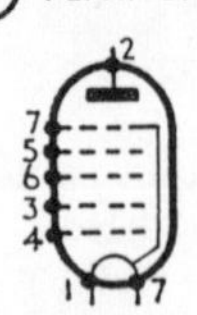

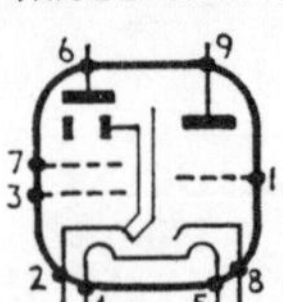

(52)

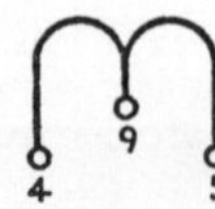

(a) A centre-tapped heater is used: pin 9 is the centre tap, pins 4 and 5 being the outer connections. This allows the heater to be connected in one of two ways:

(*i*) SERIES CONNECTED. Connect 12·6-volt heater supply to pins 4 and 5. Valve will then draw 150mA from the supply.

(*ii*) PARALLEL CONNECTED. Connect 6·3-volt heater supply to pins 4 and 5 strapped together, and pin 9. Valve will then draw 300mA from the supply.

(b) K″ Cathode No. 2 triode.

(c) (*i*) Approximately 1/7th of the hot resistance.

$$\text{Hot resistance} = \frac{V}{I} = \frac{12{\cdot}6}{150} \times 1000 = 84\Omega$$

$$\therefore \text{ Cold resistance} = \frac{84}{7} = \underline{12\Omega.}$$

(*ii*) Infinity.

(*iii*) Approximately one-half that obtained in (*i*) $= \underline{6\Omega.}$

(*iv*) Infinity.

(*v*) Infinity.

(53) The component is a point contact diode.

(a) Demodulator in a radio or television receiver, amongst many other uses.

(b) The + sign indicates the cathode end of the diode.

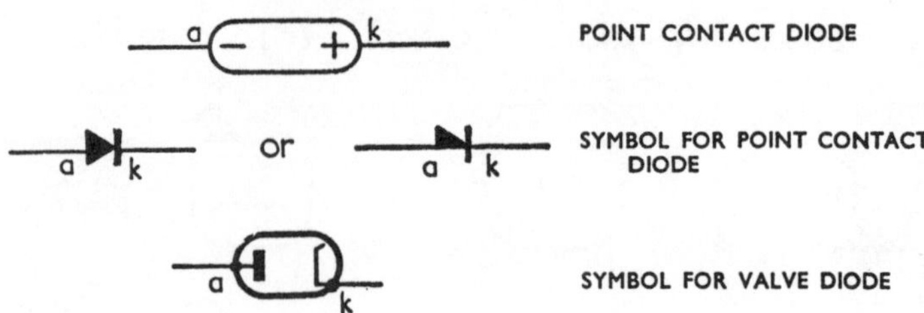

(c) A heat-sink should always be used when soldering it into circuit to avoid damage to the device. The end wires should not be bent close to body, otherwise the lead may fracture or the enclosure crack under the strain. It must not be mounted near sources of heat, such as valves, resistors, etc.

(54) (b) It depends on meter polarity. When the diode is forward biased a low resistance reading will be obtained (typically 500Ω); and when reverse biased a high resistance reading will result (typically 2MΩ).

(55) Circuit (a).

(56) The component is a transistor.

(a) Emitter; Base; Collector.

(b) The lead wire nearest the spot is connected to the collector. On some transistors the collector-wire lead is more widely spaced than the other two.

BASE
EMITTER
COLLECTOR

(c) To prevent the maximum safe junction temperature being exceeded (for certain Mullard transistors this is 75°C), otherwise the soldered joints of the emitter and collector pellets may become loose, or the indium diffuse too far into the *n*-type germanium (this may increase the "noise").

(d) For a p-n-p transistor the base is n-type.
For an n-p-n transistor the collector and emitter are n-type.

(e) OC71.

(f) (*i*) ≏ 10kΩ (*ii*) ≏ 2MΩ (*iii*) ≏ 300Ω
MEDIUM R. HIGH R. LOW R.

(g) The leakage current flowing in a transistor is affected by both heat and light. It is therefore necessary to exclude the light from the sensitive elements by means of a light-proof container, otherwise the characteristics of the device will alter. The con-container is usually either a metal cap or a blackened glass-bulb.

(h) As the transistor manufacturer generally quotes the value of $I'co$ for a particular value of voltage between collector and emitter, P is set to give this required voltage, then the value of

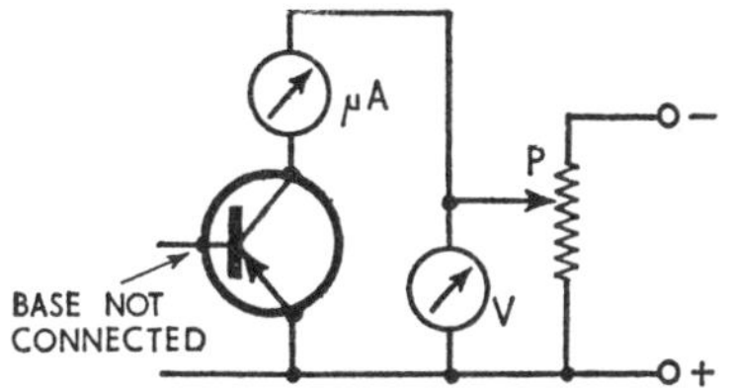

$I'co$ can be read directly from the μA meter in the collector circuit.
$I'co$ is normally of the order of tens of μAs (*iv*).

(i) Thermal runaway is a process whereby the collector current of a transistor continues to rise due to internal heating until it is limited by some external means (resistance), or until the transistor is eventually destroyed.
It may be prevented by using a stabilizing circuit which protects the d.c. working point against excessive shift.
The most common arrangement employs a potential divider, R_1 and R_2, for supplying the base potential; and an emitter resistor R_e to introduce negative d.c. feedback which increases when the temperature of the transistor rises.

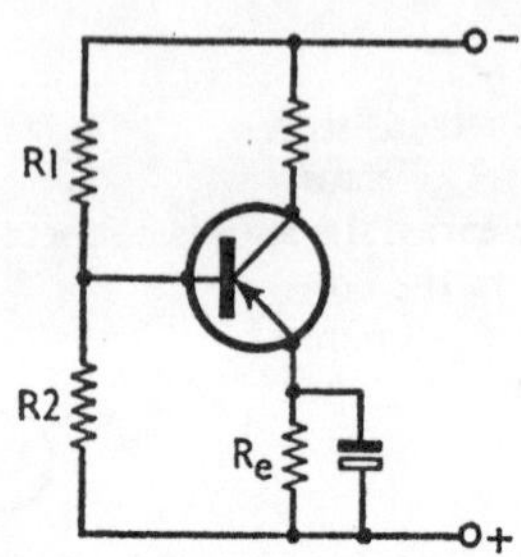

(j)

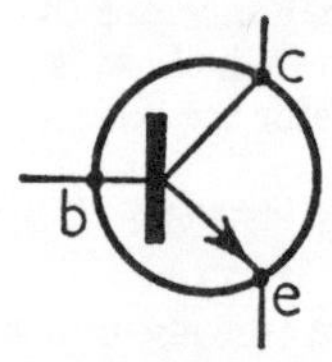

N-P-N TRANSISTOR SYMBOL

(57) The answer is 1kHz. Note that the period (p) of one cycle is 1mS ($f = 1/p$).
(58) (a) Sine-wave; (b) parabola; (c) rectangular or pulse; (d) saw-tooth or ramp; (e) square-wave.
(59) (d) is correct.
(60) (a) 300m (note $\lambda = f/v$).
(61) Waveforms (a), (d) and (f) have a d.c. component.
(62) (a) 240V.
(63) A d.c. amplifier will amplify both a.c. and d.c.
(64) An a.c. amplifier will amplify a.c. only.
(65) (a) An *AND* gate.
(b) 111, *i.e.* all three inputs must be present.
(66) (a) An *OR* gate.
(b) 00.

(67) (a) A *NAND* gate. This is an *AND* gate followed by a *NOT* gate which is an inverter.

(b) (*ii*), (*iii*) and (*iv*) may give rise to this condition.

(68) (a) A *NOR* gate, *i.e.* an *OR* gate followed by a *NOT* gate.

(b) 000.

(69) (*v*) is correct. In the diagram given below it will be noted that in order to obtain binary 1 at the output, binary 1 must be present at the outputs of the *AND* and *OR* gates. There are three choices that will satisfy this condition: 0000, 1000 or 0100.

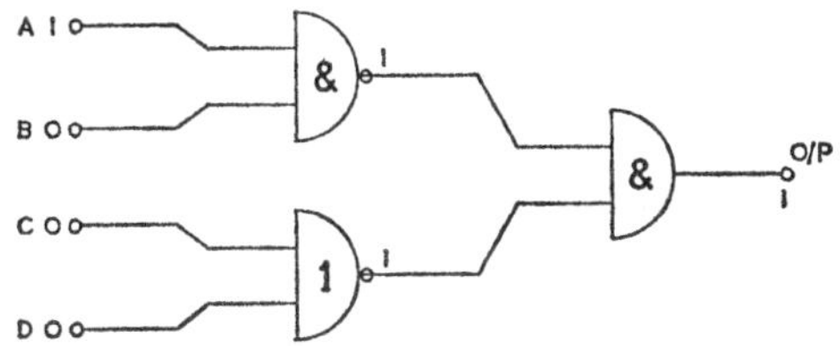

(70) (a) Emissive; (b) Resistive or conductive; (c) Voltaic.

(71) (a) Fuse; (b) Fixed Resistor; (c) Indicator Lamp; (d) Wires Crossing; (e) Wires connecting; (f) Potentiometer; (g) Inductor; (h) S.C.R.; (i) Insulated-Gate F.E.T. (n-channel); (j) Zener Diode; (k) Unijunction Transistor (n-type base).

(72) (*iv*) 100mV—200mV.

(73) (*ii*) 600mV—700mV.

(74) (*ii*) is correct. The diode must be reverse biased. Provided the input voltage does not fall below the zener (o/p) voltage a stabilized output will be maintained.

(75) Statements (*i*), (*iii*) and (*v*) are true. (Note that the steeper the slope the lower the resistance of the device; also that the characteristic is symmetrical).

(76) (a) Differentiator; (b) D.C. restorer; (c) Clipper or limiter; (d) Integrator; (e) Full-wave rectifier; (f) A.C. amplifier. (Note that the d.c. component of the input waveform does not appear in the output).

(77) Red, blue and green.

(78) (*i*) Yellow; (*ii*) Magenta; (*iii*) Cyan; (*iv*) White; (*v*) White.

(79) (a) Reverse biased.

(b) As shown in the diagram below, an increase in the reverse bias will result in a decrease in capacitance.

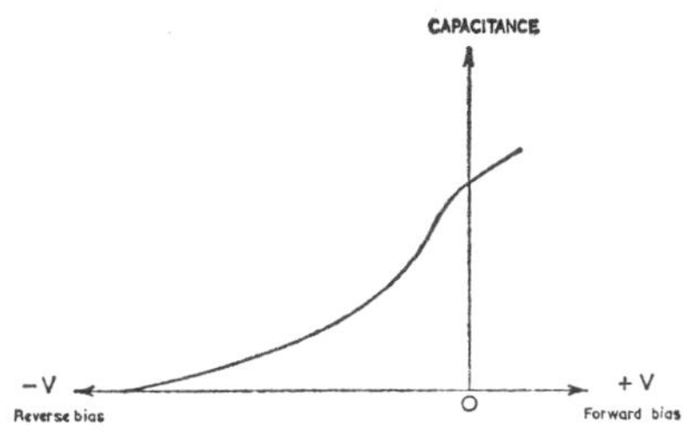

(80) (*iv*) is correct.

(81) (*i*) is correct.

(82) (*iii*) is correct. Once conduction has commenced the gate loses control and cannot be used to switch off the device. It is switched off by lowering the anode voltage so that the anode current falls below its maintenance level.

(83) (a) Block 1—r.f. amplifier, pre-selector or aerial tuning. Block 3—i.f. amplifier (1st). Block 5—a.m. detector. Block 7—local oscillator.

(b) A different type of demodulator would be required, *i.e.* an f.m. detector which responds to f.m. signals but not to a.m. signals.

(c) No change would be necessary to block 6. It would be necessary for the i.f. amplifier to work at a higher frequency (usually 10·7MHz for a domestic receiver). Also, the bandwidth of the tuned circuits would need to be greater for f.m. signals. Fundamentally, the stage functions in the same way for both a.m. and f.m.

(d) The local oscillator is tuned above the incoming signal on L.W. and M.W. by the i.f. Thus the frequency of the local oscillator would be

$$1{\cdot}11 + 0{\cdot}47\text{MHz} = \underline{1{\cdot}58\text{MHz}}$$

(84) (a) In diagram (a) the beam would be deflected upwards. In (b) the beam would continue on a straight path between the plates as there is zero p.d. between the plates. In (c) the beam would be deflected downwards.

(b) This is electrostatic deflection.

(c) (*i*) Magnetic; (*ii*) Electrostatic.

(85) (*ii*) is correct. The final anode potential accelerates the electrons to a high velocity so as to cause the screen phosphor to glow on being struck by the fast-moving electrons.

(86) (*iii*) is correct.

(87) (*ii*) is correct.

(88) (*i*) This input will cause the trace to move upwards. If the Y amplifier gain is set to a sensitive position the trace may move completely off the screen.

(*ii*) An opposite polarity d.c. input will cause the trace to move downwards. This is the usual convention which is employed in oscilloscopes: positive = upwards; and negative = downwards.

(*iii*) The trace will be deflected upwards on the positive half-cycle and downwards on the negative half-cycle. Thus the screen will display the pattern of the input waveform. Note that in the d.c. position, the Y amplifier will amplify a.c. as well as d.c. However, if the input signal contains a d.c. component as well as an a.c. component, the d.c. may cause the trace to move off the screen if the d.c. component is large compared with the a.c. component. Should one wish to inspect the a.c. component only it would be best to set the switch to a.c.

(89) If the Y amplifier gain is increased by a factor of ten the deflection sensitivity will increase by the same amount, *i.e.* to 10mV/cm. Thus with a deflection of 5cm the input signal must be 50mV peak.

(90) Maximum power will occur in the load *R* when the resistance of *R* is equal to the internal resistance of the generator. Under this condition there will be one half of the generator voltage across *R*, *i.e.* 7·5V. Thus (*iii*) is correct.

(91) (*iv*) is correct.

(92) In bunches. (*i*) is correct.

(93) (*iv*) 1500MHz.

(94) (*iv*) is correct.

(95) (*ii*) Cavities in the anode block.

(96) A transducer is a device which converts one type of signal into an electrical signal or *vice versa*. For example, a microphone converts the sound pressures (mechanical force) on the diaphragm into an electrical voltage.

(97) An analogue quantity is one which can vary continuously and has no steps. Thus an analogue measuring instrument is one which gives a smooth variation. Most measuring instruments are analogue devices. (*i*), (*ii*), (*iv*) and (*v*) are analogue devices.

(98) Waveforms (b) and (c) are digital type signals *i.e.* having steps.

(99) An *AND* gate would be required here. There would be no output signal thus the machine would not start until all five safety switches were closed.

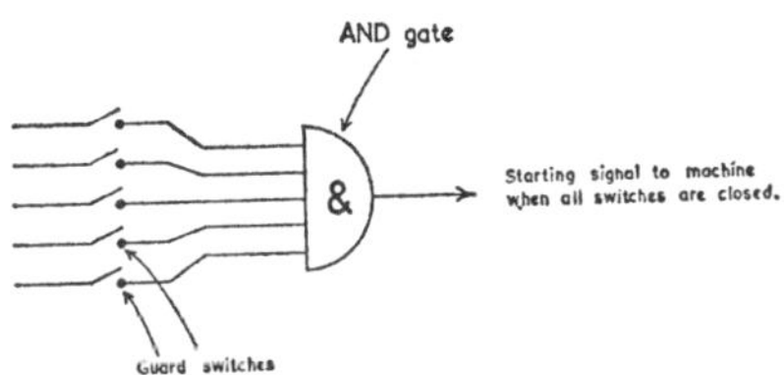

(100) (*i*) This is false. The eye responds more to some colours than others even when they are projected with equal energy. The eye is more sensitive to yellow and green than it is to red and blue.

(*ii*) This is true. The sensitivity of a photoelectric cell is not normally uniform over its operating spectrum. It often peaks at a particular wavelength and falls off either side. In some cells the maximum sensitivity may lie outside the visible light spectrum, *i.e.* the cell may be useful for detecting infra-red.

(*iii*) This is false. Sound waves in air travel at about 340 metres/sec. In water the velocity is about 1450 metres/sec.

(*iv*) This is false. Pulse radar is normally used to measure an object's distance and to determine its position. Velocity is usually measured with C.W. systems.

(101) Diagram (c) is correct, *i.e.* the discharge is exponential.

(102) (a) is correct. Essentially a fuse is fitted to prevent the apparatus and wiring from overheating to eliminate the risk of fire. At the same time it may prevent components from excessive damage.

(103) (c) is correct.

(104) (b) is correct.

(105) 5A.

(106) (a) is correct. Usually a 2A or 3A fuse is fitted. Some allowance must be given for switch-on surges.

(107) (d) is correct. The square wave which is a symmetrical waveform may be considered as being composed of a fundamental sine wave and a large number of odd harmonics.

(108) (d) is correct. $11011 = 16 + 8 + 0 + 2 + 1 = 27$.

(109) (b) is correct $11111 = 16 + 8 + 4 + 2 + 1 = 31$.

(110) (b) is correct.

$$\left(\text{Modulation index} = \frac{\text{frequency deviation}}{\text{modulating frequency}}\right)$$

(111) A megger should be used because this checks the insulation under voltage stress.

(112)

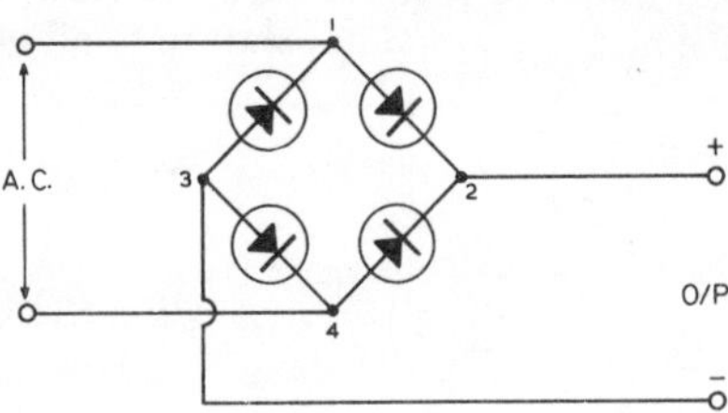

(113) (d) 0·97.

(114) (a) 50×10^{-6}S.

(115) (d) 60.

(116) (a) 50.

(117) Transistor No. 1: Faulty—Both junctions s/c.
Transistor No. 2: Faulty—Collector-base junction normal but base-emitter junction is open circuit (emitter lead o/c).
Transistor No. 3: Normal readings for a serviceable transistor.

(118) The heat radiated from a body depends upon the nature of its surface; a dull black body radiating better at a particular temperature than a shiny white one. The use of a blackened heat sink improves the rate of heat loss and assists in ensuring that the maximum junction temperature of the device fitted to the heat sink is not exceeded.

(119) The effective capacitance $= \dfrac{C_1 \times C_2}{C_1 + C_2} = \dfrac{60 \times 120}{180}\text{pF} = 40\text{pF}$

(120) The effective capacitance $= C_1 + C_2$
$= 2 + 50$ nF (2000pF = 2nF)
$= 52$nF

(121) (a) 300V. Note that the distribution of voltage varies inversely with the capacitance values.

(122) The maximum voltage permitted across C_1 is 200V. Now, with 200V across C_1 there will be 100V across C_2 since the capacitance of C_2 is twice that of C_1.
Thus the maximum voltage across A-B = 200 + 100V
= 300V

(123)

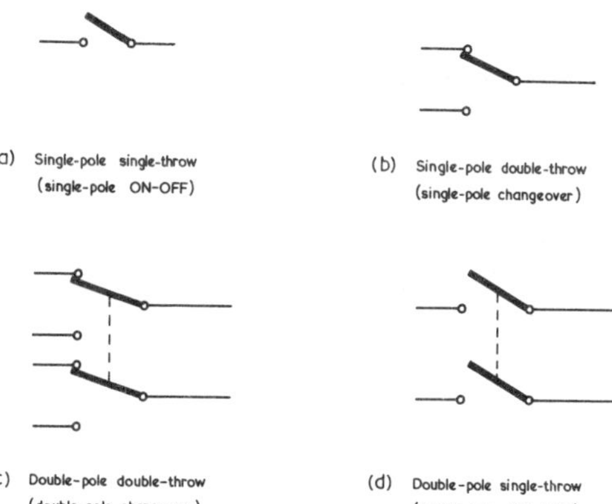

(a) Single-pole single-throw (single-pole ON-OFF)

(b) Single-pole double-throw (single-pole changeover)

(c) Double-pole double-throw (double-pole changeover)

(d) Double-pole single-throw (double-pole ON-OFF)

(124) (a) 4R7K = 4·7Ω ±10%
(b) 68KK = 68kΩ ±10%
(c) 2M2M = 2·2MΩ ±20%
(d) R68J = 0·68Ω ±5%
(e) 1ROG = 1Ω ±2%
(f) 27RF = 27Ω ±1%
Note that the last letter in the code indicates the tolerance:
F = ±1% G = ±2% J = ±5% K = ±10% M = ±20%

(125) Before the i.c. is fitted into circuit it is prudent to check that the d.c. and signal supplies to the pins are of normal magnitude; also that associated external components are in good order. Note that an excess voltage or faulty component may damage the i.c. Next, before fitting the i.c. make sure that it is the right way round

otherwise it may be permanently damaged. An indentation or some other mark at one end of the i.c. serves to ensure correct orientation. Locate the i.c. into its holder or printed-circuit board, taking care not to bend or break the pins which are quite brittle. If the i.c. is to be soldered use the minimum of solder and do not apply excessive heat.

SECTION (2) MODULE AND BLOCK FAULT-FINDING LOGIC

(1)*

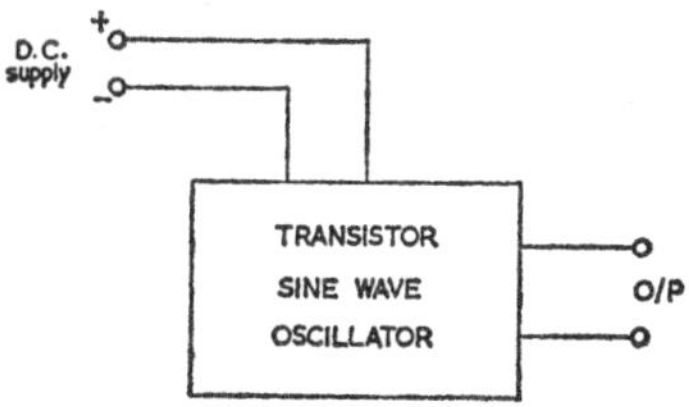

(a) Draw the waveform which will normally be present at the output terminals.

(b) What is the SOURCE of the power that may be taken from the output terminals?

(c) The frequency of the output signal is 50kHz at a level of 100mV r.m.s. Suggest two methods of detecting the presence of this signal.

(d) Should there be no output as indicated by either of your selected test methods, what check would you now make to diagnose the trouble?

(e) If the oscillator was of the valve type would there be need for any additional check to that in (d)?

(2)*

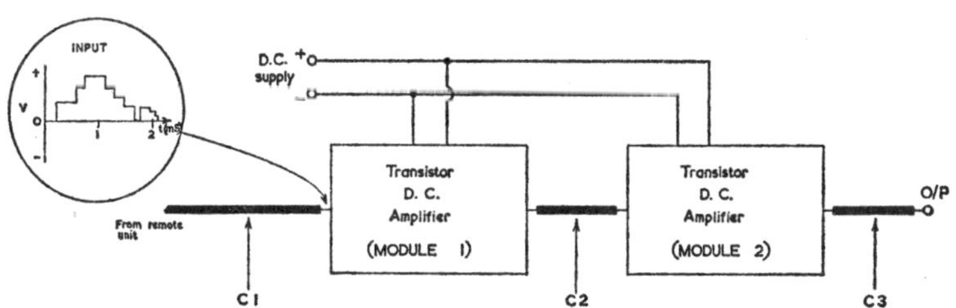

(a) When all is in order the phase of the output signal from module 2 will be:

(*i*) Same as input

(*ii*) Depends upon the number of transistors in each module and the circuit configurations employed

(*iii*) Of opposite phase to the input

(*iv*) Opposite to the input signal for module 2.

—continued

(2) *Cont.*

(b) The best way to check the phase of the o/p signal waveform would be to use:
  (*i*) A double-trace c.r.o.
  (*ii*) An a.c. valve-voltmeter
  (*iii*) A single-trace c.r.o.
  (*iv*) A digital voltmeter.

(c) A signal is obtained from the output end of coaxial line C_2 but not from the output end of C_3. The next logical step would be to:
  (*i*) Check the d.c. supply to module 2
  (*ii*) Remove module 2 and commence detailed investigation on that module
  (*iii*) Make a disturbance test on module 2
  (*iv*) Make a further signal check using the c.r.o.

(d) There is no signal at the output end of C_3. Would you:
  (*i*) Conclude that a fault lies in modules 1 or 2
  (*ii*) Carry out further signal checks using the c.r.o.
  (*iii*) Check the d.c. supply
  (*iv*) Replace modules 1 and 2.

(e) The signal is present at the input to module 1 but not at its output. Would you conclude that:
  (*i*) The defect must lie in module 1
  (*ii*) The fault must lie in module 1 or the d.c. supply to it
  (*iii*) The defect will most likely be in module 1 or the d.c. supply to it, but could lie in C_2 or module 2
  (*iv*) Replacement of both modules is bound to effect a cure.

(f) At the output end of C_3 the signal is of very low amplitude but is quite normal at the input to module 1. Which of the following tests would you make next?
  (*i*) Check the signal at the output of module 1 and if low in amplitude check the d.c. supply to the module
  (*ii*) Check the signal input to module 2 and if low test the d.c. supply to module 1
  (*iii*) Check the signal at the output of module 1 and if low replace module 1
  (*iv*) Replace both modules.

(3)

The block diagram opposite is of 8 plug-in modules which form the electronics of a piece of industrial control equipment. The input to M_1 is a sine wave of variable amplitude and frequency and the output of M_8 is a rectangular pulse of constant amplitude and duration. Modules 1—8 are concerned with the processing of the input signal and the production of the output pulse. There is no output from M_8 unless there is an input to M_1.

(a) If there is no output from M_8 would you commence logical fault-finding by:
  (*i*) Carrying out systematic d.c. checks on each unit in turn starting at M_1 and working towards M_8
  (*ii*) Replacing each module in turn commencing with M_1

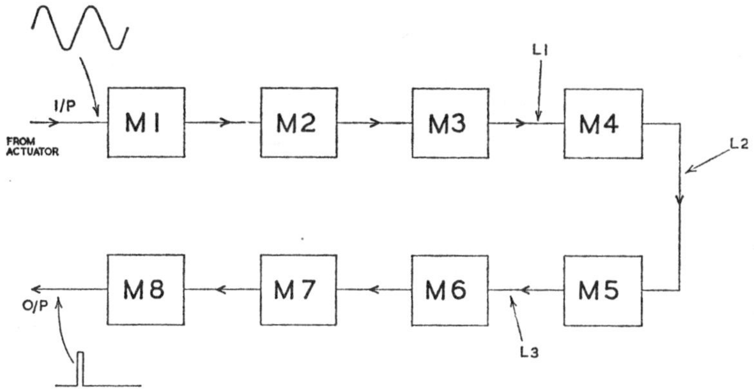

(*iii*) Checking the d.c. supply to each module
(*iv*) Checking for the presence of the signal at the input to M_1.

(b) There is a signal input to M_1 but no output pulse from M_8. Quickly to find the fault would you first:

(*i*) Check for the presence of appropriate waveform at the output of M_4
(*ii*) Check for the presence of the appropriate waveform at the output of M_2
(*iii*) Check for the presence of the appropriate waveform at the output of M_6
(*iv*) Test the d.c. supply to each module.

(c) There is no output from M_8 and initial tests carried out on the system revealed no waveform at the output of M_4 but correct waveform at the output of M_3. Would you say (assuming the d.c. supply to each module is correct) that the fault is confined to:

(*ii*) M_3, M_4 or interconnecting leads L_1/L_2
(*ii*) M_4, M_5 or interconnecting leads L_1/L_2
(*iii*) M_4 or L_1
(*iv*) L_2.

(d) If the signal from the actuator is missing due to a break down how could you check that the electronic modules are in order?

(e) Choose from the list below two tests which will quickly pinpoint the faulty area if there is no output from M_8. Place the checks in the order which you would carry them out.

(*i*) Replace each module in turn
(*ii*) Check the d.c. supply to each module
(*iii*) Check the input waveform to each module if the previous test is positive
(*iv*) Check the input waveform to M_1
(*v*) Use half, quarter and eighth-split method, checking waveforms with c.r.o. if previous test is positive
(*vi*) Feed in a test signal to M_1 and note whether or not there is an output from M_8.

(4)

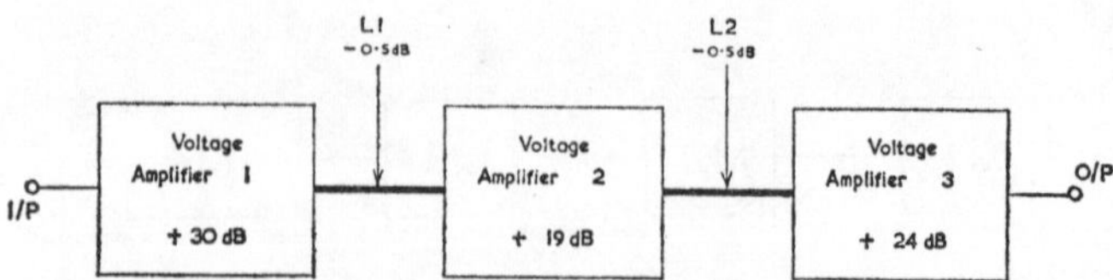

(a) What is the overall voltage gain in decibels from I/P to O/P?

(b) If the amplitude of the input signal to Amplifier 1 is 50μV, what will be the amplitude of the signal?

(*i*) at the output of Amplifier 3; and

(*ii*) at the input to Amplifier 3.

(c) Due to a fault condition if the loss introduced by the connecting cable L_1 was increased to 78·5dB, what would be the amplitude of the O/P signal with 80μV applied to the I/P.

(5)

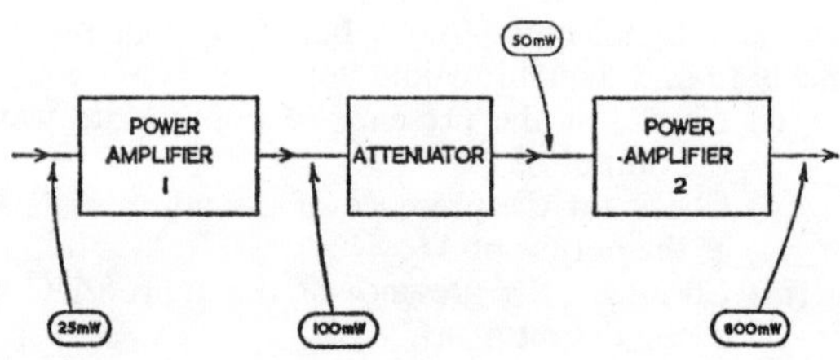

(a) Express the gain or loss introduced by each of the three blocks in decibels.

(b) What would be the power at the output of Amplifier 2 if the attenuator were not included?

(c) What is the overall power gain in decibels from input to output?

(6)

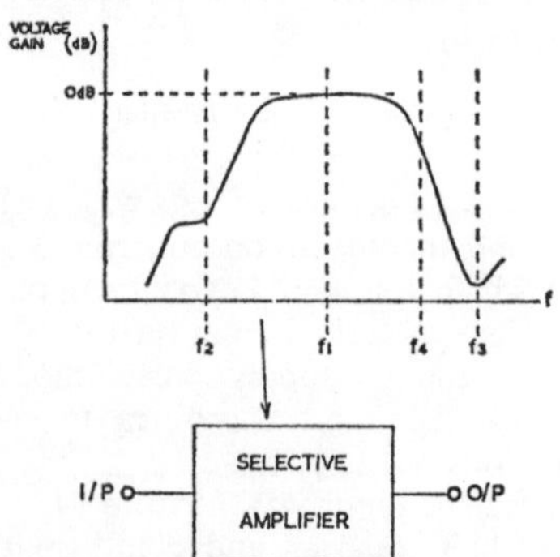

The response curve shown above is for the selective amplifier given in block form. When a signal of frequency f_1 is injected into the amplifier an output voltage of 1V is obtained. What will be the amplitude of the output signal when signals with frequency f_2, f_3 and f_4 are applied to the input (at the same level used for f_1 input) when:

(a) f_4 is 3dB down from f_1;

(b) f_3 is 36dB down from f_1; and

(c) f_2 is 6dB up from f_3?

(7)

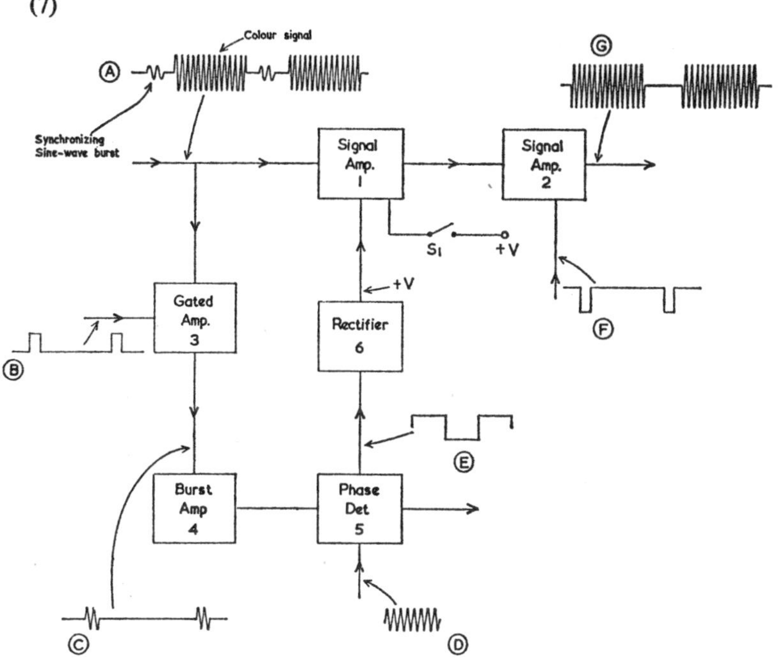

The above block diagram shows part of the colour signal processing used in a number of colour t.v. decoders. Before attempting the questions carefully read and digest the following basic facts about its operation:

(*i*) Waveform (A) is present only during colour transmissions.

(*ii*) Waveform (A) is fed to the Gated Amp 3 which operates (amplifies) only when a positive pulse [waveform (B)] is applied to it.

(*iii*) The timing of the positive pulses of waveform (B) is arranged so that the amplifier is operating during the period of the sine wave burst. Thus the output of the gated amp. consists of sine wave bursts [waveform (C)].

(*iv*) Waveform (C) is fed to the Burst Amp. 4 where it is amplified and subsequently fed to the phase Det. 5.

(*v*) The Phase Det. 5 receives two inputs, the sine wave bursts from the Burst Amp. and a continuous sine wave input [waveform (D)]. Provided *both* inputs are present then waveform (E) is available at its outputs.

—*continued*

(7) *Cont.*

(*vi*) Waveform (E) is rectified and smoothed in Rectifier 6 to provide a positive d.c. potential (+V) which is fed to the Signal Amp. 1.

(*vii*) The d.c. applied to Signal Amp. 1 makes it operational and allows waveform (A) to be amplified. If there is no d.c. from Rectifier 6, the Signal Amp. 1 will not function. After amplification the colour signal is fed to Signal Amp. 2 for further amplification.

(*viii*) S_1, which may be used for test purposes, causes the Signal Amp. 1 to operate continuously when it is closed.

(*ix*) The sine wave burst is not required at the output of Signal Amp. 2 and it is removed. This is the purpose of the negative-going pulses of waveform (F) which cause the amplifier to cut-off for a brief period. The timing of the pulses is arranged to coincide with the sine wave bursts.

(*x*) Waveform (G) (the colour signal) causes the picture on the screen to be coloured. If the waveform is missing the picture will be in black and white.

Now follow the questions [No. (7)].

(a) On a colour transmission there is no colour in the picture due to loss of waveform (G). If waveform (A) is present at the input to blocks 1 and 3 which of the following could cause the trouble:

(*i*) Faulty block 3
(*ii*) Loss of waveform (F)
(*iii*) Loss of waveform (B)
(*iv*) Faulty block 4.

(b) On a colour transmission there is no colour in the picture but waveform (C) is present at the input to block 4. Which of the following could cause the fault:

(*i*) Loss of waveform (A)
(*ii*) Faulty block 3
(*iii*) Faulty block 1
(*iv*) Loss of waveform (B).

(c) There is no colour in the picture during a colour transmission. Which of the following tests would you carry out first.

(*i*) Test Signal Amps 1 and 2
(*ii*) Check for the presence of waveform (B) and if correct check to see if waveforms (C), (D) and (E) are present
(*iii*) Check for the presence of waveform (A) and if correct check for +V out of block 6
(*iv*) Check for the presence of waveform (A) and if correct operate S_1.

(d) Sine wave bursts appear in the output of block 2. The most likely fault would be:

(*i*) Waveform (B) missing
(*ii*) Waveform (D) missing
(*iii*) Waveform (F) missing
(*iv*) S_1 permanently closed.

(e) There is no d.c. output from block 6. The cause of the fault could be:

(*i*) Waveform (D) missing
(*ii*) Waveform (A) missing
(*iii*) Fault in Gated Amp.
(*iv*) Waveform (B) missing.

(f) Waveform (E) is present but there is no colour in the picture when receiving a colour transmission. S_1 is closed but still the colour does not appear. Would you check:

(*i*) For the presence of waveform (A)
(*ii*) The operation of block 6
(*iii*) The operation of blocks 1 and 2
(*iv*) For the presence of a waveform at the output of block 1.

(8) This question deals with faults on a Binary Counter Circuit. Before attempting the problems carefully read the following basic facts concerning its operation:

A REGISTER is a row of bistable circuits, each of which can be set to a 0 or a 1 state. The state of a circuit may be determined by measuring the voltage at its output terminal. A bistable circuit uses two transistors (or valves) but it will be represented by a block as below.

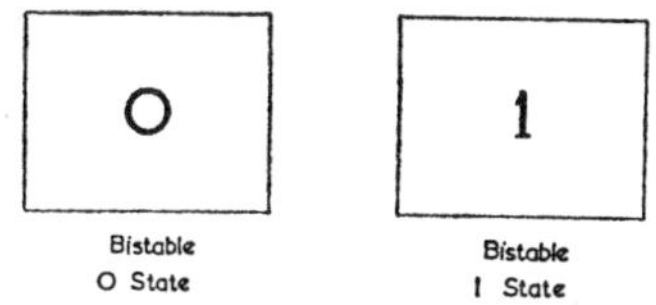

A SHIFTING REGISTER is a register in which the 0 and 1 states are all transferred one place to the right when a SHIFT PULSE is applied. See diagram below.

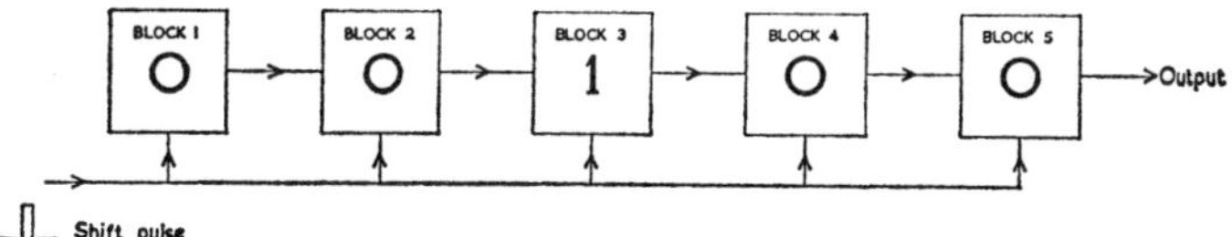

The digit in block 3 is transferred to block 4 when a shift pulse is applied. Block 3 then holds 0, which was transferred from block 2. When the next shift pulse is applied the digit is transferred to the block 5 and the block 4 reverts to the 0 state.

If such a register initially holds only 1 digit, the rest all being set to zeros, it can be used as a COUNTER or DIVIDER by feeding the output back into the left-hand block and using the shift pulses as input pulses. See diagram overleaf.

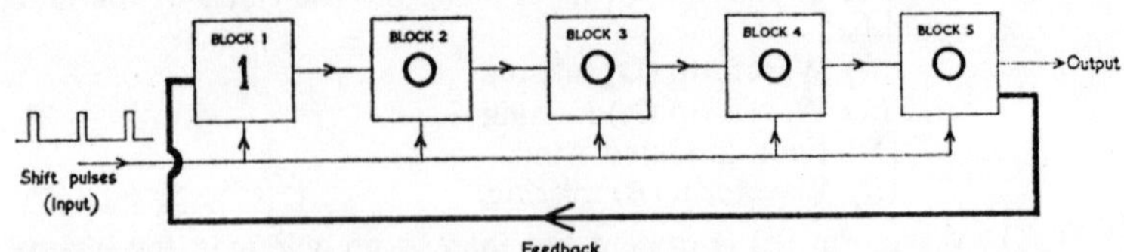

DIVIDE-BY-FIVE ARRANGEMENT

Each input pulse moves the digit one place to the right. At the 5th input pulse an output appears and is fed back to the first block. Thus the arrangement will *divide by five* or *count five pulses* since *one output pulse appears for every five input pulses.*

Questions [No. (8)] (assuming a divide-by-five arrangement as shown previously).

(a) A digit (1) is initially set in the register but no output pulse appears when three input pulses are applied. Is there anything wrong?

(b) A digit is initially set in the register but no output pulse appears after ten input pulses have been applied. How would you find the fault?

(c) A digit is set into the register and an output pulse appears at the 5th input pulse but not at the 10th, 15th, 20th . . . etc. What is the fault?

(d) A digit is set in the register and output appears on the 2nd, 5th, 7th, 10th, 12th, 15th, . . . etc. input pulses. What is wrong?

(e) An output pulse appears for every input pulse. What is wrong?

(f) An output appears at the 5th, 9th, 13th, 17th, 21st, . . . etc. input pulses. What is the trouble?

ANSWERS TO SECTION (2)

(1) (a)

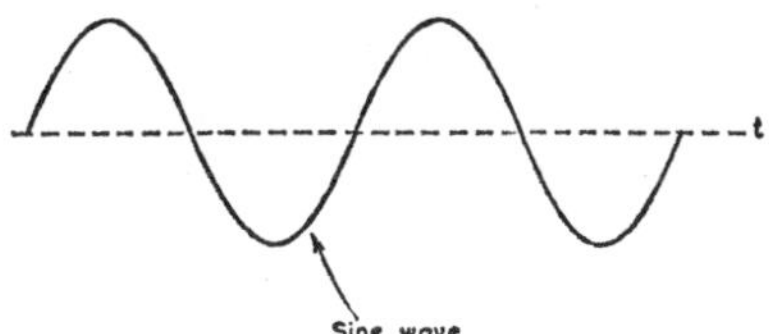

(b) The source of the output power is the d.c. supply, *i.e.* the oscillator may be regarded as a kind of converter, converting the d.c. power to a.c. power.

(c) The signal may be detected by using either a valve-voltmeter or a sensitive c.r.o. (Note that the c.r.o. responds to peak values).

(d) It would be best to check the d.c. supply first. If absent or low the oscillator will fail to function. Should it be correct then the fault lies in the oscillator or the output circuit.

(e) The valve requires a heater supply, thus an additional check is required. If the heater supply is absent or low then the oscillator will fail to operate. A quick check is to note the colour of the glow from the heater. This should be a cherry red when it is receiving the correct heater supply.

(2) (a) (*ii*) is correct.

(b) (*i*) is correct. If the input signal is applied to one trace and the output signal to the other, the phase relationship between the two is readily established.

(c) There is not sufficient information to assume that the fault is confined to module 2 as it could lie in C_3. Thus it would be best to make a further signal check using the c.r.o. [(*iv*)] By connecting the c.r.o. to the output of module 2 the area of the fault may be narrowed down. If a signal is obtained here the fault lies in C_3 (o/c). With no signal at this point the fault lies in module 2 or its d.c. supply or C_3 (s/c).

(d) (*ii*) is correct. First of all the input signal to module 1 should be checked. If absent, the fault either lies in C_1, module 1 I/P circuit or the remote unit. If present then the c.r.o. may be connected to the output of module 1 to see if a signal is present there. In this way you are able to collect quickly sufficient information to narrow down the fault area.

(e) (*iii*) is correct. Note that a s/c in C_2 or the input circuit of module 2 may also remove the signal at module 1 o/p.

(f) (*i*) is correct.

(3) (a) (*iv*) is correct. There is no point in carrying out checks on the modules until it has been established that there is an input to the system.

(b) It is often quicker when there are a large number of modules or units processing the signal to use initially a half-split method of fault location, *i.e.*, checking for the presence of the signal at the output of M_4 [(*i*)]. If the signal is correct at this point the fault lies in the signal path M_4 to M_8 and if absent the defect is most likely confined to M_1-M_4.

(c) (*ii*) is correct. Note that a s/c in L_2 or M_5 input could remove the signal from M_4 o/p.

(d) This may be done using an artificial signal source such as from a sine wave signal generator. With the output of the signal generator connected to M_1 input (actuator i/p disconnected) and its output adjusted to give a sine wave of the same nominal frequency and amplitude normally supplied by the actuator, the operation of the modules may be tested.

(e) First check (*iv*); second check (*v*). These tests will assist in isolating the trouble quickly. The i/p from the actuator must be checked first. Then by using half, quarter and eighth-split methods with the aid of a c.r.o. the fault may be narrowed down to a small section of the system.

(4) (a) 72dB.

(b) (*i*) 204·8mV (approx.). Note that for every +6dB, the signal is approximately doubled in amplitude.
(*ii*) 12·8mV.

(c) 40μV. (The system will produce an overall loss of −6dB).

(5) (a) Block 1 +6dB; Attentuator −3B; Block 2 +12dB.

(b) 1·6W.

(c) +15dB.

(6) (a) 0·707V.

(b) Approximately 15·56mV.

(c) Approximately 31·12mV (*i.e.* f_2 is 30dB down on f_1).

(7) (a) (*i*), (*iii*) or (*iv*) could cause the fault.

(b) (*iii*) is the only one of the four given that will cause the fault.

(c) (*iv*) is correct. It is most useful to operate S_1 after checking for the presence of waveform (A). If waveform (A) is correct then when S_1 is closed colour should appear on the screen provided blocks 1 and 2 are functioning. Should colour appear then the fault is confined to blocks 3, 4, 5, 6, or waveform feeds *B* and *C*.

(d) (*iii*) is correct.

(e) Any one of the four could cause the fault.

(f) The fault is confined to the signal path *via* blocks 1 and 2. As waveform (E) is present it follows that waveform (A) must be correct. Thus it would be best to check for the presence of an output from block 1 [(*iv*)]. The operation of S_1 eliminates block 6.

(8) (a) There is no fault as an output will not appear until five input pulses have been applied.

(b) Apply one input pulse using a simple battery and switch. Measure the voltage state of the second bistable (block 2). Has the 1 been transferred? If the indication is no, the second block is faulty or the connection to it is o/c. If the indication is yes, apply another input pulse and check the voltage state of the third bistable (block 3). Proceed along the register until the faulty block is found.

(c) The fault here is an o/c feedback loop. The digit that was initially set in the register would move to the right and on the fifth input pulse would appear at the output. However, with the feedback line o/c it would not be fed back to block 1 and all blocks would be in the 0 state.

(d) The register was not clear to begin with. A digit was held in block 4 which will produce an output at the second input pulse. The output will be fed back to block 1. The digit that was set would appear at the output three input pulses later, *i.e.* on the fifth pulse. The output pulse would again be fed back to block 1. Thus there are two digits going through the register at the same time.

(e) Each circuit may have been set to 1—clear the register and again. One of the bistaples may be permanently set to the 1 state (*e.g.* a transistor failure). This may be located by attempting to set each block to 0 and measuring its output. If a block is found at 1, it is the faulty one.

(f) Feedback loop connected from fourth block instead of the fifth as in (a) or connected to the second instead of the first block as in diagram (b) below.

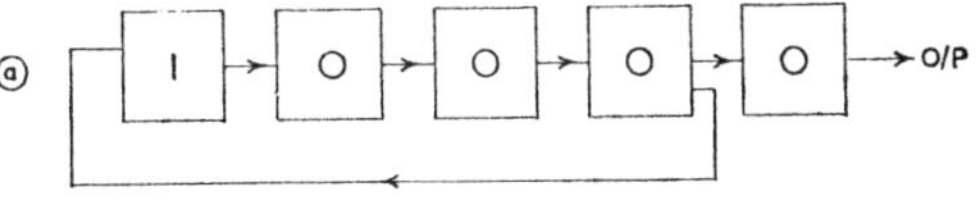

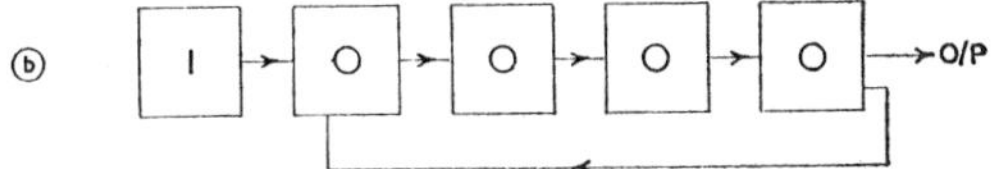

SECTION (3) SIMPLE CIRCUITS

Those questions suitable for first-year students are denoted by an asterisk (*) immediately following the question number.

(1)*

A B
R2 50kΩ±20%
R1 25kΩ±10%
R3 25kΩ±10%
C1 100pF

(a) Provided all components lie within tolerance, a typical resistance measurement across terminals *A* and *B* would be:

(*i*) 25kΩ; (*ii*) Infinity;
(*iii*) Zero ohms; (*iv*) 47kΩ.

(b) If R_3 was open circuited an expected reading across *A* and *B* would be:

(*i*) Infinity; (*ii*) 47kΩ;
(*iii*) 76kΩ; (*iv*) 74kΩ.

(c) If C_1 was short circuited an expected reading across *A* and *B* would be:

(*i*) ≃ 47kΩ; (*ii*) Zero ohms;
(*iii*) ≃ 25kΩ; (*iv*) ≃ 100kΩ.

(d) If R_2 was open circuited an expected reading across *A* and *B* would be:

(*i*) Infinity; (*ii*) ≃ 50kΩ;
(*iii*) ≃ 12·5kΩ; (*iv*) Zero ohms.

(2)*

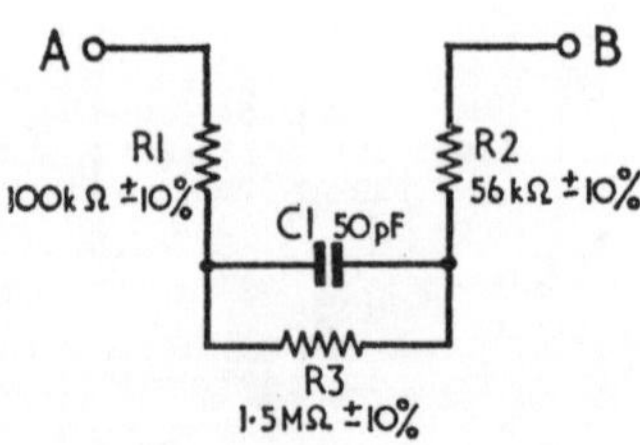

When 100V d.c. was applied across the terminals *A* and *B*, the measured current flowing in R_1 was found to be 0·65mA. A component was suspected of being faulty as it was realized that the current reading was incorrect. What component was faulty?

(3)*

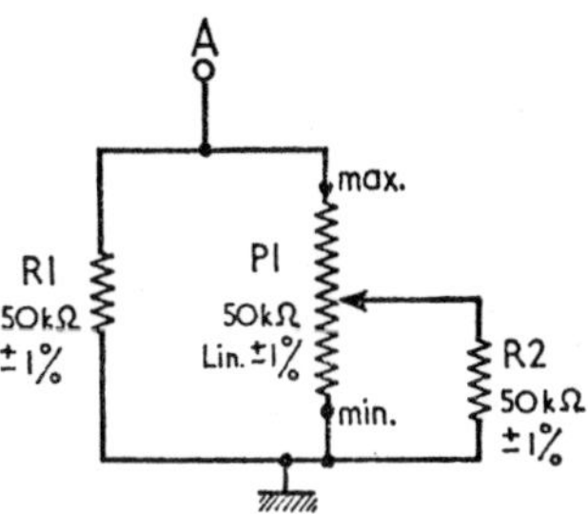

When the slider is in the MAX. position the resistance between A and chassis is 25kΩ, and when the slider is in the MIN. position the resistance between A and chassis is 50kΩ. Give two possible faults to account for the readings obtained.

(4)*

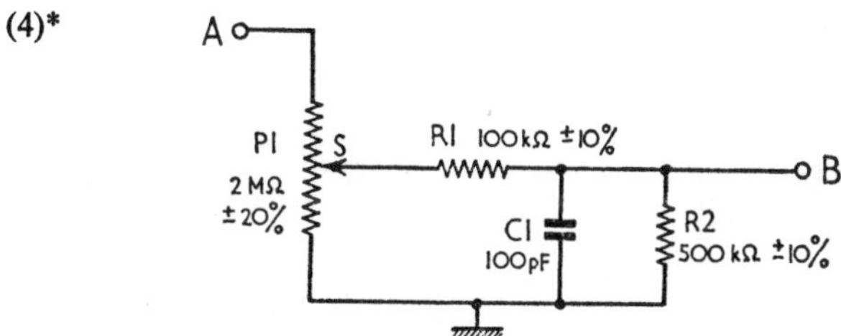

Below are three sets of resistance measurements made on the circuit above when a single fault was present in each case. From the measurements given indicate the most probable faulty component in each case.

(a) SLIDER SET TO TOP OF TRACK
Between A and chassis: 2·1MΩ.
Between S and chassis: 595kΩ.

(b) SLIDER SET TO BOTTOM OF TRACK
Between A and chassis: 2·1MΩ.
Between B and chassis: 490kΩ.
Between S and chassis: zero ohms.

(c) SLIDER SET TO BOTTOM OF TRACK
Between B and S: zero ohms.

(5)* The aerial input circuit of a radio receiver is shown overleaf.

(a) What will the resistance between A and chassis be when S_1 is switched to (*i*) M; and (*ii*) L?

(b) If the resistance was infinity when set to L, and did not alter when L_3 was short circuited, but measured 1Ω when set to M, what would you suspect as being wrong?

(c) If the resistance was zero ohms in both positions of S_1, what would you suspect as being wrong?

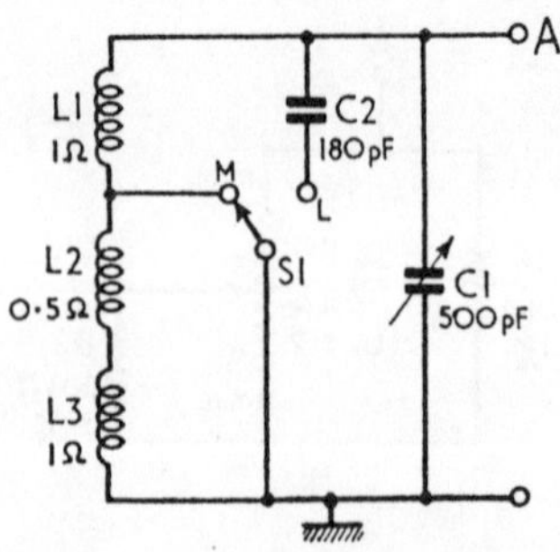

(d) If the resistance was zero ohms when S_1 was set to L, but 1Ω when set to M, what would you suspect as being wrong?

(6)

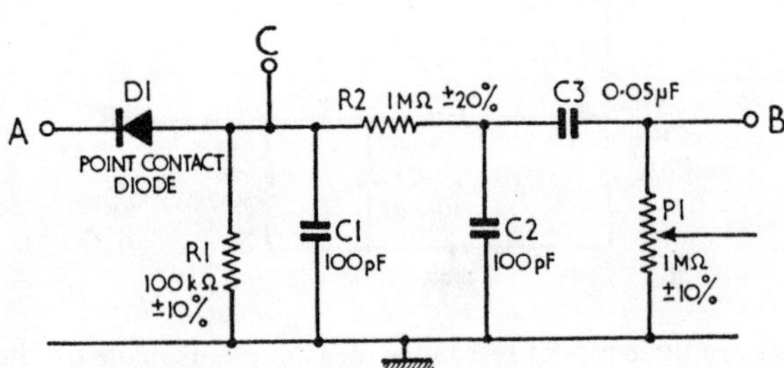

Resistance measurements made on four different detector circuits, whose circuit diagrams are the same as that shown above, are:

CIRCUIT 1

A (−) and chassis (+) = ≏ 100kΩ
B (−) and chassis (+) = ≏ 500kΩ

CIRCUIT 2

B (−) and chassis (+) = ≏ 1MΩ
C (−) and B (+) = infinity

CIRCUIT 3

A (−) and chassis (+) = ≏ 2MΩ
C (−) and chassis (+) = ≏ 100kΩ

CIRCUIT 4

A (+) and chassis (−) = ≏ 2MΩ
A (−) and chassis (+) = 500Ω

[NOTE: (−) indicates negative pole of meter battery connected to test-point.
(+) indicates positive pole of meter battery connected to test-point].

If you consider that the resistance measurements indicate a fault in any of the circuits, state the *most likely* component fault.

(7)

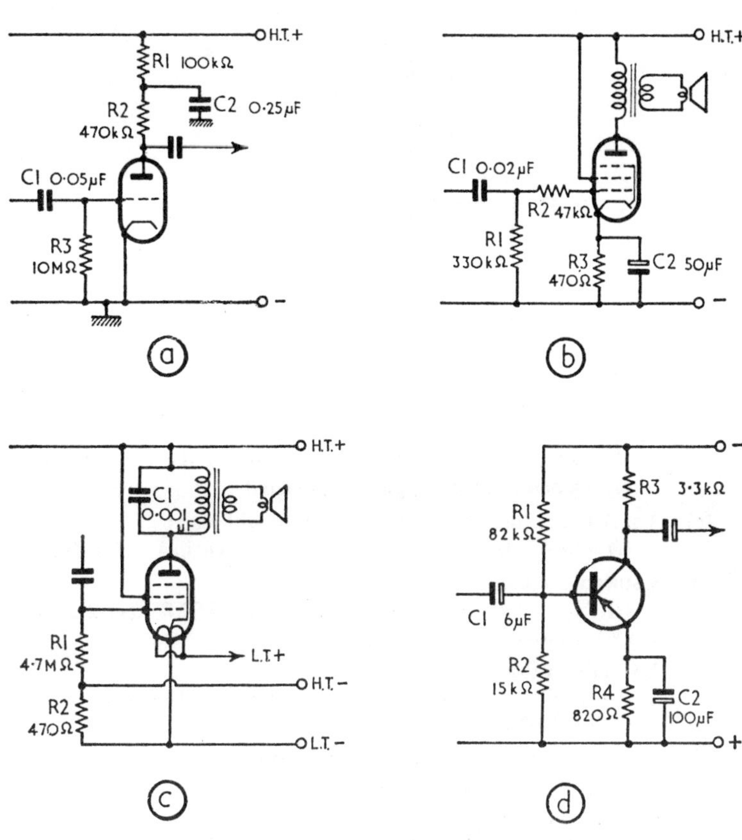

(a) How is the bias voltage obtained in each of the circuits shown above?

(b) What is the function of R_1 and C_2 in circuit (a)? How do the values of these components compare with a similar arrangement in a transistor a.f. amplifier?

(c) What is the function of R_2 and C_2 in circuit (b)?

(d) What is the purpose of C_1 in circuit (c)?

(e) Why is C_1 such a large value in circuit (d)?

(8) The circuit shown overleaf is that of an a.f. power amplifier which is functioning correctly, but no signal is applied.
The following questions should be attempted in the order given.

(a) A d.c. voltmeter connected between anode and chassis will read:
(*i*) 250V d.c. (*ii*) 150V d.c. (*iii*) 260V d.c. (*iv*) 227V d.c.
(*v*) Very low

—continued

(8) *cont.*

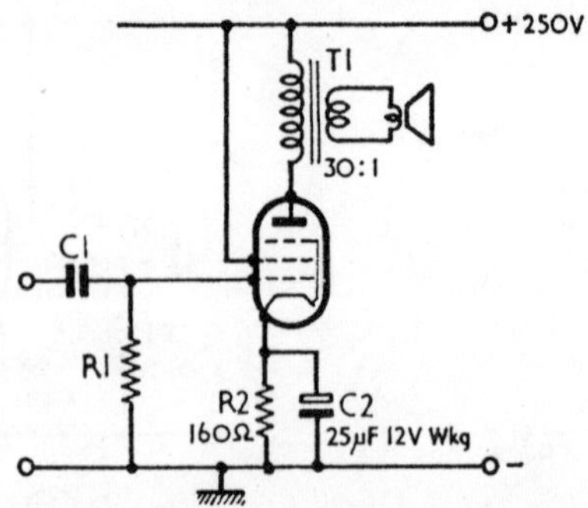

(b) A d.c. voltmeter connected between cathode and chassis will read:
(*i*) 15V d.c. (*ii*) 15V a.c. (*iii*) 8V d.c. (*iv*) 0V
(*v*) Depends upon amplitude of signal.

(c) A mA meter inserted in the anode lead will read:
(*i*) 45mA (*ii*) 50mA (*iii*) 100mA (*iv*) 5μA (*v*) 5mA.

(d) A suitable value for R_1 would be:
(*i*) 22kΩ (*ii*) 2·2kΩ (*iii*) 470kΩ (*iv*) 4·7kΩ (*v*) 2·2MΩ
(*vi*) 4·7MΩ.

(e) A suitable value for C_1 would be:
(*i*) 25μF (*ii*) 0·0001μF (*iii*) 100pF (*iv*) 4μF
(*v*) 0·00001μF (*vi*) 0·02μF.

(f) A suitable wattage rating for R_1 would be:
(*i*) ¼ watt (*ii*) 2 watt (*iii*) 10 watt (*iv*) 30 watt.

(g) A suitable tolerance for C_1 would be:
(*i*) ±0·1% (*ii*) ±1% (*iii*) ±20% (*iv*) ±2%.

(h) If R_1 is short circuited, the anode current will:
(*i*) rise (*ii*) remain the same (*iii*) fall (*iv*) cease.

(i) If R_1 goes open circuit, the cathode voltage will:
(*i*) rise (*ii*) remain the same (*iii*) fall (*iv*) cease.

(j) If C_2 goes short circuit, the anode current will:
(*i*) fall (*ii*) rise (*iii*) remain the same (*iv*) cease.

(k) If C_2 goes open circuit, the cathode voltage will:
(*i*) rise (*ii*) fall (*iii*) remain the same (*iv*) cease.

(l) If the primary winding of T_1 goes open circuit, the screen grid current will:
(*i*) rise (*ii*) fall (*iii*) remain the same (*iv*) cease.

(m) A d.c. voltmeter placed between grid and chassis will read:
(*i*) 0V (*ii*) 8V d.c. (*iii*) 12V d.c. (*iv*) 250V d.c.

(n) A d.c. voltmeter placed between grid and cathode will read:
(*i*) 8V d.c. (*ii*) 0V (*iii*) 12V d.c. (*iv*) 250V d.c.

(9)

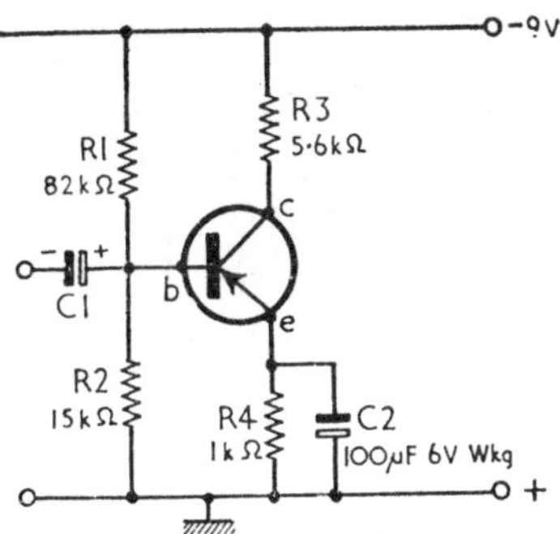

The circuit shown is that of an a.f. amplifier which is functioning correctly, but no signal is applied.

Questions should be attempted in the order given.

(a) If the collector current (I_c) is 1mA, what will a d.c. voltmeter read when connected between:

(*i*) emitter and chassis
(*ii*) collector and chassis

(b) Where would you connect a meter to read the base current.

(c) A d.c. voltmeter connected between base and emitter would read typically:
(*i*) 1V (*ii*) 0·2V (*iii*) 1000mV (*iv*) 1mV (*v*) 500μV.

(d) The base/emitter junction is:
(*i*) forward biased (*ii*) reverse biased (*iii*) has no bias.

(e) The collector/base junction is:
(*i*) forward biased (*ii*) reverse biased (*iii*) has no bias.

(f) If R_2 goes open circuit, the collector current will:
(*i*) rise (*ii*) fall (*iii*) remain the same.

(g) If R_1 goes open circuit, the collector current will:
(*i*) rise (*ii*) fall (*iii*) remain the same.

(h) If C_2 goes open circuit, the emitter volts will:
(*i*) rise (*ii*) fall (*iii*) remain the same.

(i) If C_2 goes short circuit, the collector current will:
(*i*) rise (*ii*) fall (*iii*) remain the same (*iv*) cease.

(j) A suitable value for C_1 would be:
(*i*) 0·05μF (*ii*) 0·01μF (*iii*) 100pF (*iv*) 6μF (*v*) 10pF.

(k) What is the purpose of the following components:

(*i*) R_4
(*ii*) C_2
(*iii*) R_3
(*iv*) R_1 and R_2?

(l) The transistor would be normally operating in:
(*i*) Class-A (*ii*) Class-B (*iii*) Class-C.

(10)

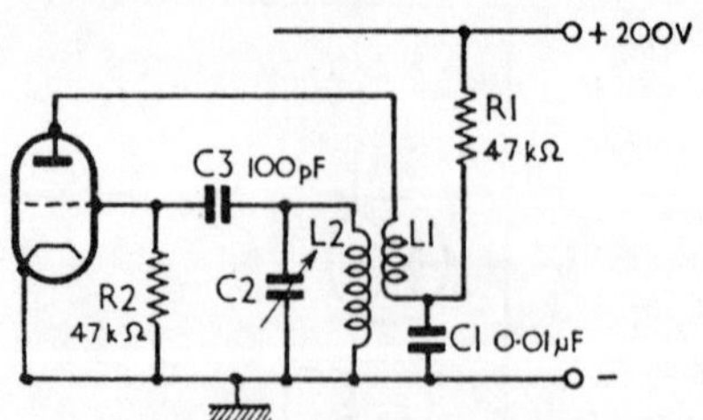

The circuit shown is that of a tuned-grid oscillator, of the type employed as local oscillator in a radio receiver, and is functioning correctly.

(a) When a d.c. voltmeter is connected between grid and chassis it will probably read:

(*i*) zero volts (*ii*) several volts positive to chassis.
(*iii*) several volts negative to chassis.

(b) What class of operation is used here.

(c) If R_2 was short circuited, the anode current would:

(*i*) rise (*ii*) fall (*iii*) remain the same.

(d) Say what would probably occur if R_2 went very high in value.

(e) Give as many fault conditions as you can think of which would result in the oscillation ceasing, or intermittent operation.

(f) Where would you connect an instrument to measure:

(*i*) anode current
(*ii*) grid current.

(g) State what would happen if the connections to L_2 were reversed.

(h) Will the amplitude of oscillation vary with the setting of C_2?

(11)

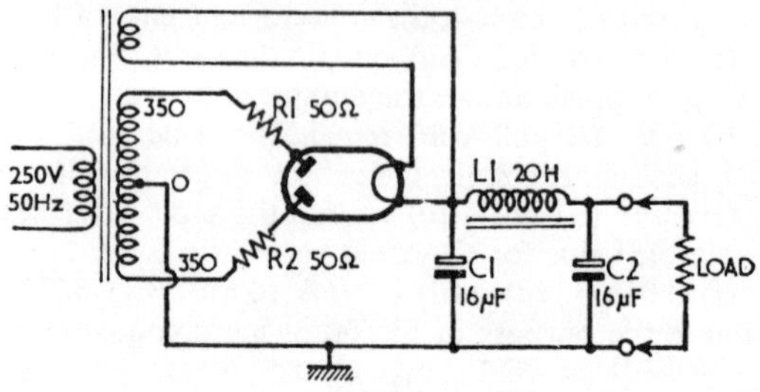

(a) State the peak inverse voltage which the rectifier must withstand.

(b) What is the purpose of the resistors R_1 and R_2?

(c) State the frequency of the ripple voltage.

(d) If C_1 goes open circuit, the h.t. output volts will:

(*i*) rise (*ii*) remain the same (*iii*) fall (*iv*) cease?

(e) If R_1 goes open circuit, the h.t. output will:
  (*i*) rise slightly (*ii*) fall slightly (*iii*) remain the same
  (*iv*) fall to zero.

(f) If C_2 goes open circuit, the hum level will:
  (*i*) increase (*ii*) decrease (*iii*) remain the same.

(g) If C_2 goes short circuit, the rectifier valve current will:
  (*i*) decrease (*ii*) remain the same (*iii*) increase
  (*iv*) fall to zero.

(h) If L_1 goes open circuit the rectifier valve current will:
  (*i*) rise (*ii*) remain the same (*iii*) fall to zero.

(12)

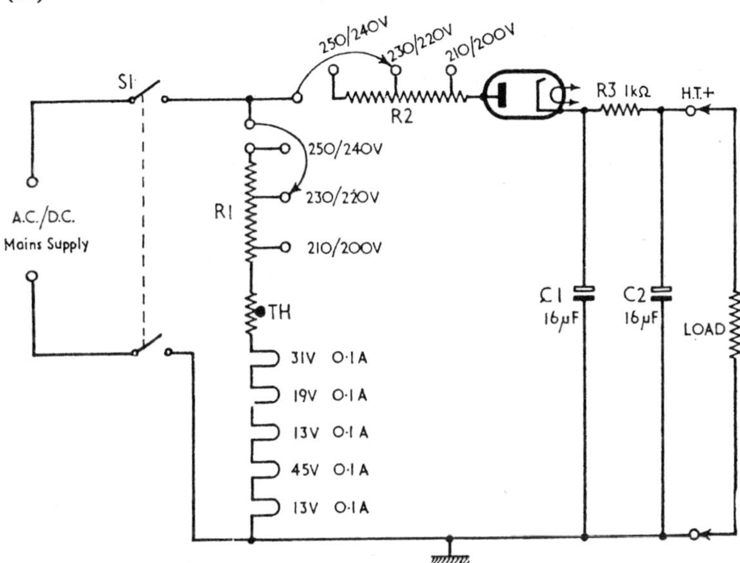

The circuit shows the power supply arrangements for an a.c./d.c. valve receiver.

(a) What form of rectification is used here.

(b) Give the function of the tapped resistors R_1 and R_2.

(c) Calculate the value of that part of R_1 which is in circuit when the receiver is operating from a 240V mains supply.

(d) State the function of C_1, R_3, and C_2.

(e) What precautions must be observed when connecting the mains supply to this power unit.

(f) Where would you connect instruments to measure the following :
  (*i*) Total h.t. current drain.
  (*ii*) The voltage drop of the smoothing resistor.
  (*iii*) Heater chain current.
  (*iv*) The h.t. resistance to chassis.

(g) If in (*i*) of (f) the current reading was greater than normal, and if in (*iii*) the current was less than normal, what would you suspect as being wrong?

(h) What is the frequency of the ripple voltage (hum voltage)?

(i) How would you measure the amplitude of the ripple voltage?

(13) Assuming that when a diode is forward biased it is a short circuit and that when reverse biased it is an open circuit, what will be the potential at points *A* and *B* on the circuits given below?

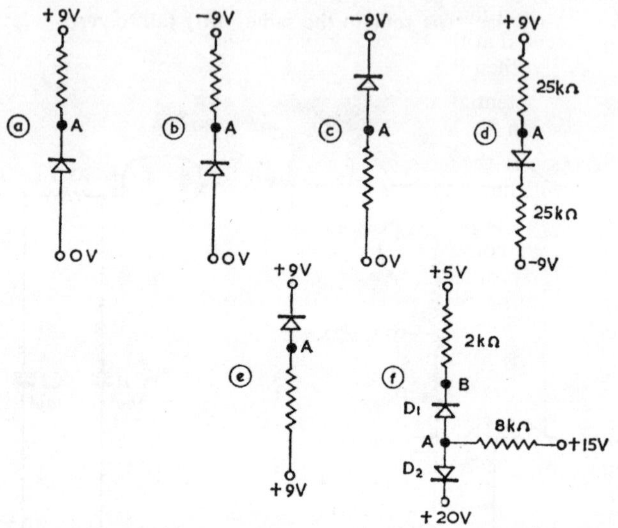

(14) In the diagram below assume that when the diodes are reverse biased their resistance is very large compared with *R* and when forward biased their resistance is very small compared with *R*.

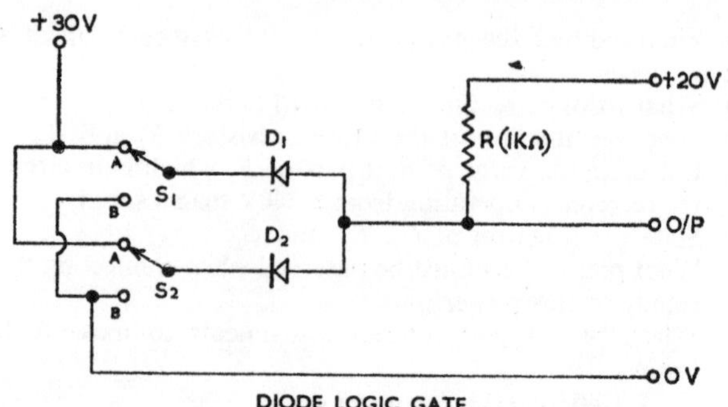

DIODE LOGIC GATE

(a) When S_1 and S_2 are in the positions shown what will be the approximate potential at the output terminal?

(b) If S_1 is in position A and S_2 is in position B what will be the approximate potential at the output terminal?

(c) What will be the approximate potential at the output terminal if S_1 and S_2 are both in position B?

(d) S_1 and S_2 are in position A but the +30V supply is missing. What will be the potential at the output terminals?

(e) Due to a fault the +30V line has fallen to +7·5V. What will be the potential at the output terminal when S_1 and S_2 are set to position A?

(f) Due to a fault the +20V line falls to +5V. What will be the potential at the output terminal when S_1 and S_2 are in position A and then B?

(g) The potential at the O/P is +30V when S_1 and S_2 are set to position A. What do you suspect is wrong?

(h) What is the maximum current that may be taken from the +20V line when the switches are in position A?

(i) When the potential at the output is approximately +20V the output corresponds to binary 1 and when OV is binary 0. What positions must the switches be in to give an output of binary 1?

(15)

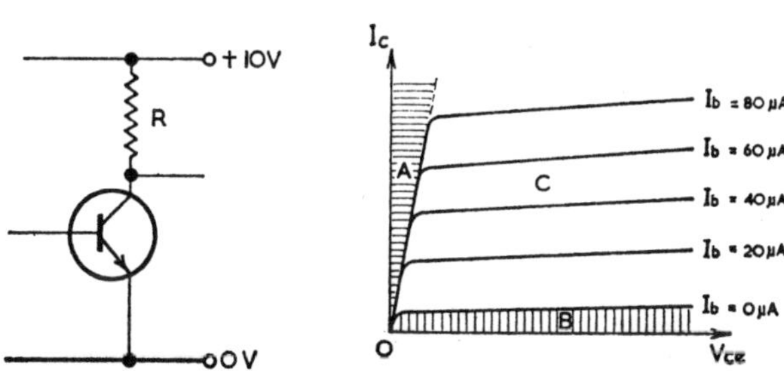

(a) When the transistor shown above is used as a switch it will be ON if the operation is confined to:
(*i*) Along line A; (*ii*) Along line B; (*iii*) In Area C.

(b) When the transistor is used as a switch it will be in the OFF state if the operation is confined to:
(*i*) Along line A; (*ii*) Along line B; (*iii*) In Area C.

(c) When the transistor is used as an amplifier so that the input signal controls the collector current and voltage, the operation will be in:
(*i*) Area A; (*ii*) Area B; (*iii*) Area C.

(d) If the transistor is used as a switch and is ON the collector voltage will be:
(*i*) Approximately +10V; (*ii*) Almost 0V; (*iii*) +5V; (*iv*) +7·5V.

—continued

(15) *Cont.*

(e) If the transistor is used as a switch and is OFF the collector voltage will be:

(*i*) Approximately +10V
(*ii*) Almost 0V
(*iii*) +5V
(*iv*) Equal to the base potential.

(f) If the transistor is "bottomed" the collector current will:

(*i*) Fall when the forward bias increases
(*ii*) Remain substantially constant when the forward bias increases
(*iii*) Increase when the forward bias increases
(*iv*) Be at a minimum.

(g) If the value of *R* is such that the collector voltage bottoms with a base current of 60μA, when *R* is slightly increased in value the transistor will bottom:

(*i*) With zero base current
(*ii*) At a higher value of base current
(*iii*) At a lower value of base current.

(h) When the transistor is operating in area A the conducting state of the junctions are:

(*i*) Emitter-base junction forward biased and collector-base junction reverse biased
(*ii*) Both junctions forward biased
(*iii*) Both junctions reverse biased.

(16)*

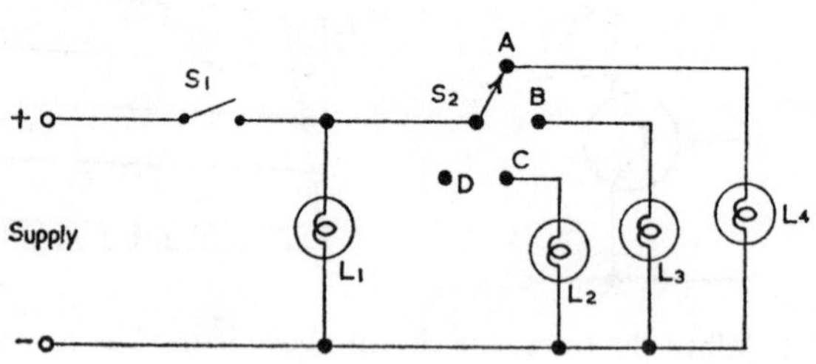

(a) S_1 is closed and the lamp L_1 is glowing normally. When S_2 is set to position A, L_4 fails to glow. The first check you would make is:

(*i*) Check the supply voltage
(*ii*) Test the lamp L_4
(*iii*) Check the voltage at S_2 wiper
(*iv*) Switch S_2 to position B.

(b) Lamps L_2, L_3 and L_4 all operate normally when S_2 is switched, but L_1 does not light. The most likely fault is:

(*i*) S_1 faulty
(*ii*) Supply faulty
(*iii*) L_1 faulty
(*iv*) O/C between S_1 and S_3.

(c) L_1 glows dimly when S_1 is closed and S_2 is in position D. If S_2 is switched to positions A, B or C the lamp L_1 goes out. Lamps L_2, L_3 and L_4 fail to glow. What do you think is the probable cause if the supply voltage is correct?

(d) S_1 is closed but L_1 does not light. Also L_2, L_3 and L_4 fail to glow when S_2 is operated. The supply voltage is correct and all of the lamps test satisfactorily. Which of the following will most likely give rise to these symptoms:

(*i*) Negative line o/c between L_1 and L_2
(*ii*) Negative line o/c between L_1 and the supply terminal
(*iii*) Positive line o/c between L_1 and S_2 wiper arm
(*iv*) S_2 high resistance contacts.

(e) S_2 is in position B. When S_1 is closed the supply fuse fails. Which of the following could cause this?

(*i*) Negative line o/c between L_1 and L_3
(*ii*) L_1 o/c
(*iii*) L_3 o/c
(*iv*) L_1 s/c.

(17)*

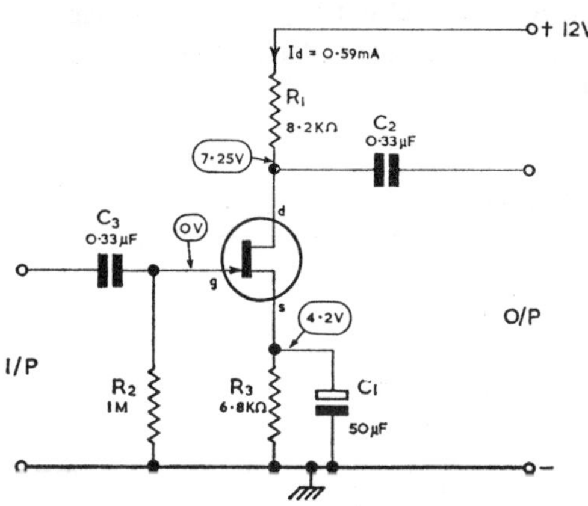

JUNCTION-GATE F.E.T. AMPLIFIER

The diagram above is that of an a.f. amplifier using a field effect transistor. The voltages given on the diagram are for normal operation and were measured with respect to chassis. No signal is applied.

(a) Is the transistor an N or P type channel F.E.T.?

(b) A typical input resistance for the transistor itself would be:
(*i*) 1kΩ; (*ii*) 500MΩ; (*iii*) 500Ω; (*iv*) 200Ω.

(c) What are the current carriers in this particular F.E.T.?

(d) Is the gate-to-source junction forward or reverse biased?

(e) What is the value of the bias voltage?

(f) If C_1 were to go s/c, the drain current (*Id*) would:
(*i*) increase; (*ii*) decrease; (*iii*) remain the same.

—continued

(17) *cont.*

(g) If C_1 were to go o/c, the drain current would:
(*i*) increase; (*ii*) decrease; (*iii*) remain the same.

(h) If R_2 were to change value to, say, 1kΩ, the drain current would:
(*i*) increase; (*ii*) decrease; (*iii*) remain the same.

(i) What would be the values of the gate, source and drain voltages if R_1 were to go o/c?

(j) If R_3 goes o/c, the drain current will:
(*i*) increase; (*ii*) fall to zero; (*iii*) rise slightly.

(k) If R_2 goes o/c, the drain voltage will:
(*i*) fall; (*ii*) rise; (*iii*) remain the same.

(l) If the transistor were to develop an internal short between gate and source, the drain current would:
(*i*) not be affected; (*ii*) rise; (*iii*) fall.

(m) With a signal applied to the input terminals the output signal of the amplifier will be:
(*i*) in phase with the input; (*ii*) in anti-phase with the input; (*iii*) 90° out of phase with the input.

(n) What effect will an o/c C_1 have when signals are applied to the input?

(18)

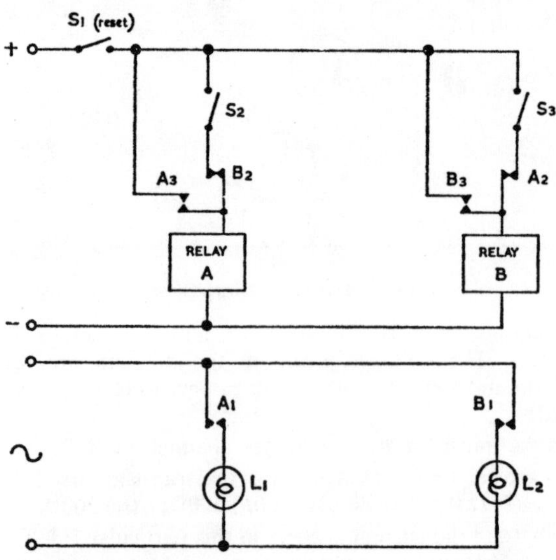

Relay contacts A_{1-3} and B_{1-3} shown in de-energized positions of relays. S_2 and S_3 close when pressed and open when pressure is released.

(a) S_1 is closed. Describe the sequence of events when S_2 is pressed.

(b) S_1 is closed but L_2 fails to light when S_3 is pressed and held closed. A possible cause of the fault would be:

(*i*) Relay *A* de-energized
(*ii*) B_3 contacts high resistance
(*iii*) A_2 contacts high resistance
(*iv*) B_2 contacts high resistance.

(c) S_1 is closed and S_2 is pressed causing L_1 to light up. S_3 is then pressed and L_2 lights up (L_1 stays on). What do you suspect is wrong?

(d) When S_1 is closed, L_2 lights up. Possible causes are:

(*i*) B_3 contacts not breaking
(*ii*) S_3 shorting
(*iii*) B_1 contacts not breaking
(*iv*) Faulty L_2.

(e) L_1 lights up when S_2 is pressed. After resetting S_1 and then closing, Relay *B* fails to energize when S_3 is pressed. Possible causes are:

(*i*) Contacts B_3 not making
(*ii*) L_2 o/c
(*iii*) Relay *B* coil o/c
(*iv*) S_3 not making contact
(*v*) D.C. supply missing
(*vi*) L_2 s/c.

(19) The diagram shows a tuned circuit L_1, C_1 which forms one of the signal tuning circuits of a v.h.f. amplifier in a radio receiver.

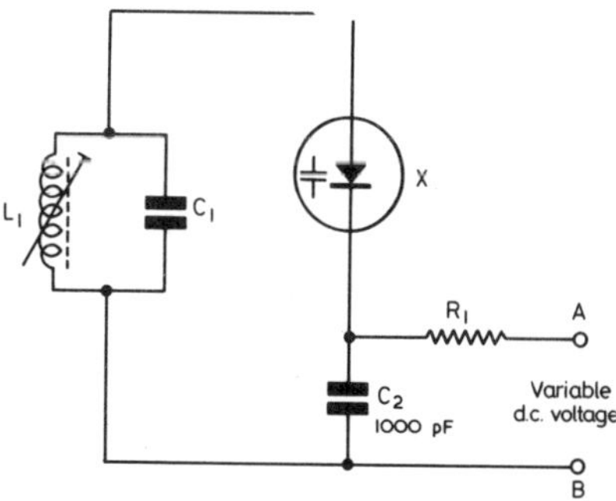

(a) What is the function of the component marked *X*?
(b) State the polarity of the voltage applied to terminal *A* (with respect to terminal *B*).
(c) If the d.c. voltage applied between *A* and *B* is at a maximum, will the tuned circuit be operating at its highest or lowest frequency?
(d) State the effect on the operation of the circuit if C_2 becomes short circuit.

(20) The diagram shows the basic circuit of a voltage stabilizer.

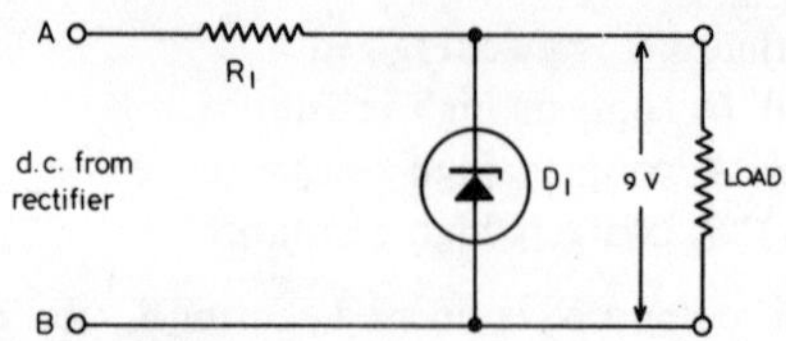

(a) What is the name of the device labelled D_1?
(b) What is the purpose of R_1?
(c) What will be the polarity of the voltage applied to terminal A with respect to terminal B?
(d) How will the power dissipation in D_1 be affected if the current drawn by the load decreases?
(e) How will the operation of the circuit be affected if D_1 goes short circuit?
(f) Sketch the essential characteristics of D_1. On your diagram indicate 9V to show its importance in this particular circuit application.

(21) The device marked X in the diagram is used for controlling the current in the load.

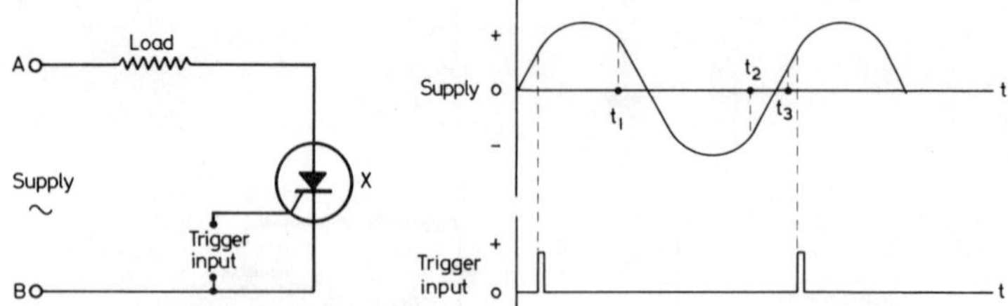

(a) Name the device.
(b) If the device is triggered at the instants shown in the diagram, will there be any current in the load at:
  (*i*) instant t_1?
  (*ii*) instant t_2?
  (*iii*) instant t_3?
(c) If the trigger supply is missing, how will the operation of the circuit be affected?
(d) Draw the voltage-current characteristic of the device X.

(22) (a) What is the function of the circuit shown below?
(b) If the peak voltage across T_1 primary is 340V, what voltage would you expect across C_2?
(c) What will be the polarity of the voltage across C_2?
(d) If D_1 goes open circuit how will the output voltage from the circuit be affected?

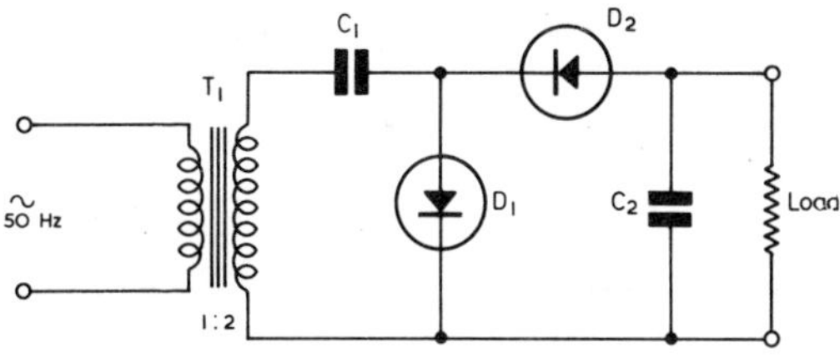

(23) (a) Which diodes in the diagram below will be conducting when terminal A is negative to terminal B?
(b) What will be the frequency of the ripple voltage across C_1?
(c) Explain the purpose of Tr_1.
(d) What is the purpose of R_2?
(e) Approximately what value of d.c. voltage is to be expected across the load?
(f) State the effect on the voltage across the load with the following faults apparent:
   (*i*) R_2 open circuit
   (*ii*) D_5 short circuit
   (*iii*) Tr_1 collector-emitter short circuit.

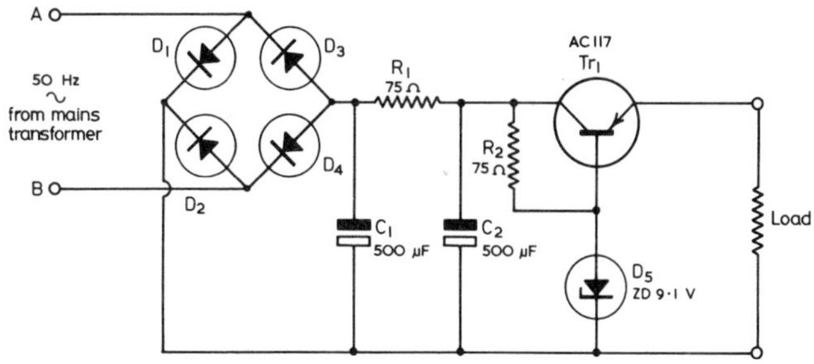

(24) (a) What circuit configuration is used for the transistor in the diagram below?
(b) What will be the normal polarity of the voltage applied to *A* with respect to chassis?
(c) What is the purpose of C_2?
(d) Does this amplifier have a low, high or medium input resistance?
(e) What is the phase relationship between input and output signals?
(f) Why is R. not decoupled with a capacitor?

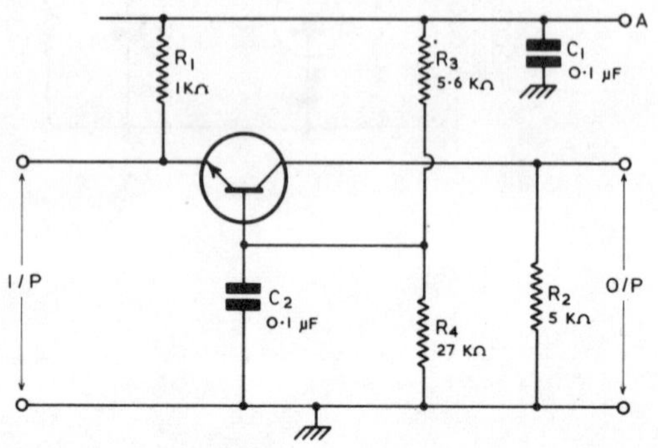

(25) What circuit configuration is used for the transistor in the diagram below?
(b) What will be the normal polarity of the voltage applied to *A* with respect to chassis?
(c) Does this amplifier have a low, medium or high output resistance?
(d) What is the phase relationship between input and output signals?
(e) If a signal of 200mV in amplitude is applied to the input, about what magnitude of signal would you expect at the output?

—continued

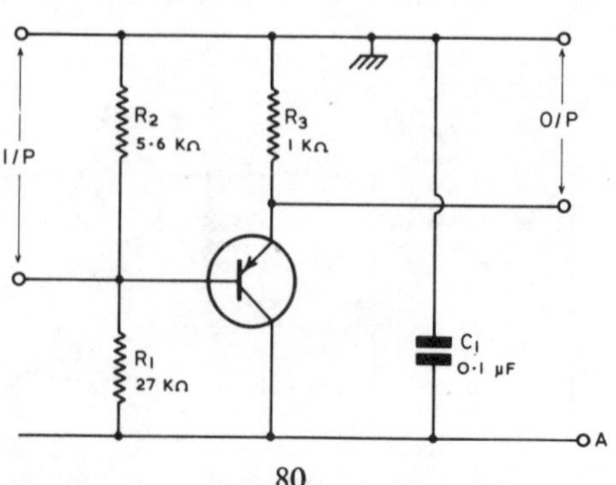

(f) Suggest a typical use for this type of amplifier stage.

(g) State the probable readings to be expected when an ohmmeter is connected between base and chassis with (*i*) the meter leads one way round; and (*ii*) the meter leads the other way round.

ANSWERS TO SECTION (3)

(1) (a) (*iv*) 47kΩ. This lies within the tolerance of R_2 and would be a typical reading.

(b) (*ii*) 47kΩ. An open-circuit R_3 will not affect the resistance apparent across *AB* since C_1 is also an open circuit to d.c.

(c) (*iii*) ≏ 25kΩ. Since R_1 and R_3 are now in series, paralleling R_2.

(d) (*i*) Infinity. Because there is now no path for d.c.

(2) C_1 short circuit. As the resistance apparent across terminals

$$AB = \frac{100}{0{\cdot}65} \times 10^3 \text{ ohms}$$

$$\simeq 154\text{k}\Omega$$ which is a likely reading for R_1 and R_2 in series obtained in practice.

(3) Either R_1 is open circuit, or there is a break in the track of P_1 (see figure below).

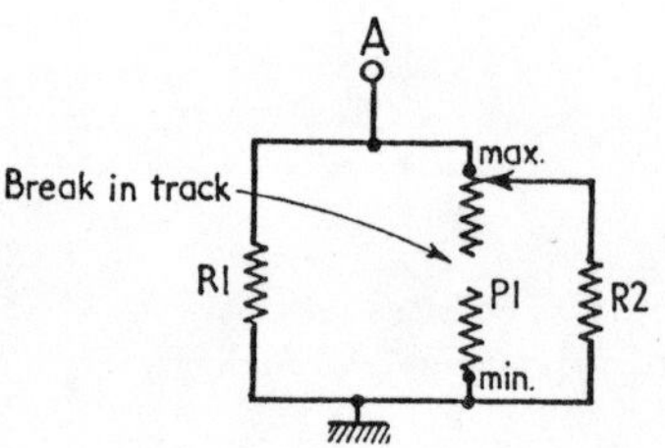

(4) (a) P_1 open circuit slider.
The first reading, with P_1 serviceable, would have been 2MΩ in parallel with R_1 and R_2 in series, *i.e.* a much lower resistance. The second reading proved R_1 and R_2.

(b) R_1 open circuit
The second reading, with R_1 serviceable, would have been R_2 in parallel with R_1. However, this reading was 490kΩ which is a typical resistance reading for R_2 and is within tolerance of this resistor. The third reading proved that the slider was making to the track.

(c) C_1 short circuit.
It is unlikely that R_1 or R_2 was short circuit.

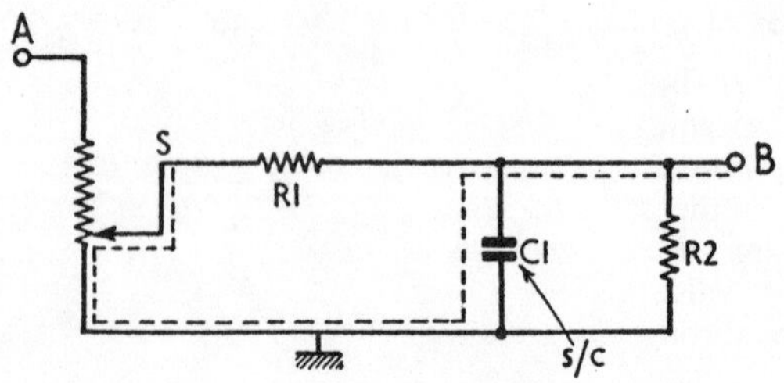

----- Meter reads zero ohms through this path

(5) (a) (*i*) 1Ω (L_2 and L_3 are short circuited in this position).
(*ii*) 2·5Ω (L_1, L_2, and L_3 have their d.c. resistances in series).
(b) L_2 open circuit. Since L_3 was proved by short circuit test, and L_1 was proved in position M of S_1.
(c) C_1 short circuit. Most likely caused by the vanes shorting.
(d) C_2 short circuit.

(6) CIRCUIT 1

C_3 short circuit. This would not be apparent when measuring from A to chassis, due to the high values of R_2 and P_1 compared with R_1, with which they would be in shunt. However, when measuring from B to chassis, P_1 (1MΩ) will be shunted by R_2 (1MΩ) and R_1 (100kΩ) in series, giving approximately 500kΩ for this reading.

CIRCUIT 2

R_1 open circuit. Since resistance between B and C should be (P_1+R_1), *i.e.* $\simeq$1·1MΩ, and the first reading proved P_1.

CIRCUIT 3

D_1 high forward resistance, as first reading, with D_1 serviceable, should be (D_1+R_1), *i.e.* a little over 100kΩ. Second reading proved R_1.

CIRCUIT 4

C_1 short circuit. Since second reading should have been (D_1 forward resistance + R_1), *i.e.* 500Ω+100kΩ, therefore R_1 is short circuited by C_1. The first reading was the reverse resistance of D_1.

(7) (a) CIRCUIT (a)

This circuit uses the bias voltage developed when grid current flows in the high value resistor R_3. The static bias thus produced is the result of the combined effects of (*i*) gas current; (*ii*) initial electron velocity; (*iii*) contact potential; and is in the order of −0·5V to −1·2V for the usual indirectly-heated valve. Therefore, to avoid distortion, this form of bias is only used where the input signal amplitude is small, *e.g.* the voltage amplifier following the demodulator of a radio receiver. It is commonly referred to as **contact potential bias, grid-leak bias,** or **grid current bias,** and can easily be recognized by the large value of grid-leak resistor employed (5—20MΩ).

CIRCUIT (b)

This circuit uses cathode bias which is produced by the voltage drop across the cathode resistor R_3, due to the steady component of the total valve space current which flows through this resistor. The grid of the valve is returned to chassis potential *via* R_2 and R_1, *i.e.* the

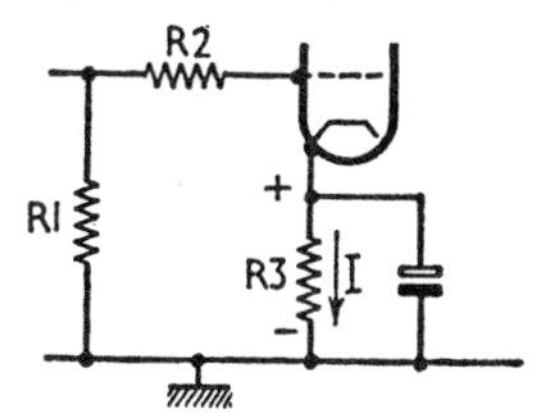

same potential as the bottom end of R_3. Hence, with reference to the top end of R_3 (the cathode), the grid is negative by a potential equal to the voltage drop across R_3.

CIRCUIT (c)

The circuit shows the output stage of an all-dry battery receiver. The valve obtains its bias from the resistor R_2 which is in the common lead between h.t.– and l.t.–; the resistor therefore carries the emission current of all valves in the receiver (typically 10mA). A drop of 4·7 volts will therefore exist across R_2 and this is used for grid bias.

CIRCUIT (d)

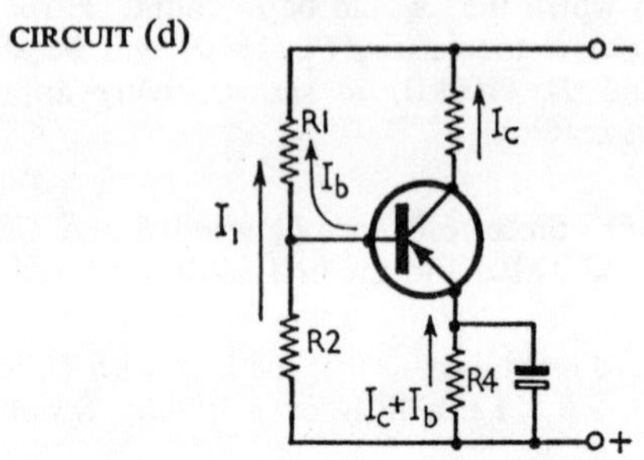

The bias is due to the p.d. that exists between the base and emitter connections. R_4 in the emitter lead carries both the base and collector currents which produce a voltage drop across it (of the order of 1V). The potential divider (R_1/R_2) carries a bleeder current I_1, and R_1, in addition, carries the base current (I_b). The potential at the junction of R_1/R_2 is arranged to be somewhat negative to the emitter potential for a p-n-p transistor (positive for an n-p-n type), by an amount of the order of 0·1V to 0·2V.

(7) (b) The function of R_1 and C_2 is to prevent unwanted coupling between stages which may arise due to the common impedance of the h.t. supply. Consider the circuit shown, where i_1 and i_2 represent the signal components of anode current of V_1 and

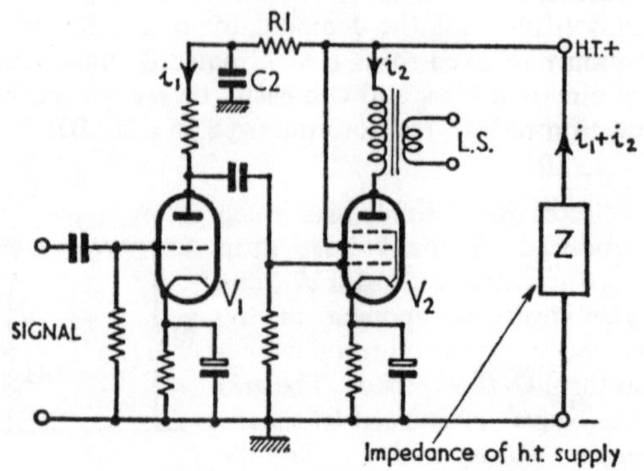

V_2, being part of an a.f. amplifier. Due to the fact that the impedance of the h.t. supply cannot easily be made zero ohms, the signal currents i_1 and i_2, flowing in the h.t. supply impedance Z, will produce a signal voltage drop. The h.t. supply voltage is then varied by the fluctuating signal voltage, giving the effect of either *positive* or *negative* feedback. (Positive feedback

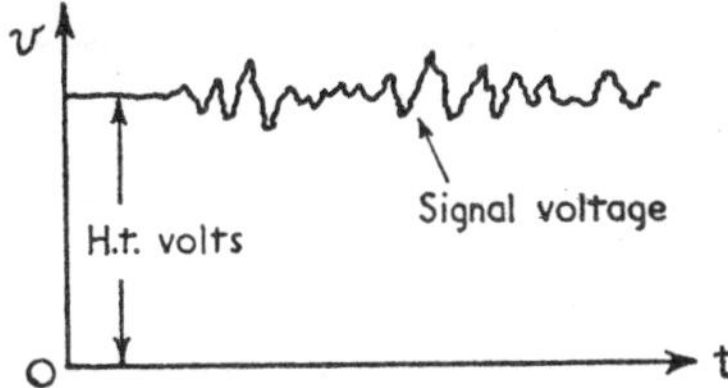

causes instability: negative feedback causes reduction in gain). The problem is usually one of combating instability (self-oscillation) and the chances of its occurring are minimized by including a simple RC filter R_1 and C_2 as shown. The filter reduces the signal variation appearing at the anode of V_1 and cuts down the risk of self-oscillation of the amplifier.

In an a.f. amplifier using valves, R_1 may lie between several kΩ and 100kΩ, whilst C_2 is usually 16μF down to about 0·25μF. It should be noted that the presence of R_1 reduces the d.c. voltage at the anode of the valve. It is because of the reduction in d.c. voltage that in a transistor amplifier, where the line voltage is usually less than 10V d.c., R_1 has a smaller value (typically 1kΩ), with C_2 made correspondingly larger (100μF) to maintain the efficiency of the filter.

(7) (c) When a power amplifier is first switched on self-oscillation may occur. The valve lead inductances and inter-electrode capacitances form tuned circuits which may burst into oscillation at frequencies well outside the audio frequency range. Although the currents flowing in the loudspeaker, due to the oscillation, do not produce audible notes, the quality of the a.f. signals handled by the amplifier may be degraded when, for example, the oscillations cause grid current to be drawn. A measure of success may be achieved in the prevention of oscillation by damping the tuned circuits so formed. This is the purpose of R_2 in circuit (b), which increases the losses at the frequency of oscillation of the grid circuit. Its value may lie anywhere from 10kΩ to 100kΩ and it must be soldered directly to the valve pin by the shortest length of lead possible.

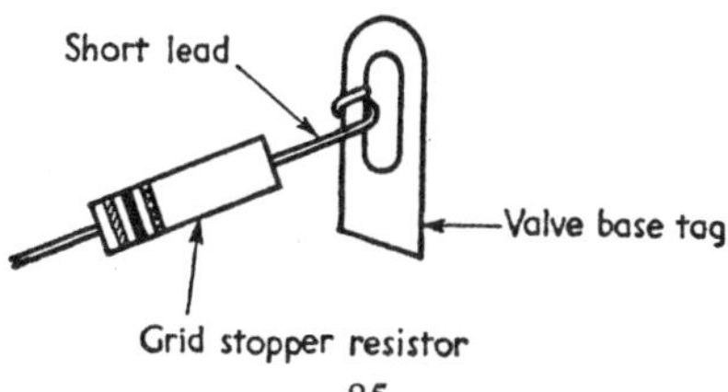

(7) *cont.* (c) The function of C_2 is to keep the potential across R_3 steady to avoid negative feedback into the grid circuit. The current flowing in R_3 can be separated into two components: (*i*) the steady component which the valve draws under "no signal" conditions; and (*ii*) a signal component which is due to the presence of the applied signal between grid and cathode of the valve. C_2 decouples the signal component of valve current, and prevents it passing through R_3. For good decoupling action the reactance of C_2 should be 1/10th the resistance of R_3 at the lowest frequency signal being applied between grid and cathode. For example, if the lowest frequency = 40Hz, and R_3 = 470Ω

Reactance (X_c) of C_2 at 40Hz should not be

$$\text{more than } \frac{470}{10} = 47\Omega$$

$$\text{Now } X_c = \frac{1}{2\pi fC}$$

$$\text{or } C = \frac{1}{2\pi fX_c} = \frac{10^6}{6{\cdot}284 \times 40 \times 47}$$

$$\simeq 85\mu\text{F}.$$

A suitable practical value would probably be 100μF. [If the lowest frequency is higher than 40Hz, then the capacitor may be smaller in value].

(d) C_1 is a fixed tone-correcting capacitor. Its function is to provide a small degree of *top cut* which is necessary when using a pentode output valve, due to the emphasis which such a valve gives to frequencies at the higher end of the audio frequency band.

(e) In an audio amplifier the coupling capacitor forms a potential divider with the input resistance of the following stage. For a valve amplifier this is effectively the grid leak resistance, since the input resistance of the valve itself is very high. In a transistor amplifier, however, the input resistance is that of a forward biased junction (base to emitter) and is very low (typically 1kΩ). To avoid loss of signal across C_1 at low frequencies (when it will have its highest reactance) the value of the coupling capacitor must be made fairly large (typically 6μF). Such a value requires the use of an electrolytic type; therefore due regard to the polarity must be made when mounting it in circuit.

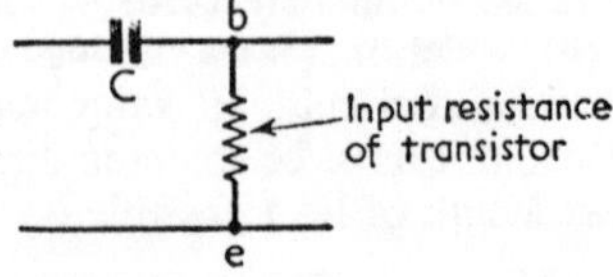

(8) (a) 227V d.c. (*iv*). As there will be a voltage drop across the primary due to its d.c. resistance.

(b) 8V d.c. (*iii*). As C_2 is only 12 volts working.

(c) Using the answer given in (b) the total valve space current may now be determined.

$$\text{Total space current} = \frac{8}{160} \times 10^3 = 50\text{mA}.$$

This will be divided between anode and screen grid. In an output stage the anode current is appreciably larger than the screen grid current, hence 45mA (*i*) is correct, *i.e.* 5mA flows in the screen grid circuit.

(d) 470kΩ (*iii*). Grid leak values for power values do not normally exceed 1MΩ, and the other values are too low, since they would normally shunt the anode load of the previous stage too much.

(e) 0·02μF (*vi*). A typical value for this capacitor.

(f) ¼W (*i*). This resistor is usually of ¼W or ½W rating.

(g) ±20% (*iii*). The value is not very critical and is a normal tolerance for a paper capacitor when used in this position.

(h) Remain the same (*ii*). The bias conditions have not been altered.

(i) Rise (*i*). The increase in anode current when this fault is apparent may damage the valve or transformer. Note that the working voltage of C_2 may be exceeded, causing it to break down. It is therefore *bad practice* to switch on with a grid leak disconnected.

(j) Rise (*ii*) There will be no bias on the valve and a large current will flow. Damage to the valve or transformer may result.

(k) Remain the same (*iii*). The purpose of C_2 is to prevent signal variations across R_2.

(l) Rise (*i*). Note that if a resistor is included in the screen grid lead, the increase in current will cause overheating, and damage may result. (To be on the safe side it is prudent to change the resistor if this fault has occurred in practice).

(m) 0V (*i*). No current flows (theoretically) in R_1. However, in practice, a very small positive voltage may be detected when measuring from grid to chassis, due to reverse grid current flow through R_1 to neutralize gas ions collecting at the grid.

(n) 8V d.c. (*i*). This, of course, is the bias between grid and cathode, produced by the voltage drop across R_2. The exact reading would depend on the resistance of the voltmeter.

(9) (a) (*i*) Voltage drop across $R_4 = 1000 \times \frac{1}{10^3} = 1\text{V}$

∴ Voltage between emitter and chassis = <u>1 volt.</u>

[In practice, the voltage, as measured, may be slightly different due to the tolerance of R_4].

(*ii*) Voltage drop across $R_3 = 5600 \times \frac{1}{10^3} = 5{\cdot}6\text{V}$

∴ Voltage between collector and chassis $= (9-5{\cdot}6)\text{V}$

$= $ <u>3·4 volts.</u>

Again, in practice, allowance must be made for the tolerance of R_3 and the resistance of the voltmeter.

(b) The meter should be inserted between the base and junction of R_1/R_2 to measure the base current, which will normally be in the order of tens of μAs.

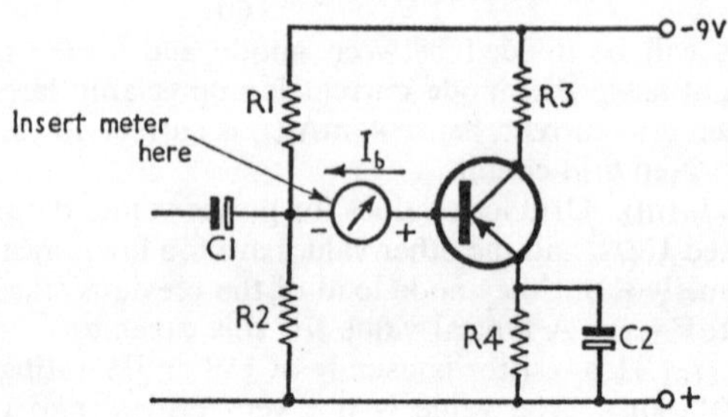

(c) 0·2V (*ii*). The voltage normally lies between 0·1—0·2V.

(d) Forward biased (*i*).

(e) Reverse biased (*ii*).

(f) Rise (*i*). Because the forward bias on the transistor will increase.

(g) Fall (*ii*). Because the forward biasing voltage has been disconnected.

(h) Remain the same (*iii*). The purpose of C_2 is to prevent signal variations across R_4.

(i) Rise (*i*). Since the forward bias will then increase. Under this fault condition the increase in I_c may result in damage to the transistor.

(j) 6μF (*iv*). A large value is required in transistor a.f. amplifiers due to the low input resistance of the transistor.

(k) (*i*) R_4 is included to stabilize the d.c. working point of the transistor against thermal changes. It performs this function by virtue of the increase in voltage drop across it when the transistor is subjected to a temperature rise. Together with the base-potential stabilizing action of R_1/R_2, the voltage across R_4 rises towards that of the base, thereby reducing the forward bias on the transistor. This in turn reduces I_c and the temperature of the device will fall.

(*ii*) The purpose of C_2 is to prevent signal variations occurring across R_4 at all frequencies handled by the amplifier. This is to stop a.c. negative feedback which would otherwise reduce the gain of the amplifier.

(*iii*) R_3 is the collector load resistor across which the output signal voltage is developed. It is normally of the order of a few kΩ.

(*iv*) The purpose of R_1 and R_2 is to supply the base potential of the transistor and to stabilize it against variations in base current. To do this the values of R_1 and R_2 are so chosen

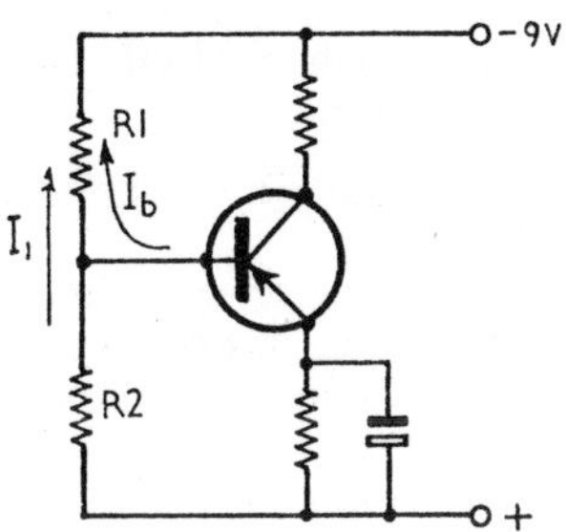

that I_1 is many times I_b. For good stabilization I_1 is often made $10 \times I_b$.

(l) Class-A (*i*). In the other two classes distortion of the signal would result.

(10) (a) Several volts negative to chassis (*iii*). This is the bias voltage produced by the flow of grid current which charges C_3.

(b) Class-C. The valve is biased beyond anode current cut-off, and the anode current consists of pulses.

(c) Rise (*i*). Because the bias is removed. This provides a useful quick check for oscillation: short circuit the grid leak and note that the anode voltage *falls* (more convenient to measure than I_a); if it does, it indicates that oscillation is taking place. It does not, of course, give any information as to the amplitude of oscillation or quality of waveform.

(d) This may give rise to a condition known as "squegging". With R_2 high in value the time-constant of the grid bias circuit will be very long, and it will then only respond to slow changes of amplitude. Under such conditions the amplitude of oscillation will increase to a large value, driving the grid well into Class-C, so far, in fact, that the oscillation will die away. As the oscillation dies away, the grid volts become less negative and when

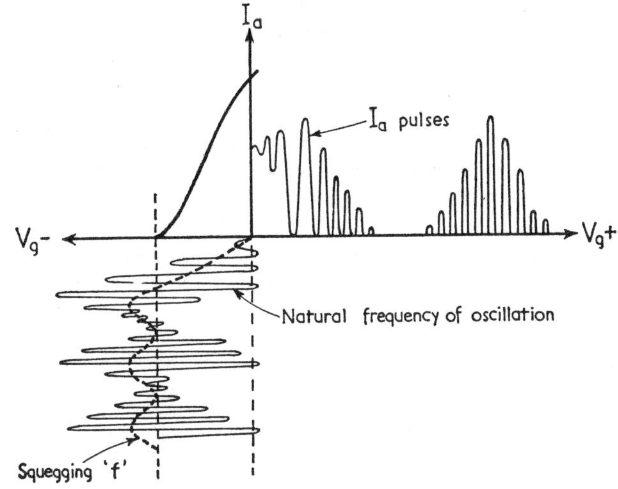

(10) (d) they reach a value less than cut-off, the oscillation recommences
cont. and the cycle is repeated.

(e) Any of the following may result in either non-oscillation or intermittent operation.

(*i*) R_1 high in value or open circuit.
(*ii*) R_2 high in value or open circuit.
(*iii*) L_1 open circuit or shorted turns.
(*iv*) L_2 open circuit or shorted turns.
(*v*) C_2 open circuit or short circuit.
(*vi*) C_3 open circuit or leaky.
(*vii*) Low h.t.
(*viii*) Low emission valve.
(*ix*) High resistance solder connections to any of components above.

(f)

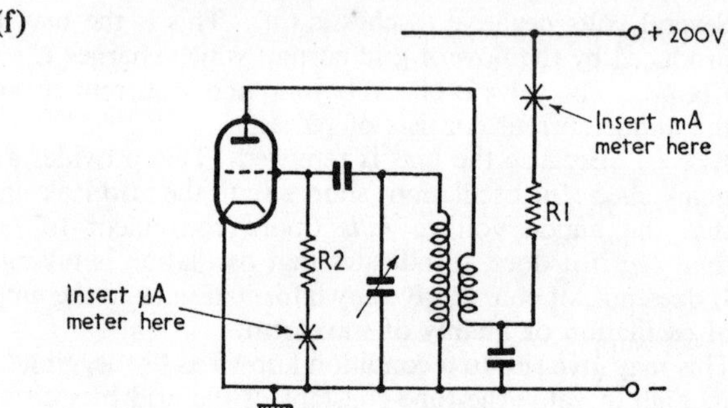

(*i*) The mA meter to measure anode current should be inserted in the top end of R_1. It is always best to insert the meter at a point where the a.c. potential is small, to prevent the instrument and its leads from upsetting the circuit conditions.

(*ii*) The μA meter to measure grid current is best placed in the bottom end of R_2 for the same reasons mentioned in (*i*). When the circuit is oscillating, the grid current will be in the order of 200μA.

(g) If the connections to L_2 are reversed, the oscillation will cease, since the feedback to the grid circuit will not be in the correct phase to maintain oscillations.

(h) Yes. In a radio receiver the amplitude of oscillation often has a ratio of about 2 or 3 to 1 over the tuning range, generally falling off towards the low frequency end of the band.

(11) (a) The peak voltage across each half of the h.t. winding

$$= 350 \times 1{\cdot}414 \text{ volts} \triangleq 495 \text{ volts.}$$

The peak inverse voltage which the rectifier must withstand is approximately (2 × peak) = 2 × 495 volts = $\underline{\text{990 volts.}}$

(b) R_1 and R_2 limit the heavy charging current which flows into the reservoir capacitor each half-cycle, so that the peak current rating for the valve is not exceeded. Manufacturers specify a minimum series resistance to be used for a particular rectifying valve; a portion of the resistance is provided by the d.c. resistance of the h.t. winding.
(c) 100c/s, *i.e.* twice the frequency of the mains supply.
(d) Fall—also the amplitude of the ripple will increase.
(e) Fall slightly—as the reservoir will only be charged on alternate half-cycles, instead of on each half-cycle.
(f) Increase, because the filtering action will be lost.
(g) Increase—a large current will flow because the d.c. output is short circuited.
(h) Fall to zero.

(12) (a) Half-wave rectification.
(b) By altering the link on R_1, it is possible to ensure that the voltage supplied to the valve heaters is constant when operating from different supply voltages. Similarly, the link on R_2 is adjusted to provide the required constant value of h.t. The resistors are so tapped that voltages in the range 200—250V a.c. or d.c. may be used with this receiver.
(c) Total voltage required by valve heaters

$$= (13+45+13+19+31) \text{ volts} = 121 \text{ volts}$$

$\therefore$ Voltage to be dropped by R_1 when operating from a 240V supply

$$= (240-121) \text{ volts} = 119 \text{ volts.}$$

The current passing through $R_1 = 0{\cdot}1$ ampere

$$\therefore \text{ Resistance of } R_1 = \frac{119}{0{\cdot}1} \text{ ohms} = \underline{1190 \text{ ohms.}}$$

(d) The function of C_1 is to improve the efficiency of rectification by raising the average d.c. output volts, appearing at the cathode of the rectifier, to almost the peak a.c. input volts. [See (a) and (b)]. The purpose of R_3 and C_2 is to remove the

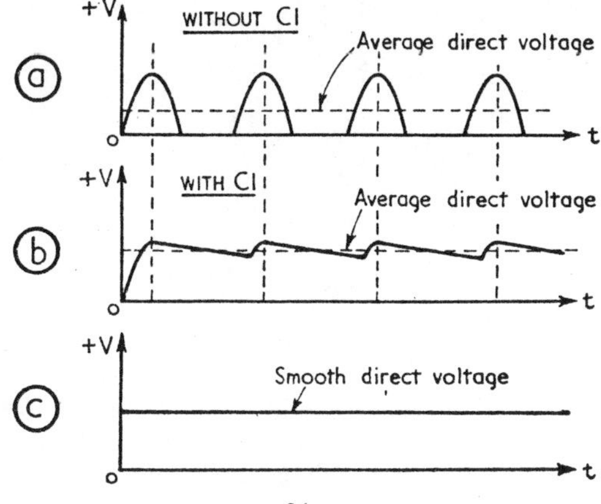

(12) (d) residual ripple voltage from (b) so that the output of the power
cont. unit is a smooth direct voltage [see (c)].

(e) Since the chassis is connected to one side of the mains supply, it is most essential to protect the user from electrical shock by ensuring that the chassis is connected to the **neutral side** of the mains. This may easily be checked by testing the chassis with a neon tester, having first ensured that the tester is working satisfactorily. Note that on d.c. mains there will be no h.t. output unless the anode of the rectifier is connected to the positive side of the mains. In some cases the negative side of the d.c. mains may be found to be "live".

(f)

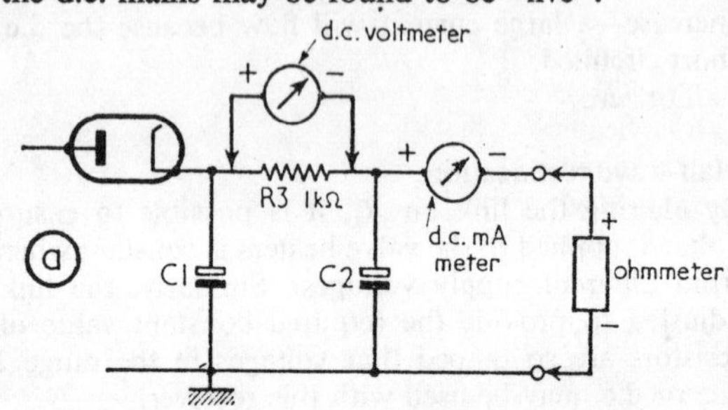

(*i*) Connect a d.c. mA meter as shown in (a). It will then read the total h.t. current, which for the usual valve receiver will be in the order of 50mA.

(*ii*) To measure the voltage drop across R_3, connect a d.c. voltmeter as shown in (a). If the h.t. current drain as measured in (*i*) is, say, 50mA, then p.d. across R_3

$$= \frac{50}{10^3} \times 10^3 = 50\text{V d.c.}$$

[The measured value will differ slightly from the calculated value due to the tolerance of R_3].

(*iii*) Connect an a.c. ammeter in series with the heater chain as in (b). A reading of 0·1 ampere should be obtained.

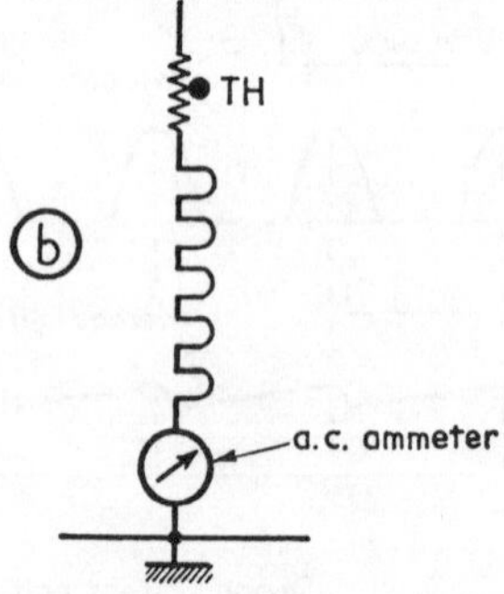

(*iv*) Connect an ohmmeter as shown in (a) ensuring first that the set is switched off. Initially, a low reading will be obtained, but it will gradually rise as the electrolytics

(12) (f) *cont.* charge to the e.m.f. of the meter battery. Eventually, a reading usually in excess of 1MΩ will result; but it does depend on the voltage divider design (if any) of the particular receiver. As a rough guide, resistance readings below about 10kΩ should always be investigated.

(g) Excessive h.t. current drain is usually caused by low insulation of the h.t. line to chassis as a result of C_1, C_2, or a decoupling capacitor being leaky. Other possible causes are:

(*i*) A valve passing greater current than normal due to incorrect bias, electrode short, or o/c grid leak.

(*ii*) Low insulation between primary winding and core or secondary of sound o/p transformer.

(*iii*) *Tracking* of wave-change switch having h.t. contacts.

If the heater current is less than normal then, provided the mains tapping is set correctly, possible causes are:

(*i*) High resistance Thermistor (Th.)

(*ii*) High resistance mains dropper (R_1).

(h) 50Hz. The same as the frequency of the mains supply.

(i) The amplitude of the ripple voltage may be measured by connecting the junction of R_3/C_2 to the *Y* AMP of an oscilloscope, having a calibrated *Y* deflection. For a well-designed power unit the amplitude will be in the order of tens of millivolts.

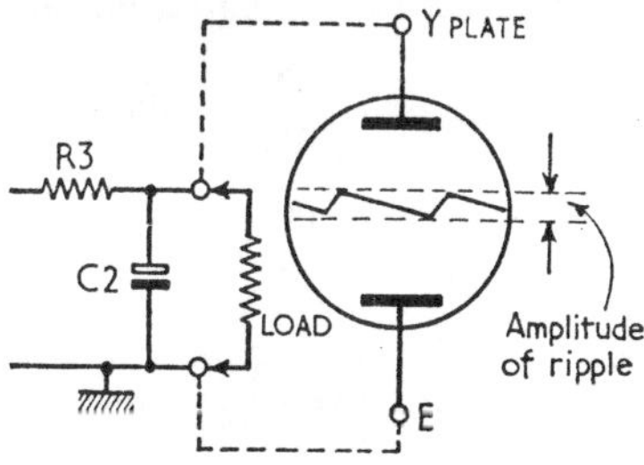

(13) (a) The diode is non-conducting thus the potential at A will be +9V.

(b) The diode is conducting thus the potential at A will be 0V.

(c) Again the diode is conducting and therefore the potential of the anode will be the same as the cathode, *i.e.* −9V.

(d) As the diode is conducting, the potential at A will assume a value depending upon the resistor values which in this case are the same. Thus the potential will be mid-way between +9V and −9V, *i.e.* 0V.

(e) The diode will neither be forward nor reverse biased and the potential at A will be +9V, as it is at every point along the circuit.

(f) D_1 will be conducting and the potential at A and B is decided by the resistor values. The potential difference between the +5V and +15V terminals is 10V, thus there will be a 2V drop across the 2kΩ resistor and an 8V drop across the 8kΩ resistor. Therefore B will be at a potential of +7V and so will point A. D_2 will be non-conducting.

(14) (a) The diodes will be reverse biased, thus the O/P potential will be approximately +20V.

(b) D_1 will be reverse biased. However, D_2 will be conducting and the O/P terminal will assume D_2 cathode potential, *i.e.* 0V. In practice it would be slightly positive due to the forward voltage drop across D_2.

(c) Both diodes will be conducting and the potential at the ouput will be approximately 0V.

(d) The diodes will be without bias and the potential at the output will be +20V, *i.e.* no current in *R*. In practice the potential would be slightly lower under this fault condition than when the diodes are reverse biased due to the leakage current in *R* which tends to increase the output voltage.

(e) Both diodes will then be conducting and the output will assume the potential of the diode cathodes, *i.e.* +7·5V (approx.).

(f) In position B the diodes will be conducting thus the potential at the output will be 0V. In position A the diodes will still be reverse biased but the output will assume the new potential of the +20V terminal, *i.e.* +5V.

(g) This would suggest that one or both of the diodes was short circuit.

(h) The resistor limits the current to a maximum of

$$\frac{V}{R} \text{ amps} = \frac{20}{10^3} = 20mA.$$

(i) Both switches must be in position A and thus reverse bias the diodes. If S_1 and S_2 are in position B, or one is in position B, the output will be 0V, *i.e.* binary 0. This corresponds to an *AND* gate and in this arrangement both diode cathodes must be positive (+30V) to give an output.

(15) (a) (*i*) is correct. The operation is along line A. Here the transistor is of very low resistance and the collector-emitter voltage is also very low. Provided the transistor is saturated, the collector voltage and current are independent of any signal applied between base and emitter. The collector dissipation is negligible.

(b) (*ii*) is correct. The operation is along line B. Here the transistor is of very high resistance and the collector current is extremely small. Again, the collector dissipation is negligible.

(c) (*iii*) is correct. Area C. Here the collector dissipation can be appreciable as there may be significant collector current with a collector voltage of several volts relative to the emitter. When a transistor is used as a switch the operation will have to pass through Area C during the transition from one state to another. To minimise collector dissipation it is necessary for the transistor to change states at high speed.

(d) (*ii*) is correct. Almost 0V: it may be as little as 0·1V.

(e) (*i*) is correct. The collector voltage will be practically equal to the line supply, *i.e.* approximately 10V, since the collector current will be negligible (less than 1μA for a silicon transistor) and in consequence the volts drop across R will also be insignificant.

(f) (*ii*) is correct. Remain substantially constant when the forward bias increases.

(g) (*iii*) is correct.

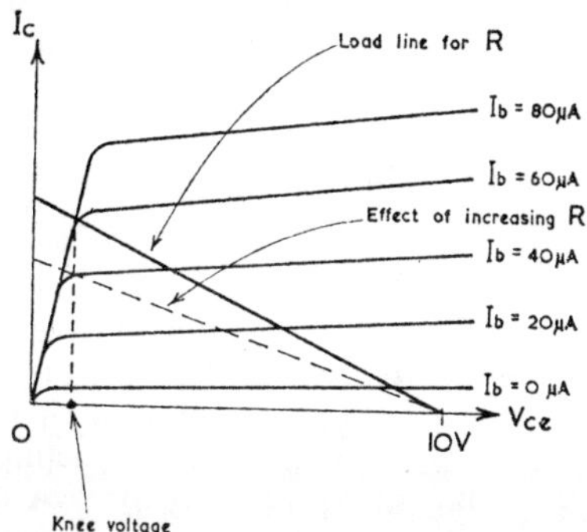

The diagram above shows a load-line for R that causes the collector to bottom, *i.e.* fall to the knee voltage at a base current of 60μA. If the value of R is increased the slope of the load-line will be less (as shown) and the collector will bottom at a lower value of base current, in this case when Ib is 40μA.

(h) (*ii*) is correct. Both junctions will be forward biased.

(16) (a) (*iv*) is correct. It would be best to move S_2 to position B (and C) to see if L_3 and L_2 light. This will give further easily-obtained information and assist in determining whether or not the defect is common to all three switch positions.

(b) (*iii*) is correct. L_1 faulty (o/c).

(c) The most likely cause is S_1 high resistance contacts, or a switch lead connection high resistance which will cause a voltage drop when L_1 draws current from the supply. Hence the voltage to L_1 will be lower than normal and the lamp will glow less bright. When S_2 is in position A, B or C the extra current demanded by L_2, L_3 or L_4 will increase the volts drop across the high resistance and reduce the voltage fed to L_1, and L_2, L_3 and L_4.

(d) Answer (*ii*) is correct.

(e) (*iv*) is correct. A short-circuit lamp L_1 would cause this symptom.

(17) (a) N channel.

(b) Usually in the order of hundreds of megohms, hence (*ii*) is correct. The impedance presented to the input terminals of the amplifier would be less and approximately equal to the value of R_2.

(c) In an N-channel F.E.T. the charge carriers are electrons.

(d) The gate-to-source junction is reverse biased.

(e) The reverse bias is 4·2V which is the source voltage. Since the gate is returning to chassis *via* R_2 it will be negative to the source by the source voltage.

(f) (*i*) is correct. If C_1 goes s/c there will be no bias voltage between the gate and source and the width of the N-channel will increase. Thus *Id* will increase (the effect is similar to a valve with no bias).

(g) (*iii*) is correct. An o/c C_1 will not affect the d.c. conditions of the amplifier, hence *Id* will remain the same.

(h) (*iii*) is correct. The d.c. conditions would not be affected thus the drain current will remain the same.

(i) With R_1 o/c there would be no current through the device thus *Vd*, *Vs* and *Vg* would be zero.

(j) (*ii*) is correct. There would be no current through the device hence the drain current would fall to zero.

(k) (*i*) is correct. If R_2 goes o/c the bias will be lost and the current through the device will rise, hence the drain voltage will fall on account of the increase in voltage drop across R_1.

(l) (*ii*) is correct. This will remove the bias as the source and drain will be at the same potential. Therefore the drain current would rise.

(m) (*ii*) is correct. In antiphase with the input. For resistive loads there is signal inversion between gate and drain.

(n) This will cause negative feedback and the gain of the stage will fall.

(18) (a) Relay *A* will be energized thus causing the hold-on contacts A_3 to close, contacts A_2 to open (rendering Relay *B* inoperative should S_3 subsequently be pressed) and closing contacts A_1 allowing the lamp L_1 to light up.

(b) (*iii*) is correct. A_2 contacts high resistance.

(c) The trouble here is that when S_2 is pressed and Relay *A* energizes, CONTACTS A_2 FAIL TO BREAK. Thus when S_3 is operated Relay *B* will also energize causing L_2 to glow. B_2 contacts will open but Relay *A* will be held energized *via* its hold-on contacts A_3.

(d) Either (*i*) or (*ii*) could cause the symptoms given.

(e) Either (*iii*) or (*iv*) could cause the fault.

(19) (a) Component *X* is a variable-capacitance diode. Its function is to tune L_1 over a suitable part of the v.h.f. band. The diode is effectively in parallel with C_1 as its capacitance is much smaller than that of C_2. By applying a variable d.c. potential *via* R_1 the capacitance of the diode may be altered, thus varying the

resonant frequency of the tuned circuit. This method of tuning a circuit is often called **electronic tuning**.

(b) The vari-cap diode must be placed in a reverse bias state, therefore terminal *A* will be positive with respect to terminal *B*.

(c) With maximum reverse voltage applied to the vari-cap diode, its depletion capacitance will be at its smallest value, therefore the frequency of the tuned circuit will be at its highest.

(d) If C_2 develops a short circuit, there will be no tuning voltage applied to the diode. Thus the tuning of the receiver will not alter, *i.e.* it will remain fixed at one frequency (beyond the low frequency end of the band). In practice, assuming that at leats two electronic tuned circuits are employed, the receiver may still tune but there will be a loss of sensitivity particularly at the high frequency end of the band.

(20) (a) Zener Diode.

(b) The purpose of R_1 is to feed D_1 with a suitable current so that it is biased to operate at a particular point on its characteristic without exceeding the maximum power dissipation for the device. The resistor drops any voltage in excess of the zener voltage, but in calculating the value of R_1 the effect of the current drawn by the load must be taken into account.

(c) As D_1 must be reverse biased, terminal *A* will be positive with respect to terminal *B*.

(d) If the load current decreases, the current passing through the diode must increase to maintain the same voltage drop across R_1. As a result the power dissipated in D_1 will rise.

(e) With D_1 short circuit there will be no output voltage across the load. Due to the increase in current through R_1 its wattage dissipation may be exceeded. The d.c. input voltage from the rectifier will probably be lower by an amount depending upon the regulation of the circuit.

(f)

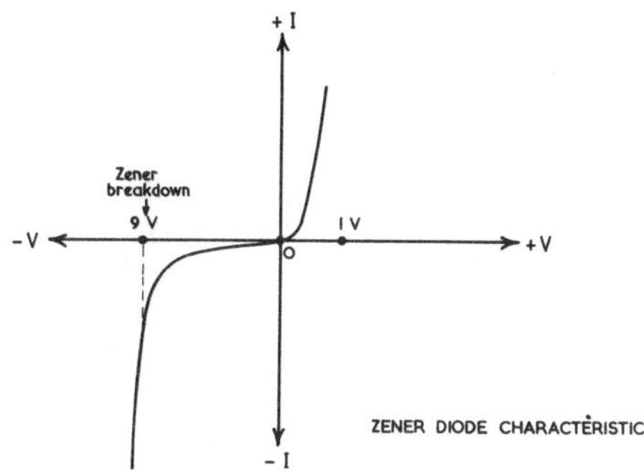

(21) (a) Silicon Controlled Rectifier (S.C.R.)

(b) (*i*) Yes.

(*ii*) No.

(*iii*) No.

(c) If the trigger supply is missing, the S.C.R. will not 'fire' thus there will be no current in the load.

(d)

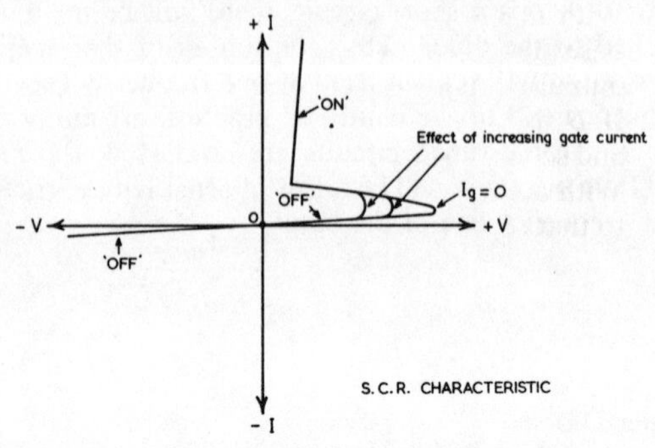

S. C. R. CHARACTERISTIC

(22) (a) The function of the circuit is to rectify the supply voltage across T_1 secondary and to provide a d.c. output voltage twice that of the peak voltage across the secondary winding (voltage doubler circuit).

(b) Peak voltage across T_1 primary $= 340V$

$\therefore$ peak voltage across secondary winding $= (2 \times 340)V$

$= 680V$

C_2 will charge to twice this voltage, *i.e.* 1360V.

(c) As C_2 is connected to the anode of D_2, the top plate of the capacitor will be negative with respect to the lower plate.

(d) If D_1 goes open circuit, the output voltage will fall to a value below that of the peak voltage across the secondary winding, *i.e.* less than 680V. The actual value will depend upon the relative values of C_1 and C_2.

(23) (a) D_2 and D_3.

(b) 100Hz.

(c) Tr_1 acts as a series regulator. Since its base is fed with a constant reference voltage from D_5, any changes in output voltage due to input voltage or load current variations will vary the emitter voltage of Tr_1. As a result, the base-emitter voltage of Tr_1 will alter thus varying the effective resistance of Tr_1. If, for example, the load current reduces tending to make the output voltage rise, the bias on Tr_1 is reduced thereby increasing the effective series resistance of Tr_1. In consequence more voltage is dropped across Tr_1 to maintain a constant output voltage.

(d) R_2 supplies D_5 with a suitable current so that it operates on the correct part of its characteristic without exceeding the maximum power rating for the diode.

(e) The base voltage of Tr_1 is D_1 zener voltage (9·1V). The output voltage will be slightly less than this as Tr_1 is forward biased. Since Tr_1 is a germanium type transistor (AC 117), the output voltage will be about 8·9—9·0V.

(f) (*i*) With R_2 open circuit there will be no voltage supply to Tr_1 base. In consequence the transistor will be OFF and the output voltage will fall to zero.

(*ii*) If D_5 is short circuit, the base voltage of Tr_1 will be zero and so too will be the output voltage.

(*iii*) With a collector-emitter short, the output voltage will rise to that across C_2.

(24) (a) Common Base.

(b) Since an n-p-n transistor is used, terminal *A* will be negative with respect to chassis.

(c) The purpose of C_2 is to 'ground' the base of the transistor to signals.

(d) Low input resistance.

(e) In-phase.

(f) If R_1 were decoupled with a capacitor, the input circuit would be shorted out to signals *via* C_1.

(25) (a) Common Collector (emitter-follower).

(b) Since a p-n-p transistor is used, terminal *A* will be negative to chassis.

(c) Low output resistance.

(d) In-phase.

(e) The voltage gain of an emitter-follower is less than unity and is commonly in the range of 0·9 to 0·99. Thus the output voltage will be in the approximate range 180–198mV.

(f) The emitter-follower stage is frequently used as a buffer stage between a high impedance source and a low impedance load. For example, such a stage may be connected between a high stability oscillator or wide-band amplifier and the low impedance circuits it is feeding.

(g) (*i*) With the meter leads one way round, the base-emitter junction of the transistor will be forward biased. Thus the reading will be effectively R_2 in parallel with the series circuit comprising R_3 and the resistance of the base-emitter junction. Assuming a forward resistance of, say, 500 ohms, the meter will read

$$\frac{5600 \times 1500}{5600 + 1500} \simeq 1180\Omega$$

(*ii*) With the meter leads reversed, the base-emitter junction will be reverse biased. Assuming a reverse resistance of, say, 2MΩ the effective resistance will be that of R_2, *i.e.* about 5·6kΩ.

SECTION (4)
FAULTS IN AUDIO AMPLIFIERS

Unless stated otherwise, all voltages throughout this section were measured between the point indicated and chassis with an AVOMETER model 8.

(1)

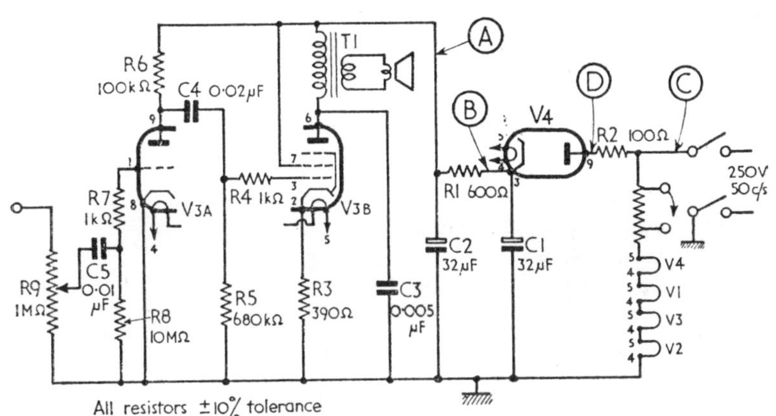

The circuit shows the power and audio stages of a four-valve receiver. When it was in good working order, the following measurements were made:
[V.V.M. = measured with valve-voltmeter].

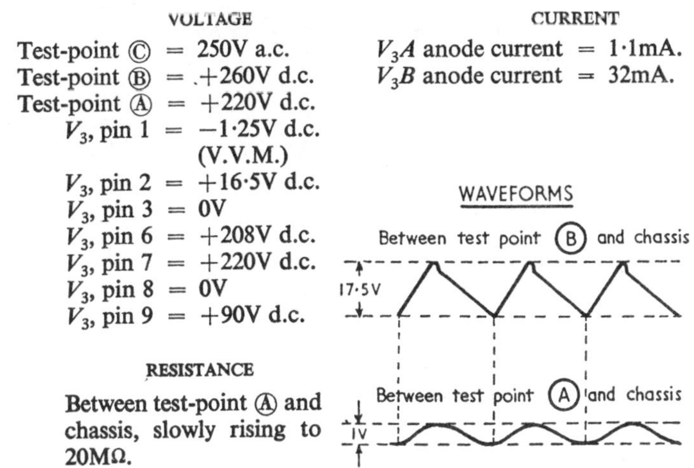

VOLTAGE

Test-point Ⓒ = 250V a.c.
Test-point Ⓑ = +260V d.c.
Test-point Ⓐ = +220V d.c.
V_3, pin 1 = −1·25V d.c. (V.V.M.)
V_3, pin 2 = +16·5V d.c.
V_3, pin 3 = 0V
V_3, pin 6 = +208V d.c.
V_3, pin 7 = +220V d.c.
V_3, pin 8 = 0V
V_3, pin 9 = +90V d.c.

CURRENT

V_3A anode current = 1·1mA.
V_3B anode current = 32mA.

WAVEFORMS

RESISTANCE

Between test-point Ⓐ and chassis, slowly rising to 20MΩ.

Tests were carried out on eight similar receivers, each having a single fault present in the circuitry shown. By carefully comparing the results of the measurements made with those given for the receiver when it was working satisfactorily, deduce the faulty component in each case.

(a) RECEIVER 1. *Symptoms:* No signals heard in the loud-speaker—hum level normal.

VOLTAGE	RESISTANCE
V_3, pin 7 = +220V d.c.	Between test-point Ⓐ and chassis: slowly rising to 20MΩ.
V_3, pin 9 = 0V	Between V_3, pin 9 and chassis: infinity.

(b) RECEIVER 2. *Symptoms:* Signals heard in the loudspeaker, but with excessive hum present.

VOLTAGE

Test-point Ⓒ = 250V a.c.
Test-point Ⓑ = +195V d.c.
Test-point Ⓐ = +170V d.c.

WAVEFORMS

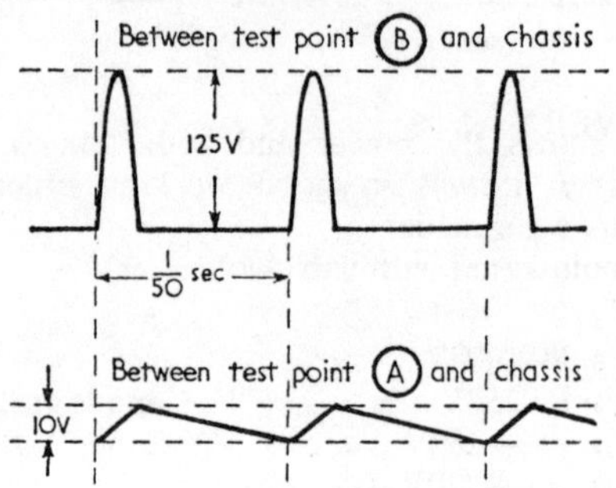

(c) RECEIVER 3. *Symptoms:* Receiver "dead", but heaters glowing.

VOLTAGE

Test-point Ⓐ = +220V d.c.
V_3, pin 1 = −1·25V d.c. (V.V.M.)
V_3, pin 2 = +16·5V d.c.
V_3, pin 3 = 0V
V_3, pin 6 = +220V d.c.
V_3, pin 7 = +220V d.c.
V_3, pin 8 = 0V
V_3, pin 9 = +90V d.c.

(d) RECEIVER 4. *Symptoms:* Receiver "dead".

VOLTAGE

Test-point Ⓑ = 0V
Test-point Ⓒ = 250V a.c.
Test-point Ⓓ = 250V a.c.
V_3, pin 4 = 250V a.c.
V_2, pin 5 = 0V

(e) RECEIVER 5. *Symptoms:* No output—hum level normal.

VOLTAGE	RESISTANCE
V_3, pin 1 = −1·25V d.c.	Between V_3, pin 3 and chassis: 750kΩ.
V_3, pin 2 = +16·5V d.c.	
V_3, pin 3 = 0V	
V_3, pin 6 = +208V d.c.	
V_3, pin 7 = +220V d.c.	
V_3, pin 8 = 0V	
V_3, pin 9 = +90V d.c.	

A 300Hz test signal was applied between the following valve pins and chassis, with these results:

V_3, pin 1: no output obtained.
V_3, pin 9: no output obtained.
V_3, pin 3: good output obtained.

(f) RECEIVER 6. *Symptoms:* Low output and very distorted.

VOLTAGE

Test-point Ⓐ = +284V d.c.
V_3, pin 6 = +282V d.c.
V_3, pin 7 = 0V
V_3, pin 2 = +0·3V
V_3, pin 3 = 0V to − 40V d.c. (increasing negatively as the volume control is advanced).
V_3, pin 9 = +89V d.c.

(g) RECEIVER 7. *Symptoms:* Very distorted output.

VOLTAGE

Test-point Ⓑ = +230V d.c.
Test-point Ⓐ = +160V d.c.
V_3, pin 6 = +140V d.c.
V_3, pin 7 = +160V d.c.
V_3, pin 2 = +42V d.c.
V_3, pin 3 = +42V d.c.

(h) RECEIVER 8. *Symptoms:* No output and R_1 overheating.

RESISTANCE

Between V_3, pin 9 and chassis approximately 102kΩ.
Between V_4, pin 3 and chassis approximately 960Ω.
Between V_3, pin 7 and chassis approximately 360Ω.
Between V_3, pin 7 and chassis (with C_2 disconnected) approximately 360Ω.

(2)

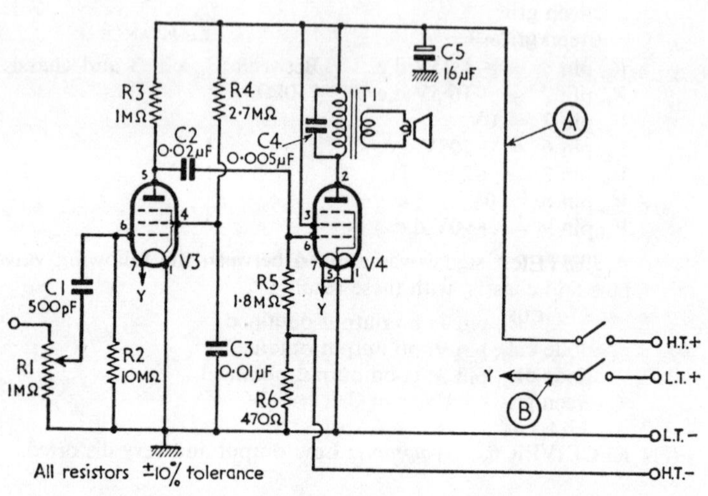

The circuit shows the audio stages of a four-valve battery receiver. When it was in good working order, the following measurements were made:

VOLTAGE

Test-point Ⓐ = +64V d.c.
Test-point Ⓑ = +1·5V d.c.
V_4, pin 2 = +62V d.c.
V_4, pin 3 = +64V d.c.
V_4, pin 6 = −3·35V d.c. (V.V.M.)
V_4, pin 7 = +1·5V d.c.
V_3, pin 4 = +28·7V d.c. (V.V.M.)
V_3, pin 5 = +21V d.c. (V.V.M.)
V_3, pin 6 = −0·5V d.c. (V.V.M.)

CURRENT

V_3 anode current = 42μA.
V_3 screen grid current = 13μA.
V_4 anode current = 3·2mA.
V_4 screen grid current = 0·59mA.
Total h.t. current drain = 7mA (for complete receiver).

RESISTANCE

Between test-point Ⓐ and chassis: slowly rising to 20MΩ.

Tests were carried out on five similar receivers, each having a single fault present in the circuitry shown. By carefully comparing the results of the measurements made with those given for the receiver when it was working satisfactorily, deduce the faulty component in each case.

(a) RECEIVER 1. *Symptoms:* No output.

CURRENT

V_4 anode current = 3·2mA
V_3 anode current = nil
V_4 screen grid current = 0·59mA
V_3 screen grid current = nil

VOLTAGE

Test-point Ⓐ = +64V d.c.
V_3, pin 4 = 0V
V_3, pin 5 = +64V d.c. (V.V.M.)

RESISTANCE

Between test-point Ⓐ and chassis: slowly rising to approximately 2·7MΩ.

(b) RECEIVER 2. *Symptoms:* Very distorted output.

CURRENT

V_3 anode current = 43μA
V_4 anode current = 0·175mA
V_3 screen grid current = 14μA
Total h.t. current drain = 3mA

VOLTAGE

V_4, pin 2 = +63·8V d.c.
V_4, pin 3 = +64V d.c.
V_4, pin 6 = −6·6V d.c.
V_3, pin 6 = −0·495V d.c. (V.V.M.)

(c) RECEIVER 3. *Symptoms:* Receiver goes into self-oscillation as the volume control is advanced.

CURRENT

V_4 anode current = 3·15mA
V_3 anode current = 42μA
V_4 screen grid current = 0·58mA
V_3 screen grid current = 14μA

Placing an 8μF capacitor across the h.t. battery stopped the oscillation, and the receiver then functioned satisfactorily.

(d) RECEIVER 4. *Symptoms:* No output.

VOLTAGE

V_4, pin 2 = +62V d.c.
V_4, pin 3 = +64V d.c.
V_4, pin 6 = −3·36V d.c. (V.V.M.)
V_3, pin 4 = +28·9V d.c. (V.V.M.)
V_3, pin 5 = +21·2V d.c. (V.V.M.)

A 300 Hz test signal applied between V_4, pin 6 and chassis produced no output from the loudspeaker.

(e) RECEIVER 5. *Symptoms:* Low output and distorted.

VOLTAGE	CURRENT
V_3, pin 4 = +28·6V d.c. (V.V.M.)	V_4 anode current = 1·8mA
V_4, pin 2 = +63V d.c.	V_4 screen grid current = 0·33mA.
V_4, pin 3 = +64V d.c.	
V_4, pin 6 = −2·4V d.c. (V.V.M.)	

(3)

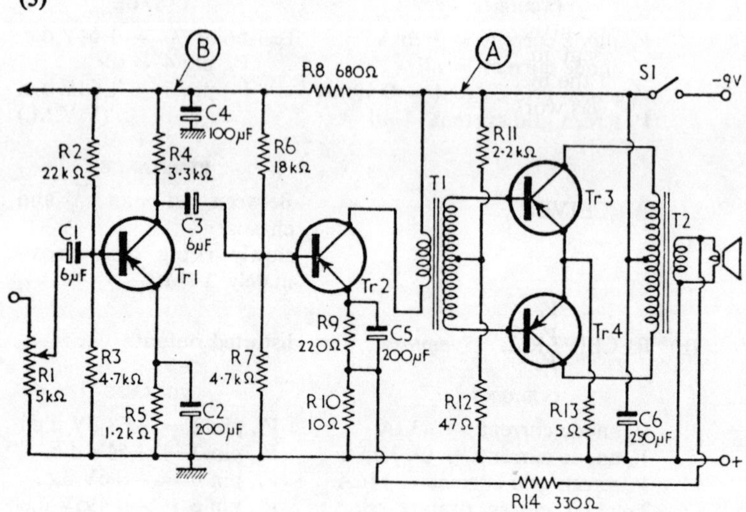

The circuit shows the audio stages of a transistor radio employing a class-B push-pull output stage. When the radio was in good working order, the following measurements were made:

VOLTAGE

*TR*1	*TR*2
V_c = −4·1V	V_c = −8·6V
V_b = −1·0V	V_b = −0·86V
V_e = −0·91V	V_e = −0·74V

*TR*3	*TR*4
V_c = −9·18V	V_c = −9·18V
V_b = −0·17V	V_b = −0·17V
V_e = 0V	V_e = 0V

Test-point Ⓐ = −9·2V
Test-point Ⓑ = −6·4V

CURRENT

*TR*1	*TR*2
I_c = 0·67mA	I_c = 3·5mA

CURRENT

*TR*3	*TR*4
I_c = 2·1mA	I_c = 2·1mA

Battery current drain = 15mA
(for complete receiver)

THE VOLUME CONTROL WAS SET TO A MINIMUM FOR ALL MEASUREMENTS.

Tests were carried out on eight similar receivers, each having a single fault present in the circuitry shown. By carefully comparing the results of the measurements made with those given for the receiver when it was working satisfactorily, deduce the faulty component in each case.

(a) RECEIVER 1. *Symptoms:* No output.

VOLTAGE

TR1	*TR2*
V_c = −0·37V	V_c = −9·2V
V_b = −0·1V	V_b = −0·12V
V_e = −0·05V	V_e = −0·03V

Test-point Ⓐ = −9·2V
Test-point Ⓑ = −0·5V

CURRENT

Battery current drain = 8mA

(b) RECEIVER 2. *Symptoms:* Output distorted.

VOLTAGE

TR1	*TR2*
V_c = −2·8V	V_c = −5·6V

TR3	*TR4*
V_c = −5·95V	V_c = −5·95V

Test-point Ⓐ = −6V

CURRENT

Battery current drain = 8mA

(c) RECEIVER 3. *Symptoms:* Output distorted.

VOLTAGE

TR1	
V_c = −0·05V	Test-point Ⓐ = −9·16V
V_b = −0·17V	Test-point Ⓑ = −5·72V
V_e = 0V	

CURRENT

TR1
$I_c = 2\text{mA}$

(d) RECEIVER 4. *Symptoms:* Output distorted and weak.

VOLTAGE

TR1	*TR2*
$V_c = -6{\cdot}7\text{V}$	$V_c = -8{\cdot}7\text{V}$
$V_b = 0\text{V}$	$V_b = -0{\cdot}87\text{V}$
$V_e = -0{\cdot}08\text{V}$	$V_e = -0{\cdot}75\text{V}$

CURRENT

TR3	*TR4*
$I_c = 2{\cdot}15\text{mA}$	$I_c = 2{\cdot}15\text{mA}$

RESISTANCE

An ohmmeter connected between the base of *TR1* and chassis read 4·7kΩ, but on reversing the leads it read 1·3kΩ.

(e) RECEIVER 5. *Symptoms:* Very distorted output.

VOLTAGE

TR2	*TR3*	*TR4*
$V_c = -8{\cdot}45\text{V}$	$V_c = -9{\cdot}18\text{V}$	$V_c = 0\text{V}$
$V_b = -0{\cdot}89\text{V}$	$V_b = -0{\cdot}17\text{V}$	$V_b = -0{\cdot}14\text{V}$
$V_e = -0{\cdot}78\text{V}$	$V_e = 0\text{V}$	$V_e = 0\text{V}$

Test-point Ⓐ = −9·2V

CURRENT

TR2	*TR3*	*TR4*
$I_c = 3{\cdot}5\text{mA}$	$I_c = 2{\cdot}2\text{mA}$	$I_c = \text{nil}$

(f) RECEIVER 6. *Symptoms:* Reduced gain.

VOLTAGE *TR2*	CURRENT *TR2*
$V_c = -8{\cdot}6\text{V}$	$I_c = 3{\cdot}6\text{mA}$
$V_b = -0{\cdot}86\text{V}$	
$V_e = -0{\cdot}74\text{V}$	

(*i*) 1000Hz test signal applied between *TR*2 collector and chassis —normal output obtained.

(*ii*) 1000Hz test signal applied between *TR*2 base and chassis—output below normal.

(g) RECEIVER 7. *Symptoms:* Very weak output.

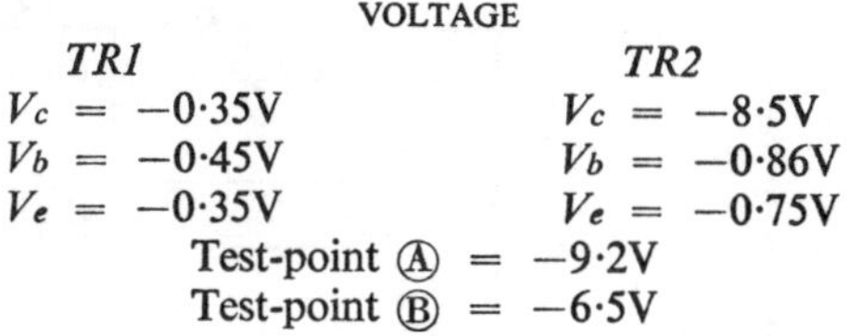

VOLTAGE

TR1	*TR2*
$V_c = -0{\cdot}35V$	$V_c = -8{\cdot}5V$
$V_b = -0{\cdot}45V$	$V_b = -0{\cdot}86V$
$V_e = -0{\cdot}35V$	$V_e = -0{\cdot}75V$

Test-point Ⓐ = −9·2V
Test-point Ⓑ = −6·5V

CURRENT

TR1	*TR2*
$I_e = 0{\cdot}25mA$	$I_c = 3{\cdot}6mA$

(h) RECEIVER 8. *Symptoms:* No output.

VOLTAGE

TR1	*TR2*
$V_c = -4{\cdot}1V$	$V_c = -8{\cdot}6V$
$V_b = -1{\cdot}0V$	$V_b = -0{\cdot}86V$
$V_e = -0{\cdot}91V$	$V_e = -0{\cdot}74V$

CURRENT

TR1	*TR2*
$I_c = 0{\cdot}67mA$	$I_c = 3{\cdot}5mA$

1000Hz test signal applied between *TR2* collector and chassis—normal output obtained.
1000Hz test signal applied between *TR2* base and chassis—normal output obtained.
1000Hz test signal applied between *TR1* collector and chassis—no output obtained.

(4)

The circuit given overleaf shows an audio amplifier, suitable for use in a record player.

(a) Give the approximate resistance readings (with the amplifier disconnected from mains) which you would normally expect when an ohmmeter is connected between the following points:

(*i*) V_1 anode and chassis.
(*ii*) V_1 control grid and chassis.
(*iii*) V_2 screen grid and chassis.
(*iv*) V_2 anode and chassis.
(*v*) V_1 anode and junction of R_6/R_8.
(*vi*) V_2 anode and V_2 cathode.
(*vii*) V_3 cathode and V_2 screen grid.
(*viii*) V_3 anode and V_2 cathode.
(*ix*) Slider of R_1 and Slider of R_{11}.
(*x*) V_1 anode and V_2 anode.

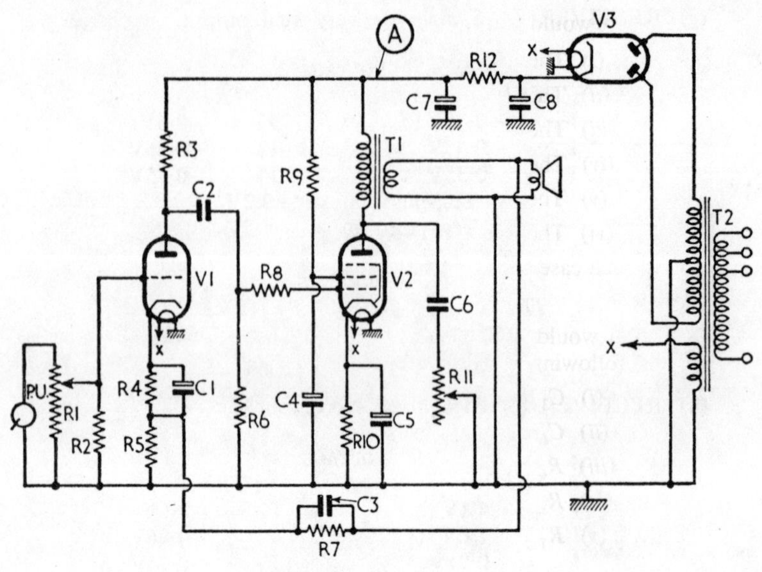

R_1	=	1MΩ log. ±20%		
R_2	=	500kΩ ±20%		
R_3	=	220kΩ ±10%	C_1	= 50μF
R_4	=	3·9kΩ ±10%	C_2	= 0·02μF
R_5	=	100Ω ±10%	C_3	= 390pF
R_6	=	560kΩ ±10%	C_4	= 16μF
R_7	=	10kΩ ±10%	C_5	= 25μF
R_8	=	47kΩ ±20%	C_6	= 0·05μF
R_9	=	15kΩ ±10%	C_7	= 32μF
R_{10}	=	390Ω ±10%	C_8	= 32μF
R_{11}	=	50kΩ ±20%		
R_{12}	=	560Ω ±10%		

T_1 primary = 500Ω

Resistance between test-point Ⓐ and chassis = 20MΩ.

(b) Give the *most likely* fault that would result in the following readings being obtained.

(*i*) Between the junction of R_4/R_5 and chassis: 1Ω.

(*ii*) Between V_1 anode and chassis: 580kΩ.

(*iii*) Between V_2 control grid and chassis: 395Ω.

(*iv*) Between V_1 cathode and chassis: 97Ω.

(*v*) Between the junction of R_{12}/C_7 and chassis: 15kΩ.

(c) Where would you connect instruments to measure the following:

(*i*) The total current drawn by V_1 and V_2

(*ii*) The total current drawn by V_2

(*iii*) The heater current drawn by V_1

(*iv*) The bias voltage for V_1

(*v*) The leakage current of C_4

(*vi*) The anode current of the voltage amplifier.

In each case suggest a suitable range for the instrument.

(d) What would be the effect on the operation of the amplifier if the following faults developed:

(*i*) C_3 becomes open circuit

(*ii*) C_6 becomes open circuit

(*iii*) R_6 becomes open circuit

(*iv*) R_{12} value rises to 5kΩ

(*v*) R_7 becomes open circuit.

Question (5) is overleaf

(5) The following questions relate to the diagram which shows the circuit of a 2-stage voltage preamplifier.

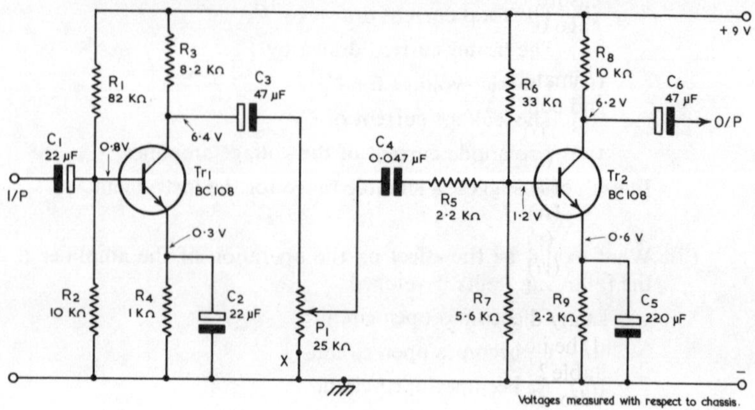

(a) If a signal of adequate amplitude is applied to the input terminals, which of the following faults will result in NO OUTPUT from the amplifier:

(*i*) C_2 o/c
(*ii*) R_1 increased to 130kΩ
(*iii*) Tr_2 base-emitter short
(*iv*) C_3 s/c
(*v*) C_4 o/c
(*vi*) Tr_1 emitter-base junction o/c
(*vii*) Line supply reduced to 4·5V

(b) Assuming the same signal conditions as in (a), which of the following faults are liable to result in DISTORTED OUTPUT from the amplifier:

(*i*) R_1 o/c
(*ii*) C_3 o/c
(*iii*) R_5 o/c
(*iv*) C_5 o/c
(*v*) R_7 reduced in value to 540Ω
(*vi*) Tr_1 base-emitter short
(*vii*) C_3 leaky

(c) With the same signal conditions as in (a) and (b), which of the following faults are liable to cause LOW GAIN from the amplifier:

(*i*) R_8 o/c
(*ii*) C_5 o/c
(*iii*) C_4 o/c
(*iv*) R_5 o/c
(*v*) C_2 o/c
(*vi*) R_3 reduced in value to 4kΩ
(*vii*) Line supply reduced to 7V

(d) If there is a break in the circuit at point *X*, what effect will this have on the performance of the amplifier?

(e) What fault symptom would you expect if C_4 developed a short circuit?

(f) To measure the base voltage of Tr_1 would you use the 1·5V or 10V range of a voltmeter having a sensitivity of 10,000 ohms per volt?

(g) Approximately what voltages would you expect at the emitter, base and collector of Tr_2 with the following faults apparent:

(*i*) R_9 o/c
(*ii*) Tr_2 base-emitter short
(*iii*) R_8 o/c
(*iv*) C_5 s/c
(*v*) R_6 o/c
(*vi*) R_7 o/c

(6) (a) How many discrete components are used in the circuit below?

(b) Would the i.c. be described as 'digital'? If not, what name would be suitable?

(c) An audio signal of suitable level is applied to the terminal marked INPUT but there is no output from the loudspeaker. Describe a series of logical tests that could be made to decide whether or not the fault lies in the i.c.

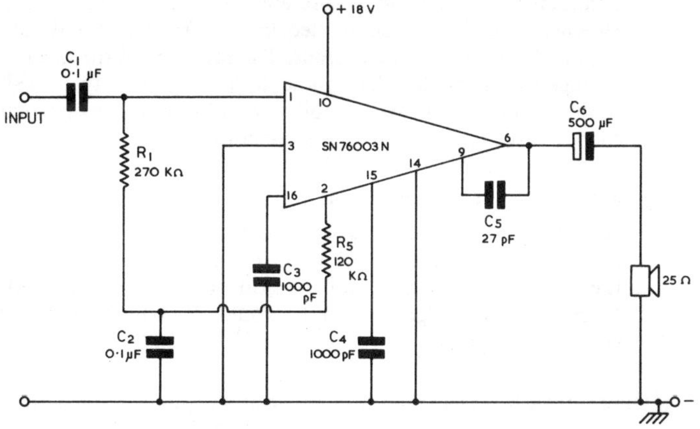

INTEGRATED CIRCUIT 5 WATT AUDIO AMPLIFIER.

ANSWERS TO SECTION (4)

(1) (a) RECEIVER 1. R_6 open circuit.

V_3A anode voltage (0V) suggests either that R_6 is open circuit or a short exists between V_3, pin 9 and chassis. The resistance measurement eliminates the short, and at the same time points to a discontinuity between V_3, pin 9 and the h.t. line.

(b) RECEIVER 2. C_1 (reservoir capacitor) open circuit.

Note the reduction in h.t. volts and increase in the amplitude of the ripple voltage, which are characteristics of this fault.

(c) RECEIVER 3. T_1 primary turns short circuit.

The anode voltage of V_3B (+220V d.c.), being the same as the h.t. line voltage, gives the clue to this fault and indicates a short circuit across the d.c. resistance of the primary winding.

(d) RECEIVER 4. Open circuit lead between V_3, pin 4 and V_2, pin 5. The voltage at test point Ⓑ (0V) suggests either that V_4 is not conducting; or a short is present between the h.t. line and chassis. The short is eliminated by the absence of p.d. across R_2, *i.e.* V_4 is not passing current. The presence of the ***full*** mains voltage on the heater chain indicates a discontinuity caused by faulty wiring or an open-circuit valve heater; in this particular case it was the wiring that was at fault.

(e) RECEIVER 5. C_4 open circuit.

As all the d.c. voltages given are normal, an "a.c. fault" is indicated. The "test signal" injections point to a fault between the anode of the triode and the grid of the pentode. Had C_4 been serviceable, "good output" would also have been obtained when the test signal was applied to V_3, pin 9.

(f) RECEIVER 6. Disconnection between V_3, pin 7 and h.t. line. The absence of voltage on the screen grid should have pointed to this fault. Grid current flow, on signal peaks, was responsible for the high negative grid volts, there being only a small standing bias on the valve (0·3V).

(g) RECEIVER 7. C_4 leak.

The positive voltage on the control grid is indicative of this fault. Note that the cathode volts "follow" those of the grid. Note also the increase in valve current, as indicated by the increase in volts drop across T_1 primary winding and R_1. A quick check for this particular fault is to short circuit R_5, placing the control grid at chassis potential, when voltage and current readings will return to normal.

(h) RECEIVER 8. C_3 short circuit.

The resistance measurements point to a low resistance between the h.t. line and chassis of approximately 360Ω. Since C_2 was proved, one must search for a possible resistance path to chassis of approximately 360Ω *via* a faulty component. In this case it is provided by the d.c. resistance of the primary winding of T_1 and the short-circuited C_3.

[The d.c. resistance of the primary winding may be found from

$$\frac{\text{Volts drop across primary (volts)}}{\text{Current through primary (amperes)}} = \frac{12 \times 10^3}{32} = 375\Omega].$$

(2) (a) RECEIVER 1. C_3 short circuit.

The resistance check between the h.t. line and chassis revealed a 2·7MΩ leak, and from the circuit diagram the most likely path exists *via* R_4 and the short-circuited C_3. The short accounts for the absence of voltage at V_3, pin 4, and the lack of anode and screen grid currents.

(b) RECEIVER 2. R_6 high resistance.

Although the total h.t. current drain reduced to 3mA, the bias voltage developed by R_6 increased to −6·6V; this can only mean that the resistor was high in value.

$$[\text{New value} = \frac{6{\cdot}6 \times 10^3}{3} = 2{\cdot}2\text{k}\Omega].$$

(c) RECEIVER 3. C_5 open circuit.

With this capacitor open circuit, the internal resistance of the h.t. battery provides a common impedance by which coupling between V_3 and V_4 can take place. A low frequency oscillation, commonly referred to as **motor-boating,** is the usual result of this fault.

(d) RECEIVER 4. Loudspeaker speech coil open circuit.

As the static voltages and currents of V_4 are normal, the fault is confined to components carrying a.c. currents, *i.e.* the loudspeaker and output transformer. This particular fault was caused by an open-circuit speech coil, but an open-circuit secondary winding or shorted turns on the primary or secondary, could have resulted in the same symptoms being apparent.

(e) RECEIVER 5. V_4 low emission.

The reduction in the grid bias voltage for V_4 is the result of the fall in the total h.t. current drain, brought about by the loss of emission of the valve.

(3) (a) RECEIVER 1. R_8 high resistance.

The low volts at test-point Ⓑ may be caused either by a short on the line or a high resistance R_8. The short is eliminated as the battery current consumption is less than normal. The low volts at Ⓑ will also cause the base volts of *TR2* to be considerably less than normal.

(b) RECEIVER 2. Low battery volts.
When the terminal p.d. of the battery has fallen by about 20 per cent of its nominal e.m.f. the battery requires replacement, otherwise any of the following faults are likely to occur: no output, weak output, distortion, instability.

(c) RECEIVER 3. C_2 short circuit.
With this capacitor short circuited, the forward bias on the transistor increases, resulting in larger collector and base currents (the increase in base current being responsible for the lower base potential). In this example the increase in collector current has caused the collector volts to *bottom*, and accounts for the distortion associated with the fault. It is possible that the increased collector current may cause permanent damage to the transistor.

(d) RECEIVER 4. R_2 open circuit
Under this fault condition, the base of *TR1* receives no potential and the collector current falls to its "leakage" value. It is the leakage current flowing through *TR1* which establishes the small p.d. across the emitter resistor. The resistance checks were included to prove that R_3 was not short circuited—the low reading of 1·3kΩ is the forward resistance of the base to emitter junction in series with R_5 (the junction being forward biased by the ohmmeter battery) with R_3 in parallel across the combination.

(e) RECEIVER 5. T_2 primary winding open circuit.
The voltages obtained point to a break between the centre-tap of T_2 and the collector of *TR4*, resulting in *TR4* ceasing to conduct. The audio currents then flowing in the loudspeaker are due solely to the operation of *TR3* and consist of half-cycle pulses (Class-B operation)—the reason for the distortion.

(f) RECEIVER 6. C_5 open circuit.
With R_9 undecoupled, negative feedback will take place into the input circuit reducing the gain of *TR2*. Note that the d.c. conditions of the transistor are unaffected by this fault.

(g) RECEIVER 7. R_4 open circuit.
The low collector volts of *TR1* suggests either that the transistor is passing excessive current or R_4 is high in value. The results of the tests show that the emitter current of *TR1* has fallen to 0·25mA, which therefore rules out excessive current as the cause of the low voltage.
In searching for a reason for the presence of a collector voltage with R_4 open circuit, one must remember that a transistor is a resistive device, and as such will possess a resistance path between collector and base. Thus, when a voltmeter is connected between the collector and chassis, a voltage reading will be obtained, the value of which will depend upon the sensitivity of the instrument and the base potential.

(h) RECEIVER 8. C_3 open circuit.
Normal output would also have been obtained when injecting at *TR1* collector if C_3 had been serviceable. The presence of the correct collector voltage for *TR1* eliminates the possibility of loss of signal occurring through a low resistance path between the collector and chassis.

(4) (a) (*i*) The resistance of R_3 plus that of the h.t. line to chassis, which for all practical purposes, would be 20MΩ.

(*ii*) From zero ohms up to approximately 330kΩ (R_2 and R_1 in parallel), depending on the volume control setting.

(*iii*) The resistance of R_9 plus that of the h.t. line to chassis, which for all practical purposes would be 20MΩ.

(*iv*) The resistance of the primary of T_1 plus that of the h.t. line to chassis, which for all practical purposes would be 20MΩ.

(*v*) The resistance of R_3, R_6 plus that of the h.t. line to chassis, which for all practical purposes would be 20MΩ.

(*vi*) The resistance of the primary of T_1, R_{10} plus that of the h.t. line to chassis, which for all practical purposes would be 20MΩ.

(*vii*) The resistance of R_9 plus that of R_{12}, *i.e.* 15·56kΩ ± tolerances.

(*viii*) The resistance of R_{10} plus that of one-half the d.c. resistance of T_2 h.t. secondary winding (say 200Ω), *i.e.* 390Ω + 200Ω.

(*ix*) Between zero ohms and approximately 330kΩ depending on the volume control setting.

(*x*) The resistance of R_3 plus that of T_1 primary, *i.e.* 220kΩ ±10% + 500Ω, which for all practical purposes would be the resistance of R_3.

(b) (*i*) C_3 short circuit: the low resistance is that of T_1 secondary winding and the loudspeaker speech coil resistance in parallel.

(*ii*) C_2 short circuit: 580kΩ is within the tolerance of R_6.

(*iii*) V_2 grid/cathode short: the reading is that of R_{10}.

(*iv*) C_1 short circuit: the reading is that of R_5.

(*v*) C_4 short circuit: R_9 is responsible for the 15kΩ reading.

(c)

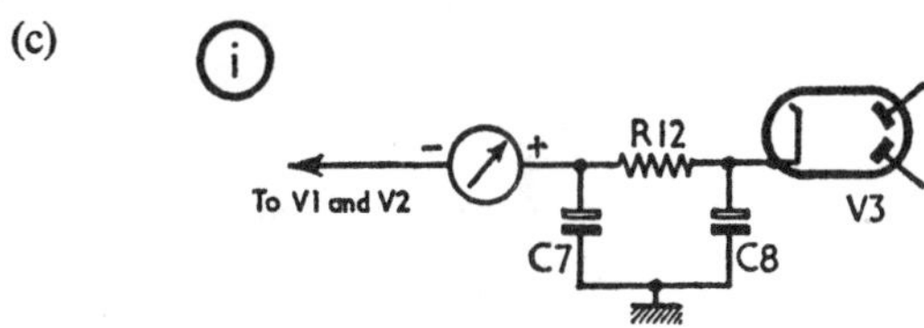

(*i*) Connect a d.c. mA meter, with polarity as shown, and set to the 100mA range.

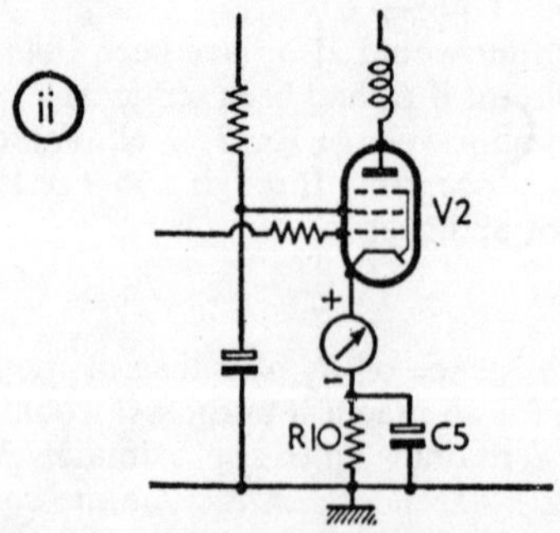

(*ii*) Connect a d.c. mA meter, with polarity as shown, and set to the 100mA range. Instrument will then register the cathode current, *i.e.* the total valve current.

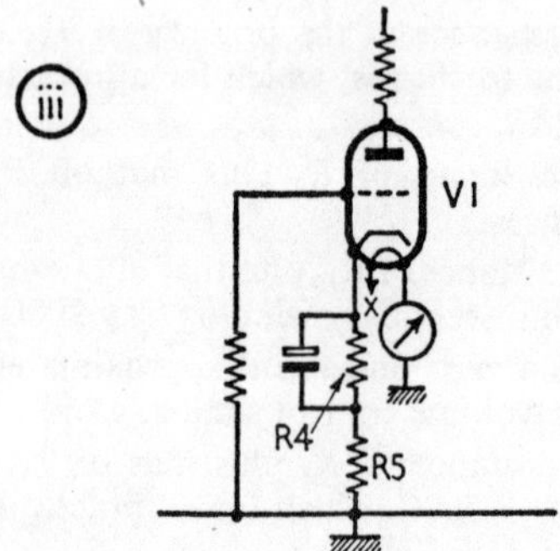

(*iii*) Connect an a.c. ammeter, set to the 1A range, as shown

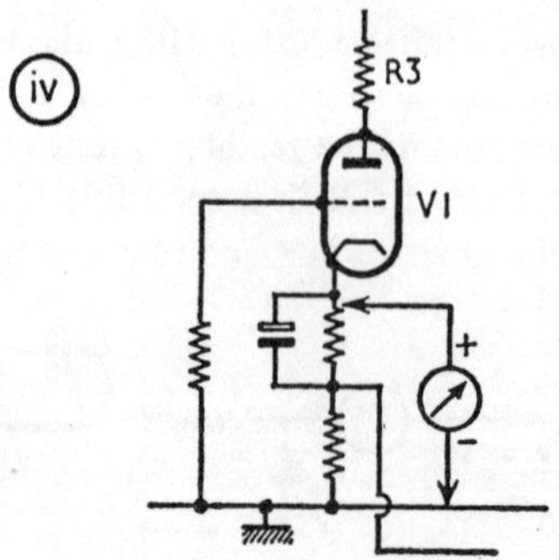

(*iv*) Connect a d.c. voltmeter, with polarity as shown, and set to the 25V range.

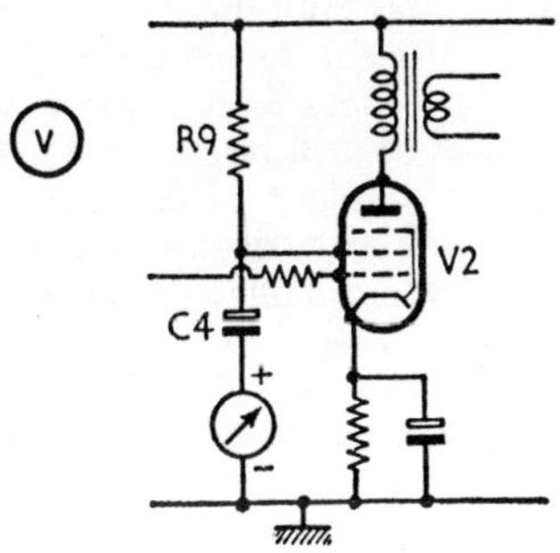

(*v*) Connect a d.c. ammeter, with polarity as shown, initially set to read mA. As the leakage current falls, reduce the range: the final reading will be taken on a micro-amp. range.

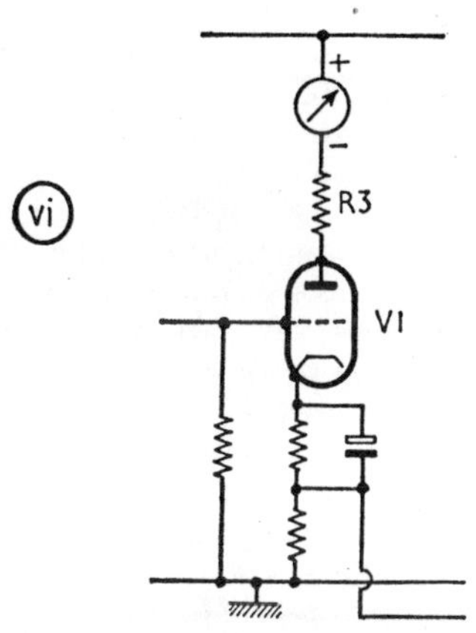

(*vi*) Connect a d.c. mA meter, with polarity as shown, and set to 10mA range: reading will be of the order of 1mA or so.

(d) (*i*) C_3 is included to provide a large degree of negative feed-back at frequencies above the audio range in the event of r.f. instability occurring within the amplifier. With the capacitor open circuit, there may be no immediate effect on the output, but should the amplifier tend to oscillate, the instability will go unchecked and the output may sound *edgy* or contain a degree of hiss.

(*ii*) If C_6 goes open circuit, the tone control (R_{11}) will be inoperative and the output will contain a greater amount of *top*.

(*iii*) The result of this fault does not always show itself immediately the power is switched on. After several minutes, however, the output is noticeably distorted, the reason being the lack of grid bias voltage. The increase in valve current which results may cause the primary winding of T_1 to go open circuit, damage the valve or cause C_5 to go short circuit (on account of the increase in volts drop across R_{10}).

(*iv*) An increase in the value of R_{12} will reduce the h.t. voltage, possibly causing loss of gain and the introduction of distortion as the result of changes in anode and bias voltages.

(*v*) With R_7 open circuit, there will be no negative feedback of audio frequencies, the volume and distortion will increase and the quality of the output will be poorer, *i.e.* sound *thin.*

(5) (a) Faults (*iii*), (*v*) and (*vi*).

(b) Faults (*i*), (*v*) and (*vii*).

(c) Faults (*ii*), (*v*), (*vi*) and (*vii*).

(d) The volume control will not function correctly. One would be unable to reduce the volume to zero although there will be some reduction in volume as the control is moved from the maximum to minimum settings (P_1 will act as a variable resistance in series with the input circuit to Tr_2).

(e) The output would sound distorted but the degree of distortion would depend upon the setting of P_1. With C_4 s/c, the base voltage for Tr_2 would be reduced as R_5 and P_1 will then be in shunt with R_7. As the volume setting is progressively reduced the base voltage of Tr_2 is lowered pushing the operating point towards the non-linear part of the transistor's input characteristic. Because of this, distortion of the signal will occur.

(f) On the 2·5V range the meter loading is equivalent to 25k Ω in parallel with R_2. This will lower the base voltage to about 0·5V. On the 10V range the meter loading is equivalent to 100k Ω in parallel with R_2. This will reduce the voltage to about 0·72V which is not such a great reuction as on the 2·5V range. Thus the 10V range will result in a truer reading being obtained because the loading is less.

(g) (*i*)

EMITTER	BASE	COLLECTOR
+1·3V	+1·3V	+8·9V

With R_9 o/c there is no transistor action. The collector current is almost zero (a small leakage current flows in the base-collector junction). The emitter voltage is practically the same as the base voltage as there is negligible drop in the base-emitter junction with the small current flowing when the meter is connected to read the emitter voltage.

(*ii*) EMITTER BASE COLLECTOR
+0·3V +0·3V +8·9V
No transistor action. Emitter and base voltages are the same. No collector-current apart from the small leakage current across the collector-base junction. Base voltage is low as R_9 is effectively in parallel with R_7.

(*iii*) EMITTER BASE COLLECTOR
+0·3V +0·5V +0·4V
No transistor action. The higher than normal current in the base-emitter junction lowers the base potential. The small collector voltage is due to the meter completing the circuit for the base-collector junction from the base potential divider.

(*iv*) EMITTER BASE COLLECTOR
0V +0·65V +0·1V
Excessive bias is applied to the base resulting in a larger than normal base-emitter current. This causes a reduction in the voltage at the junction of R_6, R_7 and a larger collector current hence the very low collector voltage. The emitter voltage is zero as there can be no voltage drop across R_9.

(*v*) EMITTER BASE COLLECTOR
0V 0V +8·9V
No transistor action. There is no bias voltage applied to the base thus the base-emitter current is zero. As a result there is no voltage drop across R_9. Only a small collector current flows this being the leakage current flowing in the base-collector junction.

(*vi*) EMITTER BASE COLLECTOR
+1·0V +1·65V +1·4V
Excessive bias voltage is supplied to the base resulting in larger collector and emitter currents. Hence the emitter voltage is higher than normal and the collector voltage considerably lower.

(6) (a) Eight (nine including the loudspeaker).
(b) No! This is a 'Linear' i.c.
(c) Check that the 18V supply is present between pins 10 and 14/3. If this is correct, test for the presence of signals at pins 1 and 6 using a c.r.o. to monitor the signal. With a signal present at pin 1 but not at pin 6, the fault is most likely within the i.c. However, short circuits in ANY of the capacitors (or faulty resistors) may be responsible for incorrect voltages within the i.c. and these could be checked before removing the i.c. In any event, it is prudent to carefully check external components before a new i.c. is fitted to avoid unnecessary damage.

CI
IN THE
KITCHEN

A fiercely addictive mystery

CATHERINE
MOLONEY

Detective Markham Mystery Book 12

Joffe Books, London
www.joffebooks.com

First published in Great Britain in 2021

Cover art by Dee Dee Book Covers

ISBN: 978-1-78931-768-8

PROLOGUE

It was the morning of Saturday, 17 October and the sun was blazing. There was something very agreeable about an Indian summer, Marjorie Poole reflected as she trudged up Dunsdon Road towards Castor Hill Park. It made you feel you'd got one over on nature for a change.

Not that she was getting much benefit from it though, she thought sourly.

Bloody Jayne Padgett and that evil-looking moggy. Why the hell was she always saddled with feeding Jayne's cat whenever Hope Academy had one of its blasted INSET days or CPD sessions or whatever they called teacher training these days . . .

Marjorie herself was a primary school teacher at Our Lady Help of Christians. But somehow Jayne seemed to be the one who was forever flitting off on courses and 'refreshers'.

Not that it was likely to save her from the chop in the long run. It was well known that Hope's senior management had the knives out for anyone over fifty, which meant her friend was firmly in the danger zone.

'I'm on the upper pay scale now,' Jayne had told her ruefully. 'They can get a couple of newly qualifieds or support staff for what they're paying me . . . It's all about the bottom line these days, so they'd be ecstatic if I decided to retire.'

Marjorie knew what Jayne meant. Long-in-the-tooth types might as well have a target pinned to their backs (though fifty was hardly old, for God's sake). But, she reflected, it wasn't just about the money. Teachers in their twenties, gagging for promotion, were far more 'pliable' whereas the likes of Jayne took no prisoners and told it like it was. Headteachers and senior managers who got their kicks from undiluted sycophancy were bound to have a problem with her down-to-earth and honest friend. Whatever else you might say about her, Jayne's overriding concern was the kids. At fifty-one, with a multitude of interests outside school and no ambition to climb the greasy pole ('the higher up you go, the further away from the classroom,' as she put it), Jayne Padgett was not the kind of teacher to be chewed up, bullied and then spat out. Which meant she was on Hope's Shit List.

Marjorie was panting as she crested the hill and arrived at the entrance to the park. Time to get back on the old SlimFast, she told herself. Just a few years younger than Jayne, she knew her own school managers were champing for a cull, in which case she would surely be in their crosshairs. Why the hell couldn't they appreciate the value of teachers with maturity and life experience? Unbelievably short-sighted. But that was the bean counters for you. Education these days was all about data and spreadsheets . . . precious little to do with child welfare.

Jayne's home was a two-bedroom first-floor apartment in a semi-circular chocolate-brick development set on the fringes of Castor Hill Park within easy walking distance of Aldbourne Village on the outskirts of Bromgrove. A bus stop directly outside the complex took Jayne straight to her job as an English teacher at Hope, so she had no need of a car. All in all, it was the ideal set-up.

Except for the pigging cat — or, as Marjorie thought of it in her less charitable moments, Jayne's 'familiar'. And to think of her christening it 'Wordsworth' . . . the name made Marjorie feel a right wally hallooing after it whenever Jayne had her on cat-sitting duties. At least the complex was

pet-friendly with a caretaker who doted on animals. So, with any luck, she'd be in and out in no time at all. The park beckoned invitingly, and she had Elly Griffiths' latest Dr Ruth Galloway mystery burning a hole in her capacious shoulder bag. An hour or two on a bench in the walled garden would be just the ticket . . .

Normally she would have met up with Jayne for their usual 'girlie' Friday evening taco-fest, but this time around her friend had been oddly non-committal, mumbling something about having 'stuff to do'. Marjorie could only hope she'd finally summoned up the courage to give that waste-of-space boyfriend his marching orders. Richard Keogh was the type who required endless propping up and Jayne didn't need any more of that. She'd cared devotedly for her mother before Margaret had to move into the Nazareth care home and now it was time for her to decompress . . . assuming that witch Judith Lipscombe from Hope Academy didn't put a spanner in the works.

Marjorie's face darkened at the thought of the new assistant head. A bossy woman built like a Sherman tank, Lipscombe was so far up management's backside it was a wonder she ever saw daylight. And it was obvious that she saw kind, down-to-earth, honest (expensive) Jayne as the sacrificial victim most likely to appease the current headteacher, Anthony 'Call-me-Tony' Brighouse.

Marjorie knew Jayne hosted meetings of Hope malcontents at her flat. 'It's a safety valve,' she'd insisted when Marjorie questioned the wisdom of such a manoeuvre. Jayne was also on the books of a local tutorial agency Top of the Class, a move guaranteed to fan the flames of managerial ire.

'You've only got to keep punching the timecard for a few more years, Jay,' Marjorie had counselled. 'Top up the old pension and then vamoose. No point giving them ammunition in the meantime.'

But Jayne's response was, unusually for her, flintily obdurate.

'I don't give a stuff how the top brass feels about me,' she had said defiantly. 'And why shouldn't I boost my

income with some tutoring? It's a free country and no reason why I can't help special needs kids whose parents want my input.'

'Management might feel a mite touchy about it, particularly after failing their Ofsted inspection for the second time running.'

But Marjorie's words fell on deaf ears.

'Tough titty. If they'd listened to some of the old guard, they wouldn't be in this mess.'

Well, Marjorie could only hope her friend was lapping up whatever pearls of wisdom came her way from the local authority guru. At least Lipscombe and her cronies wouldn't be able to say Jayne wasn't interested in the latest educational gobbledygook . . .

Punching in the code to the immaculate lobby of Cabot Court, Marjorie reflected that Jayne had it sorted.

Why make waves though, Jayney? she pleaded silently, thinking of her plump greying-haired friend whose kindness was a byword with Hope's more troubled pupils.

Now, where in the name of all the saints was that dratted cat?

Despite Jayne calling herself an 'old fuddy-duddy', her apartment was all stripped back pine flooring and minimalist décor. Marjorie invariably developed a bad case of kitchen envy whenever she swung by her friend's abode.

But not this time.

Entering the stainless-steel wonderland her heart skipped a beat.

Jayne was slumped across the granite island in the centre of the room, half standing half sitting, her ample form hunched over so as to hide her face, strands from her chignon spiralling down on either side like a cloak of invisibility. A pool of crustily congealed vomit marred the perfection of the otherwise spotless floor.

A bottle of Domestos bleach stood on the worktop at her elbow.

Marjorie knew instantly that her friend was dead.

It looked like suicide, but even as she processed the scene, she rejected the obvious explanation.

Jayney wouldn't, *couldn't* have killed herself. She was on the threshold of the next stage of her life — the 'golden years' or the 'third age' or whatever it was called these days.

Marjorie took a tissue from her shoulder bag and gently fanned the strands of hair away from Jayne's face.

They'd watched enough *CSI* for her to know she mustn't contaminate the crime scene, she thought, suppressing a wave of hysterical laughter.

Even though she was expecting it, the sight of the ugly weal around the dead woman's throat made her flinch.

Strangulation.

Murder.

A wave of almost unbearable sadness surged through her.

I knew you'd never have ended it all, Jayney. You were always a fighter. Oddly enough, she felt no apprehension for her own safety.

It was obvious Jayne had been dead for a while.

Whoever had done this was long gone.

Like a thief in the night.

Marjorie sank onto the bar stool opposite Jayne's body.

At that moment, Wordsworth appeared from nowhere, slithering and slinking about her ankles in a manner that would normally have seen her delivering a well-aimed kick at the tiresome feline.

But on this occasion, she bent down and rubbed the old warrior's moth-eaten fur.

Who did this to her, Wordsworth? she said silently. Was it Hope's bloody Stasi? Had they come for her at last?

Abruptly, she chided herself for being melodramatic. No, most likely it was a burglary gone wrong . . .

And yet . . . Jayne must have let her killer into the flat. There was no sign of a break-in. Her friend's handbag reposed next to the bread bin on the wraparound countertop with her black leather purse clearly visible on top.

Sunlight streamed into the kitchen as Wordsworth padded about mewling softly, contentedly oblivious to his mistress's inanimate form.

Don't touch the body, she told herself as though in a trance. Mustn't contaminate the crime scene.

Crime scene.

It was beginning to sink in.

Jayne Padgett was dead.

Marjorie staggered into the living room whose Juliet balcony overlooked the park.

Sightlessly, she collapsed down on the black leather armchair opposite Jayne's top-of-the-range massive Samsung TV.

Outside, a chirruping from the late-flowering cherry tree in the communal back garden was the only sound to break the peace.

Time to take stock.

Jayne had never made it to the LEA's latest training bonanza.

Instead, she had died right here in her own kitchen. Forced to drink bleach in a gratuitously prolongation of her ordeal — there was no other way to explain it.

It occurred to Marjorie that she wasn't surprised.

She knew her friend — 'Mrs Pepper Pot, that's me!' — had made enemies at Hope and further afield . . . but would they really kill her?

Wordsworth was weaving restlessly in and out around her feet, almost as though he sensed from her demeanour that something was wrong.

Marjorie got up and walked back into the kitchen, trailed by the cat.

Her heart was thumping in her chest as she stared at Jayne's body.

"Trailing clouds of glory do we come from God, who is our home . . ."

So much for the cat's namesake. There was nothing remotely glorious about that flaccid middle-aged corpse and the sheer banality of the Domestos bottle.

As if in a dream, she reached for her mobile.

All she could do for Jayne Padgett was to set the wheels in motion.

999. She made the call.

1. TEAM TALK

DI Gilbert ('Gil') Markham felt curiously indolent as he sat on the bench that he had come to think of as his in the terraced graveyard of St Chad's church, overlooking the back of Bromgrove Police Station. Basking in the October sun, long legs stretched out in front of him, he savoured the tranquillity of the Sabbath — the lull before the machinery of the latest CID investigation cranked inexorably into gear.

The vicar gave Markham a friendly nod as he headed from the church towards his rectory on the other side of the cemetery but knew better than to disturb his reflections. He was, by now, familiar with the inspector's habits and had heard about the police activity at Castor Hill Park. Apparently, a teacher had been murdered. Which meant Markham would be girding his loins — buckling on his spiritual armour — for the battle ahead.

Others might have scoffed at this description for being over the top, however the Reverend Mr Dodsworth suspected the darkly handsome but austere looking policeman had a mystical streak in his makeup. A lapsed Catholic, the vicar knew Markham was nonetheless a regular visitor to churches in and around Bromgrove. A devout Unitarian, that uncouth sergeant of his had sniggered on the one occasion the vicar

had encountered him lurking outside the church and made the mistake of alluding to the DI's ecumenical spirit.

Mercifully, there was no sign of DS George Noakes on the present occasion. Just as well, thought Mr Dodsworth, smiling benignly at Markham. As far as he was concerned, there were limits to Christian charity.

Happily unaware of the vicar's sentiments regarding his wingman, Markham was indeed summoning up his reserves of strength. It was always this way at the outset of an investigation. However 'wet' it might seem to his colleagues in CID (and Markham was under no illusions about the jealous resentment that attended his growing reputation as CID's wunderkind), the DI saw himself as a foot soldier in the eternal battle between good and evil, bearing arms on behalf of all the murder victims he had ever known — 'absolute for death' as his girlfriend Olivia Mullen, an English teacher at Hope Academy, liked to put it.

His thoughts turned to yesterday's discovery of Jayne Padgett . . .

It was interesting that Marjorie Poole hadn't for a second entertained the possibility that her friend could have killed herself, concluding immediately that this was murder even before she saw evidence to the contrary. That her friend had died by strangulation.

Likewise, before the pathologist Doug 'Dimples' Davidson got to grips with the body, he agreed with this verdict.

'A horrible way to go,' he muttered grimly on surveying the scene in the victim's designer showroom kitchen. 'Can't have been suicide.'

The bluff medic always put Markham in mind of Siegfried Farnon as played by Robert Hardy in the original *All Creatures Great and Small* — more country vet or harrumphing farmer than police surgeon. But the caustic, cantankerous exterior belied his deep compassion for the victims. 'That disinfectant would've burned her insides out . . . agonising . . . Someone must've forced it down her.'

After a further examination, from which Markham and Noakes averted their eyes, Dimples plonked himself down on one of the sleek tubular bar stools that Marjorie had so admired, ample buttocks spilling over the sides as he wriggled onto the fabric seat.

'Yes,' he sighed. 'The bleach was just a nasty finishing touch. Looks like the killer toyed with the idea of a staged suicide but some other impulse took over. Bruising on the throat and petechiae point to her having been attacked . . . and half-throttled into the bargain.' An awkward clearing of the throat. 'Looks like she's been interfered with too.'

'But she's a granny.' The DS was stupefied.

Dimples was used to George Noakes, the Yorkshireman didn't mince his words.

'Clearly you haven't absorbed the latest mantra, Sergeant.'

'Eh?'

'"Fifty is the new thirty."'

'Get out of it, doc. This one's a dead ringer for Hetty Wainthropp.' This was not as insulting as it sounded, thought Markham, given Noakes's admiration for the retired busybody of the television series.

From the way Noakes's fists were balled in the pockets of his grubby chinos, Markham could tell there was a slow burn of anger. His gaze trained on the straggling grey bun, as though afraid to linger on the foam-flecked lips and bulging eyes, the DS muttered, 'She's a teacher for chuff's sake . . . jus' minding her own business. There's a bag of books an' folders over there in the corner. Looks like she fancied a brew or summat before getting stuck in. I mean, why would anyone . . .'

Dimples, too, was angry beneath his countryman's manner.

'I'd say there was an unconsummated sexual assault of some kind,' he said gruffly. 'Her underwear's been removed and there's bruising . . . looks like he stopped short of rape.'

'Poor cow.' Noakes's tone was bleak. 'Planning a nice quiet afternoon marking essays on *Lord of the Flies* or whatnot an' then this.'

The pathologist was surprised. '*Lord of the Flies* hey, Noakes? Very observant of you.'

'Recognised the cover cos it was our Natalie's GCSE book,' came the gnomic response. 'Sort of stuck in my mind.'

Markham allowed himself a moment of amused speculation about the teenaged Natalie Noakes's reaction to William Golding's fable of masculine degeneracy. It certainly hadn't sufficed to turn the pneumatic perma-tanned beautician off men, he reflected wryly, before reproaching himself for being uncharitable. After the poor girl's experience during the Bluebell investigation, it would be no wonder if she never went on a date again. Certainly, any potential suitors would have a hard time getting past her protective father.

'Where did the victim teach?' Dimples asked.

'Hope Academy,' Noakes replied glumly. 'Reckon it must be fate the way that place gets dragged into every bleeding murder.'

Even allowing for the exaggeration, Markham shared Noakes's dismay. The last thing he wanted was Olivia being drawn into another murky investigation, especially given DCI Sidney's dislike of his 'lady friend' (an antipathy that was entirely mutual).

And this case looked like it could get very murky.

'Not a random attack, though.' Dimples looked round the pristine kitchen and back towards the flat's little hallway with its cheerful vintage rose design, a homely contrast to the high-spec modern kitchen and state of the art utensils. 'She let them in, the lock hadn't been forced.'

'Yeah,' Noakes agreed. 'There's an intercom buzzer to let folk in from downstairs. So she would've been able to check who it was. She musta known 'em . . . Hey—' he stopped short — 'didn't that teacher friend of hers — the one who found her — didn't she say Janet were meant to be

off on some training course an' that's why she had to come over? To feed the cat or summat?'

'*Jayne*,' the DI corrected mildly. Noakes was notorious for misappellations and malapropisms. His 'displacement device', Dimples called it behind the sergeant's back. 'Jayne Padgett. But you're right. Marjorie said Jayne told her she was away on a training course at Quickswood Lodge — that's the council's training centre at the university ,' Markham added for the pathologist's benefit. 'She asked if Marjorie could swing by to check on the cat . . .'

'What was she doing home then?' Noakes demanded. 'Playing truant from the conference or what?' His voice suggested that their murder victim's distaste for CPD was a mark in her favour.

'It looks like a spur of the moment thing.' Markham said thoughtfully. 'Someone must have asked to meet up and she told them to come to her flat. She most likely figured it would be okay to miss the opening session at Quickswood and slip in afterwards. You know how it is with these things . . . the introductory stuff's usually a waste of time.'

Eloquent grunts from both Noakes and Dimples greeted this assessment.

'She had her mobile out,' Markham went on. 'It's on the counter over there next to the microwave. And she had begun a text to Marjorie saying no need to drop round after all because she was going to see to Tiddles or whatever he's called.'

'Wordsworth.' Ironically, Noakes had no trouble whatsoever recalling the name of Jayne Padgett's pet.

The DS prowled the immaculate kitchen, reflecting how impressed his missus would be by the designer finish and whizzy gadgetry . . . Bit of a waste for someone on their own, mind.

'Looks like she got off on playing Mary Berry,' he said eyeing a Daewoo blender. A thought struck him. 'Did Mrs Thing say whether there was a boyfriend in the picture?'

'Ms Poole said there's a man friend,' the DI replied patiently. From the tone of her voice when she spoke of him, Marjorie Poole wasn't a fan. 'Works in sales . . . apparently he was supposed to be in Birmingham this weekend.'

'Thass no distance . . .' The boyfriend sounded promising to Noakes.

'Family liaison are on it and we'll be seeing him in due course. Kid gloves,' the DI added beadily, only too aware of the way his sergeant's thoughts were tending.

He became aware the pathologist had sunk into a brown study. 'What is it, doc?' he asked.

'The overkill . . . excuse the pun.' Dimples looked troubled. 'She was grabbed around the neck and half-throttled, so why force her to drink bleach . . . Why not just strangle her and be done with it?'

'Like you said, perhaps they planned to stage the death — make it look like suicide — but things didn't go according to plan,' Markham suggested.

Noakes tugged at his salt and pepper thatch with unnecessary vigour, rumpling it into the haystack dishevelment that attended intense cogitation. 'Mebbe the killer wanted to send a message,' he said at last.

'A message? Like what?' Dimples sounded mystified.

'Wash your mouth out . . . You've got a mind like a sewer . . . I dunno, summat to do with cleaning her act up. Mebbe that's the point of the Dettol.'

'Domestos,' Markham and Dimples said in unison.

'Whatever.' The DS cudgelled his brains. 'She could've gossiped about 'em . . .' Noakes nearly said it was the sort of thing women did but checked himself in time. Didn't want the guvnor deciding he needed to go on another of them daft diversity courses where everyone sat around pretending to be PC. 'Happen there was some sort of vendetta going on . . . school politics, that kind of thing.' From all Noakes knew of Hope — 'the swamp of fear and loathing', as Olivia Mullen was wont to call it — such a scenario was eminently feasible.

The pathologist looked scandalised. 'You think a teacher could have done this?'

'Oh, that lot'd cut your throat soon as look at you,' the DS retorted cheerfully. 'Remember the Ashley Dean case.'

The other two looked as though they would rather not take that particular trip down memory lane.

'Wouldn't making her ingest bleach inhibit any sexual interaction?' Markham enquired fastidiously.

Noakes made a face. 'Yeah, it ain't exazacly an aphro-thingy.'

Dimples' face was a picture of concentrated distaste. 'An aphrodisiac. Quite.'

'Mind you, he might be up for all of that . . . y'know get off on 'em thrashing about in agony.' The DS warmed to his theory. 'Like that poisoner bloke they thought was the Ripper — George Chapman — he had a thing for potassium or one of them chemicals . . . gives you vomiting and convulsions.'

The DI bit his lip at the look on the doctor's face as Noakes shared the fruits of his latest discoveries from Sky Crime.

'He may simply have wanted to degrade Ms Padgett.' The DI was noted for his scrupulous respect in referring to victims, and woe betide any subordinates who attempted levity or gallows humour. 'Demonstrate contempt for her as a woman.'

'Or mebbe he wanted to send us on a wild goose chase, get us looking at local sex offenders or summat . . .'

'I'm sure DCI Sidney will want us to cover that angle,' Markham said heavily. 'Leave no stone unturned.'

Dimples grimaced sympathetically. DCI Sidney (or 'Slimy Sid' as he was more popularly known) was guaranteed to prefer just about any line of enquiry which by-passed the local comprehensive school and 'respectable' citizenry in general. News of this murder would have him reaching for the sex offenders register in a flash. Better still if the trail led to a mental health outpatient clinic . . . Markham was

willing to bet Sidney had the Newman Psychiatric Hospital on speed dial.

No way would the DCI want the spotlight to fall on Hope Academy, Bromgrove University or any other civic institution likely to be tainted by murder.

The DI saw trouble ahead but kept his expression neutral. 'Time of death, Doug?'

'Tsk, tsk . . . You know better than that, Inspector.' But the pathologist's tone was indulgent. He held Gilbert Markham in high esteem, although there was almost a force-field about him that repelled familiarity. No entry. Odd that the star of CID appeared to find that old scoundrel Noakes more congenial than everyone else, but there was no accounting for tastes . . .

'I'd say she died around ten-ish, in the morning, not long before her friend arrived. Rigor hadn't started.'

'Taking a risk weren't he . . . ?' Noakes resumed his pacing. 'I mean, who's to say ole Marj wouldn't rock up an' catch him right in the middle of it . . . She had keys, so nothing to stop her barging in.'

'The arrangement was that Marjorie would come at eleven because that's when the cat had his daytime feed. Ms Padgett made a note on that calendar she has on the fridge. Also, her unfinished text mentions the time so the killer knew they wouldn't be interrupted.'

'Right.' Noakes screwed his face up, digesting this information. 'She most probl'y told 'em there was plenty of time for a cosy chat . . . *Bastard.*' Then he appeared to cheer up. 'But we're talking Saturday morning. One of the neighbours had to have noticed . . .'

'I wouldn't count on it,' Dimples said. 'They're mainly over sixties and retirees . . . the wife's aunt lived here for a while . . . quite exclusive, no riff-raff allowed.'

Privately, Noakes thought it sounded like prime curtain-twitching territory.

The DI had a pretty good idea what his subordinate was thinking.

‘You mean residents keep to themselves?’ he asked.

‘Pretty much, yes . . . easy enough to slip in off the road without being spotted.’

‘And no CCTV,’ Noakes observed glumly. ‘You’d think with it being mostly wrinklies — er, sorry, senior citizens — they’d have better security.’

‘Well, Cabot Court’s only a small development,’ Markham observed. ‘Just sixteen flats, no doubt all with entry phone, communal gardens and in one of Bromgrove’s safest neighbourhoods . . . arguably no real need.’ He looked the other two in the eye. ‘Mind you, after what’s happened here, I imagine the management company may want to reassess their priorities.’

Dimples heaved himself down from the bar stool.

‘Right you are, gents. I need to get her down to the mortuary. Okay to get the paramedics up here?’

Markham nodded assent and the pathologist headed for the downstairs lobby.

Noakes’s gaze travelled to the stiffening corpse at their feet. In life, the deceased had been a well-respected member of society — no high roller, just a kind, comfortably plump teacher whose very ordinariness no doubt offered reassurance to generations of parents and children. In death, she had no dignity, her features distorted to resemble a hideous gargoyle.

‘Who’s looking after the cat?’ The DS was gruff. ‘Wordsworth . . . Who’s gonna take him?’

‘I had a word with Marjorie. She’s getting it sorted.’ The gentleness of Markham’s tone would have astonished the lower echelons of CID who had christened the aloof inspector His High Mightiness. ‘Why don’t you get the SOCOs in, Noakesy.’

And in no time at all, the paper-suited forensic team was combing every inch of the flat.

* * *

Markham returned to the present, drinking in all the drowsy autumnal beauty that Jayne Padgett would never again behold. In that moment, the gravestones and

monuments which bordered the crooked paths of St Chad's cemetery seemed like unearthly witnesses to his pledge that he would catch whoever had dashed the cup from her lips.

A soft breeze rustled the foliage overhead. Soon it would be time to go and meet his team in CID.

His team. 'Markham's Gang', the envious sniped.

He and Noakes had somehow got their partnership back on track after it had almost been derailed by the Bluebell investigation when the DS discovered that Natalie was not his biological daughter. After that domestic crisis, his wingman had arguably acquired new powers of empathy . . . or at least that's what Markham had hinted at in Noakes's last appraisal with Sidney.

The DCI had been openly derisive. 'Empathy!' he barked, with a distinct edge to his voice. 'Your sergeant doesn't know the meaning of the word, Markham. A walking affront to the service and well past his sell-by-date. He should be thinking of retirement.'

The DI was having none of it. A mysterious alchemy bound him and Noakes together, based not only on a shared distaste for the kind of backscratching and politicking at which Sidney and his ilk excelled but on some intuitive recognition that they shared a hinterland beyond words. For all his reputation as a supremo of slobbishness, the DS had a strangely romantic, poetic chord in his nature that made him almost psychically sensitive to Markham's inner workings. Though they had never spoken of it directly, Noakes had somehow assimilated Markham's lonely history as a survivor of childhood abuse with a natural sympathy. The DI would have been at a loss to define the precise nature of their bond. He only knew that Noakes always had his back and was the only person apart from Olivia whom he allowed behind the emotional portcullis erected in his youth.

And there was the thing. Olivia adored Noakes who reciprocated in kind, exempting her from the swingeing contempt with which he generally regarded 'arty-farty types'. Perhaps it was her resemblance to the ethereal heroines he

recalled from childhood picture books. Perhaps it was the disarming roguishness that somehow got past his defences. Whatever the nature of her allure, it certainly irritated Mrs Muriel Noakes whose rampant enthusiasm for 'Gilbert' did not extend to his partner. While the two couples occasionally socialised together (Olivia complained the forced smiles gave her lockjaw), Noakes's 'missus' invariably spoke of her husband's boss in the condoling tones of one who had been snared by mere sexual attraction and thereby forfeited a true meeting of minds. 'Such a charming man . . . so easily imposed on.'

Notwithstanding his susceptibility to Olivia's charms, the DS was utterly devoted to his redoubtable wife. They had met through ballroom dancing, both being surprisingly light and elegant on their feet despite a hefty combined poundage, and it had apparently been love at first sight for Noakes.

'She were standing under this glitterball with her head thrown back laughing,' he said simply, when Olivia ventured an enquiry on the subject. 'I wanted to make her smile at me the same way.' If she had difficulty visualising Noakes's bossy, snobbish spouse in the light of winsome enchantress, Olivia had managed not to show it.

Markham's thoughts turned to the two other members of his team.

Kate Burton was the absolute antithesis of Noakes — earnest, conscientious and always smartly turned-out. The psychology graduate had to overcome parental opposition before joining the police ('no job for a woman', was her father's verdict) but was now on the fast track to success. There was a time when Burton seemed to have lost her mojo — a broken engagement played its part — but she now planned to take her promotion board in the new year and was currently an acting DI. It had taken Markham a long time to accept that Kate carried a torch for him (Olivia called him an 'emotional clodhopper' in consequence), but he was confident she had long since overcome any such feelings. 'Nah,

guv, she's still hung up on you,' Noakes pointed out slyly from time to time, but more from habit than anything else.

Burton and Noakes had taken a long time to shake down together as members of Markham's team, her politically correct sensibilities and head-prefect rectitude continually assailed by the grizzled veteran's total indifference to anything resembling twenty-first century professionalism.

But they had come to appreciate each other's qualities, not least the cast-iron loyalty to their guvnor. Noakes still looked as if he had a bad case of piles whenever Burton proceeded to quote from her beloved *Diagnostic and Statistical Manual of Mental Disorders*, while she in turn could look boot-faced at the endless breaches of decorum and good taste which were her colleague's stock-in-trade (her Queen Victoria face, as Markham thought of it — 'we are not amused'). But the old antagonism was long gone. Indeed, the DI suspected that nowadays the sparring was almost a matter of form because the rest of CID expected it.

The final member of the team, the former DC Doyle, was now DS Doyle, having sailed through his sergeant's exams. Not that this in any way affected his relationship with Noakes who, as well as being Doyle's mentor, seemed at times to stand almost in loco parentis, so regularly did the younger man pour out his romantic woes to the old warhorse over a pint or four in various hostelries (when they weren't charting the progress of their beloved Bromgrove Rovers). An easy-going character and a snappy dresser, with a degree in criminal law under his belt, the gangling 'ginger ninja' was, like Burton, on the fast track but Markham hoped to hang on to him for a good while yet.

Yes, the DI was well satisfied with the little unit which, despite Sidney's best efforts, had become his very own 'flying squadron' with several notable successes to its credit.

He looked wistfully back at St Chad's, wishing there was time to take a stroll around the cool depths of the church.

It was a squat little edifice — almost dumpy in its undistinguished soot-stained architecture — but Markham loved

it nonetheless, in particular the vivid red, blue and green wood panels in the side chapels with their trefoil and fleur-de-lys decorations, almost like a medieval solar. There was an emphasis on majesty — on the kingship of Christ — which always made him feel oddly exultant as though the legions of evil had already been vanquished.

'Battle is over, hell's armies flee;
Raise we the cry of victory . . .'

He grinned at the thought of DCI Sidney's likely reaction to these musings.

'None of your poetising, Inspector . . . Save it for your first novel.'

Sidney had never forgiven him that Oxbridge pedigree and First in PPE. 'An officer of your rank can't afford to be fey.' He made it sound like a communicable disease. 'Good honest down-to-earth legwork, that's what we need.' Markham could almost hear the nasal honk breaking through the tranquillity of the graveyard, birds twittering in the canopy overhead as though Sidney had suddenly materialised at his elbow.

With a last regretful look at the church, Markham squared his shoulders and headed for the station.

* * *

The station looked even more tired and drab than usual when Markham came in out of the sun, though he was amused to note that the miniature Zen garden Kate Burton had bequeathed to CID, with little bonsai tree, gravel, rockery and tiny rake, appeared as well tended as ever.

His corner glass-walled office with unrivalled views of the station carpark felt stuffy and stale. Yanking the sash window open as far as it would go (a measly few inches) made precious little difference, but it felt like a gesture of defiance against the penny-pinching powers that be and thus afforded some small satisfaction.

Noakes was already installed across from Markham's desk, dividing his attention between a bag from Dunkin'

Donuts and the executive pendulum toy — a stress-busting present to Markham from Olivia — in whose cradle mechanism he delighted.

Acting DI Kate Burton followed swiftly on Markham's heels, freshly washed brunette pageboy swinging and youthful button-nosed face alert with interest. Her charcoal trouser suit was immaculate, and it looked like the new glasses she whipped out of her executive briefcase — magnifying her eyes to the size of enormous brown lollipops — were a designer brand, a vast improvement on the NHS specs of yore.

The contrast with her colleague was almost comical, though Markham noted Burton's look of horror at the DS's 'casual wear' was swiftly suppressed.

Noakes was clearly losing the battle of the bulge, and it looked as though Muriel had washed her hands when it came to sartorial standards (only intervening when the threat to her social standing was too egregious to be ignored). The mismatched clobber, as Markham told Olivia later, was simply horrendous. Off-white t-shirt topped with moth-eaten mauve sweater over baggy brown cords which barely contained the swelling paunch. Little wonder that Sidney claimed he could easily be mistaken for one of Bromgrove's down-and-outs.

At least with its being Sunday, Sidney was safely on the golf course therefore unlikely to suffer a spasm of corporate dyspepsia at the sight of Markham's wingman.

DS Doyle followed hard on Burton's footsteps. Less formally dressed than the acting DI, he was nonetheless equally dapper in off-duty drainpipe jeans, skinny rib black sweater, Skechers trainers and linen jacket.

His gaze gliding over the oblivious Noakes, Markham supposed two out of three wasn't bad.

When they were finally settled — soy macchiatos for Burton and Doyle, doughnuts and cappuccino for Noakes and black coffee for the DI — Markham summarised the facts of their latest case before crisply running through the roster of suspects.

'Ms Padgett was an English teacher at Hope Academy,' he said.

Noakes's hangdog features worked convulsively but he held his peace.

'It sounds as though there were issues with Hope's assistant head, Judith Lipscombe,' the DI continued.

'The new witch on the block,' Noakes muttered to no one in particular.

'Ms Padgett also did work for a private tutorial agency, *Top of the Class*. Proprietors are Pauline and John Thornfield.'

'There's a boyfriend,' Noakes said mutinously.

'Indeed, there is.' Markham was unruffled. 'Richard Keogh, a sales executive. Though I understand from Jayne's friend Marjorie Poole that this was something of an on-off relationship.'

Kate Burton was scribbling away in a manner that had Noakes and Doyle exchanging resigned eye-rolls.

'There was a somewhat complicated family background,' the DI continued. 'Ms Padgett was adopted but had recently sought out her birth mother. According to Marjorie, her ex-husband Bill Travers wasn't very happy about this. There's a couple of half-sisters in the mix too apparently.'

Noakes's massive shaggy head lifted from his Dunkin' Donuts bag.

'Ex-husband?'

'Yes, he's Head of Science at Hope . . . Now in a relationship with an NQT from the Modern Languages department, name of Christine Bickerton.'

'NQT being a newly qualified teacher,' Burton translated punctiliously, eliciting further expressive grimaces from her colleagues.

'Anyone else who might've hated the vic?' Noakes enquired with heavy sarcasm.

'It seems there may have been problems with another teacher on the agency's books,' Markham replied.

'Problems?' Burton looked up from her notebook and frowned.

'She fell out with a colleague, Gill Dacre, also on *Top of the Class*'s books.'

'Wouldn't you jus' know it,' Noakes growled. 'That bloody school again.'

Markham seized the bull by the horns.

'There were a couple of parents, too. John and Shona Restorick. I gather they complained about Ms Padgett while she was teaching at Hope. It got awkward because she and the Restoricks were fellow-worshipers at St Jude's in Aldbourne Village.'

'*Lovely*.' Noakes's scowl was something to behold, accentuating his resemblance to a St Bernard almost beyond the point of caricature. 'So we've got school management,' he almost spat the words, 'a weirdo family set-up and this tutoring agency or whatchamacallit in the frame.'

'Correct.' Markham looked his colleagues in the eye.

'What next, sir?' Kate Burton asked politely.

Markham felt some relief at settling into the familiar groove.

'I want you and Doyle to get the incident room up and running,' he said evenly. 'Noakes and I are going to take another look at Ms Padgett's flat and then deal with the next-of-kin.'

A snort from Noakes.

'As in Jayne's birth mother Margaret Crompton — she's in a care home — and the biological half-sisters,' the DI amended. 'Then there's her adoptive mother Marian Padgett . . . It's a trifle complicated.'

And then some!

'After that, we'll look in on the boyfriend . . . see what he's got to say.'

'Got it, sir.'

Once upon a time, Burton would have resented Markham's choice of Noakes to accompany him on the initial interviews. But there was a new air about her these days, as though she was done sighing for the moon.

'We need to be ready to brief the DCI,' Markham added tonelessly.

Three faces met his deadpan.

Yeah, good luck with that!

'Right team,' he said. 'Let's crack on.'

As the team were heading for the door, Burton turned back.

'Who broke the news about Jayne to Marian Padgett and the boyfriend?'

'I did that yesterday afternoon,' Markham replied evenly.

After you sent me home to the missus, thought Noakes.

That was the guvnor for you. When it came to the godawful jobs, he never palmed them off on anyone else. Which was why the team would always go through fire for him.

Without further ado, they dispersed.

The agency investigation case had begun.

2. REVIEWING THE FIELD

That afternoon duly saw Markham and Noakes back at Jayne Padgett's flat.

The other residents turned out to be 'worse than useless', as Noakes said witheringly, having seen and heard nothing unusual. 'Not even a woman getting murdered next door. Jesus wept.'

Markham famously hated profanity.

'Sorry guv, but you gotta admit they're a waste of space . . . I mean, what happened to looking out for folk?'

'It was Saturday morning, Sergeant,' Markham observed mildly. 'No reason to clock comings and goings, especially with Ms Padgett buzzing her visitor in.'

'My missus wouldn't have missed summat like this,' the DS insisted. 'What's the point of Neighbourhood Watch if nobody gives a monkey's?'

Grimly, Markham silently agreed that precious little was likely to escape Muriel Noakes's gimlet eye. Especially not if there was the faintest possibility of scandal in the mix.

Jayne Padgett's computer had been removed for analysis, but the DI didn't anticipate any earth-shattering discoveries in that direction. Given that she was a teacher, the victim had most likely been highly discreet about what she

shared on social media, indeed may have been a thorough-going Luddite like himself and ignored Facebook and the rest of it altogether.

'It's a bit . . . well, impersonal,' Noakes said after wandering through the flat. 'Like a show house.'

Number 8 Cabot Court was undeniably somewhat sterile, especially the living room with the black leather recliner which bore a disconcerting resemblance to a dentist's chair.

To Markham, that armchair and the three-piece suite in front of a huge flat screen TV, with combined CD and DVD rack to the side and Ikea rug precisely aligned in front, spoke of a woman who strove to keep her life neat and tidy. Compartmentalised.

It was a technique he understood all too well.

The bathroom and two bedrooms — the master with terracotta-tinted walls, bookshelves and built-in-desk — were equally pristine, as though ready for inspection at any time. Perusing the bookshelves, Markham saw their content was heavily weighted towards the classics — Austen, Dickens, Trollope, Hardy — with a smattering of historical biography. Sadly, he reflected that he and Jayne Padgett would likely have found each other congenial company.

'She liked the royals by the look of things,' Noakes said approvingly, fingering a hefty tome with a picture of the queen and the Duke of Edinburgh on its spine. 'My missus is the same . . . can't get enough of Princess Di . . . reckons her dying like that were all a conspiracy cos of her having a thing for Indians. Buck House didn't want William an' Harry having a black stepdad.'

Markham could only breathe a silent prayer of gratitude that Kate Burton was spared Mrs Noakes's highly spiced insights into the Windsor's dynastic arrangements. On the other hand, these days Kate would most likely take such digressions in her stride having long since recognised that her colleague was incorrigible. Something of her 'wokeness' must have rubbed off on him, since he at least refrained from any reference to 'wogs'.

There were only two photographs in the flat, displayed in Habitat frames on the oak monks' bench beneath the television in the living room. One showed an elderly lady between two unremarkable middle-aged women, both running to fat, but well-dressed with expensive hairdos, while the other was a stiffly posed family portrait with a recognisably teenaged Jayne Padgett in dowdy school uniform — navy blue A-line skirt, matching sweater over a white shirt and striped tie plus oversize blazer (of the 'she'll grow into it' variety) — sitting between a stodgy-looking couple.

Noakes picked up the latter for closer scrutiny.

'Yeah, that's her all right. Not 'xactly the class raver, was she?'

Under the DI's cool regard, he hastily qualified, 'Mind you, that get-up don' do anyone any favours.'

'Quite.'

The DS thought complacently that their Nat had made Hope's school uniform look like the height of fashion, though this reflection was attended with some slight misgiving as to all that glamour having adversely affected her scholastic record. On the other hand, Muriel said university was overrated these days whereas a beautician would always be in demand . . .

Markham interrupted these paternal musings.

'Marjorie Poole should be here shortly. I want her to take another look around in case she notices anything significant . . . something we may have missed.'

Noakes looked about him. Now denuded of police tape and crime scene markers, the flat looked totally unremarkable.

'It's a nice gaff,' he conceded. 'When you think of some places. Remember the scuzzy caretaker at Hope an' the state of that basement? I couldn't wait to have a shower afterwards.'

Markham's skin crawled at the memory of their previous investigation.

'Ms Padgett was clearly comfortably off — a good job, no money worries by the look of it . . . only herself to worry about.'

'D'you reckon she were lonely, guv?'

Markham recalled her bookshelves. A mental traveller is never truly lonely, he thought. Not with an inner world available to supply all the life, fire and feeling that might be lacking in everyday existence.

Aloud, he said, 'I think she was self-sufficient . . . a woman who had come to terms with the hand she was dealt.' With a pang he added, 'Her life was the way she wanted it.'

The DI wandered into the master bedroom overlooking the rhododendron-lined paths of Castor Hill Park, now bathed in a pale-beaming sun which brought out all the mellow tints and golden gleams of autumn. The old mansion house owned by the Castor family was long gone, but the main entrances to the twelve-acre site were guarded by delightful lodges of various sizes once occupied by the gardeners and outdoor staff. The cottage on the western side nearest to Cabot Court harked back to the Arts and Crafts era and was clearly visible in all its gingerbread-house glory, Virginia creeper half-covering the sandstone and mock-timber facade. Markham made a mental note to have Kate Burton check out all park personnel . . . perhaps something on that Saturday morning had been picked up, some sign that all was not right at Cabot Court . . .

Back in the living room, Noakes was peering at the contents of a white-painted glass cabinet which stood against the eau-de-nil wall behind the three-piece suite.

'I like these china animals,' he said. 'Beatrix Potter or summat.'

'They're Herend,' the DI observed, wandering round to join him. 'Very collectable these days, I believe.'

'But they weren't nicked.'

'No . . . And our killer didn't bother with the mobile phone or her purse,' Markham continued. 'So this definitely wasn't a burglary.'

'I wonder why they didn't take the computer or the mobile while they were at it?' Noakes asked. 'I mean, how

were they to know she hadn't got summat incriminating on there?'

'Good question.' The DI's gaze travelled thoughtfully around the small space. 'Whoever did this might have been confident there was nothing for us to find. No evidence on her devices.'

'Or they could have given 'em the once-over jus' to see if there was owt iffy.'

'Yes, these days that would be child's play and there was time. They knew Marjorie Poole wasn't due till eleven.'

'Couldn't be sure they wouldn't leave a shadow behind on the hard drive, though,' Noakes pointed out with an air of superior knowledge. 'That's what did for Shipman, remember — cocky git forgot about clues in the software an' the techies were all over him.'

'It wouldn't matter about traces of activity on the hard drive, sergeant . . . Not if it was Ms Padgett who was forced to log on.'

'Chuffing Nora. So you reckon they made her do that before the bleach an' the rest of it . . .' Noakes was back to the hair-tugging. 'But if there was stuff about 'em on there an' next thing she turned up dead with a bellyful of cleaner, they couldn't claim it was all a coincidence . . .'

'Any halfway competent CPS lawyer certainly could.' Markham's voice was flinty. 'Especially if said legal hotshot portrayed Jayne Padgett as a neurotic woman having a crisis — pretty much anything she did could be explained away as irrational behaviour or fantasy and nothing to do with the suspect.'

'D'you think Padgett had issues then, guv . . . change of life an' all that?' Noakes was always notably squeamish when it came to talking about "women's things" or anything remotely connected with the climacteric. Markham, not for the first time, wondered fleetingly about the intimate side of his sergeant's marriage, before deciding that some doors were best left firmly closed.

‘There’s nothing here to suggest Ms Padgett was in the throes of a personal meltdown,’ the DI replied.

‘No stash of tinnies an’ no booze in the fridge,’ Noakes concurred. ‘Mind you, the SOCOs found some HRT tablets in the bathroom cabinet.’ The queasy tone was back.

‘Nothing remarkable about that, but we’ll need to check out the medical history with her GP.’

The DS was huffing and puffing in a manner that suggested considerable perplexity.

‘Lemme get this straight, guv. You think whoever did this could’ve made her go on the laptop an’ moby so they could see if she’d put anything about ’em on there?’

‘I think they were callous and cruel enough, certainly.’ Markham’s features seemed carved from marble. ‘Alternatively, they were sure that there was no risk of any digital trail leading back to them.’ Restlessly, the DI raked a hand through his thick black locks which — much to DCI Sidney’s chagrin — as yet showed no signs of a receding hairline. ‘They wouldn’t want to leave the flat carrying anything . . . less chance of a quick exit—’

‘Or someone remembering ’em.’

‘Precisely.’ Markham’s gaze returned to the cabinet and a playful dolphin figurine whose joyful exuberance was in such sad contrast to its owner’s fate. ‘For what it’s worth, Noakes, I think our killer ruled out any possibility of detection via the electronics.’

‘You think she was killed cos of summat that happened out of the blue then, guv? I mean, just lately. . . ?’

‘More that she strikes me as having been a very private person, sergeant. Discreet, circumspect . . . not the type of woman to use her devices for personal stuff.’ Markham smiled at the other’s expression. ‘Oh, I know that’s unusual these days when most people are obsessed with sharing their lives on social media.’ Natalie Noakes being no doubt of their number, he thought. ‘But Jayne Padgett’s more old-style . . . not like generation Y or Z or whatever they call the “In” crowd these days.’

Mastiff's head on one side, Noakes considered this argument.

'Yeah, you could be right, guv . . . going by them Jane Austen books an' the frumpy clothes.' Clearly the victim's sensible wardrobe hadn't impressed him. 'Hey, what about a diary? She'd go a bundle on all that scribbling malarkey.'

'I think you might be on to something there . . . One of the SOCOs said it looked like someone had gone through her desk in a hurry. All her stationery and other paraphernalia — bills and papers — were jumbled up any old how, which doesn't fit with the rest of the flat.'

'So, you think there were summat personal she wrote down that might've landed him in it,' Noakes said with satisfaction.

'It's a strong possibility.'

They were suddenly startled by the shrill sound of the buzzer.

While Noakes went to admit Marjorie Poole, Markham wandered over to the living room window with its little Juliet balcony. This had a view of the park's delightful walled garden with floral cuckoo clock, cobbled arbours and geometric flowerbeds where asters, phlox, buddleia and late-blooming anemones jostled in a riotous profusion of colour. On the wall next to the balcony was a framed picture that Markham had somehow overlooked previously — an elaborate botanical sampler whose motto struck him as unbearably poignant: 'If you chase butterflies, you may never catch them. If you rest quietly, they may light upon you.'

He wondered if Jayne Padgett had held fast to that injunction — he visualised her waiting patiently for some future epiphany when death came calling instead.

The lost metamorphosis made him all the more determined to catch her killer.

There was a bustle behind him and Noakes ushered Marjorie Poole into the living room.

'The SOCOs have finished in here, Ms Poole,' he told her. 'Let's go into the kitchen and we can have a cup of tea.'

The homely thick-set woman visibly relaxed.

'It's allowed then . . . the flat's not a crime scene anymore?'

The DI smiled at her. 'With this being largely a retirement complex and Ms Padgett's flat in such good order, we aimed to keep the disruption to a minimum.'

Back in the kitchen, Markham signalled to Noakes to take a bar stool and did the same himself, realising that Jayne Padgett's friend would derive some reassurance from being allowed to make the tea. The DS brightened considerably when a plate of chocolate digestives also materialised before them.

'We haven't yet had an opportunity of speaking to Ms Padgett's ex-husband Bill Travers,' the DI began. 'I understand his father's ill in hospital, so it can wait till Monday when we speak to the staff at Hope Academy . . . Obviously, he's been informed what's happened and Family Liaison are in touch.'

Noakes wasted no time getting down to the nitty gritty. 'How'd she get on with her ex then, luv?'

Marjorie Poole looked steadily at them. Physically unprepossessing, her unnaturally dark pudding bowl haircut with large patches of white gave her the appearance of a piebald pony. Yet there was nonetheless something pleasing about the intelligent honesty of the woman's broad bespectacled face.

'Jayne and Bill got divorced a year ago,' she answered with a slight compression of the lips.

This wasn't lost on Noakes.

'You didn't like him, then?' he enquired, munching and slurping with gusto.

'He'd traded her in for a younger, sexier model,' came the reply with some asperity. 'Oldest cliché in the book.'

'What's his new bird like?'

Marjorie didn't take offence at Noakes's bluntness. Indeed, as so often with members of the public, there was something about the uncouth lumbering sergeant that seemed to put her at ease.

'Attractive, pushy, brilliant at brown-nosing, ruthless at getting what she wants . . . Jayne didn't stand a chance.'

'There was bad blood over the divorce, then?' Markham enquired. 'Ill-feeling between Jayne and the two of them?'

'Jayne was pragmatic about things . . . aimed to move on with her life and not harbour bitterness.' Marjorie's bottom lip trembled. '"No point crying over spilt milk," she used to say.'

Noakes's piggy eyes took it all in. 'Great cuppa, luv,' he said warmly. 'Can I have another? They don' spoil us like this back at HQ, I can tell you.'

She bustled about making fresh tea, gradually composing herself.

'An' your mate was seeing someone, yeah?' Noakes made it sound the most natural thing in the world.

'That's right.' She had herself well in hand now. 'Richard Keogh. Works in pharmaceuticals . . . Greeners in Calder Vale.'

'Was it working out for her with this fella?' The DS was very casual, but his glance was keen. 'Sounds like she deserved a bit of happiness.'

'I didn't think he was half good enough for her,' Marjorie replied. 'But then,' she gave a wry smile, 'I *would* say that wouldn't I?'

'Was he like the other one then . . . a skirt-chaser?' This should have sounded salacious, but the gruff kindness in Noakes's voice took the sting out of it.

Marjorie gave a shuddering laugh.

'Oh, Jayne really knew how to pick them! She had low self-esteem, which meant she ended up with the selfish ones. *Look*,' she pleaded, 'I don't want to prejudice you against anyone before you've even had a chance to speak to them . . . doesn't seem fair somehow.'

It was confirmation of Marjorie Poole's decency that she didn't want to put the knife in.

'Was Jayne happy at work?' Markham changed tack.

'They were gagging to get rid of her,' was the forthright response.

'Why was that, luv?' Noakes was a picture of mystification. 'Experienced teacher. Aren't they crying out for folk like that?'

'*Experienced* . . . *That* was the problem, Sergeant. Experience equals expensive at a time when schools are strapped for cash and all they care about is balancing the books. For what they were paying Jayne, they could have had a couple of cheap young NQTs . . . the plan being to spit them out when they hit forty and start again,' she concluded with a touch of venom.

Noakes screwed up his hangdog features. 'Jayne wouldn't play ball, right?'

'She wasn't the type to go quietly. But they'd have got her in the end.'

The DS was curious. 'How's that then?'

'Performance management, capability procedures. It was already starting. Endless informal drop-ins and observations . . . hints about "support" programmes.' Marjorie's plain face flushed unbecomingly. 'Total garbage all of it, but the idea was to wear her down so she'd give in and resign before being pushed.'

'Nasty scam,' Noakes observed. The DS had a feeling that Slimy Sid had a similar plan for him only the guvnor kept banjaxing it.

'Yes, nasty's the word.' Markham could tell Marjorie Poole was warming to his big untidy subordinate.

'You said she had low self-esteem, but it sounds as though your friend took quite a courageous stand,' the DI observed quietly.

'Jayne felt it was a matter of professional integrity, Inspector. She told me that over the years she'd got sick of watching colleagues "disappear" because they were the wrong age, or their faces didn't fit.'

'What do you mean by people's faces not fitting,' he pressed her, though he had a pretty good idea what she meant.

'Oh . . . anyone with a mind of their own who was not afraid to stand up to management or speak out if they thought something was wrong or unfair.'

'Bit like trade unions,' Noakes surmised.

'Exactly like that,' she agreed. 'Only no one wants to be the union rep at Hope cos you might as well have 'Come and Sack Me' tattooed on your forehead.'

The DS grinned. Ole Marj might look like a bag of washing but she was a straight shooter and no mistake. Quite a refreshing change from the usual smarmy bullshit-merchants he'd encountered previously at Hope.

'So, there were issues with management,' Markham summarised.

'Well,' Marjorie bit her lip but then decided to take the plunge. 'The new assistant head, Judith Lipscombe, had it in for Jayne. I don't know all the details, but she was looking to make her name as some sort of efficiency or cost-cutting tsar—'At this, Noakes snorted with derision. 'So, she was after someone's scalp and Jayne fit the bill. There were trumped up incidents and complaints . . . plus Lipscombe had a coterie of biddable parents ready to back her up.'

'Anything official?' the DI asked.

'No, but plenty of low-level stuff aimed at making life difficult . . . Jayne said Lipscombe was working up to something big but so far she'd managed to dodge the bullets.'

'Musta been wearing,' Noakes sympathised.

'Yes, I think it was starting to take its toll . . . And she was doing tutoring on the side, building up a side-line so she had something to fall back on.'

It made sense, thought Markham, given the poisonous situation at Hope. 'Was that working out well?' he asked.

'She was with *Top of the Class*. They've got an office in Aldbourne Village. Pauline and John Thornfield. I got the feeling she wasn't mad about them, but the work was regular and they paid well.' Marjorie hesitated. 'The agency had another teacher from Hope on its books. It was a bit awkward because she decided Jayne was muscling in — you know, trying to poach students . . . sorry, I can't remember her name . . . I think it was all smoothed over in the end.'

The woman looked suddenly white and wretched, as though it had suddenly hit her that any number of people might have wished her friend ill.

With the intuitive sensitivity to an interviewee's mood which was one of Noakes's hidden strengths, the DS leaned in cosily. 'How's Wordsworth doing?' he asked.

The effect was immediate and soon they were swapping feline anecdotes, Noakes cheerfully admitting that his missus couldn't bear to have another cat after their Siamese 'Duchess' had to be put down.

Eventually returning in his own roundabout way to the matter in hand, Noakes asked casually about the photographs in the living room.

With a certain wariness, Marjorie replied, 'That's Jayne's birth mother and half-sisters. The other one was taken with her adoptive parents when she was still at school.'

'Sounds like summat out of *Long Lost Family*,' Noakes said affably. 'Never easy with them kind of set-ups.'

'You're right, Sergeant. The family situation was complicated.'

Seeing her uneasiness, Markham said gently, 'We appreciate you want to respect Jayne's privacy, but any background you can give us would be a help.'

The DI already knew the essentials, but he wanted to hear what Marjorie Poole had to say.

'Jayne was a foundling. Left outside the park gates over on the south side . . . just off Lassiter Road . . . Her birth mother had her when she was very young, but it wasn't until Jayne was in her forties that she went looking for her.'

'I take it that's the elderly lady,' Markham prompted.

'Yes, that's Margaret Crompton, Jayne's biological mother. She's in Nazareth House now. Late sixties, not so very old, but she suffers from a degenerative health condition of some kind.'

Noakes's expression suggested a degree of bafflement at this exotic family tree.

'Her adoptive dad Des died two years ago,' Marjorie continued. 'Her adoptive mum Marian Padgett lives in Aldbourne Village.'

Dad looked okay but mum had a face like a nutcracker, thought Noakes.

He grasped the nettle. 'How'd Marian react when Jayne went searching for her birth mother?'

Marjorie pleated her peasant top with restless fingers.

'She was very hurt. Bill wasn't happy about it either . . . He got on well with Des and Marian, you see.'

'How about Tricky Dicky?'

Trust Noakes to start nicknaming the suspects. Markham shot him a look. 'My sergeant means Richard Keogh,' he said.

'Oh, he wasn't best pleased either . . . thought the whole thing was undignified and resented the time she spent on it.' Defensively Marjorie added, 'But Jayne had a right to explore her roots . . . And she tried to be sensitive about it, made it clear to Des and Marian that as far as she was concerned, they were still her mum and dad.'

What about the Ugly Sisters, wondered Noakes, recalling the other picture.

'The two women in the picture with Margaret are Jayne's biological half-sisters Angela Studholme and Valerie Holmes,' Marjorie explained, almost as though she read his mind.

Something about the way she spoke suggested to Markham that they hadn't exactly fallen on their long-lost sister's neck. But, sensing Marjorie's discomfiture, he steered the conversation into more general channels.

'Nice woman that,' said Noakes afterwards as they stood in the downstairs lobby. 'But you could tell she were dead uncomfortable talking about the biological family. Don' reckon them two sisters killed the fatted calf when ole Jayney came calling . . . *No way, Jose*!'

'Well, you'll have a chance to judge for yourself, Sergeant. Family Liaison has arranged for them to join us at Nazareth House.'

'Triffic,' the DS grunted.

A door slammed somewhere in the building, making the two men jump.

'Think he'll come back here, guv?' Noakes speculated uneasily. 'Y'know, unable to stay away.'

'No, his work here is done,' came the sober response. 'But I've got drive-by patrols arranged, just in case.'

As he left, Markham turned back to look at the building. Cabot Court slumbered, peaceful and blank-eyed, in the autumn sun as though the terrible events of the previous day had never been.

3. REFLECTIONS

'Jayne was a lovely person.' Olivia contemplated their takeaway from the Lotus Garden, the Chinese local that was her current favourite. 'Chow mein or sweet and sour pork . . . or do you want some of each?'

'Some of each would be great, sweetheart.'

Sunday evening at their apartment in the Sweepstakes, an upmarket complex off Bromgrove Avenue, had come to be the couple's 'treat night' when they ate off trays in front of the television. But tonight, Olivia wanted to hear about developments in her boyfriend's latest investigation, not least as she knew Jayne Padgett from Hope.

Outside it was dark with a steady relentless drizzle, but their kitchen was cosy and aromatic from the takeaway.

Markham watched Liv with amusement as she sat at the pine table decanting noodles and pork balls from foil trays onto plates, happily munching on prawn crackers while setting out their feast. Tall and willowy, it was a wonder to him how she never seemed to put on an ounce despite a hearty appetite.

Olivia caught his eye.

'With something as horrible as this murder, I shouldn't really want all of this,' she said with compunction. 'But if anything, I'm hungrier than usual.'

‘Life goes on, Liv,’ Markham said gently, ‘and I know how it is for you teachers eating on the hoof all week. Nothing wrong with having a blow-out.’

‘You’re right about eating on the hoof,’ she agreed. ‘Our lunch hour at Hope has shrunk to about ten minutes if we’re lucky . . . And as for loo breaks, well you can forget it.’

He was relieved the subject of Hope Academy had come up quite naturally.

‘From the sound of it, Jayne Padgett was one of the good guys,’ he said. The food was hot and the noodles deliciously crispy, and Markham felt his own jaded taste buds begin to revive.

Olivia’s expression was affectionate. ‘Jayne looked prim and old-fashioned — she laughed at herself for being like Mrs Pepperpot — the old woman with the bun from the children’s series — but she was good fun . . . no interest in promotion or anything like that . . . just a hardworking classroom teacher who really cared about the kids.’

Markham recalled what Marjorie Poole had implied, about Jayne being measured for her professional shroud. ‘Did it count against her, not caring about career development?’

‘Oh, don’t get me wrong, she wanted to be the best teacher she could be. She wasn’t a chalk-and-talk merchant, and she welcomed new ideas . . . But she was different from so many of them at Hope — the ones desperate to strut round with a clipboard, boss everyone else about and stay as far away from the kids as possible.’ Olivia contemplated her glass of pinot grigio meditatively. ‘And she was *kind*, Gil. I remember she kept Kit Kats and biscuits in her room for students who missed breakfast club, and she had a reward box with little prizes for the weaker ones, kids were always turning up at her door — and it wasn’t cupboard love, they really *liked* her because she listened.’

‘Her friend Marjorie suggested the knives were out for her,’ Markham said carefully.

‘Once staff get to a certain age, schools want shot of you so they can employ cheaper people.’ Olivia flashed him

a grin before taking an enormous swig of her wine. 'They'll be targeting me too any day now.'

Markham would back his girlfriend against the apparatchiks any day.

'The name Judith Lipscombe came up.'

Olivia pulled a face, putting down her forkful of baby bok choy and mushrooms as though she had suddenly lost her taste for them.

'Lipscombe and Tony Brighouse — he's the new head — are pretty ruthless. They didn't like Jayne because she couldn't toady to save her life and she spoke up about stuff that was wrong . . . rubbish behaviour policies, excessive workload, bullying, health and safety.' Her face darkened in a manner that suggested she was running through a similar inventory of her own.

Markham interrupted these reflections. 'Did things get ugly, then?'

His partner looked troubled.

'I'd heard rumours about allegations,' she said, 'but they couldn't have made it stick otherwise Jayne would've been out on her ear.'

'Allegations?'

'Could have been anything, Gil. I wouldn't put it past that pair to plant porn on someone's computer if it meant they had an excuse for sacking them.'

'I take it Jayne hadn't opened up to any of you about what was going on?'

'She didn't confide in me, Gil. We weren't close enough friends. And anyway, I think there came a point where she just decided to keep her head down and build up her tutoring outside school.'

'Ah yes, the tutoring.' Markham helped himself to a barbecued spare rib from the plate of 'extras'. 'Apparently there was a colleague who felt Jayne was queering her pitch . . . Gill Dacre.'

Olivia raised her eyes to heaven. 'That woman's an officious so-and-so — bossy, loud, opinionated and thinks she's

God's gift to teaching . . . Also, I reckon she was jealous of Jayne's popularity with the kids. *Wow*, this prawn toast's seriously good.' Now she was tackling the extras with gusto. 'But Dacre's well in with the leadership team and there's a clique of parents in her corner. I think she stirred them up to make trouble for Jayne.'

'Would that be a Mr and Mrs Restorick by any chance?'

'My, you *are* well-informed, Gil.'

'Matt was helpfully indiscreet.'

'Ah, *now* I get it.' Matthew Sullivan was also an assistant head at Hope ('too many chiefs an' not enough Indians in that place,' Noakes griped, bemused at the number of managers). Always close, the trio had become still closer during the notorious Ashley Dean murder case when Sullivan himself had fallen under suspicion. Cheerfully un-PC, he had grown on Noakes, a process materially assisted by their mutual love of the Beautiful Game.

'D'you fancy some of this dim sum, Gil? Come on, you need to save me from myself. Otherwise I'll be *waddling* into class tomorrow.'

'No you won't.' He regarded the flushed, vivacious face admiringly. 'You'll glide in there with your usual balletic grace so no one could possibly imagine the scale of tonight's pig-out!'

She grinned then returned to the subject in hand. 'Did Matt have any idea about who could have done this to Jayne?'

'He was knocked for six, especially when I told him about the bleach.' Markham refrained from telling Olivia that there might have been a sexual motive. The case was horrific enough as it was.

She shuddered. 'I can't begin to imagine the pain.' Suddenly she had no trouble resisting the dim sum.

'She was strangled too . . . would have been unconscious very quickly.' It was small comfort, for Markham could hardly bear to visualise Jayne Padgett's death throes. *Could she have been aware of what was happening to her?* 'At some stage, she bit her tongue almost in half,' Dimples had told him in a terse phone call from the morgue. 'Wasn't raped, so

the sexual assault looks like an afterthought. Either private gratification or to get you haring off in the wrong direction.'

The pathologist concluded that the poisoning and sexual assault occurred more or less contemporaneously with death. 'Looks like they had a game plan — a staged suicide, perhaps. But then something changed. For whatever reason, the killer went off-script, Inspector.'

What was it that derailed him? Uncontrollable rage, twisted lust . . . or were they looking at a panicked attempt to simulate a sex attack?

Olivia's voice broke into his thoughts.

'Do you have any leads, Gil?'

'I'm ruling out the residents in her building. It's a small block, all elderly retirees. There's a caretaker, but he wasn't there on Saturday — part-time reservist with the Territorials and off on some team-bonding exercise.'

'Isn't there cover for when he's not there?'

'The management company normally sorts it, but for some reason there was no one on that day.' Markham smiled grimly. 'Presumably heads will roll.'

'Would it have made any difference if they hadn't screwed up?'

'Probably not.' He sighed. 'Anyway, Cabot Court's a dead end.' He bit his lip. 'Sorry, poor choice of words.'

Olivia reached across the table and squeezed his hand.

'Don't beat yourself up. It's early days.'

'Try telling that to the DCI.'

'How *is* the Slimy One?'

'We're due to brief him first thing Tuesday morning.'

She chuckled. 'Get George to wear something suitably eye-catching by way of distraction.'

'It'll take more than Noakes's dubious sartorial choices to keep Sidney off our backs. He's probably got some whizzy profiler lined up to blind us all with science.'

'Kate'll like that.'

'She always gets on with the boffins. The rest of us just find them a bloody nuisance.'

Markham toyed with his dim sum. 'I should warn you, we'll be down at Hope tomorrow morning doing interviews with Jayne's ex and the powers that be.'

'Don't forget Bill's lissom young girlfriend.'

'I take it you don't like Christine Bickerton.'

'Don't much care for either of them,' was the blunt response. 'Bill Travers is a pompous git and *she*'s always got an eye to the main chance . . . runs snitching to management at the drop of a hat with a view to making herself look better. *Yuk*! Anyway,' her voice was ominous, 'you'll be able to judge for yourself.'

Markham felt it best to leave the subject of Hope Academy for the time being.

'Jayne's family background is somewhat complicated,' he continued.

'Did you know she went on *Bromgrove Roundup* when it was still going?'

'What's that when it's at home?'

'*Honestly*, Gil, you're *hopeless*. Don't you remember . . . a sort of TV magazine programme, more upmarket than *Jeremy Kyle*, obviously.'

He quirked an eyebrow. 'That wouldn't be difficult.' Then, increasingly intrigued, 'What was she doing on there, then?'

'Well, it was a Nick Critchley piece—'

'That name rings a bell. Oh yes, wasn't he the bloke who got into trouble for sensationalism . . . exploitative reporting or some such?'

'That's the one. People who'd been on the show complained he twisted things and misrepresented them to boost the ratings.'

'But that's par for the course isn't it?'

'*You're such a cynic*.' But Olivia's tone was indulgent. 'Actually, now I come to think of it there *were* parallels with *Jeremy Kyle* . . .'

'Wasn't Kyle's show axed over something similar? I seem to remember a contestant committed suicide and then all

these folks came out of the woodwork with horror stories about how he'd manipulated them . . .'

'That's right. The mental health charities made a huge hoo-ha about it.' Olivia poured herself another glass of wine. 'Help me out here, Gil, otherwise I'm going to feel like a lush. Bad enough that I have it with ice cubes.'

With a wry smile, he complied.

'Was Jayne one of the people who complained about Critchley, then?' he asked.

'Well, hers was the last "family feature" he did, and the show bit the dust not long after that.'

'Did you watch it?'

'No,' she said regretfully. 'But I heard it was a bit of a hatchet job . . . made it appear like Jayne's blood relatives resented the upheaval in their lives when she showed up and felt displaced in their mother's affection, that kind of thing . . . The biological mother looked like some vulnerable old dear who wasn't firing on all cylinders, while the adoptive mum came across all bitter about being thrown over for someone else.'

'*Phew!*' he whistled. 'What a mess.' Then, 'That explains it . . .'

'Explains what?'

'Why Noakes and I got zilch from the next-of-kin.'

'Who did you meet?'

'Well, it turned out her biological mother Margaret Crompton wasn't well enough to see us — she's in Nazareth House with advanced Parkinson's — so we had to make do with the half-sisters.' Markham grimaced. 'I couldn't track them down yesterday — apparently there was some family shindig in Blackpool — so today was the condolence visit.'

'What were they like?'

'There wasn't really time to judge. Margaret's condition had suddenly deteriorated, so they were preoccupied with that.'

Angela Studholme and Valerie Holmes had struck Markham as two well-coiffed women with the self-assurance

of the comfortably off. Both were somewhat overweight, but on closer inspection it was apparent that Valerie had once been very pretty, the frosted blonde hair to her shoulders and a certain doe-eyed soulfulness making her more attractive in the flesh than the woman they had seen in the photograph at Jayne's flat. Angela, with her dark chignon and spectacles resembled a school librarian, but it turned out her air of competent efficiency was the legacy of her career as an administrator at the Newman Hospital. Both women exhibited a certain wariness and were difficult to read, but that was probably not to be wondered at given the circumstances.

'If they were in Blackpool yesterday, surely they couldn't have had anything to do with Jayne's murder, even if there *was* ill-feeling over the Critchley business.'

'But they didn't set off till midday, so there was time for a visit to Cabot Court.'

'You don't think they could have done something like *that* to her do you, Gil?'

'Noakes says poison is a woman's weapon.' Markham tried to keep his tone light. 'He was full of George Chapman to start with, but it didn't take long before he was regaling me with Florence Maybrick and black widow killers in general.'

Olivia giggled. 'Sky Crime's got a lot to answer for . . . So, which of them does he have down as Bromgrove's answer to Lucrezia Borgia?'

'I think he was stumped, to be honest. They were hard to read.'

'Anybody else in the mix?' Olivia looked wistfully at the pinot grigio, but *no*, even with the prospect of 9T on the morrow (T standing for 'thick as mince', as Noakes would doubtless put it), she really couldn't justify polishing off the bottle.

'Jayne had an on-off boyfriend.'

'Oh yes, Dick something or other . . . more off than on by the sound of it.'

'Yes. Richard Keogh, or Tricky Dicky as Noakes insists on calling him.'

She chuckled. 'That figures.'

'He's what you'd call a long drink of water — lean and lanky — not bad-looking if you like the undernourished type.'

Olivia thought for a moment. 'He's younger than her by a few years. Might have appealed to her maternal streak . . . she and Bill didn't have any children.'

'Did you ever meet Keogh, Liv?'

'She kept him under wraps most of the time. I saw him at a school concert once . . . didn't make much of an impression.'

'He was quite defensive with us.' Markham exhaled heavily. 'But given the way Noakesy was larding on the innuendo about cougars and younger men, perhaps that isn't so surprising.'

Olivia burst out laughing, the full-throated peal which had first attracted his notice.

'Oh *no* . . . Did he really call Jayne a *cougar*?' Overcome with mirth, she nearly overturned the remains of the takeaway.

'Well, actually it was jaguar, but let's just say Keogh got the gist.'

'God,' she spluttered. 'Jayne wasn't exactly a *Sex in the City* type.'

'Quite.' Markham took a large gulp of wine at the remembrance of their conversation with Richard Keogh.

'I imagine he clammed up after that.'

'He was supposedly in the office at his pharmaceutical company yesterday morning.'

'On a *Saturday*?'

'Catching up on paperwork apparently, though there's nobody to vouch for him.'

'*Ah.*' Olivia began tidying up, but her mind was still busy with the case. 'Did he say anything about Jayne's family set-up?'

'He and Bill Travers have one thing in common,' Markham said levelly. 'Neither of them approved of the

quest to find her birth mother. In Keogh's case, I'd say he resented another claim on her attention — he's the needy sort and whatever the dynamic was between them, it suited him to have her undivided attention . . . sounds like that changed once she started investigating her roots.'

'What was Jayne's adoptive mother like?'

Markham's visit to Marian Padgett had been curtailed by the arrival of her GP and a neighbour. No time to form a clear impression.

'Nondescript and pinched-looking . . . had some sort of nervous tic which made me glad Noakes wasn't with me.'

'Okay, well that's enough for one night!' Olivia had detected a note of despondency in his tone. 'I'm going to clear up and then we'll see what's on the box . . . maybe sample *Sky Crime* so I can impress George with my prodigious knowledge of serial killers.'

'He said something about there being a documentary about Dennis Nilsen on this evening.'

'Perfect . . . That's the charmer who flushed body parts down the drains, right? *Dyno-Rod* here we come!'

But beneath the flippancy, Markham could see she was badly shaken by that last reference.

He wandered through to his study where the curtains were drawn against the damp autumn night. The room overlooked Bromgrove North Municipal Cemetery, a place he had come to love with its ranks of old weathered headstones and monuments interspersed here and there with grotesquely baroque examples of Victorian funerary art.

But tonight he was relieved that view was screened from sight . . .

The sound of his mobile jolted him back to reality.

It was Noakes.

'I thought you had a date with Dennis Nilsen, Sergeant.'

'S'all right . . . there's plus one, see,' came the oracular reply.

'What's up then?'

‘Got a call from uniform. Suspected break-in at Cabot Court . . . sounds like one of the residents freaked out an’ made the caretaker call it in.’

‘Anything in it?’

‘*Nah*, guv. The patrol boys thought they saw some kid legging it towards the park but that was all.’

‘Is there any way of getting into the building without being buzzed in?’

‘They’ve all got individual numbers for the keypad downstairs.’ Noakes sounded uneasy.

‘What if the killer forced Ms Padgett to tell them her user code?’

‘You mean so they could come back later?’

‘Maybe they wanted to have another look round the flat.’ Markham’s mind was racing. ‘One of the SOCOs said it looked like someone had been rooting through her desk, remember.’

‘Or p’raps they were worried they’d dropped summat . . . left us a clue. But the Exhibits boys parcelled everything up after we’d finished with Marjorie . . . there weren’t owt like that knocking about.’

Markham pictured the grizzled DS scratching his chin.

‘The patrol definitely didn’t see anything significant?’

‘Jus’ this kid going like the clappers. But there’s a group of tearaways from Aldbourne knock about at night near the park . . . most likely it was one of them. Had his hoodie up so they didn’t get a look at his face.’

‘What about security at Cabot Court tonight?’

‘I’m sorting a static unit, guv . . . parked out the front so everyone gets the message an’ the coffin dodgers c’n sleep easy.’

Markham chose to ignore the irreverent reference to Jayne Padgett’s neighbours. ‘Good.’ Suddenly he felt light-headed with fatigue. ‘First thing tomorrow I want a look at the crime scene photos in case there’s anything that seems out of place, plus I need to see an inventory of the flat’s contents.’

'Right, boss.' A gargantuan yawn told him the DS was equally weary. 'How's your Olivia?'

Markham smiled to himself at the unwonted bashfulness.

'Thanks to your pep talk earlier, I've been enlightening her on the subject of famous poisoners.'

Doubtless this would make Noakes's night, if not his entire week.

'Right, guv.' A portentous clearing of the throat. 'Happen I'll let you get back to it.'

'George probably thinks we were swinging from the chandeliers,' Olivia commented when he reported this exchange.

'Not at all. He's got us down as Dennis Nilsen aficionados,' he said. 'A romp with you doesn't compare!'

She threw a sofa cushion at him as they dissolved in laughter.

Then, more seriously, she asked, 'How's it going with the forensics?'

'DNA samples are only valuable if they fit profiles on the database, Liv.'

'And there wasn't anything like that in Jayne's flat?'

'Unfortunately, no. Plus, whoever killed her was forensically aware, so we're on a hiding to nothing . . . And even if we *do* turn up evidence of family members or colleagues, cross-contamination or any one of half a dozen crime scene scenarios can explain it away.'

'So basically, you're stuffed.'

He echoed his girlfriend's mantra from earlier in the evening. 'Early days, sweetheart, early days.'

Olivia reached for the remote.

'Right,' she said, 'Dennis Nilsen awaits.' With a guilty glance at Markham, 'Bit of a busman's holiday for you, Gil.'

'Who knows what I'll glean, Liv . . . Right now, I need all the help I can get.'

With that, they curled up together on the sofa, the agency investigation temporarily banished from their minds.

4. TEMPEST

Noon the following day, Monday, 19 October, found Markham and Noakes sitting in Noakes's car in a cul-de-sac round the corner from Hope Academy. 'The less attention we attract at this stage the better,' the DI had said.

'That assembly they made us sit through was bleeding awful,' Noakes groused. 'I thought it couldn't get worse than the Helen Kavanagh crowd,' referring to a previous administration, 'but this lot came across so insincere it made me wanna *puke*. I mean all that crip crap 'bout being on a wonderful journey with Padgett an' her being an inspiration when all the time they were lining her up for a P45. An' them plastic smiles . . .' He smirked. 'It were obvious your Olivia an' Matt Sullivan hated it. The two of 'em looked like they'd smelled summat nasty when that Brighouse creep started banging on.'

'As you'll have noticed, neither Olivia nor Matt is good at dissimulation, Sergeant. A major handicap for anyone in their profession.'

Markham felt a sharp spasm of anxiety at the thought of Olivia. She had known and liked Jayne Padgett. 'It doesn't make any sense, Gil,' she'd told him that morning. 'Okay, there were the usual workplace tensions. And she put the odd

nose out of joint with her tutoring. But it was all such petty, *ordinary* stuff!'

That was the thing about Evil in Markham's experience. It was often so banal.

He had observed something more than hypocrisy beneath the plastic smiles at the school assembly.

Naked fear.

'Thing is, though, none of 'em have an alibi,' Noakes continued with relish.

The DI was thoughtful, mentally reviewing the roll call of suspects as Noakes surveyed Taggart Close and wondered if the missus fancied having their drive tarmacadamed like that one over the road . . .

Markham hadn't cared for Judith Lipscombe. Noakes had made a valid point when he talked about the stench of hypocrisy, but on the other hand the assistant head was obliged to present an appropriate face to the world no matter what her true feelings about Jayne Padgett.

She was a busty bespectacled blonde, but expensively dressed, her sharply tailored executive suit with fuchsia blouse striking just the right balance between corporate severity and feminine allure. Noakes had judged the knee-high black suede boots 'a bit S&M', but the overall effect was highly professional. Her voice was low and well-modulated with just the hint of a Northern accent.

The assistant head affected surprise at his suggestion that the school might have wanted Jayne Padgett to move on and merely opened her eyes wide when Noakes, throwing subtlety to the winds, asked if management was 'looking to pin summat on her'.

'Jayne's teaching methods were somewhat out of date,' Lipscombe told them, all sweet reason. 'And she could be defensive when support was offered.' As in supporting her out the door, presumably. 'Plus,' delicate pause, 'there was a lot going on in her personal life, so it was understandable if she took her eye off the ball.' This was a discreet reference to the whole blood-family imbroglio on which she declined

to be drawn, though her lips tightened perceptibly when Noakes got started on 'that sewer rat Critchley'. 'So undesirable for someone in our profession to get involved with the media,' she sighed.

Noakes emerged from his DIY reverie.

'Why *did* Padgett go on that TV show, guv?' he asked. 'Sounds like it caused no end of bad feeling with everyone getting the hump.'

'I believe Critchley's production company helped people search for their relatives in return for a cut of the action — filming the story as it unfolded.'

'Yeah, but I mean the bloke's a right piece of work . . . she musta known what she was getting into.'

'Who can say what was in her mind.' Markham thought of that sterile flat and the cat. 'Maybe she wanted some excitement in her life.'

'Attention seeking . . . cos of her age? Mebbe she didn't want to end up like that Bridget Jones . . . necking vodka an' crying over Chaka Khan.'

The DI was amused. 'I hadn't put you down as a fan of rom coms, Sergeant.'

'Our Nat had it on the other day,' the other mumbled. 'There's this bit where Bridget Jones has a meltdown cos she's worried 'bout turning into a saddo . . . dying alone an' someone finding her body half-chewed by Alsatians. An' with Padgett, well, it were jus' her an' Wordsworth. Don' see Tricky Dicky sticking around.'

'Ms Padgett was a well-educated middle-aged professional,' the DI mused, 'but you could have a point about her being restless and dissatisfied . . . possibly in the mood to live dangerously.' In which case she had succeeded beyond her wildest dreams, he thought with a sharp pang.

'An' mebbe Critchley or one of his team came on strong, so she thought it'd be a good thing.'

'True . . . though it was an error of judgement given his track record.' Markham twisted in the front passenger seat which, even well pushed back, failed to accommodate

his six-foot-three frame comfortably. 'He's gone to ground, but Kate and Doyle are going to chase him up once they've finished with the Thornfields at *Top of the Class*.'

'Lipscombe were dead mealy-mouthed, an' as for the ex-husband —what a prat . . . total windbag. No wonder ole Janet changed her surname back.'

'*Jayne*,' Markham corrected mechanically, reviewing the encounter with Jayne's colleagues.

Bill Travers was a well-built, self-important man, balding on top and trying to compensate with a half-hearted attempt at a beard. He accepted Markham's condolences with a perfunctory nod which spoke volumes about his feelings towards the late unlamented.

'How the hell d'you think he managed to snaffle Bickerton? Talk about punching above your weight.' It seemed manifestly unfair to Noakes when he reviewed the romantic dynamic afterwards.

Christine Bickerton was a composed young woman — expensively dressed, long dark pageboy with trendy bangs, excellent figure — whose strident Northern accent had grated on Markham's ear. She had made the appropriate noises about Jayne Padgett, but this was at odds with the dislike that flashed out when they asked how she had got on with her dead colleague. 'Of course, it was awkward . . . Jayne blamed me for the breakup with Bill, but the marriage was on its last legs long before that.'

Was it? Markham wondered. Or did you deliver the *coup de grace*?

'Things got easier as time went on and Jayne accepted the situation,' the NQT added piously. Matthew Sullivan had told Markham that the young teacher 'had her claws out' for Jayne Padgett. Looking at Christine Bickerton, the DI suspected she was past mistress of the art of being passive aggressive. But was she a killer?

'We're looking for a bloke, right?' Noakes interrupted his thoughts. 'I mean, what with Padgett having been interfered with.'

‘Not necessarily.’

‘How come?’

‘There was no semen left at the scene, but Dimples says some form of sexual activity took place.’

‘That jus’ means he couldn’t get it up . . . Them types usually can’t,’ Noakes retorted darkly.

‘It’s possible the scene was staged.’

Noakes stared at his boss.

‘You think a *woman* yanked Padgett’s undies off an’ caused them bruises.’

‘The bruises were superficial. It could have been an attempt to hoodwink us into thinking this was a sex attack gone wrong.’ Markham thought intently. ‘Dimples thinks the killer might’ve planned to stage Jayne’s death as a suicide but then lost control. The aborted sex could have been motivated by lust. Or we might be looking at a last-ditch attempt to disguise the real reason behind her murder.’

Noakes thumped the dashboard. ‘You know what Sidney’ll say. Psycho rapist on the loose.’

‘Without a doubt.’ The DI frowned, being all too familiar with Sidney’s favoured playbook. ‘But we’ve come across enough disturbed individuals to know it could be nowhere as simple as that, especially since Jayne let her killer into the flat, which suggests they were *known* to her.’

‘Sidney’ll say the perp tricked his way in.’ The DS’s perverse streak now saw him playing devil’s advocate. ‘An’ you gotta admit, none of them lot—’ he jerked a stubby forefinger in the direction of the school — ‘fit the profile . . . all too respectable by half.’

‘As you pointed out though, Sergeant, none of them have strong alibis. Well, Travers and Bickerton are each other’s, but that doesn’t count for anything, while Lipscombe and Tony Brighouse came in to Hope to catch up on paperwork.’

‘Losers,’ Noakes said succinctly. ‘I mean, why’d they come in of a weekend? Unless,’ he smacked his lips lubriciously, ‘they had an *ass-ig-nay-shun*.’ No one so adept as the DS when it came to drawing out syllables.

'They're both married.'

'So what?' Noakes countered defiantly. 'An' anyway, Brighouse looks the type.'

Tony Brighouse was what Noakes called a snake oil salesman — good-looking in a Keir Starmer-ish sort of way and very smooth.

'He'd had run-ins with Padgett,' the DS continued. 'You could tell he didn't like a woman standing up to him . . . he might've come over all *Guardian*-reading leftie but betcha he ditched all that diversity bollocks when some middle-aged biddy tried telling it like it was.'

It was a shrewd observation. Like Christine Bickerton, something had flared in Brighouse's eyes before it was swiftly banked down. Dislike? Anger? *Fear*?

'Watcha reckon to the Gillian woman?'

'Gill Dacre?'

'Yeah.' The DS shuddered theatrically. 'Wouldn't much fancy being taught by *her* . . . what a ball-breaker.'

'Parents probably see the disciplinarian approach as an asset, Sergeant,' was Markham's dry response.

'Mind, it was odd the way she suddenly played the sick card . . . like she couldn't get out of there fast enough.'

It was true. There had indeed been something off-kilter about the teacher's body language.

A faded sharp-featured blonde whose half up, half down hairstyle was too young for her, she had made no bones about her disapproval of Jayne Padgett. 'Teaching isn't a popularity contest,' she snapped acidly when Noakes enquired why the two colleagues hadn't got on, proceeding to explain that in her opinion the dead woman was 'far too keen on being friends with students when she should have maintained boundaries and a suitable distance'.

Markham recognised the green-eyed monster when he heard it and was willing to bet the woman was a ready recruit in the campaign to manoeuvre Jayne Padgett out of Hope.

And yet, Gill Dacre was clearly uncomfortable about something and visibly longing to escape, darting furtive

uneasy glances at the two senior leaders — who had insisted on being present for the interviews with staff — in a manner that suggested some strong internal agitation.

Finally, just after coffee and biscuits were brought in by two fifth-form girls — all coy sidelong looks and ill-disguised speculation about the visitors — Dacre had said she didn't feel well and asked to be excused as she had a full afternoon timetable.

There was little Markham could do but accede graciously to this request. No way did he want a complaint of police harassment landing on Sidney's desk before they had even got started.

But it was odd, nevertheless.

'Let's get Kate to check in with Ms Dacre later today,' he said. 'Then she can interview her first thing tomorrow,' he said.

'Think she knows owt, guv?'

'Something was definitely up with her but I'd say there's a strong instinct for self-preservation, so provided we keep tabs it should be all right.'

'Mebbe she jus' felt bad about being a bitch to Padgett,' Noakes said ruminatively. 'Didn't look like there were much love lost between her an' Travers. Did you see the way she looked at him an' Bickerton as she passed them on the way in? Someone's not been playing nicely in the sandpit.'

'Indeed.' Though the DI hadn't been able to work out the dynamic between the three teachers. Gill Dacre had cringed away from the couple in the doorway of the head's office, while the look she shot them was a strange compound of dislike, resentment and . . . something else that defied analysis.

No wonder Olivia called Hope a nest of vipers. And yet, with the likes of Matt Sullivan and good old Dr Abernathy in situ, all was not lost.

Noakes had an uncanny ability to read the guvnor's thoughts. 'Sullivan made hisself scarce,' he grunted. 'Can't see him enjoying tea parties with Lipscombe an' Brighouse.'

'I managed a few words earlier this morning,' the DI replied. 'Given that we're friends, Matt felt it might be diplomatic to absent himself.' Then he flashed his rare, charming smile. 'He's not a fan of SLT, though, and disliked the vendetta against Ms Padgett. In his own quiet way, he did his best to tip her the wink about any "informal support", so she was always one step ahead of the gruesome twosome.'

Noakes guffawed. 'Good man.' He thoroughly approved of Sullivan's subversive streak. 'Did he say anything about them allegations your Olivia mentioned?' As always, his cauliflower ears turned pink at this reference to Markham's partner.

'It was something and nothing according to Matt. Just this couple who felt their little darling wasn't getting Ms Padgett's undivided attention . . . The fact that there were twenty-eight other students in the class clamouring for the teacher's notice appeared to have escaped them.'

'Special needs, was she?'

'As it happens, yes.' Markham shifted impatiently in his seat. 'Matt felt Gill Dacre and the leadership team had stirred up Mr and Mrs Restorick to make trouble for Jayne.'

The DS snorted, disgusted. 'God, they're worse than the kids.'

'Yes, it's something Olivia hates. She says too many colleagues regress to the level of the playground and give the profession a bad name.'

'Well, good on Padgett for digging her heels in an' standing up to the bullies,' Noakes said stoutly.

But look what it cost her, thought the DI. Assuming there was a connection between school politics and the murder.

'What else did Sullivan have for us?' Noakes asked hopefully. 'Did he know owt about this agency lark . . . *Top of the Form* or whatever it's called.'

'*Top of the Class*.' Markham pinched the bridge of his nose, as though the whole case was giving him neuralgia. 'There was some sniping from two women whose children attend Hope and were being tutored by Ms Padgett . . .'

Noakes waited expectantly while the DI dredged the names from his memory.

'Both single parents—'

'That figures.' The DS's latent prejudices stood smartly to attention.

'Michelle Preston, she's a secretary with the council and Denise Rooney, a nurse at the Newman.'

'Chuffing Nora, not that place again,' Noakes grumbled. 'Didn't Padgett's prune-faced half-sister work there too?'

'That's right . . . Angela Studholme was an administrator there.'

'God.' The DS's expression was louring. 'Jus' so long as we don' end up having to go back there again.' He gestured expressively. 'I've had it *up to here* with the Newman.'

Recalling previous investigations, Markham could hardly blame his subordinate for this reaction.

'By the way, guv,' Noakes was temporarily diverted from the subject of Bromgrove's special hospital, 'them two women—'

'Angela Studholme and Valerie Holmes,' the DI interposed, seeing that his sergeant was groping for the names.

'Right. They're Padgett's half-sisters, yeah?'

'Correct . . . same mother, different father.'

'They didn't say owt about their dad . . . wonder if he's still knocking around.'

'Sorry, I should have said. I checked with the matron at Nazareth House and she filled me in. He died in 1999.'

'Oh.' Noakes looked crestfallen. It was obvious he had thought the family tree potentially a better bet than school politics.

'But I think you're right to wonder about the family background.'

Visible revival of stout party.

'It must have been deeply unsettling for Jayne's half-sisters when she began researching her past,' the DI continued.

'Yeah . . . On *Long Lost Family*, sometimes you get folk who are dead unhappy 'bout rellies turning up outa the blue

an' the halfies or step-kids or whatever c'n get really jealous when mum's all taken up with the kid she gave away.'

'Correct, Noakes. And there was the fact that it clearly stirred up a hornet's nest with Critchley given the broadcasting standards enquiry.'

'Plus, the school weren't happy about it.'

To say nothing of the ex-husband and on-off boyfriend.

A sharp rap at the window startled both men.

Judith Lipscombe, wearing a thin-lipped expression of disapproval, stood next to the car in a high-vis jacket.

'Sixth-formers will be heading this way in the lunch hour, gentlemen,' she said. 'And as you've already attracted a certain amount of attention . . .'

'Of course, Ms Lipscombe.' Markham bestowed his most disarming smile. 'We'll be on our way now.'

As they drove away, Noakes eyed the approaching gaggle of short-skirted girls with their Oompa Loompa fake tans. 'Jus' as well it weren't Doyle doing this end,' he declared sententiously. 'The lad wouldn't know where to look. 'S like fricking *Love Island*.'

'That's modern youth for you, Sergeant.' If the thought occurred to him that Natalie Noakes didn't exactly dress Amish in her time at Hope, the DI kept this to himself.

Noakes smirked as he looked in his rear-view mirror. 'Lipscombe looks a total *tit* in that get-up.'

'All part of a senior leader's remit these days,' Markham riposted. 'And pretty democratic of her to get out there with the troops.'

Noakes muttered something uncomplimentary under his breath. Then, 'Did you pick up owt from the crime scene photos, guv?'

The DI exhaled heavily. 'Nothing stood out,' he said. 'Nothing that looked like it would have made the killer return at any rate.'

'An' the patrol boys didn't clock any more suspicious activity outside the flats.' Noakes scowled. 'Like as not it were

jus' one of the wrinklies getting the wind up about the local scrotes.'

'How many times, Noakesy . . . "senior citizens", not wrinklies.'

The DS grinned unrepentantly.

'Do we have a description for this lad who was lurking outside Cabot Court?' Markham asked.

'Nada . . . local plod's pretty dozy . . . Jus' some kid with his hoodie up.'

The thought of that dark figure disappearing into the night bothered the DI.

'We c'n get Burton to check out all the spotty nerks Padgett taught, boss . . . then ramp things up a notch if any of 'em's on the pervy side.'

Lipscombe and Brighouse would just *love* that, the DI thought glumly. And any focus on Hope's student population would likely have the parents up in arms.

Another thump of the dashboard. 'Right boss, what next?' Noakes demanded.

'Let's hear what Kate and Doyle have for us. Then we'll think about what we're going to tell the DCI.'

'Don' suppose . . .'

'Yes, there's time for a quick pit stop at McDonald's, Sergeant.' Markham bowed to the inevitable. 'But nothing too greasy, for God's sake. We don't want to reek of chip fat for the rest of the day.'

The DS looked indignant.

'You c'n have a chicken wrap or summat, boss.' It was clear he considered this was for wimps.

Suppressing a smile, Markham looked out of the window as the car picked up speed. The day was wet and damp with sodden leaves clogging the pavements and grey skies brooding oppressively above. The DI flexed his shoulders, ready for what lay ahead.

By visiting Hope Academy, they had cast a stone into the pond. Who could say what ripples it would make . . . ?

* * *

‘John Thornfield’s got previous, boss,’ Kate Burton announced once the team was assembled in Markham’s office.

Outside his window, it was lashing a gale, no trace of that balmy Indian summer. The leylandii trees which screened the station from the high street tossed and writhed as though in some kind of encephalitic ecstasy. ‘Like they’re giving us a warning or summat.’

Noakes was not generally prone to poetic metaphor, but there was something vaguely threatening in the atmosphere and all of them felt it.

‘What kind of previous?’ Markham hardly dared hope this was the break they were looking for.

‘A community order after a bust-up with his wife. We’re talking way back in 2008, so it’s long spent, but it shows he’s got a temper.’ Burton smoothed down the lapels of her immaculate pinstripe trouser suit, wrinkling her nose as Noakes shrugged off his jacket unleashing a waft of McDonald’s.

‘Did the Thornfields volunteer this information?’ the DI asked.

‘No, but there was something shifty about him, so I ran a check afterwards.’

‘Wouldn’t safeguarding an’ all that mean he couldn’t do stuff involving kids? I mean, what about all that DBS malarkey?’ Noakes demanded impatiently.

‘He wasn’t barred from running the agency, sarge,’ Doyle explained, contemplating his new Tricker’s brogues with some complacency (definitely the right choice for an up-and-coming DS). ‘And anyway, he stayed pretty much in the background. It’s Pauline who’s the brains of the outfit.’

‘What’s *she* like then?’ the older DS asked.

‘Boxy-looking woman, but definitely the efficient type,’ Doyle said thoughtfully. ‘She was very cagey about Padgett . . . really didn’t want to be drawn on her.’

‘If Padgett found out about Thornfield’s conviction, mebbe it led to a barney,’ Noakes speculated. ‘Or p’raps she dug up summat else . . . some other secret they didn’t want anyone knowing about.’

The DI looked at Burton and Doyle in turn. 'What's your take on John Thornfield?'

'Crooked as fuck,' Doyle blurted out then blushed to the roots of his carroty hair as the fastidious DI raised his eyebrows. 'Sorry, sir. That just popped out.'

'There were definitely tensions between Jayne and the agency, boss.' Kate Burton's sense of decorum was well to the fore. No effing and jeffing for *her*.

'What about those single mums who were gunning for her?' Markham asked. 'Did that have anything to do with it?'

Burton flipped open her notebook.

'Pauline said they complained about Jayne "pumping their kids for personal information".'

Markham's brows furrowed. 'Any idea what they meant by that?'

'Not really, boss,' Burton admitted ruefully. 'She clammed up after saying this and gave us some folderol about confidentiality and data protection.'

'Padgett was the caring type,' Doyle put in. 'Hot on pastoral issues and all that . . . Maybe she had concerns about the kids' home life or something and wanted to check they were okay—'

'But the kids shot their mouth off an' these two slappers came looking for her,' Noakes finished eagerly.

Burton looked thoroughly disapproving. 'We can't make assumptions about lifestyle just because someone's a single parent,' she said in a distinctly vinegary tone.

Noakes and Doyle exchanged meaningful glances that suggested they were constrained by no such liberal sentiments.

'We need to speak to these women,' Markham said. 'Set it up will you, Kate . . . and I want you to liaise with Matt Sullivan and arrange interviews with Ms Padgett's students — very low-key and make sure someone from SLT sits in so there's no suggestion of police oppression. Also, try to arrange a meeting with Marian Padgett please, but tread softly — her GP's the prickly sort.'

The acting DI scribbled away happily. As far as she was concerned, to do lists represented the acme of felicity.

'And let's dig deeper into the Thornfields,' Markham continued.

'They're each other's alibi for the time of Jayne's murder,' Burton frowned.

'Which in effect means no alibi at all.' The DI drummed his fingers on the desk then restlessly strode to his window to watch the tempest outside.

Finally, he said, 'Let's go through everything we've got and then meet back here . . . Dimples is emailing me the autopsy report, so we can unpick that.'

'Everything's set up in my office, sir.' Now she was an acting DI, Burton had her own shoebox carved out of the opposite corner from Markham's.

'Good. Let's say five thirty for a case review. Remember, the DCI wants a full briefing tomorrow morning.'

The mere thought of Sidney made his stomach clench. 'That man's enough to give anyone IBS on the spot,' Olivia had said. Judging by the look on his subordinates' faces, they shared his sentiments.

* * *

It was almost six when they reassembled, and Burton had just begun taking them through the timeline on her trusty portable whiteboard when there came a knock at the door.

The DI swallowed an impatient retort, summoning an encouraging smile for the civilian administrator.

'What can we do for you, Sue?'

'Sorry to disturb, sir. I know you said no interruptions but there's a report come in about a body in the park . . . they think it's a teacher from Hope Academy.'

The four officers moved as one towards the door.

5. DEADLY STAKES

‘God, oh *God*.’

Markham’s team stood in the walled garden of Castor Hill Park, gazing down at the body on the bench beside the floral clock.

Kate Burton was beside herself.

‘I checked with Hope like we’d arranged, sir. It turned out she knocked off early and the TA took over . . . the cover supervisor told me I’d get through to her eventually because she was still in the building. Her mobile was switched off, but I just thought it was after-school stuff . . . clubs or meetings.’

‘She must have shot off not long after me an’ the DI showed up.’ Noakes did his clumsy best to comfort Kate Burton. ‘You weren’t to know, luv . . .’

The four detectives looked down at Gill Dacre’s body.

It was decorously positioned with knees and ankles together and calves slanted at a forty-five-degree angle — ‘ever so prim and proper, jus’ like one of the royals’, as Noakes told Muriel afterwards. The torso was relaxed and slightly slumped, but an angry red weal around the woman’s neck showed all too clearly how she had died. Her eyes were wide open and staring with an expression of surprise, while the half up, half down hairstyle had come loose, and a hank

of blonde hair fell over one cheek which looked as though it bore fresh scratch marks.

Another strangulation, Markham thought. A murderer who lunged for his victims' necks.

'Dacre were antsy when me an' the DI swung by,' Noakes said at last. 'But we couldn't tell if she were spooked by management or one of the others or what . . .'

'I spoke to the head's PA too.' Burton was distraught. 'She made it sound like Dacre was still on the premises.'

'Probl'y couldn't be bothered to check, ma'am.' This was Doyle. 'Took it for granted she was still there . . . having a brew in the staff room or hiding from management or something. If she snuck off, most likely she never bothered to sign out.'

The rain had ceased, and Castor Hill's walled garden was eerie in the gloaming, powerful arc lights illuminating the scene. The bench with its murdered occupant was situated next to a vibrant bed of dahlias, the park seeming almost to mock CID with the beauty of its bronze autumn panoply. Nearby a statue of some Graeco-Roman deity, with helmet, trident and streaming linen, observed the scene as though poised to swoop down and sweep the corpse away to some celestial region. Altogether, it was one of the strangest and most surreal settings that the team had ever encountered.

'She must've come here to confront the killer,' Burton said, looking wildly towards the little half-timbered mock Tudor lodge a short distance away.

It was a reasonable assumption, thought Markham.

On closer inspection, he could see that the front door and windows of the quaint little cottage were covered by grilles, so it was presumably uninhabited. And in the late afternoon on a damp and uninviting autumn day, the area would normally have been deserted. Moreover, the bench had a direct line of sight to the gateway which gave access to the garden, so the killer would have had ample warning in the unlikely event of anyone approaching.

'Who found her?' he asked.

Noakes gestured to a boiler-suited figure hovering in the background and puffing away on a cigarette as though for dear life.

'That poor sod over there, name of Gary Trent. He jus' came round to give the place the once-over before they locked it at half six . . . thought she were having a kip at first. Uniform took a statement.'

'I take it Mr Trent didn't notice anyone in the vicinity.'

'He were busy working in the meadow bit, that conservation whatchamacallit over on the other side . . . wouldn't normally be the one to go round checking, but they're short-staffed so he nipped across at chucking-out time . . . never expected anyone would be in here. Went over to give her a shake — sometimes they have to do that with winos or down-and-outs — before he realised . . .'

'Must be a cool customer.' Doyle tried to visualise the killer. 'Couldn't be sure someone wouldn't come blundering in on them.'

'They'd have scoped out the grassy bit at the front on the way in. Plus there's no café or bogs . . . jus' them weirdy bits of wood an' logs,' Noakes had never really seen the point of 'installation art'. 'Schoolkids an' dog walkers prob'ly don' bother with this part once it starts getting dark . If they moved quickly, nowt to fear . . . An' if anyone did rock up, they could make it look like they were helping a friend, propping her up like . . . Dacre said she weren't feeling well, remember.'

'But why *here*?' Burton asked suddenly. 'I mean, the park's not all that convenient for Hope.'

'It's right next to Cabot Court, though,' Doyle pointed out. 'Maybe the killer's local . . . someone from Aldbourne Village . . .'

'Or maybe they were drawn to this area for some reason,' Markham said.

'You mean because of a psychological connection to where they'd killed Jayne Padgett?' Burton's colour was gradually returning, her face less pinched and wan now they

were heading into profiling territory. She shoved the pageboy behind her ears. 'D'you think it's symbolic in some way, guv?'

Noakes cleared his throat. When Burton started on all that *DSM* bollocks, quoting Freud and Jung till it made him want to scream, she never knew when to stop. And his feet were turning colder by the minute.

'Here's Dimples,' he said.

The pathologist came lumbering over, his resemblance to a country vet more pronounced than ever as he grunted at them, plonked his 'bag of tricks' down and pulled on some disposable gloves.

As Davidson conducted his external examination, the detectives moved discreetly to one side, watching as paramedics erected folding screens around the bench to shield the gruesome tableau from public view.

The little gaggle at the gateway to the walled garden appeared to have swelled.

'Doyle, see if you can get the area cleared please.' The DI had an entrenched distaste for rubberneckers.

The 'ginger ninja' was about to act on this instruction when there was a sudden commotion and a tall well-built young man burst through the knot of spectators and came rushing over to them.

'I need to see her,' he panted. 'I'm Simon Dacre. They told me that's my mum you've got there.' The local bush telegraph had clearly been busy.

Using a combination of elbow and arm, Noakes steered the youth away from the paramedics' screens towards the Judas tree that overlooked some well-pruned topiary.

''Course you c'n see her, lad.' His Yorkshire burr had become very pronounced. 'The doc's just looking after her now . . . she's in good hands and one of our lot'll take you down to the hospital.'

'What was she doing out here? I don't understand. Was she mugged? Was it a druggie?' The broad slab face contorted. 'I always said to her, "Just give them whatever they

want, Mum" . . . told her not to hang on to her bag cos it's not worth it.'

'We don' think she were mugged, son. There was a teacher from her school killed the other day . . . it's most likely connected.'

'Mum was shaken up about that,' the other said slowly. 'But wasn't it a burglary?' He shook off Noakes's restraining arm, his expression darkening. 'Are you saying this is down to one of the kids from Hope? Mum's a tough teacher, but some of 'em are proper little shits . . . downright scary and there's never any backup from management.'

Noakes caught Doyle's eye.

'My mate here is going to take you to the hospital so you c'n see to it that folk do right by your mum.' The small eyes were full of compassion. 'Is there anyone we should call?'

'It's just the two of us. Dad walked out when I was a baby . . . no idea where he is now.'

Noakes's arm was back around his shoulders. 'Well, with you being the man of the house, you have to stay strong for her now.' Embarrassed, he added, 'They say a person's spirit hangs around for a while after they're dead . . . so she'll be watching.'

With this anthropomorphic admonition, Noakes escorted Simon Dacre to the gate followed by Doyle, the group of spectators parting respectfully to let them through.

The DI watched them thoughtfully. George Noakes might be a byword in CID for tactlessness and all-round recalcitrance, but he somehow created a space around the deprived and bereaved where they felt their sorrow was safe. The jowly detective with the piggy eyes and dishevelled attire might not have any answers for them, but they believed he understood at least a part of what they were feeling and genuinely cared. That authenticity was all the moment needed.

Noakes re-joined his colleagues just as Dimples emerged from behind the screens.

'Uniforms are getting rid of that mob back there,' the DS growled with a baleful look towards the gateway where

Doyle was superintending proceedings. Then he returned to the matter in hand. 'Was she interfered with, doc?' he enquired hotly. 'Don' say yes . . . not with her poor lad on his way to the morgue.'

'There was some interference, yes . . . intercrural most probably . . .'

'Whass that when it's at home?' Noakes sounded fierce, but the pathologist was imperturbable.

'Non-penetrative sex between the thighs,' he replied.

'He didn't ejaculate?' Burton asked intently.

'It would appear not.'

'Same perv who did for Padgett, then?' Noakes declared.

'Definitely a possibility.'

'Time of death, doc?' This time, Markham was confident of the answer.

'Within the last hour, Inspector.'

The DI looked around the sodden garden and found himself hoping that Gill Dacre's last physical sensations were gentle and she had time to register the soft hiss of English rain on yews and horse chestnuts . . . dusk on an autumn day . . . time to watch that dripping canopy of cypresses — a little wind in the trees — before the blood vessels burst and flooded into the brain leaving no more words. One heart-stopping moment of panic and then she was free.

He became aware of a chirping somewhere in the undergrowth — a wood thrush most probably. In that instant, he felt most acutely the fragility of existence, the absurd brevity of the bird's flight through the lighted hall, from night to night . . .

Markham knew full well the disdain his literary tendencies inspired amongst the rank and file. 'CID's very own poet laureate,' the DCI had sneered on one memorable occasion.

But he did not care two hoots.

Words mattered to him.

It was how he had built a rampart around himself to defend against the sad dark centre of childhood neglect and abuse.

And how he had ultimately triumphed.

It was also what bound him inextricably to Olivia Mullen: this excess that she claimed was uniquely Celtic and for which he felt such strong kinship — the recourse to poetry and art as an essential safety valve, releasing beauty, fortifying the soul for battle, reminding you of the evanescence of life and inuring you against its grief . . .

He sensed that words had mattered to English teacher Gill Dacre, too. That her forbidding presence in the classroom had been about her passionate commitment to passing on the torch of learning . . .

Had she passed from night to night? Or was she now safe from the tempest, basking in the warmth and light of some eternal bourn?

Noakes was blinking around at the rain-drenched garden in a way that told Markham his shambling uncouth DI was pondering those self-same questions in his own inimitable way.

Suddenly, he felt overwhelmed by a wave of affection for his prize-fighter wingman, often bewildered by the boss's meteor streak but stubbornly determined to follow wherever it led.

Not that there was anything particularly elevated about his DS's next words.

'We need to check out them spotty herberts at Hope,' he rumbled. 'Happen one of the lads she taught has a thing about older women . . . angry with 'em cos they're like his mum an' she's the boss . . . or summat like that.'

Kate Burton looked at her colleague as though he was a special needs pupil who had suddenly revealed unexpected potential.

'Interesting you should say that, sarge,' she said eagerly. 'There's a brilliant article in the *BMJ* this week about the mother complex.'

Noakes didn't exactly look as though he relished an exchange of the latest psychiatric intel.

Dimples came to the rescue.

‘We must have a talk about that m’dear,’ he said. ‘It so happens my wife’s working on a paper about the maternal power complex.’

You can count me out. Noakes couldn’t believe the pathologist was encouraging her. Mind you, with his missus being a psychologist she and Burton could have a cosy powwow about freaky teenagers and maybe flush out any likely psychos Padgett had taught at Shitty High while they were at it.

Suddenly Markham’s mobile trilled, sounding obscenely strident in the garden’s deathly hush.

The conversation was short and to the point.

‘I have to brief the DCI,’ was all he said at its conclusion, though the grim set of his mouth clearly indicated how little he relished the prospect.

Noakes looked mutinous. ‘I thought Sidney were seeing us tomorrow.’

‘In the circumstances,’ Markham gestured eloquently at their surroundings, ‘he’s bringing our meeting forward.’

The stretcher party was ready to take Gill Dacre to the ambulance waiting at the park’s north side.

Doyle was back. The DI glanced towards the entrance to the garden, observing with satisfaction that the little crowd had dispersed and two uniforms flanked the gateway.

He nodded to Dimples and the sombre group moved with its sheeted burden towards the exit, followed by the four detectives.

Was the murderer still lurking nearby? he wondered uneasily as they passed the little lodge whose diamond-paned windows winked wickedly in the spectral illumination of the arc lights.

But there was no one to be seen now, save for the white-clad SOCOs flitting silently about the wall garden, as always their paper-suited forms reminding him of giant moths.

Then they were out of the modest little park.

Lime, ash, pine. The trees swayed and bowed, paying homage almost as though Gill Dacre was a heroine fallen in

battle on some foreign field. The DI suspected she would have liked the send-off.

* * *

Markham was generally able to anticipate DCI Sidney's mood from the demeanour of his hamster-like PA Miss Peabody, but she was off with the flu and an unsmiling gorgon ushered them into the waiting room outside his office.

'*Kerr-ist*! That one looks like Maggie Thatcher,' Noakes observed in a not-at-all sotto voce as she then whisked off on some unspecified errand (tormenting underlings in the typing pool by the look of things). 'Why can't he have someone smiley an' pretty for a change?'

'Sounds like CID's training on the evils of stereotyping passed you by, Sergeant.'

'Well, I mean it's jus' downright *depressing* when they look like that an' bad for *morale*,' the DS added virtuously. 'Plus, did you see the way she eyed me up an' down, like I were summat she'd scraped off the bottom of her shoe. *Rude*, that's what I call it.'

Given the way the scent of McDonald's was now contending with a definite whiff of dog dirt (Noakes having trod on something nasty in the park), Markham was not surprised at the supercilious look Margaret Thatcher's doppelganger had thrown his DS. Despite having marginally spruced himself up for the visit to Hope, his wingman still contrived to look like a down-at-heel bookie, though even the sporting fraternity would have baulked at the lurid mustard and green multi-check jacket that simply shrieked colour blindness.

Still, he supposed it could have been worse. At least the rest of the ensemble was just about passable and he could always pretend Noakes had been on undercover duties . . . If that wasn't a contradiction in terms given his get-up . . .

In the event, when they were eventually admitted to the Presence, Sidney contented himself with a single withering look at 'Markham's useful idiot'.

The DI couldn't help his gaze wandering to the photomontage which covered one wall of the inner sanctum, the rank and file having irreverently dubbed it Sidney's Hall of Fame. According to DI Chris Carstairs, the DCI's latest 'VIP crush' was the Countess of Wessex after she had attended a meeting of Bromgrove's Police Liaison Committee. Sure enough, there were HRH and Sidney side by side in a *Gazette* photograph blown up so that it dwarfed all the other luminaries in his gallery of minor celebrities.

It tickled Markham's fancy to think that the DCI and Muriel Noakes shared a passion for all things royal, but this flicker of amusement was short-lived as Sidney embarked on his agenda of concerted damage-control.

'We absolutely *cannot* have any repeat of Hope Academy being dragged into the mire,' he rasped, tugging at the goatee that he doubtless imagined vastly augmented his gravitas and imparted a philosophical cast to his physiognomy ('the Thomas Aquinas of Bromgrove CID', as Olivia put it sardonically). Somehow that beard was never enough to distract Markham from the eczema and executive buzz cut that gave his boss the appearance of a marine with a bad case of impetigo.

'I'm afraid some exposure is unavoidable, sir, given that we have two victims who were both teachers at the school.'

'An' everyone knows they all hate each other up there,' Noakes chipped in unhelpfully, eliciting an angry glower followed by a denunciation of 'scandal-mongering' and panegyric to Hope's 'dedicated professionals'.

'The likelihood is that Ms Padgett and Ms Dacre knew the killer,' Markham said once Sidney paused for breath, before segueing into a review of the facts as they stood.

Sidney's expression darkened still further as Markham revealed Jayne Padgett's family history and the Nick Critchley angle, the DCI clearly finding it an unpalatable complication — not least as this was an episode no one at the local TV channel *Bromgrove Live* would care to see resurrected. As he

listened, the DCI clearly sensed his prospects of a flattering media profile going up in smoke.

The atmosphere turned positively glacial when Markham mentioned parental involvement in the vendetta against Jayne Padgett, specifically the clique headed by John and Shona Restorick.

'The Restoricks happen to be friends of my wife,' the DCI said frigidly with a reverential glance at the studio portrait of that Valkyrie-like lady in pride of place on his desk. 'And I should point out that Mrs Sidney has recently agreed to chair the school's Building Fund Appeal.'

Trust Brunhilde to get in on the act. Markham's heart sank but he ploughed on before Noakes could say anything about it being better to demolish awful old eyesores and have done with it.

Predictably, Sidney brightened when the DI referenced Cabot Court's mysterious prowler and the reports of juvenile delinquency around Aldbourne Village.

'And you say there was evidence of attempted intercourse?' he asked eagerly in the gratingly nasal tones that acted on Markham's nerves like fingernails on a chalkboard. 'Surely that points to a sex offender . . . Presumably you'll be looking closely at absconsions from mental health facilities and former inmates at HMP Bromgrove.'

If in doubt, pin it on some local low life.

Good old Sidney. Never knowingly guilty of originality.

'It's not necessarily as straightforward as all that, sir.'

Understatement of the year.

'While there are indicators the victims were interfered with, these could point to sexual dysfunction or even gender ambiguity.'

'Now look here, Inspector. If you imagine for one moment that I'll allow you to dredge up all that . . . *unpleasantness* about intersex individuals again . . . then you can forget it.'

The DCI had hated it when skeletons tumbled out of various closets during the New College Close investigation,

the case which dragged Hope Academy once more into the unforgiving glare of publicity. Though he parroted the fashionable diversity shibboleths — or 'fluent bollocks,' as Noakes called it — Sidney shied away from avant-garde deviance. What he wanted was your straightforward common or garden rapist from the sticks . . . emphatically nothing that suggested any sort of noxious subculture at the local comprehensive.

'Oh, nothing like that, sir, *gracious no*.' Markham forced a mirthless laugh. There was something about these ghastly interviews with Sidney which ended in him speaking in clichés. *Like some Victorian dowager*. 'It's just that the psychology appears somewhat complex given how the victims were presented and the lack of follow-through.'

Sidney was appeased. 'Ah well, in that case we can draw on the profiling unit at the university, work out the forensic *signature*.'

This was precisely what Markham had hoped to avoid, though no doubt Burton would be ecstatic at the prospect of liaising with the local David Canter.

Noakes looked distinctly underwhelmed, notoriously having no time for Sidney's expert boffins.

Before the DS could put his foot in it, Markham intervened smoothly.

'Excellent idea, sir. I'll put Kate Burton on it right away.'

He felt a spasm of self-disgust as he said this, but blindsiding Sidney had to be worth laying on the smarm.

And indeed, it appeared to have worked.

'Good to see you've got an open mind on this, Markham. Stick with the science and you won't go far wrong.'

Noakes wriggled. *The science*! Fat chance of that turning up anything useful.

Sidney's beard-stroking had settled into a more relaxed tempo.

'We'll do a press conference tomorrow, sir.' *That should do the trick*. 'Appeal for witnesses . . . "somebody's husband, somebody's son", that kind of thing.'

He couldn't believe he'd come up with anything quite so cheesy. It was straight from the Yorkshire Ripper playbook.

But Sidney was nodding magisterially.

'That's the ticket, Markham. Let's not get carried away, eh?'

This was undoubtably a patronising acknowledgement of the DI's regrettable predilection for 'hunches'.

It made him want to punch Sidney's lights out.

More salaaming and finally they were done, the DCI inclining his head as though in benediction.

'I'm heading out for a bit, Sergeant,' Markham said once they were on the other side of the door to Sidney's office. 'Need to clear my head . . . take stock.'

The DS knew what this meant.

The guvnor was headed to Doggie Dickerson's on Marsh Lane to work out his post-Sidney aggro.

'Righto, boss,' he said. 'I'll hook up with Dacre's lad an' see what gives with Dimples.'

'And get Kate to liaise with the university will you, Noakesy. As in "sticking with the science".'

The DS did his special eye roll. The one he reserved for dire emergencies. Real *Planet of the Apes* stuff.

'She'll have one of them weirdies on speed dial, boss. Leave it with me.'

And Markham was more than happy to do just that.

* * *

'Doggie' Dickerson was the most improbable health guru that it was possible to imagine — the mere mention of whom was guaranteed to elicit scowls in high places.

His boxing club in Marsh Lane (Bromgrove Police Boxing Club, to use its full title) was frequented by both the local criminal fraternity and CID's finest, the barriers between Bromgrove's usual sworn enemies obliterated by a shared passion for slugging it out in the ring.

The proprietor himself might have posed for Long John Silver or some other piratical buccaneer, such was the eccentricity of his appearance. Others might have been turned off by the peculiar horsehair wig, eyepatch and wonky yellow tombstone teeth, but Markham was long inured to Doggie's less than salubrious aspect, finding him infinitely more congenial than the pert little misses and 'buff' specimens who presided over such antiseptic amenities as *Body Works* and *Primal Training* in Bromgrove town centre.

Doggie was anathema to the DCI.

'Absolutely *disgraceful* that senior officers don't see the signal it sends out when they persist in fraternising with characters of that ilk. I wouldn't be at all surprised if he wasn't involved in human trafficking and God knows what else.'

Markham was fairly sure that Dickerson's code of ethics precluded any such criminal enterprise. Strictly low-level, that was Doggie, and CID had never been able to connect him to any big-league activity despite all of Sidney's fulminations.

Needless to say, the unsanitariness of Doggie's locker rooms and showers — the need for re-grouting being the least of it — had proved no impediment to Noakes. He and the gym's proprietor had formed a fast friendship founded on their mutual loathing of all things 'woke'.

'We should form our own political party,' was the DS's regular refrain.

'I'm not sure my blood pressure could take it,' his boss invariably replied. 'Wait till we've both retired before you and Dogs launch your project for world domination, Noakesy.'

Frankly, he wouldn't put it past the two of them.

The one area where Noakes and his guru were somewhat at odds was Doggie's recent flirtation with new age 'hocus pocus', but the departure of buxom Marlene (of bingo hall and astrological fame) had coincided with a slackening of his allegiance to Zoroastrianism, the flowing Gandalf-like tabards replaced by a dingy Doc Holliday frock coat

Since Markham was by a long way his 'fav'rite 'spector' (a dubious honour), Doggie lost no time in hastening to the

changing room reserved for 'premium customers' (thus placing them marginally less at risk from contracting hepatitis B and other viruses than his 'standard' clientele).

'Mr Carstairs is already in there warming up, Mr Markham,' he said, rubbing his hands together like some modern-day Fagin. 'Fink he's looking to get his own back for that pummelling you gave him last week.'

Perfect. DI Chris Carstairs could be counted on for a vigorous workout which would allow him to exorcise all thoughts of DCI Sidney and that shambles of a 'briefing'.

Ever conscious of the obligations of hospitality, Doggie plonked himself down on the bench opposite Markham, scenting the already fetid air with a distinct whiff of Jack Daniels.

'Hear you've got a teacher copped it next to Castor Oil Park.'

God, the old villain was worse than Noakes when it came to misnomers.

'Castor *Hill*, Dogs.'

'Yeah, that's the fella,' returned the other, not one whit abashed.

'She was famous from the telly too, 'cording to my Lil.'

Lil? Come on. Keep up, Markham.

'Thass my lady friend from the bridge club,' Doggie explained with a bashful leer.

'Bridge eh, Dogs . . . You'll be too posh for the likes of me at this rate.'

'*Hur-hur-hur* . . . You will have your little joke, Mr Markham.' The rheumy eyes watered with pleasure.

'What did your, er, lady friend reckon to that television programme then?'

'Well, she said the teacher woman tried to track down her mam who dumped her at the park gates when she was only a babby . . . But it was dead awkward.'

'How was that?'

'Well the relatives were cheesed off an' didn't really want to know . . . only went along with it for the cameras. You see,

her long-lost mam was that pleased, it was supposed to look like everyone was chuffed for her.'

I need to see a copy of that programme, the DI resolved. *There's got to be one knocking about somewhere.*

'So I take it the programme wasn't all sweetness and light?'

'*Nah*. Lil said it was kind of bitchy underneath all the nicey-nice stuff. An' some of 'em looked fit to kill. She said you could tell by the end the teacher was dead uncomfortable, like she wasn't happy with how it was going . . .'

'Interesting, Dogs, very interesting.'

The gym's proprietor was clearly pleased to have provoked such a reaction.

'The director bloke got sacked after that, didn't he?' he went on. 'An' no wonder. Lil said if the poor woman had any idea how they planned to twist things, she wouldn't never have gone on the programme in the first place.'

Doggie leaned back against the off-white wall which had a grimy tide mark where many a sweaty bonce had rested.

This was what it was all about, he thought complacently. Helping the local nick with research. And Mr Markham was always so polite and receptive.

'Also heard you've found another dead teacher.' He tapped the side of his bulbous purplish nose as though to indicate infinite sagacity and discretion.

'S'right, Dogs.' Most likely Carstairs had spilled the beans.

'But *she* didn't go on the telly, did she.' He shook his head slowly from side to side, clearly defeated by the conundrum. 'Happen one of that wild crowd from Aldbourne had it in for teachers . . . maybe they didn't like school, see.' He winced and winked in a manner that suggested "the happiest days of your life" was a monstrous fraud perpetrated on the credulous public.

'We'll be checking out the student population, Doggie, never fear.'

'Or maybe the second one was blackmailing whoever topped the first woman.' Doggie didn't watch *Midsomer Murders* for nothing.

Markham nodded gravely.

It was a hypothesis that troubled him.

All that he had seen and heard of Gill Dacre suggested an inflexible rectitude that would appear to preclude calculation or venality . . .

'Right, 'spector.' Doggie shuffled to his feet. 'I c'n see I've gave you food for thought there.'

'Indeed, you have, Dogs.' Markham began to unpack his kit. 'Perhaps you'd care to warn Mr Carstairs I'm on my way.'

With a panache that could not be exceeded by the proprietor of Bromsgrove's swankiest establishment, Doggie saluted the DI, hitched up the ends of his frock coat and headed back to the ring (no doubt by way of his frowsy 'office' with its bottle of whisky in the filing cabinet).

Time for Markham to clear his mind of everything but the cathartic prospect of a fiercely contested bout that would banish all thoughts of the DCI and an investigation that was shaping up to be the most intractable of his career.

6. STEPPING IT UP

Tuesday morning saw a return to milder weather, though the mood in Markham's office as the team assembled for the morning briefing was anything but cheerful. Even Noakes was subdued, his usual Falstaffian attire replaced with a funereal-looking (albeit shiny) suit designed to pass muster at the press conference.

Kate Burton had made an effort on the hospitality front, providing toasted bagels and decaf coffees. After cautiously examining his roll between finger and thumb as though it were some exotic delicacy (the absence of sugar or other 'topping' was a poser), Noakes soon got stuck in. Not a patch on Greggs, obviously, but could have been worse. Last time round, she'd produced the godawful granola stuff that tasted like bird droppings.

The DI updated Burton and Doyle on the meeting with Sidney.

'I've been in touch with Professor Nathan Finlayson at the university, sir,' Burton said at the conclusion of Markham's recital. Then, shyly, 'His book on erectile paraphilias was really good.'

There was a choking sound from Noakes.

No wonder the lass could never get it together with a normal bloke, he thought to himself. *Not when she always had her nose in some kinky textbook or other. Erectile paraphilias, for chuff's sake!*

But the DI was serene.

'Excellent, Kate. I can mention it at the press conference . . . assuming the professor's happy to go on the record.'

You betcha, Noakes's savage internal monologue continued. *That lot love getting their phizzes in the paper.*

'Oh yes, boss.' Burton looked enthusiastic. 'He consults at the Newman too, so it means he can cover the mental health angle.'

'Don' forget the prison,' Noakes put in sourly, setting the Newton's Cradle in motion with an emphatic clack. When the DS began fiddling with the desktop gadget, it was a sure sign of ebullience or exasperation. In this case, Markham had no doubt that the prospect of a university expert descending on them was playing havoc with his wingman's blood pressure.

Burton watched the little steel balance balls smack against each other. She looked somewhat anxious at the prospect of trawling hospital and prison records.

The DI smiled at her.

'We have to keep an open mind,' he said firmly. 'Plus, the DCI needs reassurance that we're not off on some witch-hunt against the school.'

'Do you reckon we're looking for someone on the staff at Hope, sir?' Doyle enquired. 'I mean, there was bad blood between Padgett and a few of them, including Dacre.' He looked at his notes. 'And didn't Padgett's friend say something about her inviting folk round so they could bitch about the management . . .'

'Yes, it would be interesting to find out more about that,' the DI replied thoughtfully. 'Though I've never heard of a teacher being murdered just because of tensions at the chalkface or school politics.' He recalled those apprehensive faces from the school assembly. 'But what do I know?'

Burton shivered. 'Evil can get in anywhere.'

Markham turned to her. 'When you and Doyle visit the school this afternoon, I'd like you to have a quiet word with Matt Sullivan and see what he knows about problems with management.'

He wandered across to his window and stared sightlessly out at the September sunshine before turning round to face the team.

'If we're assuming that Gill Dacre went to meet the killer, then what did she hope to achieve?' he asked.

'Blackmail?' ventured Doyle. 'She knew something or guessed something . . . and wanted money in return for keeping schtum.'

Burton shook her head. 'That doesn't fit. Dacre wasn't the type to cover for a murderer.'

'She might've done,' Doyle temporised. 'If they had some sort of hold over her. Or if there was some reason she sympathised with them.'

Burton tried another tack. 'Maybe she thought *someone else* had done it and just wanted to sound the murderer out about what she should do — ask their advice—'

'Yeah,' Noakes liked this hypothesis. 'But then she blurted summat that made 'em realise she knew too much, that she could be dangerous. So they snuffed her.'

Markham nodded. 'Something did definitely upset her when we called at the school.'

'Maybe she remembered something,' Burton suggested. 'Something she'd forgotten about . . . then she suddenly realised it was important.'

Doyle pulled a face. 'Might not have had anything to do with the school. Perhaps it was just a coincidence, her getting upset during that meeting. If her mind was elsewhere, that could be why she looked distracted.'

The DI notoriously disliked coincidences, but he had to concede the logic of this argument.

'What's with the sex stuff then?' Noakes sounded genuinely at a loss. 'Has he got a hang-up about middle-aged

teachers, had a bad experience at school?' The DS clearly had no difficulty envisaging such a scenario. 'Or is it like summat out of Freud an' he hated his mum?'

'Maybe it was spur of the moment.' Burton surprised them by skipping any reference to her beloved *DSM*. 'Maybe the act of killing was some kind of sexual trigger and he just couldn't help himself.'

'Or,' Doyle ruminated, 'it could have started out as a sexual assault and then he got angry, cos he couldn't perform.'

'Dimples can't be a hundred per cent certain on this, but he's reasonably sure in each case the interference with the body occurred either contemporaneously with death or immediately afterwards. He felt there was almost something staged about it . . .'

'You mean, to make us think it was a sex attack, boss?' Doyle asked.

The DI raised his hands palm upwards before letting them fall heavily. 'Possibly, or because of some inner compulsion . . . or elements of both.'

'Talk about a bleeding whack job,' Noakes muttered. 'An' you really think professor wossname's gonna lead us to him?' he challenged.

'I think he may provide us with insights into the forensic signature,' the DI said carefully.

'You mean shut Sidney up,' the other said rudely.

'Collateral benefit,' was the equable response.

'Are we going to say anything about sexual assault at the press conference, sir?' Burton was anxious to be clear about the script, given that she had been elected to front the occasion.

'I think you can talk about "unexplained features" and "a severely disturbed individual who needs help". Throw in a reference to Professor Finlayson for good measure and ask people to look for unusual behaviour in loved ones . . . deviations from their normal routine.'

Noakes grinned wolfishly and winked at Burton.

'The ole "somebody's husband, somebody's son" guff . . . Jus' give 'em a juicy headline an' the *Gazette*'ll lap it up.'

His colleague looked pained.

Markham shot Noakes a quelling look. 'The idea is to talk in generalities, Kate. Keep the hacks off the subject of Hope as far as possible.'

Burton looked dubious. 'What about Jayne's family background and the Nick Critchley backstory, guv. That's bound to come up.'

'If Gavin Conors has anything to do with things, it will.' Noakes and the *Gazette*'s lead 'reptile' had been at loggerheads for years, their animosity exploding into fisticuffs on one memorable occasion.

The DI was prepared for this eventuality. 'We ask them to respect the families' privacy . . . imply we'll get heavy in the event of press harassment or doorstepping.'

Noakes brightened up considerably at the notion of 'getting heavy' with Conors.

'The DCI will back you,' Markham continued. 'No way does he want local TV dragged into this.' He rubbed the back of his neck, something of a reflex with him when contemplating Sidney's machinations.

Noakes snorted. 'Thinks it'll bugger his chances of doing a slot with them dolly birds on *Bromgrove Roundup*.'

'More than likely,' the DI sighed.

'Padgett got on the wrong side of everyone with that Nick Critchley programme,' Doyle mused. 'Any of *them* could've had it in for her and then Gill Dacre twigged to something . . . maybe came across one of the relatives.'

'Fair point.' Burton nodded vigorously. 'It's a small world. Marian Padgett and the half-sisters live in Aldbourne Village just a few streets away from Dacre and the ex-husband Bill Travers worked at the same school with his new partner.'

'An' there's Padgett's boyfriend, Tricky Dicky,' Noakes reminded them. 'He's local too . . . works in Calder Vale but his gaff's on Lassiter Road.'

Kate Burton noticed the guvnor's weary air.

'I got a look at that Nick Critchley programme,' she said. 'It used to be on YouTube, but they took it off after broadcasting standards and GDPR got involved.'

'Well done, Kate. How did you manage that?' Markham asked curiously.

'One of the reporters on *Roundup* let me watch it.' The faint blush that attended her answer suggested the possibility of this being more than a casual acquaintance.

Markham was amused to detect within himself a twinge of proprietorial resentment, so used had he become to Kate Burton's hero worship.

But now she was moving on. And deep down he was glad.

Before Noakes could unleash any innuendo of the *Carry On* variety, the DI said, 'Did Critchley skew things?'

'I'd have to say yes, boss. Practically everyone came out of it badly. Padgett looked like she was unbalanced and selfish, you know, like she was doing it for her own satisfaction and to hell with everyone else . . . a sort of creepy personal crusade.'

'What about the Ugly Sisters?' Noakes didn't want *them* off the hook.

Burton looked mildly anguished at this terminology but admitted, 'Not great . . . The way the film was edited, it made them appear bitter and jealous about their mum suddenly turning all her attention to Jayne.'

'Is that what actually happened?' Doyle asked. 'Did they freak out over Padgett suddenly turning up out of the blue like that?'

'Clearly they weren't happy,' Burton replied. 'It wasn't easy for them — the whole foundling thing coming to light was difficult. Jayne was conceived as a result of date rape, which made it even worse.'

'Great for ratings, though,' Doyle pointed out. 'The more sensational the better.'

'True,' she agreed. 'And all the negative stuff — like Jayne's half-sisters not being happy — was all about boosting

the viewing figures. Angela and Valerie complained to *Ofcom* in the end. It was a complete car crash for everyone.'

'Did Marian Padgett and Bill Travers say anything on the programme?' Doyle was mentally reviewing the *dramatis personae*.

'Very buttoned-up and discreet,' Burton replied. 'But you could tell Marian was upset. Travers talked about ingratitude and turning one's back on those who'd done the most for you.'

Marjorie Poole had been aware of their resentment too, Markham reflected. So maybe they hadn't been so discreet after all.

'Can you get me a copy, Kate?' he asked. 'I'd rather go via the backdoor than storm in waving a warrant.'

'Shouldn't be a problem, sir.'

He thought back to her summing up. Car crash sounded about right, he thought gloomily, frustrated that he couldn't seem to find a way to reconcile the two halves of the investigation.

But they had to step it up a gear. Maintain momentum.

'Noakes and I need to interview the Thornfields and the two mothers who complained about Ms Padgett,' he said.

'All sorted, boss,' Burton said crisply. 'I've made an appointment for two o'clock with the Thornfields, and two forty-five with the mums, at the office in Aldbourne. Meantime, me and Doyle will check out the school to see if there were any problems with individual students. *Softly, softly*, obviously,' she added registering Markham's concerned expression.'

'What about them stroppy parents with the special needs kid?' demanded Noakes.

Burton consulted her notebook.

'The Restoricks,' she said. 'I've lined *them* up for tomorrow afternoon. They've agreed to come to the station at three.'

'Big of them,' Noakes muttered.

The acting DI ignored the interruption.

‘Professor Finlayson can give us some time tomorrow,’ she said. ‘He’s consulting at the Newman in the morning.’

Noakes and Doyle exchanged meaningful glances. Clearly neither fancied having ‘some bearded twat’ foisted on them.

‘Excellent, Kate, please set it up,’ he said. ‘And I want to see Simon Dacre tomorrow as well.’

‘Nice lad that,’ Noakes put in. ‘Proper devastated about his mum.’

‘Yes,’ the DI concurred. ‘Maybe he can give us some insight into what made Gill tick. If it wasn’t blackmail, then what would have made her agree to meet the killer?’

A knock at the door.

‘They’re ready for you downstairs, Inspector.’

Time for the press conference.

‘Right, Kate,’ Markham said. ‘It’s over to you and the DCI for this one.’

She gave a wan smile.

‘You’ll be fine. Just keep to generalities and emphasise the psychology angle.’

‘Yeah, they love all that BS,’ Noakes added cheerfully. ‘Jus’ blind ’em with science, luv.’

* * *

In the event, that was precisely what she did; assisted by Barry Lynch from the press office, the oleaginous administrator for once proving immune to the blandishments of short-skirted female journalists.

‘Ole Octopus mitts weren’t bad,’ Noakes said afterwards. ‘Came across quite business-like for a change.’

Doyle grinned.

‘He’s seeing Daphne from HR. Keeps him on a tight rein by all accounts. The fierce-looking woman who let the journos in, that was her.’

‘Oh, I’m with you now. She’s scarier than the battleaxe they’ve got covering for Peabody,’ Noakes guffawed before

breaking into Annie Lennox's famous feminist anthem, 'Sisters Are Doin' It for Themselves'.

'Bandits at six o'clock, sarge,' the ginger ninja murmured as DCI Sidney sailed by with a disapproving glower in their direction.

Noakes stopped singing abruptly. 'Stuff Slimy Sid,' he said. 'He got what he wanted, didn't he? Everyone on high alert for some kind of Peter Sutcliffe nutter an' nowt about pervsters at Hopeless.'

Doyle chuckled reluctantly. 'Yeah, well me and Burton have to get down there and check it out . . . as in see if some saddo remedial had a complex about her or Dacre.'

'Matt Sullivan'll see you reet.' The Yorkshire inflection threatened to tip into parody. 'As for Burton an' SLT, well, they'll start yakking about pastoral this, that, and the other. But *he'll* know if there's any lad with a screw loose . . . Nab him on his own while Burton's boring the tits off the rest of 'em.'

'Can I quote you on that, sarge?'

'*Get out of it*!' But this was said with affection.

Markham and his acting DI came over.

The DI's expression was not especially mirthful, but it was clear he felt the press conference had gone better than expected. 'As Mr Lynch might say, "I think we got away with it."' He smiled at Kate. 'Well done, Kate. You've won us some breathing space.'

Though not for long.

'Shall we get off to Hope then, sir?'

Doyle looked resigned. When his colleague had the bit between her teeth, there was no chance of a refreshment break.

'You do that, Kate.' Markham took pity on the gangling DS. 'But why not regroup over a coffee first. I'd say you've earned it.'

She blinked uncertainly. 'Righto, sir. I'm drawing up a spreadsheet for the alibis. We can go through those together.'

Markham bit the inside of his cheek to avoid laughing at Doyle's expression.

'Where are you up to with alibis?' he asked, ignoring the silent semaphore passing between Noakes and Doyle.

'Looks like anyone from Hope could've met up with Dacre,' she replied. 'It's all a bit easy come, easy go at the end of the school day.' She frowned. 'Staff split without saying where they'll be.'

'Can you blame them?' Noakes burst out. 'After a day at Scrote Central, they must be gagging to disappear.'

'They're supposed to sign out or let admin know the score,' she insisted stubbornly.

Noakes raised his eyes to heaven. *Right, well good luck with that.*

'What about the non-teaching suspects?' Markham enquired pacifically.

Burton looked frustrated.

'I rang around,' she said. 'Angela Studholme and Valerie Holmes were having tea at Valerie's. Marian Padgett was home alone. The Thornfields doing the books in their office, and Richard Keogh out on the road somewhere near Lancaster.'

None of them vouched for, thought Markham with a sinking heart.

'Any luck tracking down Nick Critchley?' he asked.

'Apparently he's been staying with his brother Max in Anglesey for the last fortnight, guv,' she replied. 'Reading between the lines, it sounded like he was drying out or something.'

Fit for murder? ran the refrain in Markham's mind. Instead, he asked, 'Fit to be interviewed?'

'Oh, yes. I've set it up for Thursday . . . thought we should give him forty-eight hours to get his act together, then no one can pull the "vulnerable adult" number.'

'Good work. Well, Noakes and I are due to see the two mothers who had issues with Ms Padgett.'

'That's right, sir. Michelle Preston and Denise Rooney . . . Not till two forty-five, after you've done the Thornfields.'

Noakes was clearly apprehensive that they were about to be subjected to an analysis of Burton's time and motion graphs.

‘The sergeant and I will take stock,’ Markham said easily. ‘Plot our strategy for this afternoon.’

His wingman practically sagged with relief. ‘Thassright, *strategy*,’ he echoed defiantly, ignoring the sardonic gleam in Doyle’s eye.

‘Okay, sir.’ Burton looked bemused at this ventriloquism but gathered up her things. ‘See you in the canteen,’ she told Doyle who appeared distinctly underwhelmed by her choice of rendezvous.

‘We c’n do better than the canteen, boss.’ Noakes spoke wheedlingly after the other two had left. ‘’Sides, we’ll only run into the crowd from Vice.’ Big yawn to that. ‘An’ there’s a Costa round the corner from the tutorial place.’

‘Fine, but I want you at your winning best with the Thornfields . . . Not to mention these two mothers. No wisecracks about single parents . . . otherwise we’ll get zilch out of them.’

‘Deal,’ came the prompt response. Bagels were all very well, but the DS fancied some proper grub for elevenses. With extra sugar.

* * *

Despite Noakes laying on the charm (faintly alarming in itself), Pauline and John Thornfield remained steadfastly non-committal about the two dead women.

The interior of their office in an unremarkable terrace in Aldbourne Village was swisher than Markham had been expecting, with two conference rooms leading out of an open plan area that featured adjoining Victorian partner desks and oak filing cabinets with roller shutters. A more modest walnut two-drawer writing table was clearly the secretary’s workstation, though she was nowhere to be seen when they arrived.

‘Tracey’s just going through paperwork with parents,’ Mrs Thornfield told them. ‘Obviously this has been upsetting for everyone.’

Pretty bloody upsetting for Padgett and Dacre, too. But, mindful of his promise, Noakes did not say this.

'We're reallocating students to other tutors, so it's a question of finding the right "fit".'

Spare us the sales talk, luv.

Something about Pauline Thornfield's bright professionalism and exaggeratedly Northern vowels was getting seriously on Noakes's nerves. She was a toothy silver-haired woman whose smile did not reach her eyes; they remained wary and watchful. Well groomed, though, in a Jaeger suit with extra-large shoulder pads that fully justified Doyle's designation of her as 'boxy'. On the other hand, the Northern persona would most likely make parents feel she was the motherly type.

The husband, too, was smartly dressed. Didn't look like a wife-beater, but then they never did. Tall, dark-haired and square-jawed, he bore a disconcerting resemblance to Clark Kent. Unlike his wife's, the accent was pure BBC. Doyle had called him 'crooked' and now Markham wondered about that. Was the man hiding something or had the young DS bristled at the alpha male self-assurance? It was hard to tell.

The secretary, an anaemic blonde, emerged from one of the conference rooms with a pleasant-looking couple. 'I've completed the paperwork with Mr and Mrs Carmichael,' she said.

'Thanks, Tracey.' Pauline Thornfield dismissed her with a wave of the hand. 'You can get off now.' She then bustled forward towards the couple.

'So lovely of you to send that card,' she said to the slight, fair-haired young man whose mousy looking wife was heavily pregnant.

'It was the least we could do . . . just wanted to show our sympathy.' It was an attractive West Country accent. He turned to Markham. 'Sorry, I should have introduced myself. I'm Ritchie Carmichael and this is my wife Pat. Miss Padgett tutored our daughter Pippa. Gill Dacre was her form tutor.'

Markham regarded the pair with interest, though he sensed John Thornfield was keen to get them out of the office.

'We're the police,' Noakes said bluntly. No point fannying about while Ma Thornfield gushed over mums and dads.

'Thought as much.' Ritchie Carmichael wasn't at all put out. 'Hope you find the bastard and throw away the key.'

'You weren't aware of anyone who might have borne a grudge against either of the victims, Mr Carmichael. Fallings-out . . . a personality clash perhaps?'

The other looked bewildered.

'No, there was nothing like that. The kids were always number one with them, weren't they love?'

His faded looking wife smiled tiredly. 'They were ever so nice, both of them,' she concurred. 'When Pippa was being bullied, Miss Padgett got it sorted right away.'

After the couple had left, Markham asked to see the personnel files for tutors on the agency's books. But nothing stood out, and all their questions about the families who used the Thornfields' services met with the same bland response.

Jayne Padgett and Gill Dacre were highly valued and there had never been any major problems with either of them.

'What about these two mums who weren't in Padgett's fan club?' Noakes was done with finesse. 'Mary thingy an' Doris whatsit . . . *They* weren't so keen, were they?'

'*Michelle* Preston and *Denise* Rooney.' The proprietress bared her fangs at him. 'Storm in a teacup, Sergeant, though of course I felt obliged to mention it to your colleague.' Another toothy smile. 'In the interests of *transparency*.'

'What exactly was the problem?' Markham asked politely.

'Oh, just an excess of *caring*. As Mr Carmichael said, Jayne was *devoted* to the children . . . easy for her to get a bit *intense*.'

Noakes noticed that Superman looked ill at ease.

'What did *you* make of it?'

'Oh, I leave personnel issues to my wife,' John Thornfield said. 'Where a tutor doesn't have children of her own, there's always the risk of *possessiveness* . . .'

He was a match for his spouse when it came to over-emphasising his words.

The DS looked at the man with dislike. It was obvious that John's opinion on Jayne could be summarised as: 'She was an interfering old bag who should have kept her nose out.'

They were all done by half past two, the agency bosses having steadfastly refused to be drawn on Jayne Padgett's personal antecedents.

'We knew about the television feature,' Pauline said with an expressive moue meant to convey distaste for such vulgar exhibitionism, 'but never get involved in people's personal lives.'

Another quarter of an hour till their appointment with Michelle Preston and Denise Rooney.

'We'll just take a turn round the block,' Markham said. 'Back in fifteen minutes, yes?'

The Thornfields were more than happy to see them go.

Noakes kicked a stray pebble on the gravelled path that led to the main road. 'Well, that was a big fat zero.'

The DI looked back at the agency office where a shadow moved behind the blinds at the window.

'You can understand them being circumspect,' he said.

'She's like summat out of *Dinnerladies,* an' Superman gives me the creeps.'

Markham smiled at the moniker.

'Not enough to convict them of murder, Sergeant.'

'They'd had a run-in with Padgett,' he persisted. 'You could *tell.*' More scuffing of gravel. 'Mebbe they thought her going on the telly like that made the agency look bad.'

'On the other hand, "All PR is good PR",' Markham mused. 'Maybe the notoriety had it uses . . . But you're right, it looks like everyone's closing ranks, including the parents.'

'Betcha they got rid of anything dodgy in the paperwork before we got there.'

'More than likely.'

'Superman didn't bat an eyelid when you mentioned his previous, Guv. An' as for *her* giving it that "every marriage has its ups an' downs" baloney . . .'

‘They were ready for us, Noakes.’

Markham took deep lungfuls of the peaty autumn air which seemed to carry the scent of mulch from countless back gardens.

Normally he loved this time of year, but a feeling of discouragement weighed him down.

Noakes was now kicking up leaves with childlike abandon.

‘Them two’ll have squared the mothers,’ he said finally. ‘Freebies or discounts or what have you. Pinky an’ Perky ain’t going to say owt nasty about Padgett now.’

And it proved to be true.

‘Rough as a bear’s arse, both of ’em,’ the DS said afterwards.

‘They’re doing their best against the odds, Sergeant.’

The two women with their identikit flicky peroxide blonde manes and skin-tight trousers had struck Markham as typical single mothers whose guilt about the nine-to-five routine and the absence of a father manifested itself in excessively strident demonstrations of devotion to their offspring.

‘An’ what the frick did they mean by calling Padgett “nosy”?’ Noakes demanded. ‘Has one of ’em got some kind of secret they don’ want anyone to know about or what?’

‘It sounded as though Michelle Preston’s home life featured a procession of “uncles”,’ Markham said thoughtfully. ‘Unsettling for the children . . . possibly the teenage daughter — Chelsey, was it? — sounded off to Jayne and then reported back to mum when her teacher sympathised.’

‘Manipulative little cow.’ Noakes scowled. ‘The Denise one were jus’ plain bolshie . . . Took against Padgett for being “posh”, if you ask me.’

Markham sighed. ‘Well, whatever the set-up, they were stonewalling us with a vengeance.’

‘D’you reckon one of ’em *is* hiding summat, boss?’

‘Denise Rooney is a nurse at the Newman,’ the DI said. ‘I plan to pay the hospital a visit first thing tomorrow. It’ll give us a chance to put some feelers out . . . find out a bit more about the background as well as touching base with Professor Finlayson.’

Noakes's mouth was well turned down at the corners. He hated trips to, in his words, the "funny farm". But at least it would mean ticking one of Sidney's blooming mental health boxes.

'Then we've got the Restoricks in the afternoon,' the DI continued. 'And I want to get Simon Dacre in. We *need* a break in this case, Noakesy. At the moment, we've got sod all.'

'Mebbe Burton an' Doyle will turn up summat at Hopeless . . . s'wall to wall dipsticks up there . . . Remember the Ashley Dean case.'

'Thank you, Sergeant. As it happens, I'm trying not to.'

They headed back to the car.

The late-afternoon sun glinted off the piles of leaves that Noakes had stirred up.

'Thick as the autumnal leaves that strew the brooks

In shady Vallombrosa . . .'

Markham grinned as he recalled the way Olivia quoted these words in an ironic tone of voice whenever he referred to her students at Hope.

Suddenly he felt a lifting of his spirits.

Who knew what the others might turn up?

He owed it to Jayne Padgett and Gill Dacre to press on.

7. SHADOW PLAY

That night Markham slept badly, creeping into his study very early on Wednesday morning to take stock.

In his dreams, he had encountered an obscure figure whose face he could not see.

As the figure tried to slip past, he accused it of being a man who threw no shadow behind him.

'No, that's you,' came the startling reply. '*You* are the one who has no history.'

And then the figure vanished.

Now in the grey light of dawn, Markham sat in his swivel chair looking across at the neighbouring cemetery as it swam out of daguerreotype haziness and the outlines of graves became clear.

He *did* have a history, and the visit to Aldbourne Village had brought the past flooding back despite his best efforts to keep it tamped down in a strongbox of memories that was rarely opened.

Two roads away from the Thornfields' office was the little avenue of semi-detached properties where he had led a contented existence with his mother and brother from the ages of five to eleven. Everything after that, with the arrival of his stepfather and the family's move to the outskirts of

Bromgrove, was such darkness that he had blotted it out. Then came university and the chance of a new beginning.

Though not for his brother, long lost to drink and drugs. There had been no new dawn for *him*. And the loving mother of his childhood was just a mirage. A fallen idol.

In Markham's mind, however, Jackdaw Lane was encircled in an eternal nimbus and it was always summer there . . . Logically, of course, he knew the sun could not always have shone. Nevertheless, his strange love-dream persisted as an image of vanished happiness that had troubled him insistently until he buried it in the furthest recesses of his mind.

Now, looking out at the serried ranks of graves, he asked himself what right he had to lament the loss of those faraway days when for Jayne Padgett and Gill Dacre tomorrow would never come.

As though to underline the unreality of his sun-blessed boyhood kingdom, outside it began to rain slowly but persistently, the gutters gurgling softly in protest.

Markham sighed and wandered through to the kitchen to make himself a strong black coffee, thinking hard about the two murdered women.

Had Jayne Padgett been trying to find her way back to some mystical childhood paradise, and had that quest led to murder? Did the demons of jealousy and resentment lurk somewhere within her newfound family, eventually slipping whatever leash had held them in check? Or was she killed because of something in her professional life?

Kate Burton's visit to Hope had failed to yield anything substantive — though being Kate, this wasn't for want of trying . . .

'It seems Jayne was well-liked by the students,' was her feedback. '"Firm but fair" they said, and she took a tough line with bullies . . . bit of an agony aunt for the older girls by the sound of it, though they knew the boundaries.' In other words, there was no question of her 'getting down wiv da kidz', as Doyle put it.

They hadn't picked up on any unusual vibes when meeting pupils from Jayne Padgett's classes, although Doyle privately confided to Noakes that one lad spent the entire interview scratching his crotch, undeterred by the presence of SLT. 'Lipscombe had this sickly smile nailed to her face,' he chuckled, 'and kept wittering on about him having grommets. As if that's any excuse for playing with your nuts.'

'Matt Sullivan didn't know anything useful about the group that met in Jayne's flat,' Burton reported. 'I mean, he'd heard staff got together now and again for a whinge, but he stayed well clear.'

That figured. Both Matt and Olivia had somehow managed to stay in teaching despite loathing the politics — the backstabbing and pettiness and sucking up.

'No names then,' was the DI's glum conclusion.

'Well, he said Lipscombe and Tony Brighouse had a go at Jayne for "wasting her energies on negativity" and "conspiracy theories".'

Conspiracy theories.

Markham found this an interesting choice of words. Had Jayne Padgett stumbled across something potentially incendiary . . . something that compromised SLT?

'For what it's worth, sir, I think someone put the fear of God into the staff.' Burton's frustration had been plain. 'Even that snippy little clipboard merchant Christine Bickerton toed the party line. It was all syrupy platitudes about Jane being a "committed learning journey enabler" . . . *Yeugh*!'

It turned out Jayne hadn't confided in anyone about the Nick Critchley imbroglio. 'Probably too embarrassed by the way it all came crashing down around her ears,' Burton concluded . . .

As Markham got himself some toast, his thoughts turned to Gill Dacre.

Was she a blackmailer who fatally miscalculated, or had she inadvertently blundered into a situation that sealed her death warrant? Could it be she knew something about Jayne Padgett's family history that made her a threat to someone?

Then there was the sexual assault . . .

What had prompted the killer's necrophiliac fumbling? Fury at his own impotence or obedience to some private ritual whose significance the police had failed to grasp?

Markham's head was beginning to ache, and it wasn't even six o'clock.

And now a visit to the Newman Hospital loomed. Despite Noakes's dislike of the place, some imp of perversity had impelled Markham to select his wingman for this particular trip — a truculent desire to confront Professor Nathan Finlayson with unreconstructed Noakes.

Kate Burton would be deferential, but somehow Markham didn't want that.

It felt mean-spirited to cut his acting DI out of the action, but Noakes had a genius for flicking complacent apparatchiks on the raw and jolting them into an authentic response.

And besides, Burton and Doyle were required back at base to deal with a most unwelcome development involving Simon Dacre, the bereaved son having turned up at Hope the previous afternoon drunkenly shouting the odds about how Tony Brighouse had blood on his hands.

'Yeah, he'd had a skinful, boss,' was Doyle's laconic observation. 'Didn't get near Brighouse, but he was bursting to take a pop at him.'

'Can't say I blame the lad.' Noakes was sympathetic. 'I thought Brighouse were a right smarmy bugger . . . prob'ly covering up all sorts.'

'Dacre was ranting about the place being "awash with sexual delinquents",' Burton snapped. 'Things could have got very nasty if Matt Sullivan hadn't rugby tackled him.'

Noakes beamed approval. Sullivan might be a drama teacher, but he never spouted any of that *I-feel-your-pain* bollocks in an emergency.

Doyle grinned. 'The kids loved it . . . their eyes were out on stalks.'

DCI Sidney, on the other hand, would definitely have an apoplexy should he get to hear about what had happened.

Which was why they needed to get their ducks in a row and dampen the whole thing down. Burton could be counted on for that.

'Find out why Simon was so adamant that a student had attacked his mother,' Markham had instructed. 'Is it just the school's poor reputation for behaviour or something specific she told him about a particular incident? And press him on Brighouse & Co. Did Gill have something on SLT? If so, then we need to know about it.'

Now, his breakfast finished, Markham padded back through to his study, staring at the graveyard through its veil of drizzle.

His thoughts returned once more to Jayne Padgett.

Did the reunion with her birth mother give her some happiness in the end? Or when she saw Margaret Crompton in the cold light of day, did the expectations simply shatter into a thousand pieces? Was it ultimately a story of bitter disillusionment all round?

They needed to speak to the adoptive mother Marian Padgett just as soon as her guard dog GP allowed it. Another challenge for Burton's diplomatic skills.

Markham reached for his mobile.

* * *

The Newman Hospital, situated behind Bromgrove General, was a peculiar mix of Gothic and modernist architecture, with a Victorian clock tower flanked by grey concrete polytunnels that recalled basking sharks. Not an entirely inappropriate analogy when one considered the dangerousness of certain patients in the special hospital. Even the determinedly upbeat 'art installations' on the theme of *Voyage to Recovery* ('happy-clappy shite', Noakes called it) couldn't soften the stark aspect of the place.

Inside, the aquarium-like acoustics, deadening all sound, together with the swivelling CCTV cameras and winking sensors, made Markham feel thoroughly disorientated as

though he was entering a parallel universe. Memories of past investigations bore down heavily on him, making the experience feel even more oppressive. Noakes too was visibly discomposed, darting furtive glances left and right as they were escorted along endless linoleum-floored corridors where the squeak of their shoes sounded unnaturally loud.

The DI wondered whether, given their previous history with the Newman, it might not have been better to see Professor Finlayson at the station, but the same perverse impulse that had made him select Noakes for this assignment inclined him to keep the psychologist at a distance — as though to invite him to the station would somehow amount to an endorsement of the DCI's 'psychotic stranger' theory.

At least their destination today was merely the research centre, at the other end of the building from the top-security intensive care ward, so they were spared the metal detector arch, plexiglass and steel cell doors that made even Markham's skin crawl and that no amount of Day-Glo art or 'patient amenities' could render palatable.

The office into which they were ushered was an impersonal room looking out onto one of the 'garden spaces' which, the helpful administrator told them brightly, 'aimed to bring the outdoors indoors'. Through the window they could see a ponytailed young woman listlessly raking leaves into piles, now and again breaking off to make patterns in the compost with her feet. Markham recalled doing the same as a child and wondered if this was a gardener or patient.

Professor Nathan Finlayson appeared a few minutes later somewhat out of breath. 'Sorry, it's all about hot desking these days . . . no fixed abode, that's me.'

Noakes was less than impressed by this opening pleasantry, not least as Finlayson looked pretty much like the 'bearded twat' he and Doyle dreaded having foisted on them.

And, to cap it all, the profiler was the dead spit of Harold Shipman.

'I'm not having you on,' Noakes told Doyle later in the pub. 'Him an' Doctor Death could've been twins. Gave me

the creeps . . . An' as for his voice . . . high pitched an' squeaky like a munchkin.'

Markham, too, was taken aback by Finlayson's resemblance to the notorious serial killer. He imagined the man's students must have a field day with irreverent nicknames.

But, as they talked, he found himself warming to the academic who displayed none of the bombast or arrogance that he had steeled himself to expect. Indeed, he had a shrewd idea that Finlayson guessed the predicament he was in vis-a-vis Sidney.

'Of course, you'll be wanting to rule out psychiatric patients and sex offenders,' the profiler said quietly, his Rochdale accent very noticeable. 'The unit here can help with that . . . and there's a critical care outreach team attached to the prison which can fill in any gaps.'

'D'you reckon we're talking some local fruit loop, doc?' Noakes had never learned to speak of 'service users' or 'clients' despite being sent on endless re-education courses.

Finlayson looked appraisingly at Noakes for a long moment, evidently deciding whether to take offence at the DS's less-than-PC words.

Whatever he saw in the other's basset hound features seemed to satisfy him.

'Having reviewed the crime scene photographs you were kind enough to send over, I'd say your killer has unresolved attachment issues,' he replied.

And for folk who speak English as a first language . . . Noakes's unspoken words and exasperation seemed to fill the air between them.

'These were tidy deaths.' The profiler's words came as a surprise.

'*Tidy?* Are you having a laugh?' The DS was openly derisive. 'What about the diddling? He'd tried to have sex with 'em, for chuff's sake.'

The munchkin stood his ground. '*Unconsummated* sex, Sergeant . . . And both women were found seated . . . one at her kitchen worktop and the second victim on a park bench

. . .their bodies had been repositioned after the sexual assault, correct?'

'Yeah . . .'

Despite his frustration, Noakes could see that old beardy boots had a point. When they found Dacre, she was just like the ballet dancers he'd encountered at Bromgrove Royal Court during the Baranov murder case. The ballerinas always sat like they were riding side-saddle, with their knees and ankles lined up diagonally just so . . . Same as the female royals, though with them it was all about stopping the paparazzi getting a knicker shot . . . And it was true Jayne Padgett had been propped upright, though by the time her mate found her she'd toppled over so you couldn't see her face . . .

'Then there were the shreds of paper towel found in the vomit at the first murder site,' Finlayson continued.

'Paper towel?' The DS looked at him blankly.

'I think the killer's first impulse was to clean up the mess — as though it jarred somehow.'

'You honestly think he were worried about a bit of puke after he'd strangled the poor cow an' forced bleach down her throat? Noakes's tone was incredulous.

'Yes, I do . . . Such behaviour is not uncommon with disorganised juvenile offenders suffering from antisocial personality disorders and compulsive sexual pathologies . . . the need to re-order the scene as if they are atoning for what they've done . . . Where they have murdered a parent, there will generally be an attempt to restore parent-child signifiers.' The profiler stroked his neat black beard meditatively. 'It could mean they pose the body . . . tuck the corpse into bed or prop it up on the sofa.'

'So, if they think they've killed their mum, say, they try to make it look pretty. Neat an' tidy . . . Legs together an' nowt cruddy.' Noakes was genuinely trying to make sense of this new language, his brow corrugating with the effort.

'Exactly like that, Sergeant.' The professor's tone was kind. It was obvious to Markham that Finlayson had warmed to his shambling, outspoken number two. It was somehow

always the way whenever he deployed Noakes, the DS getting straight to the heart of the matter without any frills or 'fannying about'.

'Given that the victims were both teachers, should we be looking for a teenaged male, Professor?' the DI asked. 'A student perhaps?'

Finlayson deliberated.

'As to that, I couldn't say, Inspector. It's certainly possible . . . Or the killer could be an adult who bears significant mental scars from some childhood trauma or emotional upheaval during adolescence.' He paused. 'I gather the first victim's family background is somewhat complicated . . . tensions between the adoptive family and blood relatives . . .'

You ain't wrong. Noakes's scowl deepened.

Finlayson steepled his elegant musician's fingers that were at odds with his otherwise homely appearance and regarded the two detectives levelly. 'From the crime scene photographs, both victims appeared to be wearing freshly applied lipstick.'

Noakes stared.

'*Come again?*' he said. 'Are you telling me he went all Avon lady an' whipped out a makeup bag? *Jesus.*'

The DI could tell Noakes was remembering the New College Close case.

God, Markham thought with a sharp sensation of dismay, this investigation was veering perilously close to the kind of "far out" dysfunctionality guaranteed to bring Sidney out in a rash.

'Do you mean the killer could have a fixation with conventional mother figures?' Markham enquired, thinking that if so, this was hardly likely to narrow the field.

'Yes. As I say, the suspect could be a traumatised juvenile or an adult with arrested development most likely resulting from an abusive or co-dependent relationship with a parent.' Finlayson allowed this to sink in before continuing. 'The PM reports on both deceased suggested that there may have been an attempt to close their eyes, though bilateral ptosis precluded such an outcome in the case of the second victim.'

‘Cos the killer couldn’t stand to have ’em looking at him, is that it?’ Noakes demanded. ‘Wanted to pretend they were sleeping?’

‘That’s a feasible interpretation, Sergeant.’

‘Could it be a woman?’ Markham asked quietly.

‘It could, yes.’

‘Even with the diddling?’ Noakes’s voice practically rose an octave.

‘Yes, even then . . . In fact, the impulse to normalise the crime scene might derive from a strong sense of self-disgust at any transgressive behaviour.’

‘Would you say it’s more likely to be someone young, doc?’ Noakes wanted Finlayson to nail his colours to the mast.

‘The sexual element would give much more pleasure earlier in life than later on,’ Finlayson answered. ‘On the other hand, the sexual element might only be hinted at in the early stages of a spree . . . not properly explored until later, once the killer has refined their methods.’

Noakes looked as though he wished he hadn’t asked while Markham, with a sinking feeling, registered the ominous reference to a ‘spree’.

‘Sexuality is expressed in many different ways, Sergeant,’ the professor explained, registering Noakes’s queasy expression. ‘For most of us, it involves direct contact with a partner. But for people who are unusual, it could mean sexual contact with someone who has just died. Where there has been an abusive background, a dysfunctional parent-child relationship, there may be an element of revenge . . . punishment of the mother figure.’

‘An’ you think summat like that went on here?’ Noakes wrestled with the scenario. ‘But he, she . . . couldn’t go all the way for some reason . . .’

‘It’s important to remember that sexual fulfilment can be a cerebral and mental experience, with no physical contact at all.’

Markham bit down on the laughter. A less likely practitioner of ‘Sex in the Head’ than George Noakes it would

be difficult to imagine. From the way he was looking at the profiler, it was obvious that Professor Nathan Finlayson had shot to the top of his wingman's all time pervs list.

What the hell was going on with these two murders, the DI asked himself. He didn't believe the dominant impulse was sexual, but this conversation with Finlayson inclined him to believe that the 'diddling', like the bleach, was not merely part of some attempt by the killer to send them in the wrong direction but derived from an aberrant sexual kink that could not be repressed.

'Of course, the high associated with murder can be akin to a sexual high,' Finlayson said in conclusion with a benign smile that did not exactly reassure the two detectives.

The DI recalled the need for some rear-guard action to propitiate Sidney. 'I take it you'll be looking for relevant indicators in the local databases, Professor?'

Was it Markham's imagination or did he detect sympathy in the academic's expression?

'Certainly, Inspector, we'll cross-reference using a range of key traits, though my feeling is that this isn't in fact a case of stranger homicide and your murderer will prove to be known to the victims.'

'Are you prepared to go on the record with that, Professor, seeing as my DCI rather likes the idea of a faceless killer?' the DI enquired deadpan.

As in one with no connection to Hope Academy or any other civic institution.

Finlayson chuckled. It was an unmelodious sound. Like he had a strangulated hernia, as Noakes informed DS Doyle afterwards in the Grapes.

'There are too many variables for me to be that precise, Inspector.'

Why am I not surprised? Noakes looked disgusted. *Typical boffin. Let's just sit on the fricking fence!*

The professor met Noakes's eyes squarely.

'I'm not hedging my bets, Sergeant. Nor am I interested in cosying up to your superiors.'

That'll be a first! Noakes's face expressed a rooted unwillingness to relinquish his fondly held prejudices. Such as a belief that *force majeure* in the shape of Sidney and his CID cronies was bound to prevail over common sense.

Finlayson spoke soberly, and something in his manner chilled Markham's blood.

'You're looking for someone who is likely to kill again, Inspector.'

'Cos they've got a taste for it or what?' demanded Noakes.

'Because they can't turn back,' came the measured reply. 'They'll do anything to keep their secret . . . whatever it is.'

* * *

'Dead ringer for Shipman,' Noakes burst out after they had left the hospital and were walking back to Markham's car.

'The resemblance hadn't escaped me, Sergeant,' came the wry reply.

'Come to think of it, ain't that what ole Shippers did when he went round finishing off wrinklies, tried to keep everything neat an' tidy . . . sat them in an armchair with a cup of tea an' a ciggy in the ash tray next to 'em, TV on an' the fire going . . . dead methodical, like.'

Markham found some relief in being distracted by his sergeant dipping into the *True Crime* files. When Noakes did not happen to be exasperating, his digressions could be rather informative.

'That's right,' he said slowly. 'Shipman was supposed to have "dressed the death scene", wasn't he?'

'Yeah.' Noakes grew animated. 'He allus tole the rellies it were "a nice way to go". My missus has jus' finished reading a book about him,' he added bashfully.

The DI was pretty sure Muriel Noakes would prefer not to have it known that she was an aficionado of the serial-killer genre, but felt some curiosity as to that redoubtable lady's verdict on Dr Shipman.

'Super Doc thought he were on a mission of mercy,' Noakes continued. 'Y'know doing the old folk a favour by killing 'em.'

'Wasn't there a school of thought that said he'd been traumatised by watching his mother die of cancer?'

The DS waggled his bushy eyebrows expressively. 'Yeah, proper mummy's boy. Never got over her dying when he were a teenager . . . seeing the GP come round every afternoon to inject her with morphine for the pain . . . well, it messed with his head . . .'

'You mean, he became obsessed with putting sick people out of their misery?'

'Sort of, but he did younger ones too . . . the missus said there were this case in Todmorden when he were jus' starting out . . . he injected this girl with pethidine . . . Anyway, the kid came round an' he were doing the kiss of life like some kind of loony. Summat went wrong so he panicked and didn't end up killing her.'

'Very interesting, Noakes.' Markham leaned wearily against his car, glad of the autumn chill after the antiseptic airlocks and oxygen-less corridors of the hospital.

Reluctantly he turned his thoughts back to their own investigation. 'Professor Finlayson's theory about the murderer having a mother complex is interesting and it should yield no end of potential misfits to dangle in front of Sidney, but it doesn't get us any nearer narrowing down our list of suspects. I mean,' the DI's tone turned heavily ironic, 'it's not as if any of them are likely to be forthcoming about their psychiatric history or admit to having a hang-up about their mother.'

The two men got into the car and Markham wrestled briefly with the refractory heater while Noakes pondered some more.

'Someone with a thing about older woman, then,' he said hopefully. 'Needs 'em but resents it . . . Like Tricky Dicky with Padgett . . . You said it yourself, guv, he wanted her all to himself, like she were his mum or summat.'

‘*Hmmm.*’

‘Or a kid from Hope, someone Padgett made dependent on her but then summat went wrong . . . p’raps they got too, er, friendly an’ she showed ’em the door.’

‘Remember, the professor said our offender could be either male or female.’

‘Don’ see Padgett as a lezzer, boss, even if her clothes looked a bit that way.’

‘That wouldn’t necessarily stop a female pupil developing a crush, especially if there was a lack of nurturing at home.’

‘*Nah* . . . They’d need their eyes testing.’ The DS saw the world in black and white, no room for shades in between. ‘An’ anyway, Deirdre Rooney said there were nowt like that going on with her kid . . . went red as a turkey-cock when you brought it up.’

‘*Denise*, Sergeant.’ Markham’s hands tightened on the steering wheel as he recalled the psychiatric nurse’s aggressive reaction after they swung by the Newman’s adolescent health department on their way out. ‘But yes it looked like I touched a nerve there . . . though whether it was just histrionic indignation at my floating the issue of inappropriate relationships or something deeper remains to be seen. Her daughter and Chelsey Preston were amongst the students Kate and Doyle interviewed . . . we may need to look at them again.’

‘Well, it’s the parents of that special needs kid this arvo,’ Noakes said. ‘The ones who kept whingeing about Padgett.’

‘John and Shona Restorick.’ The DI’s voice was toneless. ‘As in the friends of DCI Sidney’s wife.’

‘No way you wanna be facing *that* without fuelling up, Guv,’ Noakes said craftily. ‘There’s a Subway two blocks away.’

The DI knew when he was outmanoeuvred. And to be honest, the thought of a strong coffee before facing the Restoricks rather appealed — even if that meant watching Noakes chomp his way through a meatball marinara or some such while delivering a scurrilous running commentary on their colleagues in Fraud and Vice.

‘You’re on,’ he said.

'Champion.' With the alluring prospect of a Subway 'whopper' secured, the DS continued to mull the imponderables of their current investigation.

'D'you really think it could be a woman, guv?'

'Professor Finlayson wasn't ruling it out, Noakes.'

'She'd need muscles to lug 'em around like that . . .'

'I don't think it would require a huge amount of strength,' Markham replied thoughtfully. 'The bodies weren't moved any great distance.'

'Mebbe there were two of 'em in on it . . .'

Markham's expression darkened at the thought of co-conspirators.

'We can't put any one of our suspects in the frame as yet,' he groaned. 'Let alone two'.

The DS looked at his boss.

'You're fed up after all that psychology waffle,' he observed philosophically. 'It'll be better once you've got a bacon butty inside you.'

'Thank you, Doctor Noakes.'

The other winked at him.

'You know it makes sense.'

Markham smiled in spite of himself. George Noakes was the throwback to end all throwbacks — 'a complete bloody Neanderthal', as Superintendent Collier once put it. But nobody else suited him in quite the same way or was so adroit at shrugging off the encircling guy ropes of CID's upper echelons . . . The DS simply stuck two fingers up at the lot of them, caring about one thing only.

How to get their man.

* * *

The thought of co-conspirators and evil couplings crossed the DI's mind later as he bade farewell to John and Shona Restorick.

In truth, they were perfectly respectable, as one might expect given their friendship with the DCI's wife.

Markham hadn't warmed to them, however, finding something cold and off-putting about the pair — clearly older parents and both small of stature, with standard blue rinse for the lady and silver fox (in his dreams at any rate) for mister.

Noakes didn't hold back. 'Their Liberty,' for such was the child's name, 'sounds a right pain in the backside . . . an' a flaming hypochondriac into the bargain . . . All that about Padgett making her psoriasis flare up . . . *Kerr-ist!*'

He clocked the guvnor's wintry expression.

'Sorry boss, but it's obvious the kid's a lard bucket an' a flipping attention seeker. Well done to Miss for putting the sprog back in her box.'

The DI frowned. 'What they said was at odds with the feedback about Ms Padgett's professional objectivity.'

'So, she had a bit of a downer on the kid . . . *So what?*' It was somewhat amusing to hear Noakes become the teacher's passionate defender. 'You can't love 'em all an' it sounds like no matter what Padgett did it wouldn't have been enough for Princess Tippytoes.'

'Those parents didn't like Jayne Padgett,' the DI said. 'Not one bit.'

Noakes shrugged expressively. 'Horses for courses,' he retorted. 'An' anyway, they couldn't come up with owt specific.'

'Mrs Restorick looked as if she wanted to say something,' the DI observed. 'As though she was on the point of telling us something and then thought better of it.'

'Liberty's BMI,' the DS chortled.

'Stow it, Sergeant.' But Markham's tone was abstracted. 'We need to have another crack at those students.'

'Burton's best for that.' No way did Noakes want to mix it with Hope's 'cary shary' SLT.

'Talk of the devil,' he muttered as the acting inspector appeared in the doorway.

'Simon Dacre's ready for you, sir,' she said. 'And after that, we can review the Nick Critchley stuff for tomorrow.'

'Excellent, Kate. By the way, any luck getting hold of the *Roundup* tape?'

At this she looked troubled. 'Apparently, it's gone walkabout, sir . . . I'm leaning on them but trying to be discreet about it.'

'No matter,' the DI told her kindly. 'I read your report which gave me a clear picture . . . But if we *can* locate it, that might be useful. 'Another pair of eyes and all that.'

'Absolutely,' she nodded vigorously. Then, 'Anything useful from Professor Finlayson and the Restoricks, sir?'

With a malicious grin, the DI replied, 'Noakes is eager to fill you in, Kate.'

The DS was looking daggers, but Markham continued smoothly, 'Interesting parallels with the Shipman case. Isn't that right, Noakesy?'

And with that, he exited his office en route to the custody suite.

8. BESET ON ALL SIDES

'So you didn't get anything useful from Simon Dacre then, Gil?'

It was Thursday 22 October, and Markham and Olivia were enjoying the rare treat of a late lunch together on the first floor of Waterstones in the town centre. Outside it was blowing a gale, but the café area was cosy and practically deserted, with no risk of their being ambushed by colleagues from the station or Hope. They had both got back late the previous night and were glad of the chance to catch up.

'I love these tub chairs,' she said, snuggling into the deep red leather seat. 'So comfortable.'

On the low table in front of them were two steaming macchiatos and cheese toasties.

She sighed blissfully and helped herself to a hearty mouthful. '*Such* an improvement on our canteen and the smell of soggy cabbage.' She smiled, before returning to the matter at hand. 'Why was Simon so convinced that a *student* had attacked his mum?'

Olivia now knew about the sexual elements of the killings, Markham having shared this information with her after the discovery of Gill Dacre's body. But Simon's wild-eyed accusations had come as a shock.

Markham, too, was enjoying his toastie, a vast improvement on the anaemic sandwiches, curling at the edges, which was the best he could have hoped for back at base.

'Dacre was all over the place, shouting about Lipscombe and Brighouse being vindictive bullies.'

Olivia grinned. 'I wouldn't argue with that assessment,' she said. 'Mind you, Gill knew how to play the game. If management told her to jump, she'd want to know how high.'

'He said there was nothing they wouldn't do to feather their own nests.'

'Yep, I'm with him on that too.'

Markham raised his eyebrows. '*Corruption*?'

'*They'd* most likely call it "creative accounting".'

'He accused them of cover-ups and misleading Ofsted while he was at it.'

'Par for the course, Gil.' She sipped her drink thoughtfully. 'Did he say what they were supposed to have covered up?'

'Dark hints that it was something sexual — no idea whether he meant teachers were at it with each other or if he was talking about paedophilic activity.' Markham grimaced. 'He threw up all over the custody sergeant before we could get down to the nitty gritty.'

'Crikey.' Olivia was startled. 'What happened once he'd sobered up?'

'He was massively embarrassed,' Markham replied. 'Back-tracked big style . . . And yet,' his eyes were troubled, 'as he was leaving, he mumbled something about us having no idea what the kids at Hope were capable of. "But no idea" were his words.'

Olivia frowned. 'And that was it . . . ? He didn't explain what he meant?'

'No. I think he was desperate to get out of the station. But there was something about the way he said it . . .'

'Makes you wonder if Gill knew about something iffy going on in the school . . . She was the kind who listened at doors.'

‘Well, apparently SLT castigated Jayne Padgett about seeing conspiracies where there weren’t any.’

‘Conspiracies.’ Olivia took a long draught of macchiato. ‘That’s a pretty strong word,’ she said finally. Then, ‘Maybe it was something involving Gill . . .’

‘God knows.’ Markham sounded exasperated. ‘Burton’s reviewing what we got from the students, to see if anything jumps out. Then we may have another crack at them.’

His partner looked dubious.

‘Brighouse and Lipscombe will batten down the hatches,’ she said. ‘And Lipscombe’ll definitely start screeching about “oppressive behaviour” given half a chance.’

‘More than likely,’ he said glumly.

She tried to cheer him up. ‘Have you heard the one about the guest going home after a wedding reception.’

A smile played about the corners of his mouth. ‘Go on.’

‘She was pulled over by the police for erratic driving and the policeman cautioned her, “Whatever you say, I shall write it down and read it back in court.” To which she replied, “Please don’t hit me again with your truncheon, officer.”’

Markham chuckled. ‘Definitely a witness in the Judith Lipscombe mould.’

Olivia was relieved to see him looking brighter.

For a time, they enjoyed their toasties and drinks in companionable silence, savouring the peaceful atmosphere and the absence of bustle.

‘It’s such a strange investigation,’ Markham said at length. ‘A tale of two halves, really, and nothing seems to fit.’

He filled her in on the interview with the profiler and Noakes’s guided tour of the Harold Shipman case.

‘Dr Shipman was “Fred” to his friends, wasn’t he?’ she said idly.

Markham laughed. ‘Oh well, I’d say Noakesy qualifies as an intimate. He was a veritable mine of information . . . courtesy of Muriel.’

Olivia choked on her drink. ‘She won’t be pleased George let *that* slip . . . Bet she hides her serial-killer books

under Dickens and Tolstoy at the library.' Then, thoughtfully, she continued, 'That point about *tidy* deaths is interesting, though . . . and what your professor said about a possible mother fixation.'

'Oh, Kate Burton was in the seventh heaven of delight when she heard about it,' he grinned. 'Whipped out her trusty *DSM* before I could say "Adult Attachment Disorders". Luckily Nick Critchley's arrival called a halt to her research, otherwise I think Noakes or Doyle might have brained her with it.'

Olivia giggled. 'How did you get on with Critchley?'

'Well, he's personable and suave . . . though close up you can see the drinking has taken a toll,' Markham said thinking of those handsome features now blurred by the battle with alcohol. 'Didn't come across as bitter and twisted about the way Jayne torpedoed his career . . . Mind you, as a TV personality, he'd be an expert at hiding his feelings.'

'Any alibi for the murders?'

'Just his brother, so not the strongest.'

She was watching him closely. 'Do you see Critchley for it?'

'Noakes said afterwards he thought he was hiding something.'

'George's dislike wouldn't have anything to do with Critchley's debonair good looks and TV profile by any chance?'

Markham smiled. 'He trotted out the old "his eyes are too close together" number, but no . . . I think it was more than Noakesy's ingrained mistrust of "slebs". Kate and Doyle picked up on it, too.' He chewed meditatively on the last gooey piece of his toastie, thinking hard. 'It was when Kate mentioned having watched a tape of the programme . . . She was talking about how hard the half-sisters — Angela Studholme and Valerie Holmes — must have found it, not to mention Jayne's adoptive parents, and how tricky it made things for Jayne at school. Then Doyle said no one really knows what goes on in families. That's when Critchley

clammed up . . . the body language turned all twitchy and evasive, and he was just suddenly mad keen to get away.'

'And you couldn't work out what was bugging him?' Olivia asked, intrigued.

'We went over the interview afterwards, but nothing leaped out at us. One minute he was all relaxed and casual . . . then the next minute the shutters had come down.'

'Maybe he was embarrassed thinking back about it all . . . the big career screw-up, his reputation in freefall, that kind of thing.'

Markham considered this.

'It was more that he looked stunned . . . like he was having some sort of lightbulb moment . . . I decided to call it a day, because it was obvious we weren't going to get anything else out of him.'

'Could be the enormity of it all is hitting him,' Olivia suggested. 'Two women dead and one of them the subject of his last ever exposé.'

'Possibly.' Markham sounded uneasy.

'Or he could just have been posing, Gil . . . trying to make himself look more important by going all mysterious and enigmatic. I mean, he was known for being a bit of a git, after all.'

Markham grinned at this summing up then turned serious again.

'I advised him he needed to be absolutely frank with us. The brother was sitting out front waiting to drive him back to Anglesey, so at least he's got someone with him. Kate's going to check in with them as soon as they're back home.'

Olivia nodded then stretched luxuriously.

'Bit of a luxury, this. I feel like a prisoner out on parole. When Matt offered to take over my shift for Immersion Day, I could have kissed him!'

'What's one of them when it's at home?'

'Oh, it's all a bit of a con really. We take a break from lessons and do 'creative learning' stuff round themes like the environment or bullying . . . personally, I think it's a load of virtue-signalling cobblers, but hey what do I know?'

Markham looked at her quizzically. 'What does Matt think about it?'

'Same as me but being an assistant head, he has to play along with it . . . *literally* play along, the poor sod. At any rate, he felt I deserved a break after last year when it took me three hours to clean up my classroom and comfort the sobbing NQT the kids had locked in the storeroom next door.'

Markham burst out laughing, causing the café attendant to glance over at them in surprise.

'Well, I'll get us more drinks,' he offered. 'To celebrate your escape.'

'And a chocolate muffin.' When it came to putting away the calories, despite her willowy frame, Olivia was more than a match for Noakes.

Once they were settled, she said, 'Your mentioning Shipman reminded me — any joy with Marian Padgett's GP? Is he still blocking you from speaking to her?'

'I went round with Kate yesterday evening and it was still no dice. A neighbour was there, and she told us the GP said no visitors.' Markham grimaced. 'Looks like the lady has friends in high places. Jayne's memorial requiem is at St Jude's on Monday evening.'

Startled, Olivia paused with the muffin halfway to her mouth.

'How did she wangle that? It's only been a week.'

'The body isn't being released, but the service can still go ahead.'

'Oh, I see.' Olivia tucked into her muffin, mulling this information. 'Something like that happened when Princess Diana died, didn't it? There was the big state funeral in Westminster Abbey, but her mother and the Catholic mafia had their own mass beforehand in Westminster Cathedral.'

'It's unusual but there are precedents all right.' Markham paused. 'There's to be a casket, though . . . extraneous tissue samples from Jayne's PM and some of her adoptive father's ashes.'

'That's seriously creepy, Gil.'

'It's somewhat macabre, yes. But everything's been signed off and at least we'll get to meet the elusive Mrs Padgett afterwards.' He sipped his macchiato with a sombre expression. 'We could have forced the issue when we called yesterday, but I don't want to alienate the family at this point.'

'And at least you know where she is.'

'Well, the neighbours have a rota organised, so there are eyes on her.' He sighed. 'The incident with Simon Dacre didn't go down well with Sidney, so the last thing I need is another relative kicking off.'

'That jobsworth Lipscombe must've got straight on the blower,' Olivia said sympathetically. 'She always squeals like a stuck pig when anything threatens her precious image.'

'She and Sidney are on the same page when it comes to making sure Hope doesn't get mixed up in any unsavoury fall-out from the investigation.'

'Do you think Hope *is* involved somehow, Gil?' Olivia twirled a loose strand of red hair round and round her finger, a habit when something bothered her. 'I mean you've got two female teachers from the same school who end up horribly murdered and then the son of one of them starts pointing the finger at "weirdo" kids . . .'

Markham knew his partner had been assigned any number of problem classes.

'Do *you* see any pupil from Hope as being capable of something so awful, Liv?'

'I suppose I should be able to answer that, considering the number of "dump" groups I've been given over the years.' Her voice was steely. 'SLT are like politicians the way they dress it up by saying it's a chance to "gain varied experience" when what they're really doing is making sure *they* don't have to teach the problematic students . . . Plus it's a crafty way of pressurising older more expensive staff into leaving cos you can only take so many years of dealing with headbangers.' A grim chuckle. 'I'm prepared to die at my post just to spite them.'

‘Is it really that bad?’

She registered his frown of concern.

‘You know me, Gil. Typical English teacher . . . the queen of hyperbole.’ She weighed her words. ‘Look, I like most of Hope’s Bash Street Kids and haven’t come across too many really nasty ones. But I couldn’t speak for everyone. Sometimes staff get saddled with what are called “intervention” or “nurture” groups where the behaviour can be truly vile . . . Or if you’re a form tutor, sometimes you end up doing social worker stuff if a kid’s got mental health problems or something’s gone wrong at home.’

‘Sounds like a minefield,’ her boyfriend said sympathetically.

‘*It is.*’ This was uttered with feeling. ‘Maybe Jayne got in over her head — somehow touched a nerve with some youngster who was troubled . . .’

‘Sounds like we’re back in attachment disorder territory?’

‘Or perhaps we’re talking someone who had issues around mother figures.’ Olivia glanced uneasily around the café which was starting to fill up with some late-afternoon trade. ‘But where does Gill Dacre fit in? Did the same pattern repeat itself with her, as in did she make the same mistake and mishandle a pastoral situation? Or did a pupil with some undiagnosed psychiatric disorder just go after two teachers because something about them set him off? It seems incredible, really . . . cos there are usually red flags that pop up with volatile kids.’

‘Could Gill have found something out and then tried to talk the killer into turning himself in . . . but she lost control of the situation?’

‘I’m sure she’d have seen the danger with that scenario, Gil. And anyway, it wouldn’t sit right with her. But I *can* imagine her doing some private detecting and getting it wrong . . .’

Markham leaned forward eagerly. ‘As in having suspicions about someone and trying to do something off her own bat?’

'Ye-es . . . maybe she discussed it with someone without realising they were the killer.'

'Hmm. That's what Kate thought might have happened.' Markham massaged his neck as though bowed down by an invisible yoke. 'But then there's the whole weird set-up with Jayne Padgett's family — lots of ill-feeling, even hatred, swirling around . . . and Gill Dacre probably came across most of them seeing as she lived in Aldbourne Village. So maybe *that's* the key to it all. After all, the teaching agency people were adamant there were no issues with Padgett and Dacre on the teaching front. The worst anyone came up with was Jayne being a bit of a busybody . . . oh yes, and the Restoricks grousing that she had a down on their kid . . . something and nothing by the sound of it.'

'Occupational hazard,' Olivia agreed. 'And you're right, the long-lost family thing sounds a real can of worms. Not that Hope isn't a snake pit,' she added with a glint in her eye, 'but it just seems like Jayne's personal circumstances had the potential to blow up in her face.'

Olivia suddenly looked downcast, her vibrant features clouded with distress.

'Jayne was a kind woman,' she said. 'I just can't get my head round the idea of her making any kid angry enough to want to kill her.'

'As a theory, it's definitely a stretch,' Markham agreed. 'But there's something *not right* at Hope. I could almost feel it in the air at that assembly.' He forced himself to sound casual. 'Promise me you'll take care, Liv. No risks, okay?' He hesitated. 'Maybe you could steer clear of any one-on-ones until we've nailed our murderer?'

'Alright,' she replied slowly. 'If it could happen to Jayne . . .'

'That seems to be the general reaction,' Markham went on. 'We ran into a couple, the Carmichaels, at the teaching agency who had nothing but praise for both teachers, they said Jayne was a star when their daughter was being bullied.'

He pulled a face. 'The two single mums we spoke to weren't as fulsome.'

'Oh, I know the Carmichaels — she was a primary school teacher before getting married. It can be trickier with single parent families, they're often more defensive, like they think you're secretly critical of them.'

'Well, Mesdames Preston and Rooney didn't give us an inch.'

Olivia pulled a face. '*Those two* . . . Chelsey Preston's a poisonous little character.'

'I thought as much. The mother certainly didn't like us skirting around the issue of Sapphic tendencies.'

Olivia giggled. 'I'd have paid good money to see that interview. Take it from me, Gil, the fair Chelsey is a man-eater in the making.' She winked at Markham. 'Currently getting her hand in with the lads of 9T.'

He threw her a reproving glance, but the tenderness in it was unmistakeable.

Suddenly his mobile rang.

'Damn, I knew this idyll was too good to last.'

The conversation was short and to the point.

'That was Noakes,' he said at its conclusion. 'He's had a report of a fire at Hope.'

She caught the look on his face. '*Arson.* My god, something must have gone badly wrong with Immersion Day . . . usually it's just vandalism and threatening behaviour.'

'I have a feeling there might be more to it than that, Liv. It started in Jayne Padgett's classroom.'

* * *

Standing outside Hope Academy a short time later, Markham reflected as he always did that the building was seriously ugly . . . a soulless sixties battery farm for disaffected youth. Little wonder that Olivia and Matt commonly referred to it as 'the bunker' or 'the gulag'. Whatever the remit of the Building

Fund Appeal that Sidney had mentioned, it certainly had its work cut out.

The stormy weather had abated, and watery sunshine was struggling to break through, gilding the bank of trees that separated the building from Bromgrove South Municipal Cemetery on the other side of the school drive. The burnished horse chestnuts were the one true beauty in the landscape so no doubt, he reflected sourly, Mrs Sidney and her myrmidons had already earmarked them for the chop.

Noakes emerged from the entrance foyer trailed by Judith Lipscombe and Simon McLeish the laconic sandy-haired fire chief whose dour Northern Irish accent belied a wryly humorous personality. It was clear from the look McLeish shot Hope's assistant head that he could well have dispensed with her presence.

'False alarm, Inspector,' she said before either of the other two said a word. 'Looks like some of our pupils got *carried away* with the fun.' A determinedly caring smile. 'Immersion Day is all about multi-sensory engagement and thinking outside the box—'

'With a cigarette lighter in this case by the look of things,' McLeish put in.

Lipscombe's expression of marshmallow sweetness did not crack, but there was pure steel behind it.

'It's all about *trust*, you see . . . allowing young people to express themselves and explore boundaries in a controlled environment.'

'Can't have been that bleeding controlled,' Noakes rumbled. 'Seeing as they nearly started the towering inferno right under your nose.'

Lipscombe favoured him with a disdainful glance. Inspector Markham was very much her idea of a CID officer, but this sergeant in his awful baggy clothes (she was sure he was wearing a *vest* under that lurid yellow sweater) looked like some kind of vagrant . . . or the sort of undesirable who lurked by their playing fields ogling Hope's female pupils.

Presumably the man had hidden talents, but she was hard pushed to discern them.

With studied graciousness, she continued, 'Miss Padgett's room was meant to stay locked for the time being. Unfortunately, one of the PE department,' a theatrical roll of the eyes as though to say *what else can you expect from that lot*, 'opened it by mistake.'

'Prob'ly wanted somewhere to hide.'

McLeish smothered a grin at Noakes's aside.

Lipscombe bulldozed on with the damage limitation. 'Miss Padgett's room is on the ground floor and set up with multiple resources for *play* and drama activities. She was the designated nurture lead, you see.'

From the look on Noakes's face, the woman might as well have been talking Swahili.

Markham hastily translated.

'Ah yes, I believe she was a special needs practitioner.'

'Oh *right*, the retards.' Noakes beamed. 'Now I get you.'

The DI cringed. It didn't matter how many diversity courses Noakes attended, his un-PC vernacular never changed. And yet Markham remembered the rapport Noakes struck up with students during the Ashley Dean murder investigation — the way, like Guinness, he reached the parts others couldn't reach. Kate Burton never dropped a politically incorrect clanger, but Hope's youngsters would never have responded to her like they did to Noakes . . .

Mercifully, Judith Lipscombe operated on a principle of selective hearing, sailing regally on as though Noakes hadn't spoken.

'It looks like one of the Year Tens became a tad *over-exuberant*. Our exclusion manager raised the alarm when she was checking the ground floor classrooms after lunch . . . But all's well that ends well. Obviously, in the circumstances, we moved the children to the sports hall and dismissed them by year group.'

Markham's iron-clad courtesy was well to the fore.

‘Thank you so much for your assistance, Ms Lipscombe. As you say, it looks like disaster was averted through the quick thinking of your colleague. We’ll take it from here.’

He bowed her gravely in the direction of the entrance lobby with a mixture of charm and firmness that was impossible to resist.

Noakes watched the retreating figure with bemusement. ‘What’s an exclusion manager?’

‘The one who gets to deal with the problematic kids before they get booted out,’ McLeish informed him.

‘*Jesus* . . . What’s with all the fancy titles. In my day, it were the head and deputy head . . . An’ everyone knew what was what, including the scrotes,’ he added darkly.

‘Ah well, that’s the brave new world of twenty-first-century education for you, Sergeant,’ the fireman said deadpan. ‘All must have prizes . . . including school staff.’

Before they could embark on further philosophical debate, Markham said, ‘What’s your take on this, McLeish? Just a prank gone wrong, or something more sinister?’

‘The exclusion manager panicked and called 999 when she spotted smoke on the ground floor.’ McLeish grinned. ‘The assistant head or whoever she is had things in hand by the time we got here. Nothing to worry about and all that. Given that it was Hope and the potential connection with your murder investigation, I got tipped off about it.’

Markham picked up on something in the other’s manner.

‘What is it?’

McLeish produced a crumpled piece of paper.

‘I spotted this next to the teacher’s desk,’ he said.

Markham scanned the scrawled obscenities before passing it to Noakes.

‘What did Ms Lipscombe have to say about it?’ the DI asked.

‘Said she had no idea where it came from . . . insisted it had to be connected with some sort of role play or free

association exercise blah blah.' McLeish clearly had a similar viewpoint to Noakes where such activities were concerned.

'Role play, my *arse*! It calls Padgett every name under the sun an' says they had it coming.' Noakes was disbelieving. 'How the chuff could Eva Braun pretend this had owt to do with schoolwork?'

'I had forensics do a sweep of Ms Padgett's classroom as part of the initial evidence trawl,' Markham said. 'There was no sign of it then.'

He was suddenly revisited by an unwelcome recollection of the youth caught skulking near Cabot Court before making off into the night . . .

Was it conceivable that their killer could be a *teenager*? The very idea sent chills up his spine.

'Most likely it's just some kid with a sick sense of humour.' But McLeish too looked uneasy.

Noakes was glowering at the building behind them. 'How come the fire alarms didn't go off?'

'Not working for some reason.' McLeish's expression was grim. 'I'll be looking into that. But I'd say this wasn't arson — more like it was just some kid messing about . . . they legged it through the window when they heard the exclusion woman screeching in the corridor.' He scanned Hope's facade with a shrewd gaze. 'Whoever got busy with the cigarette lighter wasn't necessarily the same kid who scribbled that stuff about the teachers . . .'

'So, you reckon there's *two* nutters on the loose . . . That makes me feel *so* much better,' Noakes retorted with heavy sarcasm.

McLeish smiled wryly. He was used to George Noakes letting off steam, or 'venting' as caring Judith Lipscombe would doubtless have put it.

'Would the fire have got out of control if it hadn't been spotted?' Markham asked.

'No. This one was too small, just a couple of paper towel spills in the bottom of the bin. On the other hand,

if Laughing Larry hadn't been interrupted.' He gestured expressively as his words hung in the air.

* * *

Back at their cars, the two detectives took stock.

'I don't like this,' the DI said. 'I don't like it at all. Seems to me that the fire-setter and poison pen are one and the same person.'

'Trying to draw attention to themselves . . . *acting out,* the psychologists call it.'

'Indeed?' Markham suppressed a smile at his sergeant referencing the medical science.

'Yeah. We were wondering if it could be a kid did the murders . . . Burton were full of that Mary Bell while you were out at lunch, y'know, the lass who were eleven when she killed them two toddlers.'

His voice was gruff, and Markham recalled with amusement how the two vastly different colleagues had bonded over their shared fascination with true-crime documentaries.

'What did Kate have to say about Mary Bell?'

'Jus' that she broke into the local nursery after murdering the first kid an' scrawled graffiti saying she'd done it. Then she kept popping up all over the show, pestering the family an' asking if she could see the little lad in his coffin . . . She even boasted about being a murderer in the playground at school an' drew weirdy pictures in her school exercise book . . .'

'But nobody took any notice?' Markham prompted.

'Well, not until she killed the second one.'

'I take it Kate thinks there are some parallels with our investigation?'

'She said Mary Bell sort of tried to tidy up after one of 'em . . . piled up bricks or summat round him as if she were tucking him into bed . . . said he'd wake up in time for tea — kind of like she were in denial about what had happened.

Big time.' Noakes shuffled his feet. 'S'like the way our two were left . . .'

'From what I recall of the Mary Bell case, there was a profoundly dysfunctional mother who dabbled in prostitution.'

The DI stared into space, deep in thought. *There it was again*. That motif of the mother.

But they couldn't be sure the one they sought was a child . . .

The sun had gone in and it was starting to get cold. It seemed to Markham that the bunker regarded them with supercilious indifference.

'Let's get back to the station,' he said. 'We'll review everything we've got and then decide on an action plan.'

'Burton's done one of them freaking evidence boards,' the DS said resignedly.

'Cheer up, Noakesy. I'll give you an hour for refreshments.' Noakes instantly brightened. 'But then I want you and Doyle back on it.'

Watching his colleague climb into the car — no doubt already planning his sugar-heavy 'refreshment' — the DI felt as though the investigation was becoming more obscure by the hour. Perhaps Kate Burton's 'crazy wall' would shed some light.

9. BLINDSIDED

In the event, Kate Burton's 'crazy wall' didn't throw up any tangible leads, but it at least had the merit of helping the team to thrash out all the different scenarios.

It felt like a constructive session, only interrupted by a bad-tempered call from Richard Keogh to enquire why the police had been 'snooping' round his place of work.

'I just called Greeners to check out Keogh's trip to Lancaster, sir,' Doyle told the DI. 'Didn't want to take his word for it. I tried to be discreet.'

'Quite right, Sergeant,' Markham reassured him. 'Interesting that Mr Keogh was so sensitive about it.'

There were no other distractions — save for some amicable squabbling over their takeaway — and they continued to review the case until Noakes's prodigious yawns indicated it was time to adjourn.

'Did Matt Sullivan give you anything on nutters at Hope?' the DS enquired of Doyle as they were finishing up, ignoring Burton's disapproving frown at this decidedly inappropriate language.

'He seemed genuinely mystified, sarge,' was the reply. 'I mean there's lots of troubled kids, but he never noticed

any of them stalking Padgett or Dacre . . . didn't remember anything hinky going on . . .'

'When I went back over the student statements, there *was* something . . .' Burton riffled through her notes. 'Yes, here it is. Chelsey Preston said, "So long as you didn't do anything wrong, Miss Padgett was always in your corner. You couldn't count on Mrs Dacre to take your side, but it was different with Miss Padgett. She understood about keeping secrets."'

Doyle looked confused, clearly struggling to decode the teenage angst. 'I wonder what she meant by that.'

'Sounds very different from when I was at school,' Burton said. 'It was always "them and us". None of this stuff about teachers taking your side or being in your corner.'

'Yeah,' Noakes chipped in. 'But these days everyone's obsessed with letting it all hang out an' adults being friends with the kids.' Derisive gesture. 'I remember getting leathered an' Mister Sykes — that was our head — shook hands with me afterwards . . . No hard feelings, see.'

The DI was amused to note that Burton looked appalled. *That explains a lot*, her expression seemed to say.

'With my lot it was the old, "This hurts me more than it hurts you" routine,' he laughed. 'As you say, Kate, it's a different world nowadays.'

Doyle joined the debate. 'Bit iffy that stuff about keeping secrets, though,' he said thoughtfully. 'I mean, wouldn't a teacher get into trouble cos of safeguarding?'

'Depends on the secret, I suppose,' Burton replied, before adding, 'By all accounts Jayne Padgett was a true professional. I don't see her doing anything unethical.' She looked down at her notes. 'Chelsey's the attention-seeking type — a drama queen, if you ask me. Hinting at a mystery could be a way of putting herself in the spotlight.'

'Agreed.' Markham massaged knotted muscles. 'What about Denise Rooney's daughter?'

'Caitlin?' Burton checked the notebook again. 'She didn't mention anything about secrets. Just said Miss Padgett

was,' more air quotes, '"very protective and big on people doing the right thing . . . talked about jealousy and envy being deadly sins when they were doing PHSE". That's the pastoral side,' she explained registering Noakes's scowl. 'Form tutor stuff and personal welfare.'

'Could mean bleeding anything,' Noakes grumbled. 'Teenage girls go in for bitching an' special friends, yeah?' A certain proud look in his eyes suggested that one Natalie Noakes might well have been queen bee of her own little circle. 'Padgett could've been clamping down on bullying like them parents said, y'know, guv, the ones we saw down at the teaching agency who said she looked out for their lass.'

'More than likely,' Markham concurred. 'But that's strong language . . . *Protective* . . . *Big on doing the right thing* . . . *Talking about jealousy and envy being deadly sins* . . . All very moralistic.'

'Maybe she was thinking of her family background and all the resentment that got stirred up,' Doyle suggested.

'Them half-sisters had their noses well put out of joint when she arrived on the scene,' Noakes mused. 'Happen she were thinking back to all the unpleasantness over that an' the Nick Critchley programme . . .'

'Anything significant from any of the other students?' the DI asked Burton.

'Let me see, guv.' She rammed her glasses more firmly onto her nose. 'Nothing else about secrets or deadly sins. A few of the girls said Jayne was "dead religious" but to be honest, they'd probably say the same about anyone who went to church or sandwiched some R.E. into form time. Apparently, she went in for Bible stories, like the Ten Commandments . . .'

'Quite a refreshing change from the usual secular diet.' There was something flinty about Markham's expression as he said this. 'Maybe that put her at odds with SLT and their liberal agenda.' He thought wryly of George Orwell's "old maids bicycling to Holy Communion through the morning mist" . . . Something told him that Judith Lipscombe and

Tony Brighouse wouldn't want anyone of that complexion delivering their all-singing, all-dancing curriculum for the twenty-first century. Too 'unwoke' by half . . .

'Talking of religious values, it's the requiem for Jayne at St Jude's on Monday evening.' He decided not to mention the casket and ashes element. 'Naturally, we'll be attending.'

Noakes and Doyle were visibly disappointed. Bang went their plans for a few pints and a review of the weekend's football.

'There's a buffet reception afterwards,' he slipped in by way of sugaring the pill.

'Well,' Noakes said virtuously, changing his tune. 'I s'pose it's only right an' proper. What with her being a churchgoer an' all.'

The DI stifled a smile as he thought of the Christian carnivora with his DS heading the charge towards the cooked meats.

'Just remember, best bib and tucker please.'

Burton and Doyle stared with rapt interest at their shoes at this injunction.

'Like we wouldn't make an effort,' Noakes muttered indignantly. 'A mark of respect innit,' he added with a reproachful sniff.

'Indeed.'

Just so long as nothing turned Sidney's basilisk glare their way.

'We need to have another crack at Richard Keogh tomorrow,' the DI told the team. 'I'd like you and Doyle to do that interview please, Kate, along with Bill Travers and Christine Bickerton.'

'See if Travers has a thing for his mum,' Noakes said with a wink at the po-faced acting DI.

'More like find out about any bust-ups they may have had with Jayne or Gill,' Markham said severely. 'And push Travers on Jayne's family set-up . . . tensions between the adoptive and biological members, that sort of thing. We'll get Angela Studholme and Valerie Holmes in after that.'

‘I’ll speak to Professor Finlayson,’ Burton said eagerly. ‘See if he can help with profiles of Mr Travers and the girlfriend.’

Whatever Noakes and Doyle felt about the criminal profiler, it was clear one member of the team was enthusiastic. Seeing the ferrety glee with which Noakes was watching the blush that spread across Burton’s neck and his nudging of Doyle, Markham wondered if there was more to it than professional admiration, ruefully determining that he would not be a dog in the manger. Besides, Finlayson had struck him as a decent sort with none of the preening self-regard he was used to when it came to Sidney’s usual picks.

‘Good idea, Kate. Right, let’s down tools . . . Back here eight a.m. sharp tomorrow.’

And with that they went their separate ways, Burton loftily ignoring the unsubtle semaphore that passed between her two colleagues.

* * *

They were back at the evidence board the next morning, mobiles switched off, when a frightened looking secretary interrupted proceedings and beckoned Markham into the outer office.

On his return to the team, the DI’s face was so pale that Burton rose in alarm.

But he waved her back into her seat.

‘Nick Critchley is dead,’ he said without preamble.

‘You *what*?’ Noakes’s mouth hung agape. ‘How come? I thought he was staying with his brother.’

Burton, too, looked poleaxed.

‘I checked in on them last night, boss, after they got back to Anglesey,’ she insisted. ‘Spoke to both of them at around seven thirty once we were finished here. They were fine . . . making dinner. The TV was on in the background and everything sounded normal.’

‘Where did they find him, boss?’ Doyle asked. ‘Was it suicide?’

'His body was discovered this morning by the cleaner at a flat they co-own in the town centre,' came the answer.

Noakes was incredulous. 'What, you mean *here*? In *Bromgrove*?'

'Apparently he told his brother he needed some space to "sort his head out". Then later on he heard the car driving off and realised Nick had taken it.' The DI sounded hollow, obviously still in shock. 'It wasn't uncommon for them to use the flat as a bolthole when times were rough. Max didn't think anything of it.'

'Not even after two women fricking copped it an' it turned out one of 'em had been on that poxy TV show?' Noakes's empurpled face clashed horribly with his fuchsia sweater. 'What kind of moron is he?'

'The kind who didn't think his brother had anything to worry about,' Markham replied mechanically, though his thoughts were racing. 'Look,' he squared his shoulders, 'there's no point speculating . . . Dimples is waiting for us over there.'

'It's jus' like with Dacre.' Noakes was adamant. 'Critchley *twigged* summat. He musta repressed it an' then it came up from his subconscious . . . he didn't remember properly till we were having a go at him about his weirdy programme an' them whacko families he covered.'

Burton nodded approvingly at the reference to repression and Critchley's subconscious. Clearly some of her interest in the workings of the unconscious mind had rubbed off on her hitherto famously resistant colleague.

'If Critchley remembered something, he could've arranged to meet up with the killer, sir,' she said eagerly. 'From what we know of his programme, he doesn't strike me as the sort to think twice about blackmail. Plus, I got the feeling they weren't exactly flush.'

'Must've been confident he could handle the killer.' Doyle too was willing to be persuaded. 'Did he tell Max anything about what he was up to, sir?'

'Doesn't sound like it,' Markham said. 'Played his cards close to his chest.'

Dead man's hand.

It suddenly occurred to the DI that Max's ignorance had most probably saved his life . . .

With a visible effort, he continued, 'Let's not jump to any conclusions. I want to hear Dimples' take. Critchley had issues around drink and drugs, so best to approach this with an open mind.'

'Sidney'll go apeshit if he thinks the TV big boys are gonna get dragged into this,' Noakes opined with cheerful malice.

'For the time being, the official line is "tragic accident" or "unexplained circumstances",' the DI said firmly. 'We examine the body in situ and then we get Max in. Any leaks or speculation and I will come down *hard* on whoever is responsible.'

Judging from the set of his jaw, they had no doubt that the DI meant it.

'Right, we'll take your car, Kate. And let's keep our phones turned off. That way, we're incommunicado.'

His day of reckoning with the DCI would come, but in the meantime guerrilla tactics were called for.

* * *

The first-floor flat owned by the Critchleys was situated in a mews block in one of the town centre's backstreets. The exterior with its wisteria-clad white stucco was charmingly picturesque but inside was what Doyle called 'pure Harrods showroom', furnished in a corporate style with no personal touches.

Dimples was waiting for them with the body. The deceased Nick Critchley was sitting in an overstuffed armchair in the living room, head thrown back, eyes shut and an almost peaceful expression on his face.

'He died sometime late last night, from an overdose of Seconal,' the pathologist said briskly. 'Mixed with cocaine and alcohol.' He gestured towards the kitchen. 'The SOCOs

have bagged the paraphernalia and what have you. Looks like it was quite the little party.'

'Any sign of force, Doug?'

The medic shot Markham a keen look.

'Interesting you should say that. I'd say he was grabbed by the throat, and there's evidence of an attempt to scrub vomit off the carpet — they made quite a good job of it. But I reckon your man would have been in no fit state to get out the marigolds.'

Noakes was entranced.

'Another one,' he breathed. 'Another *tidy* death. The victim looking like he's sleeping an' then the killer cleaning up the puke, same as with Padgett.'

'Figure your killer is a bit of a Mrs Hinch on the side eh, Noakes?'

The DS scowled at the pathologist's quip. 'Professor Finlayson from the Newman says this one don' like *mess*,' he declared stubbornly. 'Gotta mean he's OCD or summat . . . mebbe a germaphobe like Donald Trump.'

The DI crouched down to view the stain then straightened up.

'You're sure he couldn't have done this himself, Doug?'

'By the time it came to the vomiting, I'd say his coordination would have been all over the place. He wouldn't have been able to stand up let alone start mopping up the carpet. Of course, it's possible he threw up earlier because of a dodgy stomach or some such, but it's my opinion the vomiting was caused by that cocktail of drugs forced down his throat and by then—'

'He was too far gone for a spot of Shake n' Vac.'

'Got it in one, Noakes.'

Doyle contemplated Critchley's supine figure intently. 'So, you reckon someone slipped him a Mickey Finn and counted on us thinking it was an encounter that got out of hand — maybe something sexual?'

The pathologist considered the corpse. 'I'd say that's feasible.'

'But then they couldn't help themselves or maybe something made them panic . . . and they tried to clean up the mess?' Burton pursed her lips as she mentally recreated the scene.

'What kind of screwball gets busy with the Brillo?' Noakes looked as though it was quite beyond him. 'Mebbe it's a woman after all . . .'

'Or someone acting on autopilot . . . someone with a strong compulsion to sanitise what has happened.' Dimples too was clearly intrigued, his countryman's features expressing bafflement at the peculiarly well-ordered tableau in front of him.

'Thass what the prof said,' Noakes told him. 'Like somehow they were trying to say sorry for what they did . . . though he figured it were summat to do with their childhood an' stuff.'

'He looks so *relaxed*,' Burton ventured. 'As though he's just having a snooze or something.'

'He didn't know much about it, m'dear,' the pathologist reassured her kindly. 'I'm reasonably sure the PM will be straightforward. You can leave it to me,' he added hastily, well aware of Burton's disconcerting penchant for attending autopsies in the interests of furthering her scientific education.

Two paramedics had come through from the hallway and were hovering with a stretcher.

'I'd better get down to it,' Dimples said. 'You go and have a shufti at the rest.' He gestured vaguely in the direction of the other rooms.

Afterwards, the detectives stood outside on the pavement watching while two uniforms cordoned off the little cul-de-sac.

The autumn sun was glowing overhead, turning the wisteria a glorious copper-red so that it seemed to blaze with inner fire. 'S'pretty that,' Noakes said, his eyes following Markham's gaze. 'The poor sod didn't deserve to die home alone, totally out of it an' chucking his guts up.'

'Do you think it happened like Dimples said, boss?' Doyle was keen to hear the DI's verdict.

Markham's face was still limestone-pale, but the response was calm enough.

'He seemed fairly sure Mr Critchley was helped on his way.'

Burton looked up and down the street. 'There wasn't any sign of someone else having been in the flat,' she said thoughtfully.

'No forced entry, so Nasty Nick must've let him in.' There was no venom in Noakes's use of the nickname. It was just his usual coping strategy kicking in. 'What's the use of pigging SOCOs combing the place anyway?' he demanded angrily. 'Unless our bloke's in the system already, it's jus' pissing in the wind.'

That was the problem, thought Markham gloomily. With a forensically aware murderer, plus the intricacies of trace evidence and cross-contamination to contend with, they were groping in the dark . . . at least until they had someone in the frame when there was a chance of making all the pieces fit.

'Right, back to base,' he said. 'I want Max Critchley brought to the station pronto and obviously,' an involuntary grimace, 'the DCI will have to be briefed given that the media outlets will be all over this story.'

'Bags I not do Sidney,' Noakes said mulishly.

'Sorry Noakesy, you're with me. I still want Kate and Doyle to take Richard Keogh and the love birds at Hope, and we need to speak to Jayne Padgett's half-sisters once Max and Sidney are out of the way.' As he said these words, it struck the DI that they sounded callous — as though Max Critchley was simply a counter to be moved around the criminal investigation board . . . like one of the markers on Kate Burton's crazy wall.

But they were running out of time.

Three bodies in just under a week.

And this last death was totally out of left field . . . as though the shadowy killer they sought had gleefully watched

them narrowing their sights on Hope while the real action lay elsewhere.

'I want alibis for everyone in respect of last night,' the DI instructed.

'Whass the point of that?' his wingman groused. 'They'll all say the same — in bed with their other half . . .' He rolled his eyes. 'Or if it's Brighouse, most likely someone else's other half.'

'The point is that we cover all the bases, Noakesy.'

And hope like mad that one of them lets something — *anything* — slip.

As they made their way to Kate Burton's car, the DI heard Nathan Finlayson's words echo in his head.

You're looking for someone who is likely to kill again . . . They'll do anything to keep their secret . . . whatever it is.

It was rare that Markham didn't wait for a victim's body to be stretchered from the crime scene. But this time he couldn't bear to bow his head as a third corpse was borne past him to the morgue. Dimples would see that everything was done with due respect.

We'll get him, Nick, he vowed, before repeating to himself the well-worn mantra.

We only have to be lucky *once*. The bastard who killed you, Jayne and Gill has to be lucky *all the time*.

* * *

'So you knew he was going to the flat in Bromgrove when he left you yesterday evening, Mr Critchley?'

Max Critchley had none of his brother's good looks.

Mister Potato Head, Noakes thought sourly as he watched the thick-set man opposite process the question.

'I guessed that's where he was headed . . . he didn't say so in as many words, but it's what usually happened when he got wound up.'

'What was he wound up about?' There was a note of menace in Noakes's enquiry.

The other shrugged helplessly.

'Dunno. He disappeared into his study when we got back from the station. I've no idea what he was doing. It sounded like he was watching something on his computer . . . maybe a promo DVD of himself or something like that.' And now the man's voice thickened with deeply felt regret. 'He'd convinced himself he was going to break back into television, see.'

'Even after the big balls-up with *Roundup*?' The retort was blunt, but Noakes's tone was softer now as he watched the doughy features working with distress. '"Never say die", yeah? Well, respect to him for that.'

The DI took over. 'When your brother left the house, did he have anything with him?'

'A padded envelope — a jiffy bag or something like that — I figured it was DVDs . . . thought he planned to go through them again later, on his laptop when he got to the flat.'

Markham and Noakes exchanged glances.

No DVDs had been found in that sterile showroom apartment. There was a laptop, but preliminary reports from technical support had failed to disclose anything useful.

The DI was willing to bet they would find nothing of any use in the Anglesey house.

But *something* had sparked a memory with Nick Critchley, had triggered a train of association that led him to his lonely squalid death . . .

An interview with one of Jayne Padgett's disaffected relatives, perhaps?

Or was it some snippet that had come his way as a 'roving reporter'? He had been a presenter on *Bromgrove Schools Bulletin*, with a slot on the local evening news, for many years before making the big time with his controversial true-life documentaries for *Bromgrove Roundup* . . .

Could it be the key to it all was contained on video footage that had never seen the light of day but somehow

represented a threat to the killer? And if so, what did that footage show?

Or was this information about Critchley taking a package back to the flat in Bromgrove merely coincidental? Who knew? Perhaps he'd merely intended to put an end to it all while browsing past hits from his glory days and then either he'd thrown the DVDs away before arriving at the flat or the killer had taken them.

Whatever was in that padded envelope, Markham was sure it had been the currency for blackmail. Critchley had suddenly realised he had struck pay dirt and hastened to cash in.

Looking over at Noakes, the DI saw this conviction reflected in his wingman's eyes.

'Did Nick say anything to you earlier that evening before he set off for the flat, Mr Critchley?' Markham asked. 'Anything at all? Please think carefully, this could be very important.'

Max Critchley scratched his thinning pate. He could have earned good money as a Wayne Rooney lookalike, Noakes reflected uncharitably. He was willing to bet that was a hair weave and all . . .

'Well, he *did* say something, but it didn't make much sense . . .'

'Go on, Mr Critchley.' The DI was warm and encouraging, his easy manner belying the urgency he felt.

'He said something like, "I should have seen it right away. It was right there staring me in the face, and I missed it. "'

'Missed *what*?' demanded Noakes.

Their interviewee passed a hand over his face top to bottom in a curious gesture as though to wipe out the last forty-eight hours.

'I don't know. But whatever it was, he looked excited about it.'

'Could he have been drinking or using drugs before he left the house?' There was no way of pussyfooting around the

issue, but as he observed Max Critchley's stricken expression Markham felt a pang of compunction.

'I wouldn't have said he was high or anything like that. We had a bite to eat — Spag Bol and garlic bread. Your colleague rang while we were getting it ready, actually. I had a beer, but Nick just drank water. *Look*,' the tone was suddenly fierce, 'he was trying to get himself back in shape, show people he wasn't just some sad old has-been. He told me he had something in the pipeline that was going to help with his comeback . . .'

'You're sure those were his words, Mr Critchley . . . "something in the pipeline"?' Markham interposed swiftly.

'Yeah,' with a hint of defiance. 'I said so, didn't I?'

'Forgive me if it sounds like I'm cross-examining you,' the DI said with his usual grave courtesy. 'I know this must be terribly painful, but we're trying to form a picture of your brother's state of mind.'

'He didn't kill himself, did he?' Max Critchley's voice was suddenly surprisingly authoritative. 'He'd already touched rock bottom and the only way was up. He wasn't finished . . . not by a long way.'

'Nick had taken drink and drugs,' Markham said carefully. 'But there are indicators to suggest the presence of someone else in the flat.'

'*Someone else*?' Max Critchley leaned forward looking alarmed.

'Was Nick in the habit of meeting anyone there,' the DI asked. 'A lover perhaps?'

'No, it was off limits to everyone 'cept us two. Besides,' the bitterness in his voice was unmistakeable, 'everyone dropped Nick like he had leprosy after *Roundup* fired him. The wind from all the doors slamming in his face could've knocked him over. He certainly found out who his friends were.'

'How were things financially?' Markham asked.

Their interviewee saw where this was going.

'You think he was trying to blackmail someone?'

'Might he have been tempted to try something like that?' The DI's voice was gentle. 'If he needed capital to reboot his career, say.'

'This has got something to do with those teachers who were murdered, hasn't it?' Max Critchley's eyes were dull with despair. 'You think Nick knew something and tried to get money from the scum who did it . . . like he was the sort of bloke who only cared about number one.'

'We're not judging your brother, mate.' Noakes's voice was gruff with awkward sympathy. 'If you ask me, he had a rough deal back in the day. That feature he did on Jayne Padgett likely got the viewer ratings rocketing an' then everyone at HQ turned all prissy an' holier than thou cos the PC brigade got the wind up. Same as when Princess Di died an' everyone had a go at the paparazzi, calling her a saint an' saying the newspaper boys weren't fit to lick her shoes . . . when only the day before they couldn't get enough of all that stuff about her being a tart an' a fruitcake.' He whistled. 'Talk about changing your tune. Slimy hypocrites, the lot of them. My missus said that Lynda Lee-Potter were a disgrace . . . slagging Di off for being a home wrecker, then the minute she died making her out to be Mother Theresa.'

Markham started to despair at Noakes's tangential musings, but a shy smile had spread across Max Critchley's homely features, so that for a moment he appeared almost personable.

'Mum loved the royals,' he said. 'Dead now, along with our dad. She was a great fan of Princess Di . . . read everything about her.'

The DS nodded approvingly as though to acknowledge membership of a very exclusive club.

'You're right about the way they turned on Nick, Mr Noakes,' Critchley continued, 'It was really scuzzy cos the bosses *knew* he had to have an angle — that's what made folk watch the programme — there'd be no point tuning in if everything was all nicey-nicey. What people *really* wanted to see was relatives at each other's throats.'

‘A bit of aggro,’ Noakes concurred sagely.

‘Exactly.’

Once again, the DI marvelled at his colleague’s instinctive gift for building a rapport with even the most resistant witness. It was something that simply couldn’t be taught, this ingrained empathy with injured souls. The uncouth DS possessed this strange ability to create a pool of intimacy and hold troubled interviewees in a protective private circle.

It worked like a charm with Max Critchley.

‘Nick hated the Padgett woman,’ he confided. ‘He said she *knew* what she was getting into and then blamed him when it all turned out wrong.’

‘Would that resentment have clouded your brother’s judgement, Mr Critchley?’ Markham asked quietly. ‘Enough to make him enter into some kind of bargain with Jayne Padgett’s killer?’

‘It might, especially if he thought they were hard done by . . . or had a raw deal like him.’ Critchley shuffled uncomfortably on his chair. ‘Look, I heard there was another woman murdered too. I don’t know how Nick got his head round keeping quiet about whoever did it but he must’ve squared it with himself somehow . . .’

‘Did your brother ever mention the name Gill Dacre?’ Markham pressed.

‘Not that I remember, no. That’s the second one, right?’

‘Yes. She and Jayne taught at the same school. Hope Academy. They were also on the books of the same tutorial agency.’

The DI watched Max Critchley’s face closely but detected no sign of recognition.

‘Perhaps they were involved in something dodgy together. Perhaps it was something bad and maybe Nick knew what had gone on. He covered the schools beat at one time, you know.’

The wretched man was clutching at straws, but there was integrity in him too.

'Look, Nick was damaged but he was trying to fight his demons and build a better life. If he saw the chance to make a quick buck,' he took a deep breath, 'then yes, I reckon he'd have taken it and tried not to think about the rest.'

'I appreciate your honesty, Mr Critchley.' Markham's eyes were soft. 'Nick's mobile wasn't in the flat, but were you aware of him calling anyone before he went out?'

'I heard him talking to someone in his study . . . no idea who it was, though.'

'D'you reckon he'd have needed a drink or summat to . . . chill . . . before sealing the deal?' Noakes asked.

'Yeah. I can see him needing to take the edge off before getting down to brass tacks.' A homely phrase for blackmail.

After they had arranged for a car to take Max Critchley home, the two detectives mulled over the meeting.

'So, the bastard got Nick practically comatose then forced those bennies down his throat,' Noakes said. 'Mister Sleazeball takes one risk too far. *Perfect.*'

'Only it wasn't, because they couldn't resist cleaning up the vomit,' his boss said consideringly.

'Won' be enough to convince Sidney that this was victim number three.' The DS's scowl was even more ferocious than usual. 'No way does he want the *Gazette* sounding off about a serial killer with links to Telly Land . . . You jus' wait an' see, guv. He'll want us to go with the whole sad sack alkie scenario.'

And so it proved.

The DCI was adamant that there could be no press release linking the death of Nick Critchley to the murdered teachers. Even when Markham pointed out Dimples' observations, he was having none of it.

'Not *conclusive* though, eh Markham,' he honked, the eczema seeming to take on a more threatening hue as he skewered the two detectives with a deadly stare. 'Nothing to say this wasn't an encounter that went wrong. And after all,' he widened his eyes, in a manner presumably designed

to demonstrate pious solicitude, 'given the man's tragic fall from grace, perhaps it isn't so surprising.'

The DI knew when he was on a hiding to nothing.

'I'll refer enquiries to the press office, sir,' he said.

'You do that, Inspector. I've had some interesting data come through from Professor Finlayson.' With an oracular shake of the head, '*Very* interesting . . . Looks like you have a promising psychiatric template to work from.'

The DI thanked God for the profiler's Janus-like dexterity.

Sidney's gaze rested momentarily on Noakes in a manner that suggested Markham's subordinate was himself potentially a specimen worthy of psychiatric study. Then, with a regal wave of the hand, they were dismissed.

'D'you see the way he looked at me?' the DS asked afterwards. 'Like I belong in the Newman or summat.'

'Well, as the Newman and Professor Finlayson are coming up trumps for us at the moment, Sergeant, I'm feeling quite benign about the place.'

The DS grinned.

'Yeah, ole beardy boots has bought us some time all right.' He yawned. 'What now, boss?'

'Let's call it a day.' *And what a day.* 'No doubt Burton will touch base shortly. We can tackle Jayne's half-sisters tomorrow.'

'You haven't forgotten tomorrow afternoon have you, guv?'

Noakes's face was a study in hurt reproach.

'Me an' the missus . . . The *Thé Dansant*,' he said. Only the way he pronounced it, the words were hardly redolent of continental glamour. 'You remember . . . you an' Olivia are coming to see us at the Town Hall Gardens.'

God, Olivia would crucify him for this. Quite literally *crucify* him.

'Looking forward to it, Noakesy,' the DI said with unnatural heartiness. 'Watching you and Muriel trip the light fantastic will be delightful . . . raise our minds to higher things.'

Much gratified, his wingman lumbered off home.

Sighing, he made his way back to his office. Now alone, Markham felt an unaccountable restlessness.

As though he had *missed* something, he thought despondently.

Outside it was growing dark, but he decided to leave his car and walk home. He could pick it up in the morning. Perhaps a tramp through Hollingrove Park would dispel his premonition of impending doom.

Flipping off the light, he left the station.

10. HIGHS AND LOWS

Olivia didn't crucify her boyfriend, but the price of her attendance at Town Hall Gardens was a Saturday ramble up Bromgrove Rise in driving rain.

'Princess Anne said, "There's no such thing as bad weather, only unsuitable clothing",' she announced crisply as her partner grumbled his way up the hill.

The sally forced a reluctant grin from him. 'You're turning into Muriel Noakes,' he muttered.

'Well, I need to brush up on my small talk for this afternoon. I mean, *honestly,* Gil . . . What the hell is a *Thé Dansant* anyway?'

'I believe it's a sort of sedate tea dance. Apparently the Edwardians invented it as a respectable way for young people to mix and flirt without needing a chaperone. It was quite glamorous back then whereas nowadays it's just older couples pushing each other round the floor, that kind of thing.'

'You're not exactly selling it to me, sweetheart.' She grinned. 'Anyway, I thought George and Muriel were Latin specialists. Aren't we going to see a bit of Latin? You know, some rumba or cha-cha-cha?' They had reached the top and she pulled back the hood of her cagoul, holding her face up to

the heavens with the rain whipping long red tresses across her face, like Cathy to his Heathcliff, thought Markham with an inner smile. But without all the nineteenth-century drama. 'Don't they do the energetic stuff nowadays?' she demanded.

'Well, I gather they're more on the ballroom side right now. Reading between the lines, I have a feeling Muriel's gone off flashing her knickers in public.'

She snorted with laughter.

'Ah, the old skirt flying up problem . . . What about George?'

'Oh well, it's a case of to hear is to obey, but he takes the slower stuff every bit as seriously I think he's looking forward to showing you his rise and fall.'

Olivia giggled again.

'How *are* things at Chateau Noakes these days?' Then, more seriously, 'Does George ever talk about the Bluebell case?' This was the investigation during which the Noakes's domestic fault lines were exposed and Natalie Noakes nearly fell through the cracks.

'No . . . but he admitted when we were on the Sherwin College investigation that the wheels had come off. Word on the grapevine is that they had therapy of some sort, but family omertà means Noakesy doesn't talk about it.'

'Muriel's snobbishness, you mean. Wouldn't do for her chums at the WI to get a whiff of them having *mental health issues* . . . That's strictly for the "plebs".'

Markham threw her a reproachful glance and she softened apologetically.

'All right, all right. I promise I'll be good as gold today . . . in raptures over her one-two-three and all that.'

He chuckled. 'No need to overdo it, love.' When Olivia's sense of mischief got the better of her, things risked getting out of hand. 'If you're not careful, she'll have you signed up for waltzing classes in no time.'

'Muriel doesn't like me enough for that.' Her voice turned arch and brittle at once. '*Poor Gilbert Markham*,' she quoted, in a surprisingly passable imitation of Mrs Noakes.

‘*Such easy prey for a certain type of woman . . . Never stood a chance once she had him in her sights.*’

‘Now, Liv.’

‘Sorry, dearest, but you know that’s what she thinks . . . plus, she gets all cosy and conspiratorial with you while flashing me these dirty looks. It really sets my teeth on edge.’

‘That’s because her husband is your “liege man of life and limb”,’ he said dryly.

‘Hmmm.’ She shook the tangled hair out of her eyes, gazing across at the woodland which bordered the hill on one side. ‘Do you reckon Natalie knows she’s not George’s biological daughter?’

‘He worships the ground she walks on,’ Markham said slowly. ‘I think he wouldn’t want her to know the truth about her paternity for fear it might change her feelings towards him.’

‘And Muriel would probably want to keep shtum about skeletons in the cupboard,’ Olivia observed. ‘Therapy’s supposed to be based on telling the *truth*, isn’t it? Whoever’s counselling them has got their work cut out.’

They turned around and arm in arm began the descent back down the tussocky slope, taking care not to skid on the mud and leaves.

‘Is George finding this investigation difficult, Gil?’

‘In what sense?’

‘Well, there’s the thing with Jayne Padgett, you know, adoptive versus biological family. It must’ve touched a nerve with him.’

‘Not so that you’d notice,’ came the wry reply. ‘He’s been so entranced with his Shipman and true-crime parallels that he’s had no time to brood on his personal situation. The latest discovery has been Mary Bell and *her* mother complex.’

Olivia burst out laughing and clutched his steadying arm. ‘*Priceless* . . . Next thing you know, he’ll be a convert to the cause of criminal profiling.’

‘Ah, there’s a way to go on that front.’ A rueful grin. ‘Though Kate appears to have fallen hook, line and sinker for our consultant psychologist.’

'*Excellent*. High time that Kate . . . moved on.'

The rain was easing now, so they headed for one of the benches at the foot of the Rise. Above them the drenched furze and gorse undulated and shifted like a pale-gold sea, sandy paths crisscrossing the moorland so that it resembled a giant quilt.

'Okay, admit it, this has done you good,' Olivia challenged him. 'You looked totally knackered last night.'

'Well, I certainly feel sharper . . . but alas no nearer to getting a handle on the case.'

'Kate didn't come up with anything useful from Hope, then?'

'Bill Travers wouldn't be drawn on rows or rifts.' Markham sighed. 'And apparently Christine Bickerton behaved like some sort of geisha, looking up at him through her eyelashes like he was God. Plus Lipscombe and Brighouse stuck to them like superglue, yakking away about duty of care to staff and pastoral responsibility.'

'As in making sure they didn't come out with anything incriminating, you mean.' Olivia looked grim.

'Precisely . . . Mind you, Travers managed to stick it to the ex by talking about her not realising the hurt she caused with her choices in life . . . That was Bickerton's cue for crocodile tears and platitudes about missed opportunities for forgiveness and reconciliation.'

'Yuk. They sound like a pair of creepy Pentecostalists. What about Gill, did they say anything about her?'

'I gather she sounded off in the staffroom about the unprofessionalism of workplace relationships. Kate wondered if maybe she had concerns about Travers abusing his authority — he'd been Bickerton's PGCE mentor, so potentially a sticky wicket.'

'Not enough of a reason to kill Gill, though . . .'

'That school was Gill Dacre's life and she probably had the inside track on everyone's secrets from SLT down,' Markham replied.

'You could say the same about Jayne. She'd been there for donkey's years . . . knew Hope inside out.'

‘But what did they know that was so dangerous?’ Markham looked up at the overcast skies as if petitioning the deity for help. ‘Fraud? Sexual impropriety? Worse?’

‘Did Kate have any luck with the students?’

‘Nada. The girls in particular struck her as attention-seekers . . . by the end of it, she couldn’t tell fact from fiction.’

‘*Huh*, I know what she means.’ Olivia slipped her hand into the pocket of Markham’s Barbour, drawing him closer. ‘I’m sorry, Gil,’ she said softly. ‘No wonder you’re fed up.’ Then, ‘What about Tricky Dicky?’

‘He’s a cold fish . . . Travelled to Lancaster on the day Gill died, but he was back at Lassiter Road by four thirty—’

‘Just round the corner from the park.’

‘Yes, so he had opportunity but as to *motive* . . . He came to the station first time round, but Kate and Doyle called on him at home yesterday.’

‘What’s his place like?’

‘Immaculate apparently. . . everywhere spotless and just so. Doyle said you could tell he was uptight about them bringing mud in on their shoes . . . dying to get the hoover out.’

‘Blimey.’ Olivia was taken aback. ‘D’you think he’s your neat freak?’ A nervous giggle. ‘Spawn of Shipman or something . . . ?’

Markham grimaced.

‘Something about it spooked Kate and Doyle . . . They said he was very buttoned-up and defensive . . . impossible to read really. Flared up when they tried to probe about his relationship with Jayne. Told them, “Everything was perfectly fine in the bedroom department thank you very much.”’

‘TMI.’

‘Indeed. One interesting detail was that he claimed Jayne was “emotionally over-invested” in her students.’

‘Emotionally over-invested . . . What did he mean by that?’

‘Your guess is as good as mine.’

‘Maybe he was saying she cared too much about the kids’ circumstances,’ Olivia mused. ‘Took too much on herself.’

‘The Thornfields implied something of the sort and those two single mothers seemed to think she was sticking her oar in.’

Markham watched his breath vanish upwards into the cold air. It seemed to him in that moment as though all his theories were equally insubstantial.

‘On the other hand, Doyle called him the kind of self-absorbed prick — I prefer the word narcissist — who thinks everything should revolve around *him*. That’s why he resented Jayne looking for her biological family—’

‘Because he was no longer the centre of attention.’

‘Exactly.’

‘Poor Jayne.’ Olivia’s voice was compassionate. ‘She was very bad to herself when it came to men. God knows what she saw in him. But then, we never know what goes on behind closed doors with other people . . .’

Markham had a weird feeling of *déjà vu*.

‘That’s what spooked Nick Critchley,’ he said suddenly.

‘What?’

‘What you just said about not knowing what goes on in private . . . Kate said something similar to him and next thing the shutters had come down and he started behaving oddly.’ He went on to tell her about the meeting with Max Critchley.

‘Nick must have known a damaging secret about someone,’ Olivia said when he had concluded his recital.

‘It looks that way . . . assuming Dimples is right about his death not being accidental.’ Markham explained the pathologist’s reservations.

Olivia whistled. ‘I’m guessing Slimy Sid is holding out for “unexplained circumstances” or,’ she assumed an exaggeratedly funereal demeanour, ‘“tragic accident”.’

‘Well, all we’ve got to go on is evidence of some vomit having been cleaned up . . . Dimples says Critchley’s motor functions would have been shot to pieces, so he couldn’t

have done it . . . On the other hand,' Markham frowned, 'no doubt there'll be an expert somewhere willing to prove the contrary.'

'Him having something on the killer fits, though, doesn't it?' she insisted. 'I mean, coming over all furtive and shooting off to Bromgrove like that.'

'Purely circumstantial, I'm afraid. But who knows . . . ? Maybe he *did* entertain a visitor — a lover or someone else — and they were the one to clean up before legging it because he was comatose. If so, Mr or Ms X won't exactly be in a hurry to come forward, and half of Bromgrove could have trailed through the place for all we know . . .'

She squeezed his hand.

'Any chance of co-opting your helpful profiler on this one? Get Kate to flutter her eyelashes at him . . . maybe he can come up with something to convince Sidney.'

Markham chuckled at the notion of puritanical Kate Burton resorting to such stratagems, then said soberly. 'It wouldn't do any good. You see, I think Sidney has . . . aspirations to break into television and this latest development might ruin it for him.'

'*Television*?' Olivia was incredulous. 'As in snuggling up to one those nubile presenters on the breakfast sofa? *A creep like Sidney* . . . Tell me you're joking!'

'Stranger things have happened, sweetheart. Look at talking heads like John Stalker . . .'

'The thought of Sidney as a pundit-for-hire! But you're probably right. God knows he's conceited enough.'

'He's not exactly confided in me about his post-retirement plans, but I get the feeling he fancies the idea of media exposure. Dragging Bromgrove TV into a lurid serial-killer narrative could nix it for him . . . And in any event, he doesn't want it looking as though we aren't on top of this case . . . a third death isn't good for the optics.'

'Hmm.'

As they sat there, two young mothers strolled by with their little girls warmly bundled up against the autumn chill.

The parents sat on a neighbouring bench while their offspring set about making walls and rooms from soggy drifts of leaves, gleefully shuffling the mulch with their feet and exclaiming over the progress of their fantasy houses.

A memory tugged at Markham.

The ponytailed gardener at the Newman making patterns on the ground . . .

Was that where they should be looking? Mentally ill patients . . . ? Could Sidney be right after all?

'Penny for them, Gil?'

'Oh, I was just going round in circles . . . wondering if we should be looking at "fruit loops" after all.'

'You're picking up bad habits from George,' she laughed. 'Fruit loops!'

'Kate Burton would be appalled,' he agreed. 'But what she doesn't know won't hurt her.'

For all the lightness of this reply, Olivia sensed his dejection.

'Have you got any more from Jayne's family?' she asked.

'Her adoptive mum Marian Padgett should be out of medical purdah on Monday for the requiem. We'll be able to speak to her afterwards provided she's up to it.'

'What about the biological relatives?'

'The half-sisters have been hard to pin down, but Valerie Holmes said we could call round five-ish.' He pulled a face. 'Something to look forward to after the *Thé Dansant*.'

'Just so long as you don't leave me stranded with Muriel. I don't mind admiring her pivots and chassés and all the rest, but that's it.'

He grinned. 'Noakesy nurses the happy delusion that you and she are destined to become best friends.'

'My devotion to George has its limits — that woman's a samurai in disguise. And as for Little Miss Botox . . .' She sat up in alarm. 'Natalie's not going to be there is she, Gil?'

'*Relax* . . . She wouldn't be seen dead with all the crusties.'

'So that's what it's come to.' She pulled a mock tragicomic face. 'Too uncool for Natalie Noakes.' Then with a

mischievous sidelong glance. 'I suspect she'd make an exception in your case, sweetheart.' If the nauseating simper she affected around Markham was anything to go by. 'What girl could resist the strong, silent type . . .'

'Stop stirring, Liv.' But it was said affectionately. 'After what she went through last year, Natalie's most likely renounced men altogether.'

Despite Noakes's daughter having been the victim of a sex attacker, Olivia had a feeling it wouldn't put a stop to her amorous adventures. However, she let it pass.

'Come on,' she said. 'You can take me to Costa for a bun and a hot drink . . . call it a reward for providing moral support under the glitterball.'

'My pleasure.'

Somewhat stiff after their interlude on the bench, they walked slowly to the car park, watching indulgently as more children arrived to scoop up leaves and create make-believe castles.

Markham suddenly felt an aching nostalgia for the loss of childhood innocence . . . when the world shimmered with exciting possibilities and no shadows fell across his path.

Then he noticed the sadness in Olivia's grey-green eyes.

The tragedy of a botched abortion — a secret which nearly blew their relationship apart — meant she could never have children of her own.

He kissed her hand before tucking it into the pocket of his Barbour, silently banishing ghosts from the past.

They were nearly at the car park entrance when Markham looked at the landscape behind them where a solitary muffled figure was now toiling up the hill, wreathed by autumn mist.

Suddenly the image of the hooded figure glimpsed near Castor Hill Park after Jayne Padgett's murder came to him, as though conjured by the mysterious spirits of the Rise.

He felt something resonate inside him like the chord of a harp.

'What is it, Gil?' Olivia asked curiously, feeling his tension.

'Just saying farewell to the ancestors or whoever are the guardians of this place,' he replied with an effort to sound casual, though that strange vibration continued to hum inside him like the message from another world.

And then it was gone.

He smiled at her.

'Right, I've done communing with the druids . . . I think we're both ready for hot chocolate.'

'With toasted marshmallows.'

'Like Noakesy, you drive a hard bargain milady . . . Marshmallows it is.'

* * *

As it turned out, the *Thé Dansant* went reasonably well.

Muriel, her dyed blonde hair teased and backcombed to within an inch of its life, had clearly decided to be gracious. And, for her part, Olivia reciprocated after an initial doubletake at the sticky-out purplish taffeta number with glittering lurex bodice, only emitting a strangled cough when Markham pronounced Mrs Noakes 'a vision in mauve'. The thing about her boyfriend was that this old-world courtliness came so naturally to him that he was able to keep up his end without succumbing to hilarity.

Noakes looked very smart too in a vintage double-breasted suit with black and white two-toned shoes that carried only faint overtones of 1940s gangsterdom. His collar and cuffs were crisply starched, and the salt and pepper hair brilliantined into submission, so that all in all he presented an appearance dramatically at odds with his everyday dishevelment.

'You could give that Craig Revel Horwood and the *Strictly* guys a run for their money, George,' Olivia told him, eliciting a blush of pleasure.

A little jazz orchestra serenaded them with feel-good melodies from a raised bandstand as couples — a mix of

amateur and professional, Noakes confided proudly — glided round the dance floor in the well of the room.

Olivia took stock.

It might not have been the Waldorf Astoria (more Bushby Berkeley musical) — the plastic aspidistras and fake greenery were definitely a bit naff — but in its way the spectacle was quite charming. A display board at the entrance proclaimed that this event was sponsored by the Bromgrove Women's Institute and the Vernon Johnson School of Dance (mercifully not the Bluebell), while tables lining the shallow circular balcony that overlooked the dance floor were immaculately styled each with its linen tablecloth and winter posy centrepiece. Teenage waitresses circulated with prosecco, 'non-alcoholic cocktails', dainty canapés and cakes. Unlimited hot drinks were available from serving trolleys wheeled by ebullient bosomy caterers, and in no time at all there was a cheerful buzz.

As ever, Olivia was surprised by how well Muriel and George Noakes moved together. For such a well-upholstered couple, they were astonishingly light on their feet as they dipped, swooped and spun. Intriguingly too, they had eyes only for each other when immersed in the dance — no coy glances at the spectators by contrast with some of the other amateur couples.

'They're very good,' she murmured to Markham.

He grinned wickedly, gesturing at his printed programme.

'I believe everyone's invited onto the floor for a Ladies' Excuse Me,' he told her.

'Oh God, not audience participation . . . Isn't that the dance where people swap partners?'

'The very one . . . And I think we'll have to do our duty, Liv.'

Just as well they'd got changed, she thought balefully. Though maybe if they'd stayed in jeans and sweatshirts, they'd have been spared this rigmarole.

Heigh-ho. Better get stuck into the prosecco before the evil hour was upon them . . .

As it turned out, she and Markham acquitted themselves quite creditably on the dance floor. Muriel looked as if she was about to expire from gratified pride when Markham gravely cut in on Noakes and requested the pleasure, while Olivia held out her arms and asked, 'Will you risk it, George?'

The problem was, Noakes was so overcome by the felicity of partnering his heroine that he held her like bone china and immediately developed two left feet, embarrassing himself by constantly stepping on her toes. Luckily, this amusing byplay escaped Muriel's beady eye owing to her being engrossed with Noakes's handsome boss.

Over cups of tea afterwards, conversation flowed easily . . . Noakes's normally bossy overbearing wife was touchingly eager to give them the inside track on ballroom dancing, and Olivia thought how much she preferred her like this. In between hoovering up as many canapés as he could get away with, Noakes chipped in with entertaining asides about some of the professionals in attendance so the time passed very pleasantly. The trauma of the Bluebell case seemed a million miles away.

The final number of the afternoon comprised an exhibition tango performed by a couple from the Vernon Johnson School. The girl was much younger than her swarthy partner, but the pairing nevertheless projected a sultry chemistry very much in keeping with the origins of the dance.

Olivia was interested to note Muriel's brittle expression as she applauded mechanically at the end of the performance.

'You're not a fan of these two then, Muriel?' she asked, curious to know what had occasioned the disapproving reaction. 'Are they together in real life?'

'He's her stepfather.' A pregnant pause then, 'Not that you'd know it from the way they carry on . . . It's the talk of the Pro-Am circuit . . .'

'Oh.' Olivia wasn't sure how to react. 'He's a professional dancer?'

'That's right.' Muriel wasn't in the habit of getting confidential with Gilbert Markham's ditzy girlfriend, but it was

a juicy piece of gossip and she relished being the one 'in the know'. 'Paul met his wife Della on the competition circuit. They got married, but she retired after her first child. He was looking for a new dance partner, so Della suggested her daughter from a previous marriage. Clare was only fifteen when they started training together, but she was a quick learner.'

A quick learner. To Olivia's ears, the words seethed with dark subtext.

'She's still only seventeen,' Muriel continued, watching the hard-featured teenager being congratulated by another dancer while the thick-set older man stood with a possessive hand on the small of her back. 'But still waters certainly run deep in her case.'

As though aware of Muriel's disapproval, the young woman looked up at their table, shooting the group a defiant glance before saying something to her stepfather and pirouetting coquettishly off the dance floor.

'I had no idea the dance world was such a hotbed of intrigue,' Markham said easily, for something about the little interlude had clearly flustered Muriel Noakes. Her husband chimed in with an anecdote about the portly trumpeter ('there's bottles of voddy in his music case') and the talk moved to last year's infamous walkout by the bandleader at the South Yorkshire Dance Festival.

But the story lingered in Olivia's mind, as did Mrs Noakes's palpable unease.

'Perhaps when Muriel looked at that girl, she saw herself,' she suggested to Markham afterwards.

'What, you think she mixed it with Casanova types?' he replied, mildly startled by the notion.

'Not after George, no.' Olivia was in no doubt that Noakes was the woman's safe harbour. 'But maybe some playboy came on to her when she was a schoolgirl or something like that.'

It was difficult to imagine She Who Must Be Obeyed as a gymslip charmer, but there were good bones beneath the

lacquered bouffant, stout corsetry and all the rest of it. And on the dance floor with her husband, a luminous vitality transformed her from the suburban snob of caricature into something altogether more appealing . . .

'More likely she was thinking of Natalie,' Markham remarked. 'Quite a lot of backstory there I should imagine.'

'Hmm.' Olivia was far from sure that Natalie Noakes's penchant for unsuitable lotharios was ancient history. 'At any rate, sequins and spangles must hide a multitude of sins if a bloke that age can sweep a seventeen-year-old off her feet.'

'Maybe he's just a very pelvic dancer.' They burst out laughing.

They were still chuckling when they reached Markham's car five minutes later.

'Right sweetheart, you were a regular trouper back there . . . I could see it did wonders for Noakesy's morale and, who knows, maybe you and Muriel are headed for the Big Thaw.'

She made an unladylike noise that sounded very like 'Humph'.

'I'm going to drop you back at the Sweepstakes and then call on Valerie Holmes with Noakes,' he went on.

'Think you'll get anywhere with her and Angela?'

'I'm not optimistic but, given how they've stonewalled us, we've got to try.'

'*Guv! Guv!*'

Noakes was heading towards them, back in 'civvies' and looking as dilapidated and disreputable as ever, his ballroom persona packed away with his two-tone tango shoes.

'Thank chuff I caught you,' he puffed.

In the half-light of the council car park, Markham noticed his normally florid wingman looked unnaturally pale and felt a prickle at the base of his spine.

'What is it?'

'Burton just called me. That Shona Restorick's been found on the tow path down by the canal with her head smashed in.'

For a moment, the DI just stared at him blankly.

It was the last name he expected to hear.

'You remember, boss? The parents of that special needs kid . . . the one with the daft name who said Padgett caused her skin complaint . . . Libby or Lissy or summat.'

'Liberty,' he said, snapping into instant recall. 'They said Jayne had a down on her.'

'That's them.' Noakes was relieved his boss was back on it. 'Well, we need to get down there right away.'

'We'll take your car, Noakes.'

Markham turned to Olivia whose white face was wraith-like in the gloom, grey-green eyes full of concern.

'Don't worry about me, I'll wait for Muriel and drop her home.'

Noakes made one of his Sancho Panza shuffling bows in her direction and then the next minute the two men were gone, leaving her there staring after them into the darkness.

11. ANCIENT HISTORY

The stretch of water in question was not strictly speaking a canal, being merely a tributary of Calder Vale Canal, which skirted Aldbourne Village.

Victorian lamp posts lined the narrow towpath at the end of which was a landing-place overshadowed by tall birches resembling the ghosts of trees. The area had a spectral appearance. Even the water seemed like a phantom river.

Further along, powerful arc lights next to the little swing bridge illuminated a scene of horror.

Shona Restorick's corpse lay face down on the bank a few feet away from the footpath, next to a blood-spattered, whimpering Jack Russell. The back of her cranium was a pulpy mess, the consistency of ground minced beef. Dimples Davidson was squatting on his haunches next to the body, probing delicately with gloved fingers.

'*This one* ain't tidy,' Noakes breathed hoarsely as they looked at the sticky glutinous brain tissue. 'He really laid her out.'

He bent down to the dog which made a feeble effort to lick his hand. Heedless of forensics, he whipped off his grubby parka and wrapped it around the shivering animal.

A gowned and masked SOCO came forward but uttered no reproach for the way Noakes had trampled over the crime scene. 'I'll see he's looked after, sarge.' A pair of arms reached out to take the bundle from him. 'You can leave it to me.'

'I don' need the anorak back, luv,' Noakes said gruffly. 'Jus' keep him warm.'

The pathologist got to his feet.

'At least there's no doubt about this one,' he said grimly. 'She was grabbed round the throat from behind and then whacked with great force . . . I'd say he used a wheel wrench or something similar.'

'Didn't kill the dog while he was at it, though,' Noakes observed.

'Presumably, he was an animal-lover,' Dimples said sardonically.

'Who found her?' the DI asked.

'Another dog walker.' The doctor jerked his head towards a pair of rotting gates that led ramblers across Aldbourne Common back to the village. 'Elderly gent. He was pretty shaken up . . . Your colleagues are dealing with him.'

Burton and Doyle had clearly wasted no time on receiving the call from Markham.

Noakes squinted at the rank undergrowth which bordered the path. 'How long has she been dead?'

'The body's warm and she's still bleeding . . . I'd say she was attacked within the last hour.'

The DS looked about him.

'What was she doing taking a walk here anyway?' he muttered angrily. 'Sitting duck for a mugger or some other nutcase.'

It occurred to Markham that the location would perfectly fit the DCI's notion of a local delinquent or escaped mental patient being responsible for the attack, but in his own mind there was no doubt. This was the work of their triple killer.

Kate Burton approached with Doyle.

'I've taken a statement from the dog walker, sir,' she announced without preamble. 'He didn't see anything.'

‘Did he know Mrs Restorick, Kate?’ the DI asked.

‘Only to nod to. They both live in the village. Usually she’s with her husband, but tonight . . .’ Her voice trailed off as she looked at the crumpled body on the ground.

‘Have we been able to locate Mr Restorick?’

‘He’s at home with a cold, sir,’ Doyle said. ‘That’s why she was on her own.’

‘Family Liaison are with him, sir.’ Burton swallowed hard as Dimples and two SOCOs levered the remains onto a stretcher, a third officer bagging what looked like a substantial chunk of pinkish-grey brain tissue.

‘This time of night, what was she thinking of?’ Noakes continued to mutter.

It was one of his idiosyncrasies to blame a murder victim for carelessness when it was the murderer he really wanted to slam up against a wall.

‘It’s not that late, sarge,’ Doyle pointed out, ‘and this footpath’s popular with local kids . . . She’d have felt safe.’

With a sharp pang, Markham remembered his own childhood fantasies of creating a private den along the canal-side.

Doyle had said the place was popular with children. It made him think of the Castor Hill prowler . . .

‘Did our dog walker see anyone hanging around?’ the DI asked Burton.

‘He *thinks* there was this girl having a cuddle with her boyfriend over by the gates when he took the short cut from the village, but he didn’t really take any notice of them and they weren’t there when he came past on his way back.’

‘School kids?’ Noakes too was remembering the mystery lurker.

‘He can’t be sure. The girl had long hair and the lad was wearing a beanie . . . Said he didn’t want to look like he was gawping at them.’

‘Poor old sod.’ Noakes was sympathetic. ‘It’s a case of eyes front, otherwise you get accused of perving.’

‘Did he hear anything?’ From the way he asked the question, it was clear the DI didn’t hold out much hope.

'A gurgling sound . . . But I mean, it's next to the river so . . .' Clearly Burton didn't want to contemplate the possibility that this might have been Shona Restorick's death throes.

Dimples and his gruesome cargo were ready to leave.

'Good luck with this one, Markham,' the pathologist said gravely. 'I hope you get him soon. She was only a tiny woman . . . it was complete overkill.'

Overkill. The same word he had used when examining Jayne Padgett's corpse.

The team formed an awkward guard of honour as the stretcher departed and then resumed their huddle.

Noakes looked down at the blood-soaked earth.

'He didn't get the Brillo pads out for *this one*.'

'It must have been an ambush, Sergeant.' Markham's voice rang with conviction. 'For whatever reason, he was unable to contrive a meeting in private so took his chances here.'

Doyle digested this. 'Stalked her you mean, boss?'

'Most probably, yes.'

'Points to 'em being local,' Noakes said. 'Knew her routine with the dog . . . confident enough to jump her out here in the dark and make a quick getaway. Tried to make it look like a mugging.'

'Could be,' the DI conceded.

Noakes irritably kicked the bole of a tree and then winced in pain. Burton and Doyle met each other's eyes in a rare moment of complicity.

'Like the doc said, she were only diddy,' their colleague growled. 'So a woman could've done it . . . happen even a kid . . .'

'Dimples said he thought they used a wheel wrench,' Burton mused.

'Perhaps they just nicked it out of someone's garage,' Doyle put in. 'Maybe even used it deliberately to make us think it was a bloke . . .'

'It's a fricking disaster,' Noakes concluded. 'An' you c'n bet the DCI'll go hell for leather with the escaped fruitcake angle.' He shot a sly sidelong glance at Burton. 'Better tell

your bearded wonder to come up with summat useful pronto . . . else Sidney's mitts will be all over this . . . He might even set Bretherton or Collier on us.'

Three faces fell. The thought of 'Blethering Bretherton' and 'Carp Face Collier' — their least favourite superintendents — muscling in was not calculated to raise spirits.

'Mercifully,' Markham said faintly. 'It's the weekend, Noakesy.'

They all knew the DCI's weekends were sacrosanct, being reserved strictly for golf, brown-nosing and family. In that order.

'But I take your point,' he added wryly. 'No doubt there will be a barrage of apoplectic messages zinging into my email first thing on Monday morning.'

Burton shivered. 'What now, boss?'

The mist that had wreathed Bromgrove Rise earlier in the day was back, but Markham found it less romantic now as he surveyed verges clogged with bracken and weeds. The canal-side felt dank and mouldy, as though its sodden vegetation had broken out in a cold sweat on beholding Shona Restorick struck down.

He felt an overpowering urge to get away from the place.

'We were meant to call on Valerie Holmes at five,' he said wearily.

'Oh, I found something out about her, guv.' Burton brightened at the memory.

'What was that, Kate?'

'Harassment warning for sending nasty emails to Jayne Padgett.'

'Well, well. That's very interesting,' the DI replied.

'You sure?' Noakes challenged his colleague. 'She didn't look the type for that kind of caper.'

'Honest, sarge, it's on the PNC and all,' was the prompt response.

Markham felt a resurgence of energy. 'Any other details?'

'We did some digging and found out Valerie was a TA at St Jude's Middle School before she retired . . . Actually,

it was Doyle who got the lowdown from the school secretary.' Kate Burton was always generous in giving credit where credit was due.

The ginger ninja endeavoured to look suitably modest but was clearly pleased at this acknowledgement.

'The secretary got off on the idea of helping to solve a murder,' he told them. 'Plus, you could tell she never liked Valerie . . . Said she had a mean streak.'

Markham was thoughtful. 'Well, I think we can deduce it hit her and Angela hard when Jayne turned up out of the blue and became the focus of their mother's attention—'

'Not to mention stirring up a shitstorm with the TV programme,' Doyle interrupted eagerly. 'Mega-embarrassing in front of all her nice respectable friends.'

'Shitstorm. Quite.' The DI rarely favoured the vernacular, but on this occasion he had to admit it was an apt description. 'Just remind me, Kate, did Valerie display any open animosity towards Jayne on that tape you watched?'

'The hostility was there, guv, but it wasn't overt. You got the feeling Critchley was trying to needle her, bringing up ancient history to make her flip. He said something about an unhealthy relationship with food making her insecure and paranoid, which was why she felt threatened when Jayne appeared on the scene.'

'Ah yes, I remember you mentioned that in your report. An eating disorder, wasn't it?'

'That's right, when she was younger, but it's not uncommon with girls at that age.'

True, Markham thought as he watched the acting DI's serious face, but from her light tone he doubted Kate had suffered through a similar sort of 'phase'.

'Anyway, Critchley made this tasteless crack about her being like John Prescott — you know, that overweight Labour politician. When he said he had bulimia, people joked he couldn't be doing it right.'

Noakes guffawed. 'Ackshually that's quite funny.'

'Not to an ex-bulimic with low self-esteem it isn't,' the acting DI countered frostily.

'She must really have *hated* him for that,' Doyle said.

'Angela probably loathed him too,' Burton continued. 'He hinted that she had OCD . . . said he kept expecting her to pop up on *How Clean Is Your House* . . .'

'D'you reckon *she*'s our control freak then?' Doyle was enthralled by the possibility. 'If she's as screwy as all that, then maybe she couldn't stop herself trying to clean up after the murders.'

Burton shrugged eloquently. 'Who can say? They didn't throw a wobbly on the programme despite all the snideness, but it had to have hurt. And it was obvious they were really upset finding out their mum had basically *abandoned* a baby and then kept it a secret all those years. At one point Valerie says it felt like she had suddenly become a stranger.'

'They were both devoted to Margaret Crompton, though,' the DI mused. 'That's a private nursing home she's in . . .'

'Oh yes,' Burton confirmed. 'Their dad died when they were in their teens, so it was just the three of them. It's been a year or so since the Critchley programme, which meant there was time for the dust to settle. By all accounts they made their peace with it before her health really went downhill.'

The acting DI sounded authoritative but now she wondered. Had the dust really settled given all that lingering bitterness and the Ofcom investigation? Had the two sisters seen what happened not merely as a betrayal of them but also of their father? Were Jayne Padgett and Nick Critchley sacrificed for some twisted notion of family honour? And, if so, where the hell did Gill Dacre fit in . . .

'Okay, good work, Kate,' the DI said, nodding to his colleague before addressing the whole team. 'Now, we're getting cold out here so I want you to start checking alibis in person . . . Shona Restorick was killed just a short time ago and it was a disorganised attack by comparison with the

other murders. Look for signs of agitation or strain . . . any indication that the killer's mask is slipping.'

'I'll brief Professor Finlayson,' Burton said with a hint of colour in her pale cheeks.

Noakes leered amiably at her. 'Tell him we need summat juicy for Sidney while you're at it. Lemme see . . . "The Butcher of Castor Oil Park Strikes Again" . . . Anything so long as it don' put poshos or friends of Sidney's missus in the frame.'

Burton smiled thinly. 'He aims to please,' she retorted then turned puce with embarrassment on realising what she had said.

Before it developed into a Benny Hill moment, the DI interposed smoothly, 'Noakes and I are going to check in on Mr Restorick and then pay Valerie Holmes a visit.'

'I'm not dressed for doing the condolence wotsit,' his wingman protested.

'You'll do just fine,' Markham told him firmly. 'Obviously if you were still in your dance togs, it would be a different matter.' He turned to the other two. 'Olivia and I were at Town Hall Gardens watching Noakesy and his lady wife dance for charity.'

Once upon a time, Kate Burton would have felt hurt at her exclusion from the DI's 'magic circle' but now, when she tentatively pressed the inner wound, it no longer ached.

It gave her a queer feeling of mingled disappointment and relief that her passion for Markham no longer blazed as it had previously but had now finally subsided into a tranquil regard. Sometimes she was almost disgusted with herself for healing so quickly, but deep down there was comfort in the abatement of her fever and the unspoken assurance of mutual esteem. Gilbert Markham would always be her professional lodestar, but his face would no longer take over the whole sky.

Now she smiled at Noakes. 'Get the guvnor quickstepping did you, sarge?'

'He weren't bad,' her grizzled colleague pronounced with the air of a connoisseur. 'But Olivia's a natural, took

to it like . . .' The phrase "a duck to water" somehow didn't suffice to convey his idol's balletic grace. ' . . . a swan,' he concluded sheepishly.

'Thanks for the commendations, Bruno Tonioli,' the DI said dryly. 'The important thing is that you look respectable enough for seeing Mr Restorick.' The ratty tweed jacket didn't bear close inspection, but at least it was no longer topped by the horrible parka. 'Once we've seen him and Valerie Holmes, we'll wrap it up.'

'I'll look in on Mrs Restorick's PM if Dimples does it tomorrow, sir.'

Doyle looked mightily relieved to hear Burton's offer.

'Only if you're up to it, Kate,' the DI said gently. Watching Davidson wield his Stryker was hardly the ideal way to spend the Sabbath. At bottom he wasn't keen on her doing every PM that came their way, but on this occasion he did not demur.

'I might get something more on the killer's pathology, sir.'

Noakes's piggy eyes gleamed.

'Summat to share with our very own Cracker?' he insinuated.

The acting inspector was suddenly in a great hurry to get to her car.

* * *

Olivia chuckled heartily when Markham relayed the exchange to her later that night as they shared the fish and chips he had picked up on the way back from the interview with Valerie Holmes.

'Good for Kate,' she said. 'Give George an inch and he'll take a mile . . . No way does she want him sniffing round this budding romance.' Then she stopped abruptly. 'I feel guilty laughing like this with you when that poor woman is congealing on a shelf in the morgue.'

'Life goes on,' Markham said gently. 'Eat your mushy peas.'

She smiled weakly. 'D'you remember that story about Peter Mandelson — you know, Tony Blair's creepy enforcer — going into a chippy and asking "for some of that lovely guacamole"? Just imagine doing that in Bromgrove town centre. You'd end up eating your chips through a straw!'

Now it was Markham's turn to laugh.

'Oh, they're getting very genteel down at the Abbey Friar . . . You can order coleslaw with your saveloys these days.'

'You know, I can tell,' she laughed. 'But seriously, this is actually very good, Gil. I feel I can face a marathon session of marking tomorrow on the strength of it.' She paused. 'Don't talk about it if you'd rather not, but how did it go with Mr Restorick?'

'He didn't seem able to take it in, but that's often the way.'

'What about Liberty?'

'On a sleepover, her aunt brought her back. She seemed dazed too . . . kept asking if we were sure her mum was really dead and what about Elvis.'

Olivia was bemused. 'Elvis?'

'The dog.'

'God, how awful.'

Markham ate some more battered cod, savouring the fat white flakes and the greasiness.

'Liberty said something was bothering her mum . . .'

Olivia was startled. 'How did she know?'

'She said Shona took Elvis out for a walk last Tuesday evening and then, as soon as they'd got home, she went back out with him again.'

'Maybe she just felt he needed some more exercise.'

Markham considered this. 'It's possible. But according to Liberty, that's what's her mum did when she was upset about something.'

Olivia frowned.

'A displacement mechanism,' she said slowly. 'At least that's what I suppose a psychologist would call it.'

Markham took a long swig of Pepsi. 'I'm inclined to agree with Liberty,' he said. 'When we spoke to the Restoricks on Wednesday, I had the feeling Shona was trying to decide whether or not to tell us something . . . Maybe that's what she was turning over in her mind the previous night when she did double duty with Elvis.' He bit his lip. 'I have to admit I didn't take to the woman, but now I wonder if I mishandled the interview . . . somehow let my antipathy show so she backed off and decided to keep shtum.'

'The Restoricks were nobody's favourite parents,' Olivia comforted him.

'Except for Mrs Sidney,' Markham said glumly. 'The DCI made sure to let us know.'

'Bollocks to that, Gil . . . No, I'm sorry,' she added as he raised his eyebrows at the unladylike outburst, 'the Restoricks were seriously tricky . . . Just about everyone at Hope had run-ins with them at one time or another. I remember when I tried to help Liberty with her weight — as in suggesting it wasn't a good idea to munch her way through crisps and sweets all day long — Shona made such a stink that I very nearly ended up on capability. I know we shouldn't speak ill of the dead and all that, but being besties with Mrs Slimy doesn't make her a saint in my book.'

'Nor mine, Liv,' said Markham, privately admiring the indignant sparkle of the grey-green eyes. 'Interesting that her weight seems to have been an issue for Valerie Holmes too,' he added casually.

This intrigued his partner, as he knew it would.

'Bulimia,' she exclaimed after Markham had recounted the fruits of Kate Burton's research. 'Or does George call it "the Princess Di disease"?'

'I'm sure Valerie would prefer to think of it in those terms,' he said wryly. 'But apparently Nick Critchley made it sound a whole lot less refined . . . As in "the John Prescott disease".'

Olivia nearly choked on a chip as Markham expounded full details of the Critchley exposé. 'God, I wish I'd watched

it,' she said. 'I'd heard on the grapevine it was bad but this sounds even worse. Utterly poisonous . . . Mind you, Valerie's pretty poisonous too, harassing Jayne like that.'

'Yes,' he said slowly. 'Looks are deceptive in her case. She's a real cat, though she kept her claws well sheathed during the interview.'

'How did she react when you brought up the harassment?' Olivia asked curiously.

'Never turned a hair. Just gave us a whole load of guff about being vulnerable and emotionally bruised . . . the usual victim razzmatazz . . . She had Angela there "for moral support" and the two of them quoted the Ofcom report at us like they'd learned it by heart.'

'Does the report exonerate them then?'

'Well, let's just say it's not a bad plea in mitigation . . . And the two of them made it clear there's a sympathetic GP onside to confirm their "trauma".' Lethargically, he speared the last piece of his cod. 'They're cool customers and no mistake.'

Olivia gave him a sympathetic look before reaching for the wine. 'This Châteauneuf-du-Pape is seriously good, Gil. Sure you don't want to join me?'

'I'd better stick to Pepsi, sweetheart. Just in case I have to fend off Sidney later . . . can't afford to be slurring my words.'

'Isn't he usually invisible at weekends? You know, off schmoozing anyone likely to bag him a gong.'

'I have an uneasy feeling someone may roust him from his lair . . . Maybe Gavin Conors once he gets hold of Shona Restorick's death. It's bound to leak.'

'*Ah*,' she said in a tone of deep comprehension, 'now I'm with you. Just try not to hate me for having another glass. It's surprisingly good with chips.'

'I'm sure Peter Mandelson would agree about the necessity of choosing the right wine to accompany a chippy tea,' he laughed.

'And, with tomorrow being Sunday, no need to worry about a hangover,' she said happily. 'Will you have to go into

the station tomorrow, Gil?' she added guiltily, looking at his tired worn face and heavy eyes.

'I need to run through the alibis.' And hide from Sidney.

'Did anything promising turn up?'

'Nobody was out for an evening ramble by the canal, if that's what you mean. Sorry sweetheart,' Markham realised that he had spoken with some asperity. 'It's a case of same old, same old . . . The only one of them out and about was Richard Keogh and he was headed for a date with a "lady friend" in Calder Vale.'

Olivia took a gulp of wine as though to rinse a bad taste from her mouth.

'God, he's a fast worker. Jayne's only been dead a week.'

'Indeed. He didn't arrive at the Pheasant till half eight, so there's an unaccounted period of time.' Markham sighed. 'But I'm sure he'll come up with something that'll be difficult to challenge, and with everyone else seemingly vouched for . . .' He began clearing away their plates. 'We may need to broaden our suspect pool. Start from scratch and see who else may have had an axe to grind against Jayne. She has to be the key to it all.'

'D'you think Shona Restorick could have attempted some kind of blackmail?' Olivia asked doubtfully.

'No . . . Nick Critchley was the blackmailer. I think with Shona and Gill Dacre it was a case of them *knowing* something . . . stumbling across something that meant the killer couldn't allow them to live.'

Despite the warmth of their cosy kitchen diner, Olivia shivered.

'You make them sound totally ruthless.'

'Well, Professor Finlayson says they're determined to hang on to their secret at all costs and we're four victims down.'

Seeing her lovely face full of consternation, he came to a decision.

'Sod it, Liv. Go on, pour me a glass of red. Pepsi doesn't quite cut it tonight. If the DCI calls, I'll feed him some of the data Finlayson emailed me earlier.'

She smiled.

'That man's turning into something of an ally, isn't he?'

'He's rumbled Sidney's game, that's for sure,' Markham replied with grim satisfaction.

'As in "Don't Frighten the Horses".'

'Precisely . . . It's highly unlikely our killer is a hospital outpatient or some local low life but Finlayson passed along some names for us to check out plus a slew of data . . . hopefully enough to give the impression we're not sniffing around Bromgrove's respectable citizenry.'

'With Sidney you must feel like you're living in *Groundhog Day*, Gil.'

'Well, the predictability means we get the chance to . . . manage his expectations, shall we say.'

'A master bullshitter that's you.' Olivia was now rooting round in the fridge. 'There's some cheese here if you can manage it after all those chips.'

'I believe I can force myself.'

It was a civilised conclusion to their meal and for a time their talk passed to other things.

Finally, Olivia yawned and stretched.

'So, you're running through those alibis tomorrow then,' she said wistfully.

''Fraid so . . . And then I'm going to check out the client base for *Top of the Class*.'

She rubbed her eyes. 'You reckon the *agency* holds the clue to it all?'

'Jayne and Gill both worked for the Thornfields. There was something slippery about that pair . . . it just made me want to take another look. Kate's got a list of their customers for the last five years, so we'll start there.'

'Are you going to bring the Thornfields in?'

'We haven't got enough on them yet, more's the pity. Turns out they know Angela Studholme and Valerie Holmes from way back. Valerie let it slip when we were round there before.'

‘Blimey, Gil, what are the odds of *that* . . . them being friends with Jayne’s blood family . . . ?’

‘It’s an interesting coincidence. Apparently they all knew each other from Aldbourne Village, but it was only when the Critchley programme came out that people clocked the connection with Jayne.’

‘It must have been humiliating for Valerie and Angela, the family’s dirty linen coming out like that?’ Olivia observed.

Markham nodded. ‘Bill Travers and Marian Padgett weren’t happy either,’ he said.

‘You’ll be seeing Marian after the requiem at St Jude’s tomorrow, right?’

‘Yes . . . Kid gloves, obviously, but we can’t keep her on ice indefinitely.’

‘She’s not a suspect, though, is she? I mean . . . Jayne’s *mother*?’ Olivia asked uneasily.

‘Adoptive mother, sweetheart.’

‘Yes, I know . . . But let’s face it, Marian’s the one who gave her a home and did everything for her. She’s the parent in the real sense of the word.’

‘In which case, Jayne reaching out to her birth mother could have felt like the ultimate rejection.’

Olivia nibbled on her Saint Agur.

‘True,’ she conceded. Then, after a moment’s further thought, ‘Jayne’s adoptive dad died around the same time the whole long-lost family thing kicked off, didn’t he?’

‘Des Padgett died two years ago — not long before Jayne got involved with the Nick Critchley project — but according to Kate’s research he found out she was checking out her biological roots.’ Markham spread some Cambozola on a cracker. ‘He was already a sick man, but there was some suggestion that Marian felt he went downhill faster after that. Bill Travers was very tight with them both and agreed with her.’

‘As far as I’m concerned, nurture trumps nature,’ Olivia said firmly. ‘I’m not surprised Marian was bitter. But was she

really bitter enough to *kill* her own daughter . . . ?' Her tone was incredulous.

Not on her own, thought Markham making further inroads on the cheese.

'Do you know if Jayne's biological father's still on the scene?' Olivia asked.

'The date rapist? Margaret Crompton said he didn't stick around, and no one's found any trace of him.'

'Just as well,' Olivia muttered darkly. 'I take it Margaret won't be attending the requiem on Monday, Gil.'

'Far too frail,' he confirmed. 'And in any event, she wouldn't be welcome. I gather it's strictly a Padgett family production.'

She laughed. 'With walk-on roles for you and the rest of CID.'

'Well, the DCI and assorted top brass will be there, pips gleaming.'

She snorted. 'With a *caring* press conference to follow perhaps?'

'Something like that . . . carefully curated to avoid any inference that we're tracking a serial killer connected to Hope, Bromgrove TV or the higher echelons of society.'

'What you need is an accommodating local psycho who'll cough to all of it.'

'Working on it as we speak, dearest,' Markham riposted sardonically. 'So *inconsiderate* of Bromgrove's delinquents not to step up to the plate.'

'I'll come with you tomorrow, Gil,' she grinned. 'Of course, this means you'll owe me.'

'Naturally.'

'But in the circumstances, I feel you need me there for solidarity.' A mischievous smile. 'Plus, I get up Sidney's nose, so from that point of view it will be a pleasure.'

Markham had a feeling that Olivia's infamous moniker for Sidney — Judas Iscariot — might somehow have reached the DCI's ears courtesy of George Noakes.

Suddenly the light in her delicate face was dimmed.

'Sorry, I'm being flippant, dearest, but I also owe it to Jayne. She was my colleague, but I was too self-absorbed to realise she was in trouble.'

'She didn't confide in people, Liv . . . sounds like she preferred it that way.'

'I remember once when we were in the staffroom, she said that "ultimately we're all on our own" . . . There was something sad about the way she said it.'

'Jayne was religious, wasn't she . . . a practising Catholic? That means she believed in the Lord of the dead and the living,' he said gently. 'So, in the final analysis she's *not* on her own.'

Olivia was touched. Looking at Markham's handsome but careworn features, she reminded herself that he never forgot all those who met untimely ends.

'I remember reading this book about Jackie Kennedy,' she said with an attempt at lightness. 'She said the Catholic Church is at its best only at the time of death. The rest of the time it's just silly little men running around in their dark suits. But Catholics *know* death . . . and if it weren't for the children, they'd welcome it.'

'There you go,' he said, endeavouring to match her tone. 'Jayne's got the full might of the Church behind her!'

Olivia squeezed his hand.

'Enough of the case,' she told him. 'Go and slob in front of the box while I make coffee.'

Nothing loath, Markham did as he was told.

Monday would come soon enough.

He would forget tangled ancient history for tonight.

12. A GLIMMER OF LIGHT

'Do dogs have nightmares?'

Kate Burton now knew George Noakes well enough to realise that this was not a philosophical enquiry and he was thinking of Elvis the Jack Russell. The acting DI kept to herself the fact that, after Shona Restorick's PM, *she* had a bad dream in which the dog had licked his owner's brain tissue from the sodden riverbank.

'I think they probably do, sarge,' she said cautiously. 'I remember reading about it in one of my psychology modules . . . something about them "acting out" during REM sleep.'

'That's rapid eye movement,' Doyle interjected, keen to demonstrate that his colleague was not the only university graduate on the block.

'What about Shona Restorick's dog, then?' Noakes mumbled. 'Will he go doolally cos of being alongside her when she were murdered?'

Burton bit her lip, struck anew by how the good and the comical were inextricably blended in her colleague's character. A noted dog-lover, the DS had never managed to persuade house-proud Muriel Noakes to entertain the notion of a family pet (*the smell, the mess*!). Certainly, it was

hard to imagine Muriel or Natalie doing duty with a pooper scooper. The DS undertook dog walking for Bromgrove's canine charity, the Best Friends Society, but would dearly have loved to keep his own mutt at home.

Suddenly, out of nowhere, Burton experienced a huge wave of affection for her irascible colleague. There was no doubting he could be a horror — only the other day she'd heard a female DI say Noakes was like some low-budget version of Donald Trump — but she saw the vulnerability beneath the awfulness and knew she would miss him when the time came to move on. Every CID had its 'throwback', but George Noakes was in a class of his own.

'Elvis will probably work the bad memories out of his system over time,' she told him gently. 'And Liberty's on hand for walks and lots of outings, which should help.'

'Don' see that kid getting off her backside anytime soon,' was his gloomy prognostication. But nevertheless he looked somewhat brighter for Burton's reassurance.

It was Monday evening, and they were waiting for Markham to emerge from his office so they could set off to Jayne Padgett's requiem.

'What's the boss doing?' Doyle asked.

'On the blower to Sidney,' Noakes grunted. 'To see if we can dodge a press conference.'.

Doyle looked confused. 'Isn't the DCI coming to church with the rest of us?'

'He's been held up in Birmingham at the BAME seminar,' Burton said crisply. Then, registering Noakes's blank expression, 'The focus group for Black, Asian and Minority Ethnic issues.'

He made a disgusted sound.

'I hate all that lefty bollocks . . . an' lumping minorities together like they're all the same, it's bloody patronising if you ask me.'

Burton was inclined to agree with Noakes as far as that went, but she didn't want to get him started on a rant against wokeness.

'They probably start every session by making folk swear allegiance to Lenin,' Doyle joked provocatively before subsiding at a glare from the acting DI.

'*Anyway*,' she said heavily, 'the top brass won't get back in time so we're representing CID.'

She reflected that it was a pity Sidney wouldn't get to see Noakes's new formal wear, Muriel and the DI having joined forces in a cunning pincer movement aimed at smartening him up. His unswerving predilection for double-breasted numbers of a type last worn by Nikita Kruschev was unfortunate, but on this occasion he really looked almost the business and for once the haystack hair was behaving itself. There was nothing to be done about the jowly mastiff features and resolutely belligerent expression, but the DS would pass muster down at St Jude's.

Markham emerged from his office looking suave and immaculate as ever. Jealous detractors could mutter 'tailor's dummy' all they liked, thought Burton, but there was nothing dandyish or effete about her boss. He was barely aware of his physical impact, however a personal fastidiousness coupled with exquisite taste ensured that all eyes were invariably drawn to him no matter what the occasion . . . a fact that didn't exactly enhance his relationship with the DCI.

'What gives with Sidney?' Noakes asked, taking the bull by the horns. 'Do we have to do a poxy press conference or what?'

'I've persuaded him it would be better to leave it till later in the week, so we don't spark a panic . . . He's agreed we can have till Wednesday.' Burton noticed that, despite the pinstripe suit and perfect grooming, Markham was breathing hard.

'What happens in the meantime, then . . . We jus' wait for a miracle?' Noakes enquired sarcastically.

'We push for a breakthrough,' the DI said resolutely. 'I want to bring the Thornfields in tomorrow morning.'

'You reckon Superman's good for it, guv?' his wingman asked eagerly.

‘Not so much that,’ the DI replied. ‘But when Kate checked through the agency’s customer records, it looked like there must be other paperwork we never saw.’

Doyle looked dubious. ‘How can you tell?’

‘The records are all neatly typed up,’ Burton told him, ‘but there’s this cryptic scribbled shorthand in the margins with initials and numbers which look like references to other documents.’

‘An’ you think they’ve got dirt on folk cos of this weirdy Da Vinci Code set-up?’ Noakes pressed.

‘Well it feels like they’re keeping something back . . .’ Burton frowned.

‘Could they be blackmailing people?’ Doyle wondered.

The DI leaned wearily against the door jamb. ‘I’d have thought that was too risky,’ he said. ‘But they’re the kind to store up information, secrets . . . on the off chance it might come in useful. Nothing so crude as blackmail, but maybe some kind of leverage if they wanted a favour. Some of the parents on their books are well-heeled—’

‘So it don’ hurt to know what they get up to in private.’ Noakes’s imagination was fired up by the scenario.

Markham straightened up with an effort. ‘Could be I’m barking up the wrong tree, but both Jayne and Gill worked for that agency, so I want to dig deeper with the Thornfields.’

‘An’ they know the Ugly Sisters,’ Noakes added. ‘All cosy an’ . . .’ He groped for a word.

‘Incestuous,’ Doyle suggested.

‘Mebbe that’s a bit strong, lad,’ his mentor replied, ‘but yeah, kind of . . .’

‘Right team, we should head off to St Jude’s,’ the DI said. ‘Let’s take our own cars, then we can shoot off home afterwards and be fresh for tomorrow morning.’

‘We’re still going to the eats afterwards, right?’ Noakes asked anxiously.

‘Yes, there’s something laid on in the parish hall next door, but we don’t want to give the impression we think it’s an “all you can eat” jolly for CID.’

''Course not.' Noakes was affronted. Noting the capacious jacket pockets, Markham couldn't help reflecting that they were ideal for secreting sausage rolls.

Well, the DI thought resignedly, he'd take what he could get. At least Burton and Doyle — both snappily attired in suits by Ted Baker and Hugo Boss respectively — created the right impression and were now adept at providing cover whenever Noakes went off-piste. Not that those shrewd piggy eyes were likely to miss anything amiss with their suspects, no matter how many hors d'oeuvres he put away.

Burton's mind was on strategy rather than snacks. 'How're we going to play it with Marian Padgett?'

'We need to be sensitive,' the DI said. 'On the other hand, it's imperative that we speak to her.'

'Surely we can rule her out,' Doyle exclaimed 'I mean, she's Padgett's mother!'

It was an echo of Olivia's protest the previous night.

'Don' count for owt these days,' Noakes sniffed. 'It's wall-to-wall killer mums on them true-crime documentaries . . . An' anyway, she's the adoptive mum.'

Markham really didn't feel up to engaging in a nature-versus-nature debate. At least not with George Noakes.

'There was a lot of residual bitterness from the Critchley programme,' he reminded them. 'Especially if Marian held Jayne responsible for Des Padgett dying before his time.'

Doyle thought about this. 'Yeah, reality TV often means a truckload of damaged people,' he observed. The newly minted DS was no cultural snob. 'It's kind of addictive to watch,' he confessed, 'but there's something sick about how it can ruin lives. I mean, look at *Love Island* and those suicides.'

'Precisely,' Markham said.

'But Marian's an old woman,' Noakes objected.

'She's seventy-six, which isn't all that old these days, Sergeant,' the DI pointed out. 'If she was in a rage or experiencing a psychotic episode, it could have produced an unnatural upswell or surge in strength.'

'She could have been on something,' Burton speculated. 'Or there could be another person involved.'

'Like a contract killing.' Noakes scoffed. '*Gangsta Granny*!'

'It feels a bit of a stretch,' the acting DI said ruefully.

'We haven't really considered a conspiracy,' Markham said slowly. 'But there's nothing to say this couldn't be joint enterprise . . .'

Noakes ran through possible pairings. 'Lipscombe an' Brighouse . Bill Travers an' his fancy piece, Bickwotsit. The Thornfields. Tricky Dicky an' whoever he's shacked up with. The half-sisters. Them single mums who had a down on Padgett . . . Christ, I c'n jus' see them doing Thelma & Louise. The Restoricks . . . only,' he came up short with a guilty duck of the head, 'she's copped it.'

Burton rumpled her nut-brown pageboy into disarray before carefully smoothing it back into shape, a sure sign of agitation. 'All of them had some reason to dislike or resent Jayne, but unless we're missing something — a tipping point — I can't make the step from that to murder . . .'

Doyle too was fidgety, restlessly unfastening and fastening the top button of his natty waistcoat. 'Maybe there's a hidden element. Some factor we haven't considered.'

'Like what?' Noakes demanded.

His younger colleague shrugged helplessly. 'Dunno, sarge.'

'Maybe there's another person,' Markham said.

Three pairs of eyes were riveted on the DI.

'Someone who's gone under the radar so far,' he continued.

'A killer teen?' Noakes asked. 'Or mebbe more than one?'

'It's possible,' Markham said. 'That's one reason I wanted to widen the net. Professor Finlayson raised the possibility of this being the work of a traumatised juvenile. Oh, I know,' he held up a hand as though to forestall objections, 'he talked about adults with arrested development too . . . But Jayne Padgett and Gill Dacre were teachers, and I can't help feeling their role in the community is somehow significant.'

'More than the long-lost family hoojah?' Noakes challenged.

'Maybe that was just the ideal camouflage,' his boss suggested. 'A perfect distraction from what was really going on.'

'So, he — they — struck it lucky.' It went strongly against the grain with Noakes for killers to catch the breaks.

It was clear the guvnor's theory made sense to Burton. 'All the family issues swirling around might have been a convenient smokescreen.'

'Does this mean we're back to square one?' Noakes looked ready to punch a hole in the wall. 'As in that fricking school with its whack jobs . . . Hey,' he wheeled round on the DI. 'Mebbe it's the kid who did the fire an' that graffiti about Padgett.'

'The same lad who was hanging round the park just after Jayne was murdered,' Burton murmured. 'But who is he?'

'No red flags came up when we checked out the students,' Doyle mused. 'They all seemed kosher . . . not the brightest bulbs in the box, granted.' Out of the corner of his eye, he observed Burton stiffen. 'But no one looked like they had it in them to do *that*,' he concluded hastily.

'When Kate trawled the agency's records, it was apparent that quite a few students from Hope had used the service,' the DI told them. 'All totally innocuous on the surface, but there could be a bigger picture.'

'Sidney won't like you going after the families,' Noakes observed trenchantly. ''Specially not if they're posh.'

'Yes, it's a minefield,' Markham agreed. 'I don't want to mix it with the families. But I'm hoping Pauline Thornfield might give us something.'

'What makes you believe Bet Lynch'll cough, guv?' Noakes asked curiously.

'Just a feeling. Now I think back, she had the same look as Shona Restorick . . . Like there was this niggle at the back of her mind . . .'

As he said this, he could almost hear the DCI's nasal honk: 'Don't give in to that famous flair of yours, Inspector . . . Next thing, you'll be doing stunts for the *Gazette*.'

Given Sidney's celebrity cravings, surely this would be a case of the pot calling the kettle black.

But still, Markham knew he had to be careful.

'I'm relying on something having touched a chord in Mrs Thornfield's mind,' he said. 'If we approach her sympathetically, perhaps we can find out what it is.'

He was pinning his hopes on there being something latent, unformulated, maybe even unthinkable, that was dormant in Pauline Thornfield's subconscious . . . something ready to rise up before her in one devastating conviction . . .

'Come on.' He jerked himself out of this reverie. 'We're due down at the church.'

* * *

St Jude's was a late nineteenth-century Catholic church built in the Gothic style with a single nave and various side chapels.

The interior could best be described as baroque Italianate, its most distinctive feature being a semi-circular two-tier reredos behind the altar crowded with statues of saints and angels, with cherubs' heads floating above the heavenly assemblage.

Markham rather liked the effect, though Olivia said it reminded her of a catacomb with all those niches. Noakes's verdict when it came was entirely in character. 'Why do holy folk allus have to look miserable.'

The rose window and pointed arches were dark on this October evening, but lamps and candles shed a soft patina on statues to the left and right of the altar, creating an almost intimate atmosphere. On the far left of the nave was a Lady chapel adorned with a remarkable painting of the Madonna; dressed as a medieval noblewoman in flowing blue kirtle and billowing ivory veil which reached to the ground, she stood in front of

a white canopy held at each corner by an angelic trumpeter. With her long almond shaped eyes and sensuous mouth, she was more siren than sanctified virgin. Not a single curl escaped from beneath the veil with its golden circlet. The blue gown was high-necked and long-sleeved. Yet to Markham she radiated a mysterious allure that was the very opposite of celestial.

The trestle with a square rosewood box rested at the bottom of three richly carpeted shallow steps flanked by two vintage metal jardinières holding fragrant lily of the valley.

'It's not a proper coffin,' muttered Noakes who clearly hadn't read Markham's email explaining that there would be a casket containing Jayne Padgett's tissue samples mixed with her adoptive father's ashes.

In a hurried undertone, Burton outlined the position, eliciting an appalled 'Gross!' It was clear from his expression that Doyle, too, was boggling at the trestle with squeamish distaste.

The congregation occupied a few pews at the front of the church, the detectives seating themselves discreetly towards the back. A few minutes after their arrival, Olivia slipped in next to Markham looking elegant in a dark trench coat with her long red hair tucked into a snood. Smiling briefly at Burton and Doyle, she distinguished Noakes with a fingertips kiss which made him beam with pleasure before relapsing into his usual expression of lugubrious suspicion.

As always on such occasions, Markham found that individuality was subsumed in a sea of black but nonetheless managed to identify most of the mourners. Jayne Padgett's half-sisters were notable by their absence, but the Hope Academy contingent were all there, Christine Bickerton leaning heavily on Bill Travers as if for support while Judith Lipscombe adopted a similar pose with Tony Brighouse. 'Like they think the poor sods are bookends,' observed Noakes.

Matthew Sullivan was there too, along with a little gaggle of students. Two big-haired girls persisted in snuffling noisily into their sleeves until he whipped out the Kleenex, while three gawky looking lads — all acne and shuffling

awkwardness — gawped round at the statues and stations of the cross as though this outing was on a par with time-travel to the Stone Age.

Richard Keogh appeared uncomfortable, wearing an ill-fitting black suit that contrasted unfavourably with the expensive wool coats around him. Various parents, among them the young couple Markham had encountered on his visit to the agency, also seemed somewhat out of it, fidgeting nervously as though unsure what to expect. Denise Rooney and Michelle Rooney were there too looking, as Noakes informed Doyle, 'like a pair of WAGs', all kohl eyeliner and witchy blonde extensions.

Pauline and John Thornfield slipped in just before the start of the service. Both of them appeared ultra-smart in what to Markham's keen appraisal looked like bespoke tailoring. Clearly their educational franchise was doing well. As the opening hymn struck up, Pauline turned round and met the DI's eye with a strangely imploring expression.

Pauline's my best bet, he thought with renewed conviction. Somehow that agency holds the key to it all.

Marian Padgett stood surprisingly erect, flanked by a praetorian guard of well-heeled senior citizens. Hatchet-featured she might be, but she was elegantly dressed in black cashmere and with her flattering blow-dry looked as if she had stepped straight out of the hair salon.

The requiem itself was dignified, conducted by an Irish priest whose lilting brogue imparted warmth to a clearly sincere eulogy. With good old-fashioned hymns played by a more than competent organist, it struck Markham that this was exactly the kind of send-off Jayne Padgett would have wanted. Unpretentious but omitting none of the rubric which had been so precious to her. Proceedings concluded with the celebrant, two altar servers and Mrs Padgett processing into the vestry behind a deacon who carried the rosewood box.

‘What’s happening now?’ Doyle enquired uncertainly as organ music continued softly in the background and the mourners resumed their seats.

‘I imagine some private ceremony of committal,’ Markham replied easily.

The young DS looked as though he wished he hadn’t asked.

Noakes wriggled impatiently. ‘D’you think the padre’s given ’em permission to keep the . . . bits an’ bobs here in the church?’

Bits and bobs. Kate Burton perceptibly winced.

‘The Padgetts were obviously very good to their parish,’ Markham answered. ‘It wouldn’t surprise me if there’s some special arrangement for Jayne’s remains, especially since her body isn’t being released.’

‘’S like Ground Zero,’ Noakes declared solemnly.

‘How d’you mean?’ Doyle was baffled.

‘After the Twin Towers thing on 9/11 . . . that’s how they managed funerals when all they had left was tufts of hair an’ bits of skin. They did proper burials for ’em. The full monty. Even if it were jus’ the top of someone’s scalp.’

Doyle looked as though he could happily have dispensed with this piece of lore, his eyes darting to the vestry door with furtive fascination.

‘Do we jus’ wait for ’em to come out then, boss?’ Noakes knew what the guvnor and Olivia were like in old churches. They’d end up being dragged round every statue and picture if they didn’t look lively.

Olivia’s eyes twinkled.

‘I think it’s meant to be a time for quiet prayer and reflection, George, though I imagine the police are excused.’

‘Cushty. We might as well go next door an’ get some grub . . . Funerals allus make me peckish.’

After their colleague’s grisly revelations about obsequies for the victims of 9/11, neither Burton nor Doyle looked as though they particularly fancied tucking into the cold meats.

Nevertheless, the detectives and Olivia adjourned to the parish hall where a very decent buffet was laid out with an extensive range of hot and cold finger food including quiches, sandwiches, pork pies, mini pizzas, savoury eggs, chicken goujons, sausage rolls and crisps, as well as scones, Victoria sponge and fruit cake. Tea and coffee were dispensed from giant urns, while trolleys were generously stocked with red and white wine and soft drinks. Middle-aged ladies with hospitable expressions stood next to piles of plates and napkinned cutlery.

'Ma Padgett's not stinted on the wake, I'll give her that,' Noakes said approvingly as he surveyed these offerings.

'Don't let him guzzle everything in sight,' Markham murmured to Olivia. 'Sidney and the top brass are stuck in Birmingham, but the last thing we need is someone regaling them with a description of my sergeant treating this as an episode of *Man v. Food*.'

She giggled. 'He's incorrigible, but I know what he means about funerals making you hungry. I could eat a horse.'

With that she sidled up to Noakes who gallantly gestured her to precede him. One of the nicest things about his boss's girlfriend was the way she enjoyed her food and didn't do the niminy-piminy thing about only liking lettuce leaves and salad. Soon the pair were chuckling conspiratorially over chicken skewers and cheese sticks.

Gradually, the rest of the congregation trickled over to the hall and soon there was a friendly, albeit subdued, buzz.

No one was in any hurry to talk to Markham and his team, apart from Marjorie Poole who exchanged a few cordial words, but that was hardly surprising in the circumstances.

There was no sign of Marian Padgett either.

Despite hostile glances from the principal Hope Academy mourners, Markham determined to stick it out. The officiating priest arrived and duly circulated along with his deacon, courteously greeting Markham and winning

brownie points from the DI for a few well-chosen words about the deceased.

And still the DI waited.

Kate Burton was at his elbow.

'Are we going to hang on for Marian then, sir?'

'Father O'Toole said she'll be along shortly. Apparently, she's lighting a candle for Jayne in the Lady chapel.'

At that moment, Pauline Thornfield approached them. Out of the corner of his eye, the DI had noticed her inching closer by degrees but gave no indication of the exultation he felt.

She wants to get something off her chest.

'I need to see you, Inspector,' she said softly, almost without moving her lips.

'Certainly, Mrs Thornfield. Shall we say tomorrow at eleven?'

He noticed the woman's upper lip under the peek-a-boo hat and veil — a secular equivalent of the Catholic mantilla — was beaded with sweat and she appeared rigid with tension.

They had barely concluded this exchange when they were joined by her husband and the Carmichaels, Markham suddenly recalling the surname of the couple from the agency. A few more parents came over and spoke warmly of Jayne Padgett, their genuine emotion contributing to Markham's favourable impression of the memorial service. Oddly, Pauline Thornfield appeared anxious to detach herself, even when the talk turned to *Top of the Class*, with several mums and dads giving testimonials of the most flattering kind.

She wants out of here, Markham thought. But why?

He felt an overpowering urge to steer the woman away from the gathering and coax it out of her.

But instinct told him it was not the right time. She had to do it in her own way and in her own time. Moreover, something had frightened her . . . or maybe someone . . .

Casually, he walked to the buffet with Burton. Under cover of helping his colleague to a slice of quiche, he

murmured, 'I want surveillance on the Thornfields . . . discreet as you like, but regular checks from when they leave here till she shows up in CID tomorrow.'

'On it as soon as we're out of here, boss.'

They made desultory chit-chat over the canapés, all the while watching and waiting.

Doyle ambled over, nodding significantly towards the doorway. Now Noakes came to join them, his pockets bulging with illicit baked meats.

Marian Padgett had arrived.

The team waited as she moved amongst the mourners, dispensing a graceful word here, a polite acknowledgement there until she reached the detectives. The DI mentally accorded her full marks for not sheltering behind her GP or other male supporters, though he guessed that they were no doubt present hovering in the wings.

'Thank you for coming,' she said simply. Then, 'There's a little meeting room behind the kitchen. We'll be more private in there.'

Several pairs of eyes followed them as they followed the chief mourner out of the hall.

* * *

Half an hour later the detectives stood in St Jude's car park.

'That's a bitter woman,' the DI said, 'but I don't think she's our murderer.'

'Marian was virtually estranged from Jayne when she was killed,' Burton mused, 'but if her GP was with her at the time Shona Restorick was attacked . . . that's a pretty solid alibi.'

'Who's to say Dr Kildare ain't lying?' Noakes looked mutinous. 'By the sound of it, they're pretty thick . . . p'raps even having a thing.'

'Maybe so, but if he confirms Marian's account, with no one to say otherwise . . .' Markham shrugged eloquently. 'It'd be difficult to challenge.'

‘Marian admitted she’d rowed with Jayne over the phone.’ Doyle thought hard. ‘Went at it hammer and tongs by the sound of things. She talked about ingratitude and selfishness . . . more or less blamed Jayne for Des having that final stroke. And she’s strong too — wiry — pretty good for her age . . . could easily have overpowered Jayne if she took her by surprise.’

‘Yeah, an’ she could’ve handled Dacre an’ Critchley no problem.’ Noakes clearly hadn’t liked the bereaved parent. ‘She’s got what it takes . . . a real ice queen. Didn’t show any emotion about her own daughter . . . All that stuff about children being a gift an’ God taking ’em away if he wants. Creepy.’

‘I think she was keeping a tight leash on her feelings, Sergeant.’ The DI had sensed mingled fury and regret ruthlessly banked down behind a facade of frigid propriety and religiosity. ‘There was an angry fall-out with Jayne, no doubt about it,’ he went on, ‘and she has to live with the fact that hurtful things were said between them with no chance to reconcile or repair the rift.’

‘Seemed to me like she’s doing all right.’ Noakes was, as ever, reluctant to give ground. ‘Reckon she’s a dipso an’ all . . . She were slurring her words at the end.’

‘I think she’s on medication,’ Burton put in. ‘Father O’Toole said something about her being treated for depression.’

‘Don’ mean to say she couldn’t have murdered Jayne, an’ then she had to fix the others cos they were on to her . . . otherwise, bang goes her nicey-nicey lifestyle. All the posh neighbours pointing the finger . . . again.’ Noakes warmed to his theme. ‘Yeah. Couldn’t face being a social outcast. Like the prof said, she had to go on killing to keep her secret.’

Burton was divided between pleasure at Noakes’s deference to Professor Finlayson and personal scepticism at the notion of Marian Padgett being the killer.

‘She’s a cold fish all right,’ the acting DI conceded, ‘but somehow I can’t picture her for it, sarge.’

'Jus' being devil's wotsit,' Noakes replied with the dignified air of one who'd seen it all and, what's more, had the t-shirt to prove it.

'Quite right too, Sergeant.' Markham smiled at his wingman. 'It's essential to have someone play devil's advocate lest we rule anyone out too hastily.'

'The bleach.' The grizzled DS was encouraged to go on. 'Y'know . . . Like I said when we looked at the body, guv. Could be a message? Summat about sin an' wickedness . . . Wash your mouth out.' With a burst of inspiration. 'Didn't them Catholic nuns in Ireland do stuff like that? You know . . . the ones who ran orphanages an' homes for girls who went off the rails.'

Olivia had drawn near while they were conversing and picked up the tail end of this exchange.

'You're right about that, George,' she said. 'I remember it, too. The Magdalen laundries scandal, wasn't it? There was a film too. *The Magdalen Sisters* . . . very hot on sin and guilt.'

As DS Doyle later put it, CID's very own Buffet Slayer looked as though he might melt into a puddle on the spot.

'Yeah, that's the fella,' he beamed at her. 'So, I figure mebbe Marian were tapping into all that religious crip crap . . . punishing Jayne for betraying her an' Des . . . y'know, honour your mother an' father. She could've been saying summat about Jayne being dirty an' all cos her mum had her after being raped.'

Olivia smiled at him. 'I can see where you're coming from,' she said as a wave of pink rose up his beefy neck.

Burton decided to interrupt the love-in.

'The bleach and the other stuff . . . wanting to tidy the scene and make it neat. It doesn't have to be a religious hang-up. Nathan,' now it was *her* turn to flush, 'I mean, Professor Finlayson, thought it could relate to unresolved sexual trauma in the killer's past. And anyway,' she added before Noakes could interrupt, 'all the research on parental homicide suggests a parent wouldn't want to inflict gratuitous suffering.'

Noakes's face expressed intense mistrust of academic research, but he acknowledged the point. 'Bloody horrible way to go, bleach,' he said. 'Ole Ma Padgett . . . well, she'd have to have a strong stomach for that.'

'Jayne died from strangulation,' Burton said impatiently.

Noakes looked mulish. 'The bleach has to mean *summat*,' he insisted.

'No doubt you're right about that,' Markham put in, 'but as yet we don't know the significance.'

'So where does all this leave us?' Burton demanded.

'I feel Pauline Thornfield's on the brink of telling us something,' the DI replied.

'Like what?' Noakes demanded.

'I don't know, Noakesy. Look, this has been a case of two halves,' Markham continued. 'Jayne's family circumstances were exotic . . . headline-grabbing. But she was a teacher—'

'Like Gill Dacre,' Doyle said eagerly. 'Both of them working for the agency.'

The DI nodded. 'And I can't help thinking everything leads back to that . . . her role as a teacher.'

'You mean fricking Hope Academy,' Noakes said glumly.

'There could be a connection to Hope,' Markham replied levelly. 'Or we could be looking at a student from there who was on the agency's books at one time.'

'Sorry, I forgot to say, there's a prayer service for Jayne and Gill at Hope tomorrow, boss.' Burton slipped in guiltily.

Markham ignored Noakes's agitated semaphore. 'What time, Kate?'

'Half eight, before lessons start, guv.'

'We can fit that in before Pauline Thornfield,' Markham told them firmly.

Noakes and Doyle exchanged disgruntled glances.

'We've got till Wednesday before Sidney brings in the big guns,' the DI said. 'Who knows, something from Hope may give us a way in with Pauline Thornfield.' He faced

them down. 'This is it, folks. Now or never. If I'm right about Pauline, there's still a chance . . .'

'I'll go through those files again in the morning, guv.' Burton sensed the guvnor's urgency.

'If she gives us a name . . . just a name . . . we can set a trap,' Markham said with more confidence than he felt.

There being nothing left to say, they headed for their respective cars. Above them, a gibbous moon watched the scurrying figures.

'Is this it then, Gil?' Olivia asked once they were en route to the Sweepstakes. 'You're pinning everything on Pauline Thornfield?'

'I've got nothing else, sweetheart,' came the quiet reply. 'But when that woman turned round and looked at me tonight, it felt like a glimmer of light. Now we've got twenty-four hours to reel her in.'

As the silent streets sped by, Olivia prayed that he was right.

13. COUNTDOWN

Tuesday 27 October was a gloriously bright day with clear blue skies and sunshine. The air was mild and sweet-smelling, with a hint of autumn compost and bonfires, and the grass verges that lined the driveway to Hope Academy were covered by a crunchy carpet of gold and russet leaves. Even the sight of the 'bunker' as it loomed into view couldn't crush the optimism Markham felt . . .

The DI was aware he could be clutching at straws, but something told him this was the day the team would have a breakthrough. He had dreamed of Jayne Padgett the previous night, which seemed like an omen. The teacher had been sitting in Castor Hill Park's walled garden at sunset near the floral cuckoo clock, Wordsworth the cat purring in her lap. As he walked along the gravel path towards her, she raised a hand to her throat and gestured as if to remind him that she had been strangled. Neither of them spoke, but he heard two words clearly, as if they were projected onto his mind by magic lantern.

Innocence betrayed.

Olivia had been intrigued when he told her.

'It was over in seconds,' he said. 'I called to Jayne to stay, but she just became fainter and fainter — dissolving into

the twilight — until she wasn't there anymore, and then the garden vanished.'

'Do you think it's significant that you saw her in the garden?'

'I reckon it's because I had been thinking of her and Gill Dacre. The park was special to Jayne because it's where she was abandoned as a baby, and the walled garden's where we found Gill's body.'

'Innocence suggests a child.' Olivia tried to puzzle out the enigma. 'A child who was somehow betrayed. Maybe she meant herself . . . abandoned by her real mother, estranged from her adoptive mother . . . Or she could have been referring to something done to her as a child. Cruelty, abuse?'

'It's possible, Liv. Or she might have been thinking of a child she cared about . . .'

'One of her students?'

'Could be . . . maybe a pupil who'd been hurt whom she tried to protect.'

'What if it was bigger than that, Gil? What if she meant kids were being betrayed at Hope because of wrongdoing . . . some sort of corruption?' She bit her lip. 'I never noticed anything like that . . . but then, I wasn't looking for it. Mind you, these days I feel like I wouldn't put anything past them.'

At that, he had laughed. 'I'm flattered you take my dreams so seriously, darling Liv. Sidney would give me short shrift if he caught me talking like this.'

'Oh, I can just imagine Judas Iscariot's take on it.' Olivia spoke through her nose, capturing the DCI's adenoidal drone to perfection. '"Let's have none of this soothsaying nonsense. You're a policeman not a medium, Inspector."'

'He's implacably opposed to flights of fancy, that's for sure.'

Olivia's imagination, on the other hand, had clearly been fired by her boyfriend's possible psychic experience.

'How did Jayne look, Gil? Was she happy or sad?'

‘That’s the thing, Liv. She smiled at me as though she knew how I felt . . . almost like she was telling me I was on the right track and to keep going.’

‘I presume you’re not going to share this with George and the others?’

‘God no, they wouldn’t know what to say. Pretty much in Sidney’s camp when it comes to that kind of thing. Noakesy would no doubt tell me I can always set up as a fortune teller if it doesn’t work out for me in CID.’

Speak of the devil, now here came his wingman lumbering across the car park.

Noakes regarded the school’s exterior with disfavour. ‘Hideous ain’t it?’ he grunted. ‘Wonder what they’ll replace it with once that building fund gets enough dosh.’

‘An even worse carbuncle most likely.’

The DS regarded the guvnor suspiciously. It appeared to him they had scant grounds for good cheer, and yet the boss seemed oddly chipper. Happen he and Olivia had made a night of it . . . Hastily, Noakes turned his thoughts from the X-rated direction in which they were tending.

Burton and Doyle had arrived, looking the picture of executive chic, which was just as well given that Noakes’s ensemble of baggy mushroom cords, yellow check shirt and mustard jacket was unlikely to win any plaudits for snappy dressing.

Noakes went straight on the offensive. ‘What’s supposed to be happening at this prayer service thingy then?’

‘It’s more like a glorified assembly really, sarge,’ Burton told him. ‘With all the rumours flying around and Shona Restorick’s murder, I think senior management want to calm things down a bit. And, after Jayne’s requiem, they figured the school ought to commemorate Gill Dacre somehow.’

‘Plus they get brownie points with the parents and governors for being ever so caring.’ Doyle’s cynicism had come on in leaps and bounds since he joined Markham’s team.

‘D’you think Pauline Thornfield will show up, guv?’ Noakes asked.

‘I can answer that,’ Burton said crisply.

Of course you can. Noakes and Doyle did an inner eye roll in unison.

'I checked who's coming,' the acting DI told them. 'There's a dozen or so visitors and she's one of them.'

'Fair enough, I suppose,' Markham said. 'Gill tutored kids from Hope privately via *Top of the Class*, so stands to reason the agency's boss might want to attend. Bit of PR for her company into the bargain.'

'Actually boss, I don't think Lipscombe and Brighouse were very keen on it,' Burton informed him. 'Having staff working for the agency kind of flags up the school's deficiencies. You know, like it's an admission the teaching isn't good enough to get kids through their exams, so families have to get help from outside.'

'Ah.' The DI took this in.

'But apparently she insisted on coming,' Burton explained. 'Told Lipscombe she owed it to Dacre to represent the agency . . . blah blah.'

Doyle frowned. 'Bit pushy wasn't it?'

'Mebbe she's got an ulterior motive.' Noakes was scanning the school's unprepossessing facade. 'Wanted to convince herself about something, check someone out before she spoke to us.'

It struck Markham as a shrewd observation.

'Yes,' he said slowly. 'I don't see either of the Thornfields putting themselves out for prayers at a school assembly unless there's a game plan.'

Burton considered this scenario.

'Who is she checking up on? The senior leaders, a teacher, one of the kids?'

Noakes shrugged. 'Not got a clue. Mebbe she'll make a move . . . try an' have a word with whoever it is.'

The DI looked at his watch.

'Right, let's get in there,' he said. 'See who Pauline speaks to.'

* * *

But in the event, Pauline Thornfield spoke to no one.

Back in the car park, three quarters of an hour later, the detectives were frustrated.

'Not a dicky bird.' Noakes was disgusted. 'Jus' sat an' flapped her lips along with the rest of 'em.'

'Odd, though,' Doyle commented. The way she stared at the kids when they were singing that whiny piece whatshisface composed for Gill.'

'You sound more like DS Noakes by the day, Sergeant,' Markham said dryly. 'If you're referring to Mr Cunningham, the Director of Music, then I thought it wasn't bad. At least the choir looked as if they meant it.'

'Not like Lipscombe an' Brighouse,' Noakes growled. 'Them two fair make me sick. Somehow it ended up being all about them an' not that poor cow.' He thought for a moment. 'At least Matt Sullivan came up with some nice stuff about her . . . stories about the kids she'd helped an' all that.'

'Yes, that was the one redeeming feature really,' the DI agreed.

Impatiently, Burton brought them back to the woman under scrutiny. 'Doyle's right about Pauline, though. She practically took the skin off those kids' faces the way she was staring at them.'

'Did you notice if she was staring at any particular pupil, Kate?' The DI knew it was a long shot.

'From where we were sitting, I couldn't be sure,' she said reluctantly. 'It looked like Pauline was checking out the back row of the choir, but I'm not positive about it.'

However, Markham had great faith in her powers of observation. 'Did you recognise anyone?'

'We interviewed five of the kids when we had those meetings with the students Jayne and Gill taught,' she replied.

Suddenly the DI felt that strange tingle in his palms which portended a breakthrough.

'Were any of them tutored via the agency?'

Burton screwed up her face, thinking intently.

'I remember Jayne gave the two lads some coaching after school, but that wasn't through *Top of the Class*. Out of the girls, I think two of them were using the agency for their GCSEs . . . Yes, that's right . . . Pippa Carmichael and Cathy Byrne.'

Markham's face fell. 'Not Chelsey Preston then? You know, the one you said was manipulative, who stirred things up by saying Jayne was sympathetic about the home situation . . . landed her in it when the mother kicked off.'

Burton was disappointed too. 'No, Chelsey definitely wasn't one of them, boss. Not the kind of girl who'd want to be in the choir.' She frowned. 'If any kid was going to be mixed up in something dodgy, I'd have put money on Chelsey . . . or Caitlin Rooney.'

'Isn't Caitlin's mum the one who works at the Newman?' Doyle enquired.

'Correct.' The DI's expression was shuttered. 'She sent us away with a flea in our ear when we probed what was going on at home.' He thought for a second before quickly resetting the team's focus. 'So, what do we know about these other two girls?'

Burton cast her mind back. 'Pippa was in Gill's form. Jayne tutored her through the agency. She seemed a nice normal kid, giggly and immature, just your average fifteen-year-old. She's not particularly academic, but no issues aside from being bullied at school.'

'We met her mum and dad when we called round the agency, boss,' Noakes put in. 'They said Padgett sorted the bullying.'

'So they did,' Markham recalled the young father and his pregnant wife. 'The parents seemed decent, nothing but good things to say about Jayne.' He looked up at the elms and birches that lined the school drive, their skeleton limbs in stark contrast to the thick drifts of leaves beneath. 'What about the other girl — Cathy Byrne?'

'Again, boss, just your standard teenager. A bit gauche and awkward like Pippa . . . no clashes with teachers.' Burton

blew her fringe upwards as though suddenly hot with frustration. 'I checked out all the kids we interviewed with Matt Sullivan. There was nothing on the school system which suggested anything out of the ordinary. None of them had got so much as a detention from Jayne or Gill. Apparently, Cathy could be a bit lippy with some staff, but no major disciplinary issues.'

'Maybe we've got it wrong and it wasn't the *kids* Pauline was staring at,' Doyle ventured.

'How d'you mean?' Noakes challenged.

'Well, there were teachers on that raised bit at the back of the choir. Bill Travers and Christine Bickerton were sat directly behind the last row of kids. Brighouse and Lipscombe were a few places down from them next to the stairs . . .'

'So, they could shimmy up an' down to that bleeding lectern thingy,' Noakes observed sourly.

Markham tried to visualise the school assembly hall with its stage and the tiered seating rising up behind it. The team had been down in the well of the auditorium, over to the right.

'We were sitting side-on,' he said slowly. 'From that angle it might have looked as if Pauline was fixated on the kids—'

'When she was really eyeballing a teacher,' Doyle finished eagerly.

The DI appeared lost in thought. 'Who can say . . .'

'Let's hope she shows at the chuffing station so we can stop the guessing game,' Noakes groused.

'I noticed Pauline didn't speak to anyone, which was odd,' Burton commented.

'Not really,' Doyle countered. 'If Brighouse and Lipscombe didn't want her there cos the agency showed them up, then she might've felt uncomfortable.'

'She's thick-skinned that one,' Noakes objected. 'It'd take more'n Lipscombe's sour puss to put her off.'

'The shifty husband wasn't with her,' Burton ruminated.

'Maybe it's him she's frightened of?' Doyle suggested.

'Or maybe she hasn't told him about this because he wouldn't want her making waves,' the DI offered an alternative scenario. 'If he's done anything he shouldn't, then he'll want to stay well out of our orbit.'

'Pauline was definitely scared.' Burton had been struck by the woman's demeanour. 'A couple of parents were coming over to speak to her at the end, but she just shot off—'

'Like she had a rocket up her arse.' Noakes nodded vigorously. 'They looked dead surprised, but happen they'll think she were too upset to stay an' chat. I mean, Padgett an' Dacre worked for her after all . . . stands to reason she'd be a bit emotional.'

Markham regarded his team steadily. 'We're sure Pauline didn't make contact with anyone before she went?'

'No boss,' three voices said in unison.

'And you've got surveillance on her in place, Kate?'

'Yes, sir. DI Carstairs lent me two of his DCs. They're taking it in shifts.'

'What if she ducks out of the interview?' Doyle asked.

'She won't.' Markham couldn't say why he was so certain, but something of that strange premonitory dream was still with him and once again he heard those words: innocence betrayed.

'You seem very sure, boss.'

Noakes was watching him curiously. For all his reputation as CID's resident gorilla, he was sensitive as a tuning-fork when it came to intuiting the guvnor's moods. He took Markham's habit of communing with the dead in his stride and, despite occasional scoffing raillery, deep down he respected the poetic tendencies which made the DI such a rarity. It made him proud to be the nearest thing Markham had to family . . . Him and Olivia. The mere thought of it set him in a glow.

And now he sensed the DI had seen something or heard voices or had a visitation. It was typical of his devotion that Noakes didn't feel any resentment at missing out on such uncanny intelligence, taking it for granted that supranatural

enlightenment was only to be expected in a man so richly endowed as his boss.

'Pauline Thornfield is going to hand us the key to the mystery,' the DI said firmly. 'And once we have that, then we'll have our killer.'

'You reckon she's going to give us a name then, guv?' Doyle sounded as though he hardly dared to hope it would be so simple.

Markham struggled to articulate his conviction. 'I think maybe she's been trying to make sense of details that have bothered her about someone . . . signs she may not have even have consciously acknowledged until someone lit the fuse . . .'

'. . . by saying something that made the pieces fall into place,' Burton finished for him.

'That's right, Kate.' Despite the sunshine, Markham's face was sombre as he added, 'Gill Dacre, Nick Critchley and Shona Restorick made the connection, too, and were killed for their knowledge. With Pauline Thornfield, I think we can break the cycle.'

Doyle looked back at the gulag-like sixties building behind them. 'Do you think the killer knows she's on to them? What if she's given the game away?'

'I don't think she's alerted them. If they were in there,' Markham jerked his head towards the school, 'all they would have seen is her getting emotional. As Noakesy said, there's nothing unusual about that, given the two teachers worked for her.'

'And she was careful when she spoke to you at the wake, sir,' Burton pointed out. 'Very discreet about it.'

Doyle was growing restive. 'So, it looks like we can narrow it down to the killer being connected to a kid from Hope—'

'Or one of the teachers,' Noakes concluded dourly.

Burton frowned. 'Don't forget Richard Keogh was at that assembly,' she said. 'And Jayne's half-sisters were there, too, along with Marian Padgett.'

'The halfsies an' Ma Padgett looked straight through each other,' Noakes chortled. 'Should have seen 'em in the foyer afterwards . . . all that bollocks Lipscombe spouted 'bout it being a time for healing didn't cut much ice.'

'Wonder why she invited the half-sisters,' said Doyle. 'Bit tactless in the circumstances.'

'Mebbe they insisted on coming, to get their own back for not being invited to the service at St Jude's.' It was clearly a dynamic that appealed to Noakes's dark sense of humour.

'Or Hope's managers could have hoped for some favourable publicity,' the DI mused. 'I believe I saw one of the *Gazette's* features team lurking next to the chair of governors . . . Perhaps Ms Lipscombe decided to take the sting out of Critchley's sensationalism by posing as the bringer of reconciliation.'

'God, I wouldn't put it past her,' Noakes grunted. Then, in an arch falsetto, '"Where there is hatred let me sow love. Where there is injury, pardon. Where there is sadness, joy."'

Doyle grinned. 'Didn't Maggie Thatcher say that?'

His mentor smirked triumphantly. 'Ackshually, it's Saint Francis of Assisi.'

Burton just couldn't help herself. 'I think Mrs Thatcher quoted it when she became Prime Minister. Brought her a lot of flak for being self-righteous.'

'Well, Lipscombe's the dead spit of Maggie,' Noakes said cheerfully, 'so that's bound to be the kind of tripe she'd give the *Gazette* . . . "*Bringing two warring families together*" . . . Pass the sick bag!'

The word 'families' seemed to strike Doyle. 'What if Jayne had an illegitimate child or something . . . And what if the kid turned out to be a student at Hope and someone didn't want it to come out. And what if—'

'*Whoa, tiger*!' Noakes held up a pudgy hand. 'You've been reading too much Jo Nesbo,' he said kindly. 'An' anyway, Padgett couldn't have children, could she?'

As far as Markham could recall, Jo Nesbo's plots were more concerned with blood-boltered psychopaths than

family relationships, but Noakes had brought the name out with a flourish (further evidence of Muriel's secret reading matter perhaps?).

'Jo Nesbo's one of Olivia's favourite authors,' he said to Noakes's considerable gratification. 'Very gritty stuff.' The DI turned to Doyle. 'I think at the heart of this case there's a secret involving a child. But as to whose child and what happened . . .' he raised his hands and let them drop, 'I'm in the dark.'

Doyle's flush of embarrassment receded.

'I know it sounded a bit melodramatic, boss,' he mumbled.

'So much of Jayne Padgett's personal history *is* highly coloured that I think it worked in the murderer's favour, Sergeant,' the DI told him. 'But I've come to think Jayne's family antecedents aren't really at the core of this case.'

However, Burton wanted to keep all options on the table. 'Even though there's so much bad blood between the different relatives?'

'There may have been murderous feelings swirling around,' Markham conceded. 'Maybe even violent passions . . .'

'Yeah, we know Val really wanted to stick it to Padgett,' Noakes said. 'I mean, the *cheek* of her barging in an' trying to be their ole mum's blue-eyed girl!'

'The long-lost family stuff is so emotive . . . almost *romantic* with that story about a foundling being abandoned at the park gates. Easy to buy into it and miss another strand.'

'Like the Yorkshire Ripper,' Noakes pronounced.

Three pairs of eyes stared at him.

'Y'know . . . all the CID top brass getting sucked into the drama of it . . . that ole codger George Oldfield doing chinwags with the killer 'bout them playing chess with each other an' taking each other's pawns an' all that cobblers. S'why they got hung up on the hoaxer bloke, Wearside Jack. They couldn't see what were under their bleeding noses.'

It was quite a long speech for Noakes, and he was flushed by the time he had finished.

‘You’ve been reading Michael Bilton,’ Burton said, almost accusingly. ‘*Wicked Beyond Belief.*’

Noakes shuffled modestly as though to admit guilty as charged.

‘Yeah, I had a shufti. The best bit was he didn’t waste time on trying to work out why Sutcliffe was a weirdy perv. He tole all about the blokes who tried to catch him. Dennis Hoban an’ all them old-style coppers who knew what was what.’

Kate Burton’s expression was perfectly intelligible to Markham.

Misogynistic to a man.

But it was a measure of how far she had travelled that the acting DI regarded her colleague with an expression almost akin to tenderness.

‘Yes, it was good the way Bilton concentrated on the policemen,’ she said. ‘I mean, why shouldn’t *their* stories matter?’

Noakes beamed at her.

‘Too right, luv. Some of ’em gave their lives to that investigation . . . an’ then they were fricking crucified afterwards cos the high ups wanted scapegoats.’

‘You’re right, sarge, it was very unfair.’

Noakes bridled delightedly, clearly well pleased at the deference shown to his role as the team’s Elder Statesman.

Doyle was encouraged to philosophise. ‘Strange isn’t it how crime fiction always makes the criminals more important than the folk trying to catch them.’

Markham smiled. ‘I don’t subscribe to that scale of values,’ he said quietly. ‘The victims come first and my team a close second. As for the murderers . . . nowhere.’

‘You felt sorry for some of ’em though, guv,’ Noakes said, thinking of the George Baranov case at Bromgrove Royal Court.

‘Of course, Noakesy. “To err is human, to forgive divine.”’ The DI smiled at his little troop. ‘Come on,’ he said, ‘we’ve got a small window of opportunity here and I

don't want to waste it. Pauline Thornfield will be with us in,' he glanced at his watch, 'just over an hour or so . . . I want us to make it count.'

'Otherwise, we get saddled with the Two Goons,' Noakes growled.

Markham's lips quirked. 'Well, the idea of Superintendents Bretherton and Collier taking over strikes me as an unmitigated disaster . . .'

Heartfelt murmurs of assent all round.

'So, it behoves us to be ready for whatever Pauline Thornfield has to say.'

'I'll brief Professor Finlayson,' Burton said eagerly.

Noakes and Doyle exchanged glances of mingled lubricity and forbearance, however the older man was feeling unusually benign towards his eager-beaver colleague and contented himself with a grunt that might have meant anything.

'Thanks, Kate. We may need to move quickly in terms of getting the DCI onside, so it would be good to have the prof available.' The DI prayed that there would be something substantive to present to Sidney.

'D'you think we'll be laying a trap . . . like with the Bluebell.' Noakes stuttered slightly as he mentioned the infamous dance studio investigation, but his boss appeared not to notice.

'I think so, yes. If Pauline gives us a name, then we'll have to move quickly.'

'Warp speed ahead,' Doyle said nervously.

'Precisely.' Markham appeared ice cool, but his palms were sweating. It was Pauline Thornfield or bust.

The group dispersed.

'Didn't see your Olivia in there,' Noakes muttered to Markham.

The DI smothered a smile. He might have known his wingman would have kept a weather eye out for the 'hopeful lady of his earth'.

'She was standing at the back of the hall, Noakesy. Rounding up the stragglers.'

'Might've known Lipscombe would shove her in the background, didn't want anyone else stealing the limelight. Least of all a looker like your Olivia . . .'

Noakes turned puce as he uttered this testimonial, but again Markham appeared not to notice his embarrassment.

'Well, there's no danger of Liv ever having a mid-life crisis with you in her corner,' he said lightly.

With that, they moved towards their respective cars, Noakes exhibiting a distinct bounce in his step.

* * *

Half past eleven saw the team in an interview room at the station with Pauline Thornfield.

Markham sat at the table opposite her with Kate Burton next to him. Noakes had agreed to this arrangement without demur. 'Makes sense to do it with a woman,' he said reasonably. 'She'd be intimidated with two blokes.' He and Doyle sat at the back of the room next to the door, the two men making themselves look as small as possible (not easy in either case).

Once the formalities had been completed and coffee and sandwiches brought for their interviewee, the DI gently opened the crucial dialogue.

'We want you to take your time, Pauline,' he said reassuringly. 'You're here of your own free will and can call a halt at any time. If you feel you need a break or want to consult with someone, just say the word.'

He was privately taken aback by how the proprietor of the agency appeared to have aged in a matter of hours, the toothy ebullience and brash assurance gone as though they had never been. Even the shoulder pads of her executive business suit seemed limp as the proverbial lettuce leaf.

'It was when I spoke to Angela Studholme at St Mary's Cathedral the other week,' she said, her voice sounding almost rusty as though it was difficult to get the words out. 'We're both on the flower arranging committee . . .'

'When was that, Mrs Thornfield?' Markham didn't like to interrupt her flow, but he wanted absolute clarity.

'Last Sunday. It was in the afternoon and we, well, we got to talking over all that had happened. Jayne being murdered and everything . . .'

'Perfectly natural.' The DI gave her the smile he reserved especially for nervous witnesses.

'It was only afterwards when I thought about what she'd said . . .'

Markham felt the blood singing in his ears. *This was it. This was it.* But his expression of polite neutrality never wavered. They might have been chatting over blooming cucumber sandwiches at a tea party, was how Noakes put it afterwards.

'And what was that, Mrs Thornfield?'

'She said how awful it was the way Jayne started out in life . . .'

The DI waited patiently.

'With her mother being raped by a cousin. Angela said you wouldn't want to go researching your roots if it led to you finding out you were the product of rape and abuse . . .'

Burton sat up. Jayne Padgett having been born as the result of rape was no secret thanks to *Bromgrove Roundup*, but that it was a family member came as news to her.

'The TV documentary said it was date rape,' she interjected. 'There wasn't any mention of a relative being involved.'

'Angela said thank heavens Jayne had enough decency left not to wash all the dirty linen on prime-time television though, God knows, the programme was bad enough as it was.'

The DI let her catch her thoughts for a second before prompting, 'You mentioned abuse?'

'Yes. So, according to Angela, incest ran in the family — the blood family that is — but everything was kept under wraps.' Pauline drained her coffee cup, her hand clutching it for dear life.

'Would you like another, Mrs Thornfield?' The DI smiled charmingly. 'In CID we drink so much of the stuff we might as well take it intravenously.'

The woman visibly relaxed. 'No, I'm fine thanks, Inspector. Just a bit jittery . . . You see, it was only afterwards I made the connection.'

Suddenly the atmosphere in the stuffy interview room was electric as the four officers waited.

She dabbed her upper lip with a handkerchief.

What came next was totally unexpected.

'I was never really happy about the Carmichaels,' she said. 'Something wasn't right.'

'Hey up, luv.' Noakes lurched forward to join them at the table, dragging his chair with him. 'Rewind a bit will you. Thass the young couple me an' the guvnor met down at your office . . . What've they got to do with it?'

Innocence betrayed.

The words seemed to hum in the air and suddenly Markham knew what was coming.

'It was the way Ritchie acted round Pippa, it always made me feel uncomfortable. Like there was some kind of . . . understanding between them . . . And then when I heard Angela talking about incest, it all clicked into place.'

'Incest!' Noakes looked dumbfounded.

Out of nowhere, Markham remembered DS Doyle talking about the way the investigation's overlapping strands all seemed to lead back to Aldbourne Village and the same group of people. Incestuous he had called it.

Noakes had found his voice. 'Are you telling us that Ritchie Carmichael's screwing his daughter?'

'Pippa's his stepdaughter, Sergeant . . . Sorry, I thought you knew.'

'No, we bleeding didn't.' A vein was pulsing in Noakes's forehead. He looked accusingly at Burton who shook her head. 'Not in the files and Hope didn't flag it up,' she said.

'No reason why it should have created any ripples,' the DI shot his wingman a quelling look, 'unless something made you uneasy.'

Wind your neck in, Noakesy.

The DS didn't retreat but he readjusted his pug-like features.

'Sorry luv,' he said. 'What you said came a bit out of left field.' Then, with avuncular kindness, 'Good on you for sussing it. But then that's your field ain't it . . . safeguarding.'

The woman held his gaze. Once again, Noakes had known which chord to touch.

'It was the standing too close . . . holding hands . . . the way they looked at each other when they thought Pat didn't notice. Somehow, when Angela was telling me about Jayne's birth family , well, it was like I had a revelation or something . . .'

Markham thought back to the young couple. The pleasant fair-haired husband with his rounded West Country vowels and the faded pregnant partner. Looking back on it, there had been something cowed about her . . .

Now Doyle drew his chair forward to join the party.

'Are you saying Ritchie Carmichael killed Jayne Padgett, Mrs Thornfield?' he asked, loosening the collar of his shirt down as though excitement had him by the throat.

'I think Jayne must have found out. I remember her saying that every family has its secrets. She told me she had ideas for a novel . . . wrote everything down in a notebook.' The woman gnawed her lip. 'But I never imagined . . . incest and child abuse.'

The DI remembered the desk in Jayne Padgett's flat that the SOCOs were convinced had been rifled.

'Jayne weren't the kind of woman to let it go, yeah?' Noakes's gruff tones could be very kind. 'She wouldn't jus' put it in a diary . . . I reckon she'd want to do summat about it.'

As in nail Ritchie Carmichael's balls to the floor.

'I think she'd have spoken to Pippa,' came the faltering reply. 'That was Jayne's way. She was in a privileged position with access to kids' homes . . . no way would she want to go charging in. Pippa's a quiet, sensitive girl . . . very self-contained and domestic. Jayne would've wanted to tread carefully.'

Self-contained.

Domestic.

Tidy.

The DI recalled the break-in at Cabot Court . . . the figure in the hoodie running off into the night . . . the compulsive tidying of the crime scenes . . . the girl with long hair canoodling by the canal around the time Shona Restorick was murdered.

Very quietly Markham said, 'Do you think there is any possibility that Pippa could be involved in these killings, Mrs Thornfield?'

It was the thinnest whisper. 'Yes.'

There was no time to waste.

The DI reached across the table and briefly squeezed her hand.

'We have to bring them in, Pauline.'

'I know.' She licked dry lips. 'I wasn't sure till this morning when I went to that assembly . . . But when I looked at Pippa, I just knew.'

Back row of the choir. So Burton and Doyle had been right.

'What can I do?' Her voice was barely audible.

'We need you to set a trap, luv.' Noakes's piggy eyes seemed almost to hypnotise their interviewee. 'You have to tackle Ritchie's missus. That'll bring things to a head cos then you're a threat to his big secret getting out.'

'I don't think I can do it, Sergeant.'

'You gotta.' When the DS spoke in that tone, resistance was futile.

'Mrs Thornfield, Jayne and three other people are dead.' Markham allowed this to sink in. 'Like you, they must have guessed something or found it out . . . we won't know how it was until we apprehend the killer.'

Burton leaned forward. 'We can protect you,' she said earnestly. 'But we have to bring Ritchie Carmichael into the open.'

'Can you do it, luv?' Noakes's meaty paw reached across the table and, in defiance of all CID etiquette, gripped Pauline Thornfield's hand hard.

She looked pale but determined as she met the DS's eyes. 'Yes, Sergeant. I can.'

14. THESPIAN CHALLENGE

After that, things moved quickly.

Pauline Thornfield was whisked off for more refreshments and a comfort break while Markham's team adjourned to his office. One of the civilian staff was dispatched to Greggs for drinks and snacks (clearly the occasion demanded brain fuel superior to the mundane canteen fare), and the four detectives hunkered down for their conference.

'How was he able to get away with it right under his missus's nose?' Noakes demanded wrathfully as he plonked himself down opposite the DI. 'With her expecting an' all.'

'That's the point, sarge.' Doyle coiled his lanky frame into a chair. 'It would have been easier for him to—' here he shot a wary glance at Burton — 'avoid, er, the intimate side of things on account of her being pregnant. He could claim he was being considerate.'

Noakes thought about it. 'Yeah, she looked ready to drop the sprog . . . dead tired an' washed out.'

'If it was a difficult pregnancy, then she'd just want some peace and quiet,' Burton said. 'No family dramas or rows. Even if she did wonder whether something was going on, she'd have turned a blind eye.'

Noakes still struggled to get his head around it. 'If he were having it away with the stepdaughter, Pat musta twigged summat was up. I mean, they were sharing the same house for chuff's sake.'

'If the abuse has gone on for a while, then Ritchie and Pippa will have become adept at hiding their liaison,' the DI said.

Doyle frowned. 'I wonder where they met . . . away from the house, I mean.'

At these words, Markham felt the hair rise on the back of his neck as though someone had stroked it.

An image flashed into his mind.

'I can think of one option,' he said slowly. 'Those cottages in Castor Hill Park would have been ideal.'

'What, you mean them funny little black an' white houses, the Hansel an' Gretel jobbies?' Noakes asked. 'But they're all boarded up.'

'Not all of them,' Burton said. 'The park staff said there'd been problems with break ins and prowlers.'

'Lemme get this straight.' Noakes continued to wrestle with the conundrum. 'Are we saying that Pippa was up for all of this? Not a victim or coerced or owt like that?' He stared at the DI. 'How d'you reckon it happened an' who did what?'

Markham took a deep breath as they waited expectantly.

'We can't know the truth without a confession, but for what it's worth this is how I see it.' The long, elegant hands flexed as he weighed his words.

'I believe Jayne Padgett somehow found out what was going on with the Carmichaels . . . saw something or heard something that disturbed her when she was over there tutoring Pippa. Most likely she threatened to tell Pat.'

'Why didn't she just tell Pat straight away?' Noakes demanded. 'It were kiddy fiddling, an' with her being a teacher . . . well, you'd think she'd be right on it.'

'Maybe she wasn't totally sure,' Burton put in. 'Could be she wanted to wait until she'd got the whole story out of Pippa before saying anything.'

‘Plus, Pat was pregnant,’ Doyle added. ‘She might have been nervous about speaking to her in case the shock made her go into labour or something like that. Or she could have thought about contacting social services first and wanted to get her facts straight.’

‘I think that’s right,’ the DI agreed. ‘After the hoo-ha about Critchley and the long-lost family saga, Jayne would have erred on the side of caution. She might even have hoped that once they’d talked things through, Pippa would leave the family home and contact social services off her own bat.’

‘So, Jayne hesitated,’ Burton said. ‘Didn’t want to go charging in like a bull in a china shop.’

‘Precisely, Kate.’ The DI’s face was momentarily downcast. ‘But that hesitation was fatal because Pippa told her stepfather—’

‘An’ Ritchie decided he weren’t going to have some nosy ole biddy spoil their fun.’ Noakes set the steel balls of Markham’s desktop pendulum toy swinging with an angry slap.

Just then the team’s refreshments arrived, creating a bustle as they divvied up the drinks and goodies; Burton — for once — was glad to join Noakes and Doyle in bingeing on sugary treats while Markham, ever austere, confined himself to black coffee.

‘So Ritchie and Pippa joined forces to murder Jayne,’ Markham resumed his account.

What about the bleach an’ the sex stuff, guv . . . the interference with Padgett, you know, down below?’ Noakes’s expression was dark. ‘You’re not telling me a teenage girl wanted a ringside seat.’

The DI’s voice was steady. ‘If Pippa was a willing partner in the sexual relationship with Ritchie, then she might have flown into a vindictive rage over what she saw as Jayne’s meddling . . . might have taken a sadistic pleasure in seeing bleach forced down her throat.’

His wingman persisted. ‘What about the sexual assault?’

‘It suited them to make it look as though Jayne was attacked by a would-be rapist. They may also have derived

some sort of sexual kick from degrading her.' Markham paused. 'Or Ritchie might have sent Pippa off to another part of the flat while he . . . gratified himself.'

'Either way, it's fricking gross.' Noakes looked for a moment as though his sugar-topped yum-yum was about to reappear, but a swig of coffee dealt with the nausea and he was once more intent on fitting the jigsaw together. 'Is Pippa the one who broke into the flat afterwards an' then legged it across the park . . . the kid in the hoodie the uniforms thought were a lad?'

'I believe so, yes.' Markham too was relieved to move on from the subject of sexual assault.

'She returned to Cabot Court for some reason,' he said.

'But she and Ritchie didn't have anything to worry about,' Doyle objected. 'The IT guys reckon the killer forced Padgett to show them what was on her mobile and laptop before making her drink bleach and the rest of it. If there wasn't anything incriminating, why would Pippa need to come back?'

Burton put down her tea. 'I think I can answer that. When I asked Exhibits to let me check out the contents of the flat, it turned out there was an earring found on the floor under her desk.'

'So what?' Doyle was puzzled. 'Nothing to say it wasn't Padgett's.'

'It didn't look like the kind of thing a middle-aged woman would wear' she retorted. 'I think it came from *Accessorize* . . . dangly and sparkly . . . not like the plain gold studs and the rest of the stuff in Jayne's jewellery box. I assumed it was just a fashion mistake, but now I think it could have belonged to Pippa. She must've panicked when she realised she'd dropped it in Jayne's flat . . . worried in case we traced it back—'

'When, ironically, none of us hotshots clocked the discrepancy,' the DI observed wryly. 'There was no risk to her at all.'

Burton tried to imagine the episode through Pippa's eyes. 'She's a teenager, impulsive, didn't think it through.'

‘She’s seriously screwy,’ Noakes said. ‘Mebbe she wanted to relive what happened with Padgett . . . scrawl on the walls or summat . . . Hey,’ with a sudden realisation, ‘it must have been her who started the fire at Hope an’ wrote that stuff. Betcha she fancied going back to the flat for a gloat.’

The DI closed his eyes briefly as Noakes flew this kite. Pray heaven, no.

‘What do you reckon happened with Dacre then?’ Doyle wanted to see where the DI’s hypothesis led.

‘I wasn’t entirely sure until Kate mentioned Pippa’s jewellery,’ Markham replied. ‘But now I begin to see how it might have happened.’ He sipped the lukewarm coffee, trying to order his racing thoughts.

‘You’ll remember we were puzzled by Gill suddenly coming over sick when we were interviewing her,’ he said.

‘That’s right,’ Burton concurred. ‘It was just after those two fifth-formers came in with coffee. *My god* . . . Now I see.’

‘See what?’ Noakes had no time for show and tell.

‘It was Pippa, sarge . . . *One of them was Pippa.*’

The DS was none the wiser. ‘What about it? How could Dacre have guessed she had summat to do with Padgett getting murdered?’

Markham took over the narrative. ‘I think she was wearing something of Jayne’s,’ he said. ‘And Gill recognised it.’

‘It was a cross and chain, boss,’ Burton said eagerly. ‘I can see it now. She had it tucked inside her shirt, but when she leaned forward her top button came undone and you could see . . . I noticed because the cross had an opal in the centre . . . it was rather nice.’

The DI nodded. ‘It must have given her a thrill to wear something of Jayne’s right under our noses.’

‘But why would she risk it?’ To Doyle it didn’t seem logical. ‘Panicking about getting an earring back in case we traced it to her but then prancing into school wearing something she’d nicked from Jayne’s flat . . . doesn’t add up. I mean, there was always the chance someone would remember Jayne wearing it.’

'These days teachers aren't supposed to wear a cross at work,' Markham said. 'I recall Olivia telling me Hope banned staff from wearing religious emblems in case anyone was offended.'

'Daft sods,' muttered Noakes.

'I'm pretty sure Jayne never wore it to work,' the DI continued. 'So Pippa would have felt quite safe.'

'Only for some reason Dacre knew it was Jayne's. How come? Oh, hang on . . .' Noakes cogitated intently, the beetle brows knitted. 'They were both God-squadders . . . could've seen each other at church. An' Hope's Thought Police can't stop you wearing whatever you like when it's outside school,' he concluded triumphantly.

'She still took a chance,' Doyle muttered.

'I think we'll find Pippa is a thrill-seeker,' Markham commented grimly. 'And it was just her bad luck that the button on her shirt came unfastened.'

Noakes narrowed his eyes. 'Yeah, I remember her now. A big lass . . . heavy on top . . . bursting out of her kit. Prob'ly that's what attracted Paedo Boy in the first place.'

'Gill must have confronted Pippa, and then the girl somehow lured her to the park . . . where Ritchie was waiting.' Burton shuddered.

'So it was Pippa did all the pointy toes stuff with Dacre . . . Christ,' Doyle whistled. 'She's probably into ballet or tap dance or something like that . . . Sorry, sir.' Too late he remembered Markham's famous dislike of expletives and blasphemy.

'It's all right, Sergeant.' The DI's tone was mild. 'I'm finding it pretty hard to get my head round all of this too.'

'She's a sick little bitch.' As ever, Noakes called a spade a spade. 'Mopping up Padgett's puke with kitchen towel an' doing the Brillo pad number at Critchley's the same time as she were watching Carmichael finish 'em off . . . The bearded wonder's going to have a field day when he gets her on the couch.' He registered the acting DI's affronted expression. 'Sorry luv,' with an ingratiating leer, 'I know you an' him have summat going.'

'Stop digging, Noakesy,' Markham said firmly. Kate Burton, lips firmly compressed, was visibly counting to ten. Doyle just grinned.

'I think you're right, that poor child is deeply disturbed,' the DI continued.

His wingman was indignant. 'How c'n you be sorry for her?'

'Because I suspect she's a victim just as much as the others in this case, Sergeant.' Markham's gaze was remote. 'Children are what we make them to be. And, on so many levels, society fails to protect them.'

Noakes regarded his boss intently, understanding in a flash of illumination that Markham was also speaking of himself.

'Yeah,' he said gruffly. 'She were groomed an' all that . . . the bastard must've messed with her head.'

'Do you remember telling me about Mary Bell, Sergeant?' Markham asked. 'I believe you and Kate saw some parallels between that case and this investigation.'

Both the DS and acting DI were hooked.

'Well, when Mary Bell was tried for murder in an adult court, she was called a twisted killer . . . a psychopath,' the DI told them. 'But nowadays the pendulum's swung back the other way and people understand she was just a small, bewildered child horribly let down by the social care and justice systems . . . indeed, by just about everyone who should have intervened to help her.' Gently he added, 'I'm not saying we should just let the victims ebb from this tale, but I think we should have compassion for the child caught up in the murk of it.'

'Fair enough,' Noakes spoke up stoutly thinking of both Markham and 'our Nat'.

There was a pause.

'Why did Critchley have to die, boss?' Doyle asked as the silence threatened to become uncomfortable.

'Max Critchley said Nick dived into his study when he returned home after we'd interviewed him. Max thought he

was watching a DVD on his computer . . . And then he headed back to their flat in Bromgrove with something in a jiffy bag—'

Burton leaned forward eagerly. 'Plus, Max said Nick told him there was something he should have spotted . . . something staring him right in the face only he hadn't realised its significance at the time.'

'Correct, Kate.' Markham moved from his desk to the window, resting his back against it as he turned to face the team. 'When we were interviewing Nick, DS Doyle commented that one never really knows what goes on in families.'

'I remember. That's when he got antsy and clammed up . . . couldn't wait to get away.' Doyle's freckled face was alight with excitement.

The DI smiled at the youngster. 'At the time, I presumed it must have had something to do with the long-lost family debacle — the ructions with Jayne's half-sisters and her adoptive mother . . . That was the fractured family we were focused on . . .'

'But Nick was thinking of the *Carmichaels*,' Burton said. 'Another family entirely.'

Markham took up the story once more. 'Going back to the mysterious item in that jiffy bag . . . There must have been extra footage from the *Roundup* programme . . . maybe shots setting the context for Jayne's story—'

'That's right,' Burton confirmed earnestly. 'They call them establishing shots.'

Know-all. But Noakes didn't say it.

'So, he had film of the Carmichaels,' Doyle breathed.

'Yes,' Markham agreed. 'It would have made sense for the documentary to include material about the families whose children were tutored by Jayne . . . local colour and all that . . . then some of it ended up on the cutting room floor.'

'But mebbe stuff niggled.' Now Noakes was caught up in the narrative. 'There was summat at the back of Nasty Nick's mind, summat creepy he'd noticed 'bout Pippa an' Ritchie. Guess it takes one to know one . . . An' then two

teachers were murdered an' he saw the chance of making a few bob.'

'Yes, I think it was blackmail,' Markham said. 'Nick was desperate to rebuild his career, remember. Sadly, it overrode all sense of morality . . . or self-preservation.'

'D'you reckon Pippa turned up at the flat with Ritchie?' Doyle wondered.

'I suspect she was lurking somewhere nearby and he let her in once Critchley was safely out of it,' the DI replied.

Burton's thoughts turned to the final victim. 'What about Shona Restorick?'

'We don't know what put her on to Pippa and Ritchie, but clearly something rang alarm bells.' The DI returned to his chair, stretched languorously and then clicked into analytical mode once more. 'Maybe Pippa slipped up . . . told Liberty something that found its way back to Shona.'

Noakes considered this. 'Mebbe Liberty saw that necklace . . . the crucifix thingy.'

'Or Liberty might have noticed something odd about the way Pippa and Ritchie behaved around each other,' Burton suggested. 'They could have got careless . . . been more blatant . . . arrogant because they figured they were getting away with murder.'

Doyle liked that idea. 'Perhaps Pippa kind of boasted she knew stuff about Padgett — what her flat looked like . . . stuff she shouldn't really have known cos Padgett only ever tutored kids in their own homes.' He turned to Burton. 'That's right, isn't it?'

The acting DI nodded. 'Yes, she was strict about it . . . never wanted students in her flat . . . the agency preferred it that way, too.'

The DI found this a plausible scenario.

'I can envisage Pippa running off at the mouth,' he said. 'Becoming excitable and hyper-adrenalized by the murders . . . so she became indiscreet.'

'It's a bleeding wonder ole Ritchie didn't do for her an' all,' Noakes exclaimed.

'Oh, I think it's possible that something might have happened to Pippa in the not-too-distant future,' the DI said consideringly. 'An overdose . . . a tragic accident. He has no intention of leaving his wife, and if Pippa ever threatened to tell—'

'It would have been curtains for her.' Doyle was aghast.

'It's called looking out for number one, lad,' Noakes said brutally. 'Happens all the time.'

'Yeah, but like the boss said, she's just a child.'

'A very dangerous child,' Markham amended.

'The courting couple down by the canal where we found Restorick, the long-haired girl and the lad wearing a beanie . . . that must have been them . . . Ritchie and Pippa.' For Doyle, the pieces were all coming together.

'I think it had to be, yes,' Markham confirmed.

'Somehow it feels unbelievable,' Burton said slowly. 'This perfectly ordinary bloke with two-point-four children on a killing spree.'

Doyle was startled. 'Has he got other kids then?'

'Figure of speech,' the acting inspector said with a shaky laugh. 'It's just his stepdaughter and the one they're expecting . . . but you know what I mean.'

'We do, Kate.' The DI rubbed his eyes savagely as though to clear them. 'When Noakes and I visited *Top of the Class*, the Carmichaels seemed the epitome of normality.'

'Though come to think of it, she didn't have much to say for herself,' Noakes said. 'It was him did all the talking.'

'Well, if we're right about Ritchie, we need to do something,' the DI pointed out.

'Like what?' Doyle asked simply.

Markham's lean dark features were intent on some inner vision. 'Noakes said it before,' he concluded. 'Pauline has to voice her suspicions to Pat Carmichael. But we don't want her to come on too strong . . . Pat's in denial and we need it to stay that way—'

'Otherwise, she might go off at half-cock an' accuse hubby, leaving us with a dead woman on our hands,' grunted Noakes.

'A dead pregnant woman,' Burton reminded them.

'Pauline needs to come across like she's just being officious,' the DI told them.

'Shouldn't be too much of a stretch,' was Noakes's sour aside.

'Kind of like virtue-signalling you mean, boss.' Burton had caught on quickly. 'Telling Pat it's important people don't get the wrong idea and maybe her husband's a bit too touchy-feely with Pippa . . . Not that she thinks anything inappropriate is going on, perish the thought, but you can't be too careful about appearances yada yada yada.'

'Perfect,' the DI said admiringly. 'I never knew you had so much guile, Kate! But then I forgot about your studies in psychology.'

Noakes was keen to show he, too, was no slouch when it came to psychological insights.

'You want Pauline to act like a bitch, is that it, guv? Mebbe give the impression she's jealous of what Pat has — dishy bloke, nice house, child on the way — an' wants to upset her with a bit of second-hand gossip about hubby.'

'Excellent, Noakesy . . . Now we're really motoring.' When it came to guile, his wingman was second to none. 'That's precisely the script I want Pauline to follow . . . mildly salacious and self-important with it.'

'Like she wants to put Pat in her place . . . make her feel uncomfortable . . . inferior.' Now Doyle was enthused. 'Then Pat goes running to Ritchie and has a whinge but it's easy for him to reassure her.'

'Absolutely like that.' Markham pulled a wry face. 'I'm assuming the Carmichaels do in fact have all the trappings so it's not unfeasible for Pauline to have an attack of the green-eyed monster.'

'He's the facilities manager at Aldbourne Health Club.' Burton had the facts at her fingertips. 'Perks and discounts a-go-go.'

The DI was pleased. 'Ideal.'

'Think Pauline can do it boss?' This was Doyle.

'She'd better,' Noakes rumbled.

'Ritchie's bound to suggest that he and Pauline meet up,' Markham developed the plot. 'So, when that happens, we need Pauline to act all coy and fluttery — give the impression she's up for a spot of dalliance in return for keeping her mouth shut. We'll tell her to suggest they meet somewhere picturesque . . . romantic.' Noakes mimed throwing up but the DI ignored the byplay.

'One of those Art Deco cottages in Castor Hill Park,' Burton suggested.

'Perfect,' Markham approved. 'Easy for us to mount discreet surveillance in the park and it's one of the killing zones, so hopefully he'll be emotionally out of whack.'

'What happens when Gnomeo an' Juliet are face to face then?' Noakes demanded.

'She's got to come on to him,' the DI said slowly. 'Needy, insinuating, a bit tearful . . . on the verge of turning nasty if she doesn't get what she wants.'

'He'll be repelled,' Burton said with conviction. 'From the look of Pat and Pippa, he likes to be the one in control when it comes to women, not backed into a corner.'

'Yes,' Markham agreed. 'Pauline needs to ratchet things up fairly quickly . . . suggest she can make trouble for his family.'

'It's asking a lot of her acting skills, boss,' Doyle put in quietly.

They pondered the undeniable truth of this observation.

'She has to start off nice but turn threatening,' Burton mused. 'Maybe even come right out with it and demand to know if he's been inappropriate with Pippa, say something contemptuous about men who are so pathetic they go after teenage girls instead of women their own age.'

'What if he stays cool, plays for time, says he'll think about it . . .' Doyle was considering every angle.

The DI ruminated. 'I think if Pauline can somehow catch him on the raw and press the right trigger points, he might be provoked into attacking her. Remember, this is a man who's

murdered four times, he's bound to be feeling the heat. It's possible he even craves the sexual release of another kill.'

'Yeah, if them cottages are where he goes for a bit of the other, he'll be well up for that.'

'Sometimes you sound like a walking seaside postcard, Noakesy,' the DI admonished his number two ruefully, 'but essentially yes, I think that particular setting is likely to have its effect on Mr Carmichael.'

'What about Pippa?' Burton asked. 'Do you reckon she'll be along for the ride?'

'Maybe he'll decide to handle Pauline himself,' Doyle said. 'Let Pippa sit this one out, insist she stays with her mum in case Pat gets the wind up.'

'Hmm.' The DI thought hard. 'Yes, he may want to put some space between them at this point.' He pushed the thick dark hair back from his forehead and stood up. 'Right, now we need a script for Pauline.'

'I'll get on to it, sir,' Burton responded crisply. 'Professor Finlayson should be able to give us some cues,' she added, eyes firmly averted from her colleagues.

Noakes seemed to be trying not to smirk but then succeeded without difficulty upon the DI announcing that the two of them would go and brief DCI Sidney.

'Back here in one hour,' Markham told them. 'And then we mobilise.'

* * *

Later that afternoon, just after half past four, Markham's team waited tensely in shrubbery behind a semi-derelict lodge on the west side of Castor Hill Park, listening to the exchange between Pauline Thornfield and Ritchie Carmichael.

A bloodshot Jaffa sun was setting just beyond the dark line of trees that bordered the park's perimeter. To Markham's fraught gaze, it seemed to leech into the horizon, staining it crimson as though the park lay under some wicked spell.

'She's played a fricking blinder,' Noakes breathed in reluctant admiration. 'All that treacly bleating . . . Carmichael hasn't even checked her for a wire.'

That had been their biggest gamble — counting on Pauline Thornfield, with her blend of sanctimony and prurience, to convince the killer this was just a sad menopausal woman desperate for love. No one else in the picture.

'He's got a stutter,' Doyle whispered. 'Quite a bad one.'

The DI had never noticed this when they encountered the personable young parent at the agency's office. It must mean that their quarry was unravelling.

Go on, Pauline, he said to himself. *Keep pushing.*

And then there it was.

'You fucking b-b-bitch.' The sibilant growl was so unexpected as to be shocking. 'What makes you think I'd ever go to bed with the likes of you.'

There was a crash — the sound of something being violently overturned. An intake of breath.

His colleague's heads swivelled towards Markham who held up a hand.

Not yet, he signalled. Not yet.

'Stand by,' the DI whispered urgently into his transmitter to the SWAT team waiting in the early evening darkness.

'I'll make sure you never see your family again, you pathetic little man,' Pauline Thornfield hissed with convincing malevolence. Kate Burton and Professor Nathan Finlayson had clearly rehearsed her till she was word perfect.

Give us a confession, Ritchie. We need a confession.

'D'you think I give a f-f-fuck about your threats . . . You have any idea who you're d-d-dealing with, you old hag? D'you really think I'm worried about slitting your wrinkly old throat when I've already killed those other interfering b-b-bastards?'

That was it, they had him.

'Go, go, go!'

Then a piercing scream rent the night.

'*Daddy*!'

It was all over in minutes.

As instructed, Pauline Thornfield had wielded the pepper spray in the cobwebbed front room of the derelict lodge known as Reynolds Cottage. But she missed her target who had a knife to the throat of his stepdaughter in the same instant that armed officers came bursting through the rotten front door.

Another terrible shriek and Ritchie Carmichael thudded to the floor, taken out in a heartbeat by the marksman who never missed.

* * *

'How did it turn out Pippa was even there?'

The following afternoon saw the team and Olivia together in their favourite hostelry, the Grapes, where Denise the bosomy landlady — ever susceptible to the handsome inspector's aloof charm — protected the detectives' privacy like a tigress, shooing away other patrons and ensuring the group had their favourite booth in the back parlour or "snug".

Outside was cold and crisp but it was cosy in their secluded sanctum, with a roaring fire which caused the wall-mounted horse brasses, curios and nautical knick-knacks that were the landlady's pride and joy to wink and glow against the oak wainscoting with their most hospitable lustre. Uneven wooden floorboards creaked and groaned as though defying all the vagaries of fashion, while ancient timbers overhead seemed to shift and settle in an age-old rhythm designed to soothe even the most cantankerous customer.

The DI's 'gang' were content to nurse their drinks as they recovered from the events of the previous day. G&Ts for Olivia and Kate. Châteauneuf-du-Pape for Markham. Cobra and Kingfisher for Noakes and Doyle (as chasers for a curry later on).

Kate brought Olivia up to speed.

'The Carmichaels live in Cuckoo Lane, parallel to Rockbourne Drive,' she explained. 'Those properties have adjoining back gardens.'

Olivia began to see where this was going.

'Undercovers clocked Pippa going in through the front door and settled down to watch,' Burton continued. 'Unfortunately—'

'They didn't stake out Rockbourne Drive,' Olivia said.

'Correct . . . Pippa went through the garden of the property behind and asked the neighbours if she could sneak out through theirs, fed them some rigmarole about being grounded and wanting to dodge her mum. They were used to Pippa's antics . . . never thought anything of it.' Burton scowled into her drink. 'So, there was a screw-up and heads will roll.'

'They're big rambling semis along there, aren't they?' Olivia observed. 'And don't the Black Woods start at the end of Rockbourne?'

'That's right,' Doyle told her. 'They had a uniform posted at the entrance to the woods just in case . . . didn't realise she might cut through the neighbours'.'

Olivia was puzzled. 'How come the uniform didn't clock her leaving?'

'Pippa wore a wig,' Markham said. 'Mid-brown shoulder-length bob, cut with a fringe and glasses . . . A totally different persona. You wouldn't have recognised her.'

'An' she came out with two of the neighbours' kids, so it looked like three youngsters hanging out together,' Noakes put in. 'She gave 'em some baloney 'bout being involved with this bloke who got off on dressing up an' disguises. They thought it were hilarious . . .'

Doyle put down his beer. 'You could say it was fortunate Pippa showing up.'

'*Fortunate*! How d'you make that out?' his mentor demanded.

'If it hadn't been for her screaming and distracting him like that, Carmichael would most probably have slit Pauline Thornfield's throat.'

'Our guys would have taken him out before there was any chance of it,' Noakes asserted confidently.

The ginger ninja raised his sandy eyebrows as far as they would go before returning to his lager.

'What'll happen to Pippa?' Olivia asked softly.

'Funny farm,' Noakes told her bluntly. 'An' I hope they throw away the key.' Registering her distressed expression, he cleared his throat and added gruffly, 'She needs help an' even then there's no saying she'll ever be right.'

'She was spitting and kicking like a wild thing when they dragged her off Carmichael's body,' Doyle said with a shudder.

'Plus, she were shouting every obscenity in the book.' And quite a few Noakes had never heard of. 'An' now in the Newman she's practically . . . what do they call it . . . ? Yeah, catatonic.'

'They think she's in deep shock,' Burton amplified. 'To start with she kept laughing her head off as though it was all this huge joke, and then she mostly retreated into herself . . . hardly said anything at all.'

'Selective mutism.' Noakes flourished this terminology with quite an air.

Markham smothered a smile at Burton's expression. Clearly his wingman had been dipping into the *Diagnostic and Statistical Manual of Mental Disorders* on the sly.

'Something like that,' she agreed. 'But Professor Finlayson has child trauma counsellors lined up.'

'Her bleeding mum's gonna need counselling an' all,' Noakes muttered.

'When do you reckon Carmichael started on Pippa?' Doyle asked Burton.

'Nathan thinks it may have been when she was very young . . . maybe even as early as four or five.'

Silence fell over the little group.

'Did the murders all happen the way you imagined?' Olivia asked by way of distracting them from sickening thoughts of child abuse. 'What made Shona Restorick suspicious?'

'Pippa told Liberty about Jayne's high-spec kitchen,' Markham replied. 'Something on the lines of who'd have

thought an old crone like that would have a *Daewoo blender*, Bodum coffee maker and top-of-the-range granite work tops . . . Liberty mentioned it to her mother. It most probably got Shona wondering about Pippa. She might already have noticed something off-key about that family. Liberty says she told Shona that Pippa's dad was always tickling her and it was a bit odd. Of course, hindsight's a wonderful thing and Liberty might be embroidering things for our benefit, but I think she *did* sow a seed of doubt in Shona's mind . . . and the poor woman acted on it.'

'As for the other deaths, it's likely we were pretty much on the money about everything,' Burton confirmed with grim satisfaction. 'We'll never know exactly what was on the footage Nick Critchley took with him to his flat, but it must have been something compromising . . . something that might have offered a reason for Pippa's teacher to be concerned about the girl.'

Olivia listened attentively as Kate Burton filled her in on the other deaths and the clues that had eventually led them to Ritchie Carmichael's door.

'We've given Jayne's cross and chain to Simon Dacre,' Markham said quietly. 'Marian Padgett agreed he should have it in memory of his mother.'

'How's Pat Carmichael coping?' Olivia asked.

'In bits,' Noakes said bluntly. 'The poor lass never suspected owt . . . thought Ritchie walked on water.'

He mentioned nothing about the hours he had spent the previous day sitting with the bereaved woman as she contemplated the wasteland of her life.

Markham looked round the table at his friends. 'It was a tale of two families,' he said. 'The long-lost family with all its melodrama . . . And that other family, superficially normal but equally lost, living the dream in their house on Cuckoo Lane.'

'If it hadn't been for Pauline Thornfield plucking up the courage to come to us, we might never have solved this case,' Doyle observed soberly.

'She played her part well,' Markham agreed.

'Loves the attention,' Noakes grumbled. 'Betcha she's all lined up for a cheesy spread in the *Gazette*.'

'Not if Sidney gets there first,' his boss chuckled.

Olivia smiled roguishly.

'A toast to the agency and to Pauline,' she exclaimed. 'For rising to the thespian challenge!'

They raised their glasses and laughter rang out around the room, banishing the shadows.

THE END

ALSO BY CATHERINE MOLONEY

THE DI GILBERT MARKHAM SERIES

Book 1: CRIME IN THE CHOIR
Book 2: CRIME IN THE SCHOOL
Book 3: CRIME IN THE CONVENT
Book 4: CRIME IN THE HOSPITAL
Book 5: CRIME IN THE BALLET
Book 6: CRIME IN THE GALLERY
Book 7: CRIME IN THE HEAT
Book 8: CRIME AT HOME
Book 9: CRIME IN THE BALLROOM
Book 10: CRIME IN THE BOOK CLUB
Book 11: CRIME IN THE COLLEGE
Book 12: CRIME IN THE KITCHEN

Thank you for reading this book.

If you enjoyed it please leave feedback on Amazon or Goodreads, and if there is anything we missed or you have a question about, then please get in touch. We appreciate you choosing our book.

Founded in 2014 in Shoreditch, London, we at Joffe Books pride ourselves on our history of innovative publishing. We were thrilled to be shortlisted for Independent Publisher of the Year at the British Book Awards.

www.joffebooks.com

We're very grateful to eagle-eyed readers who take the time to contact us. Please send any errors you find to corrections@joffebooks.com. We'll get them fixed ASAP.

Printed in Great Britain
by Amazon